OSLG

SO-ACA-914

JAN   2014

North Sea Requiem

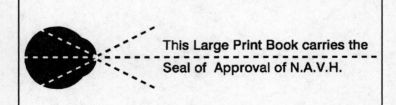

This Large Print Book carries the
Seal of Approval of N.A.V.H.

NORTH SEA REQUIEM

A. D. SCOTT

THORNDIKE PRESS
A part of Gale, Cengage Learning

Detroit • New York • San Francisco • New Haven, Conn • Waterville, Maine • London

GALE
CENGAGE Learning·

Copyright © 2013 by A. D. Scott.
Thorndike Press, a part of Gale, Cengage Learning.

ALL RIGHTS RESERVED
This book is a work of fiction. Any references to historical events, real people, or real places are used fictitiously. Other names, characters, places, and events are products of the author's imagination, and any resemblance to actual events or places or persons, living or dead, is entirely coincidental.
Thorndike Press® Large Print Crime Scene.
The text of this Large Print edition is unabridged.
Other aspects of the book may vary from the original edition.
Set in 16 pt. Plantin.

LIBRARY OF CONGRESS CATALOGING-IN-PUBLICATION DATA

Scott, A. D.
    North sea requiem / by A. D. Scott. — Large print edition.
        pages ; cm. — (Thorndike Press large print crime scene)
    ISBN 978-1-4104-6504-7 (hardcover) — ISBN 1-4104-6504-7 (hardcover)
    1. Journalists—Scotland—Fiction. 2. Highlands (Scotland)—Fiction. 3. Large type books. I. Title.
    PR9619.4.S35N67 2013b
    823'.92—dc23   2013037242

Published in 2014 by arrangement with Atria Books, a division of Simon & Schuster, Inc.

Printed in the United States of America
1 2 3 4 5 6 7 18 17 16 15 14

For Maeve Nolan

"Stormy weather,
Since my man and I ain't together,
Keeps raining all the time."
— "STORMY WEATHER"
BY HAROLD ARLEN AND TED KOEHLER

PROLOGUE

Mrs. Frank Urquhart was dead set against the Sabbatarians. What right did religious folk have to tell others they couldn't do anything other than pray on a Sunday? How could they dictate no hanging out washing on a fine day — which Sunday often was?

Here I am with the whole of the shinty team's shorts an' shirts, and I'm expected to leave the washing until Monday? No chance. God must be a man, she always complained. *No woman would ignore grass stains and mud stains, to say nothing of the blood, for two whole days.*

It was Saturday night; she was waiting for the water to boil in the washhouse attached to their council house on one of the new schemes of homes built for decent working families.

They'll need a good long soak this week, she thought as she sorted through the big wicker hamper, the one with the leather

9

handles that was delivered to her house a couple of hours after the match ended if it was a home game, Monday if it was away.

The smell didn't bother her — she was a nurse. This job she accepted as her duty, her husband being the manager of the town shinty team.

"Would you look at yon?" she muttered when she reached in for the socks, "one of those eejits has left his boot in with the dirty washing."

When she pulled the boot from the pile and found a foot in the sock inside, she screamed loud enough and shrill enough to set the dog barking, her daughter running, and wake her husband up from his chair in front of the fire, where he was dreaming of the team winning the competition and drinking whisky from the silver Camanachd Cup itself.

Her daughter, Morag, who was sixteen and a replica of her mother, ran in to see what the noise was about. She almost threw up at the sight, but had the sense to relieve her mother of the boot — and the foot — and lock it in the pantry out of reach of the dog. But not before her father, the feared coach, had seen the end stump of the leg and passed out on the washhouse floor, where Nurse Urquhart used an already bloody pair of shorts to stem the flow from the cut on his forehead. Then Morag called the police.

The confusion in the ensuing forensic investigation came about because no one dared mention that Coach Frank Urquhart always fainted at the sight of blood.

ONE

For once, Hector Bain, the *Highland Gazette*'s photographer, was first in the office for the obligatory Monday morning news meeting. He needed to match the names of the players to the shots from an unusually high-scoring shinty match the previous Saturday.

The team list, written in Hector's tiny wee script that even he had trouble deciphering, was in the cheapest notebook available, a school jotter, which Hector bought by the dozen. The prints and the contact sheet were in the plain brown envelope preferred by the legal profession, with a red ribbon wound around a circle of cardboard the size of a half-crown piece.

"Right," he was muttering, "this is definitely Willie Fraser, the captain." The captain looked like a thug. But then again, so did most of the shinty team when on the field.

Hec scratched his head, hoping his carrot-colored hair would cause whatever Celtic goddess was the patron of memory to look favorably on him and give him a clue to who the other players were.

Last Saturday's game had been fast and furious — games in the Highland League were legendary for their competitiveness. By halftime, Mrs. Urquhart, a nurse as well as the coach's wife, had been busy, her first aid kit almost empty.

Shinty is the game of warriors — so many players believed. An ancient game, predating the Celts, it gave birth to ice hockey; it reawoke the fiercesome rivalries that had all but died out with the dispersal of the clan system. Team rivalries were intense; the games fought as fiercely as ancient clan battles but with a small concrete-hard ball and double-sided hockey-style sticks instead of claymores.

The phone rang. Hector ignored it. Fiona the receptionist called up the half-spiral stone staircase, "Hector, pick up the phone, it's for you."

Even though there was no one else in the reporters' room, and no need to feel embarrassed, Fiona's voice made him blush.

"Hello, Hector? It's me, Frankie Urquhart."

14

"That was a great game on Saturday," Hector said. Frankie was a friend as well as a neighbor.

"Aye, well, it was. But we lost, so ma dad's no' in the best of moods. Listen, I'm phoning you from work so I can't be long. I just wanted to tell you that Sergeant Patience wants to know why you took a picture o' the leg my mother found in the shinty boot."

"Sergeant Patience?" Hector was not happy to be involved with Sergeant Patience again; their truce was fragile. "Do you still have the leg?"

"Naw, the police took it away. Took the whole hamper and we don't know when we'll get it back. Dad is livid 'cos we don't have spare shirts and we're away to Kingussie next Saturday."

"Pity."

"Aye. Dad wants you to write about what happened in the newspaper, ask if anyone . . ."

"Has lost a leg?" Hec was laughing at his own joke when Joanne Ross and Rob McLean, reporters on the *Gazette,* walked in. "I'll get Rob to talk to your dad," said Hec and hung up.

"No favors," Rob said, "I am not writing up some stupid story so your pals can have their names in the paper."

15

Rob and Hector and Frankie had known one another since primary school, and although Rob regarded Hec as nineteen and sixpence in the pound, they were all good friends in the known-each-other-since-in-their-prams kind of way.

"Suit yourself." Hector turned to Joanne, who was sitting next to him, wondering if it had warmed up enough to take off her scarf and Fair Isle beret.

"Mrs. Ross . . ." His ginger-cat-colored eyes fixed on her. "My friend Frankie Urquhart, his mum found a boot in the shinty team's dirty washing and there was half a leg in it wearing their team sock, and I took some pictures." He shook some prints out of a large brown envelope onto the table.

"Horrible!" Joanne shuddered, not wanting to examine the picture of the severed limb too closely.

"Brilliant!" Rob was staring at the pictures, seeing a good story and even better headlines of the "legless" variety. Somehow Hector had managed to capture the end of the stump in vivid Technicolor — even though the film was black-and-white.

McAllister, the weekly newspaper's editor, and Don McLeod, the deputy and chief sub editor, walked in. The town bells struck nine o'clock, and McAllister started the news

16

meeting.

"Right, what have we got for this week?" McAllister wanted the meeting over with because he had a bad case of chilblains and his feet were horribly itchy. *Serves me right for buying those newfangled nylon socks — they don't even keep your feet warm.*

"I've got these." Hec pushed the shots across the table to the two editors. A miniature cloud of cigarette smoke hovered above them, the tall, narrow room being too cold for smoke to rise.

Don McLeod, a short stubby man who, after many weeks in gaol for a crime he did not commit, looked all of his sixty-six years. Chain-smoking did not help his health, and his skin had taken on a distinct tobacco tinge. "What team is thon sock from?"

"Our local," Hec said.

"Great." Being a man of Skye, any team other than his island team was Don's dire enemy when it came to shinty. "So, Hector Bain, in less than thirty words" — he poked a particularly lurid close-up with his wee red editing pencil — "how did you come by these pictures?" He said this knowing it was impossible for Hec to tell the simplest story in less than ten minutes.

When he had finished, McAllister was glad Hector Bain was the staff photogra-

17

pher, not a reporter; for Hec, putting events into sequence was impossible.

"So the coach, Mr. Urquhart, where does he live?" the editor asked.

"Two doors down from me in Dochfour Drive." Hector registered McAllister's impatience rising to nine on a scale of one to ten. "The team was playing at home on Saturday. Mrs. Urquhart does the washing for the team . . ." It was the only way the coach could ensure every one of his part-time players turned up in full team strip. "And when she found the leg she screamed and ma granny went round to see what was wrong, but it was her husband Frank Urquhart who was bleeding, 'cos he'd hit his head, and this leg, it was lying on the floor, so . . ."

"Since you take your camera everywhere," said Don, eager to get on with the news meeting.

"Probably sleep with it," Rob quipped, and was rewarded with the sight of Hec going as red as his hair.

"I took a few shots, but Frankie, that's my pal, had to call the doctor for his dad Frank 'cos his head needed stitches, then police came . . ."

Hector didn't say, but when he recognized his nemesis, Sergeant Patience, climbing out

18

of a police car two sizes too small for his ample body, he jumped the fences between the back gardens, ran home, and hid in his studio cum shed cum washhouse, putting up the red No Admittance sign before developing the film of the leg in the shinty sock and boot.

"This is my story," Joanne announced. "Rob isn't interested."

"I am so," Rob protested. "Plus I played shinty at school, so I know the rules."

"This is front page plus page three, so both of you are on it." McAllister scribbled a note on his running sheet. "Rob, do a lead story and a background filler on the Shinty — interteam rivalries, who would want to sabotage the team, and all that. Joanne, you interview Mrs. Urquhart."

"I can get some great headlines on this." Don was pleased. He started to scribble.

"Next?" McAllister asked.

"I have something that might be interesting . . ." Joanne began, when Mal Forbes, the new advertising manager, walked in.

"Sorry I'm late, chasing up an account," Mal said before taking a chair at the far end of the table. He was too new in the job for friendship, but all agreed he was efficient and hardworking, and after only two months had the advertising rolling in. He was polite to the others, but secretly considered Rob McLean frivolous, Don McLeod too old, and Joanne to be a grace-and-favor appointment on the *Gazette,* her being the "very good friend" of McAllister. Hector he totally ignored except when he needed him to take a picture to help sweet-talk a customer into taking a bigger advertisement.

Joanne thought Mr. Malcolm Forbes resembled a weasel; his shiny black slicked-back hair oozing Brylcreem, his shiny three-piece suit bought from a national chain of cut-price tailors, and his ridiculous briefcase, more suited to a high court judge than an advertising manager, irritated her. But it was his condescending manner to all things female that vexed her. She could say nothing; condescending males were ten a penny and Mal was no worse than most.

Stop being so unreasonable, she told herself. *Most men think women should stay in the kitchen.*

"I've a double page booked for this week," Mal announced, "and what with all the rest of the ads, we'll need four more pages."

"No . . ." McAllister groaned, "I mean — good for you, Mal. But what we'll fill the pages with heaven only knows." He turned to Joanne. Since McAllister and Joanne started courting, he was careful to not show favoritism in the office. To her this came across as distant; to Mal Forbes, she was still McAllister's fancy woman. The others hadn't noticed much change in their relationship.

"It's this notice in our classified section . . ." She hesitated, no longer confident it was interesting.

"I've a good-size ad for flour booked to run for four weeks opposite the Women's Page," Mal interrupted, looking straight at her. "Maybe Mrs. Ross could do some recipes. The advertisers really like your page. My wife does, too." He saw the flush spread across her cheekbones and assumed she was pleased at the compliment. "Now, if you'll excuse me, I've clients to call on." He was off his chair and out the door and running down the stone staircase without waiting for an answer, leaving Joanne struggling, wishing she could come up with a witty retort.

Recipes! she thought. *And the worst is, none of the others see anything wrong with his suggestion.* She well knew very few, women included, would see anything wrong in a woman being told to pursue recipes rather than a severed leg in a shinty sock.

"Sorry, Joanne," McAllister apologized, "but we need something to fill those pages."

"I'll ask my mother-in-law for her recipe for plum duff, shall I?"

This was meant sarcastically, but Don said, "You make one to test the recipe, then I can have a piece. I love a good plum duff." He nudged her with his elbow. She laughed. Good humor was restored all round.

"Right," McAllister said, "let's find out all we can about this leg. It's looks like a story that could . . ."

"Run." Don, old sub editor that he was, couldn't resist.

Rob decided it was best to speak to Sergeant Patience in person. "He's upstairs wi' Detective Inspector Dunne," the constable on the desk said.

"I'll wait." Rob settled down with a copy of yesterday's *Sunday Post,* but didn't have time to finish the comic section, as the galumphing steps of the police sergeant could be heard coming down the stairs from the detectives' room.

The desk constable gestured with his head towards Rob, and the sergeant looked at the reporter. He too gestured with his head and mouthed, *outside.*

"DI Dunne will go too far one day," the sergeant complained. "He's banned smoking in the office."

22

Rob, being a nonsmoker and knowing how small the detectives' offices were, sympathized with the detective inspector.

"We have pictures of the leg in the team sock and boot." Rob knew there was no point in denying Hector's intrusion into the crime scene.

"One day, I'll get that little twerp Hector Bain."

"Aye . . ." Rob was about to say "the bane of your life," but he needed the sergeant's good grace.

"The leg was at least three days dead before it was cut off," Sergeant Patience said. "DI Dunne is going to call McAllister and ask for your help 'cos so far, none o' the hospitals has lost a leg."

"You want us to publish an appeal asking if anyone has lost a leg?"

"Aye." The sergeant smiled, for once seeing the humor in the situation. "Mind, it's probably some eejit's idea o' a joke."

"Or a threat."

The sergeant looked at Rob. "Do you know something I should know?"

"No. That was a guess. I mean, it is shinty. You know how seriously the teams take the Camanachd Cup. But the Highlands isn't Glasgow, it's not Celtic versus Rangers."

Rob and the sergeant were amused by the

story: they knew shinty rivalries. They knew the players — in the main, young men from scattered communities of the Highlands and Islands; they knew the games were a chance to blow off steam, to travel, to have an after-game drink or seven, but sabotage, threats, and physical damage were always confined to the field. So this leg business was most unusual.

"Are the police going to make a statement?"

Sergeant Patience considered this. "Naw. It's no' as though it was a fresh leg. As I said, it's probably just some o' the lads up to mischief an' taking the joke too far."

"Not much of a laugh if it was your leg. I mean, you'd be very attached to your leg . . . if you were alive when you lost it."

"Aye, there is that." They grinned; the case had to be investigated, but both appreciated the joke.

Over the next days the gossip about the foot in the boot ran around the town, the glens, the islands. In the telling and retelling the story became so garbled, everyone was avid to read the full account in that week's *Gazette.* The edition sold out by midday. And although the newspaper account added to the mirth and speculation and puns and bad jokes, no one came forwards to claim the leg.

For Joanne, the most mortifying part of that week's edition came the day after publication.

McAllister congratulated the team, telling them the paper had sold out. "And there's a real controversy brewing in the letters to the editor." He winked at Joanne as he said this.

Normally she would pretend she didn't notice, whilst loving the attention he paid her. This time she was wary; *something in his grin,* she thought.

"Aye," he continued, "there's been some irate letters complaining that the ingredients in the plum duff recipe are no' the 'real' plum duff."

Joanne was furious. "It's my mother-in-law's recipe. You can't get more authentic than that."

"First a potential war between shinty teams, now the battle of the bakers, I'm loving this." Don McLeod was chortling.

"Aye, and my mother-in-law will be up in arms if you dare publish even one criticism of her recipe." But Joanne had the grace to laugh. And the sense to know that Don McLeod and John McAllister's policy was "publish and be damned," then sit back and enjoy the controversy.

Two

Joanne always hated February: cold, damp, miserable — in other words, *dreich*. To her dreich was the alternative name for February — the *r* rolling off the tongue, the *e* elongated, the *ch* said at the back of the throat as though there was a terminal illness lurking there — dreich. The only bright spots of the month were the first shoots of snowdrops pushing up through the frost and snow, the spring lambs cavorting in the fields on the lower farms, and the river that ran through the town, threatening to burst its banks with the volume of melted snow.

Joanne was discovering that that week's copy of the *Highland Gazette* — plum duff recipe and all — had caused quite a stir.

For the people of the Highlands, Skye and the smaller islands, Loch Ness, and the fault line of the Great Glen, the story of the leg was a major talking point and a major mystery, and the telephone at the *Gazette* barely stopped ringing all day.

In a quiet moment between phone calls — mostly asking about the recipe or the foot — an advertisement registered with her, principally because it was run in the Lost and Found section:

Seeking friends and colleagues of the late Robert John Bell, USAF, based at RAF Kinloss 1951 to 1952.

The notice had run twice without Joanne paying it much attention, even though she always read all the classified adverts, believing they gave a true sense of the state of a community. She loved the Goods for Sale ads. The notices. The Lost and Found. The sadness. The optimism. The crushed dreams.

FOR SALE Unwanted engagement ring.

LOST Dearly loved pet rabbit. Answers to the name of Fluffy.

FOUND Set of false teeth in drinking fountain at bus station.

NOTICES Lovat Scouts who served in the Faroe Islands — reunion dinner.

It was this that made a local newspaper. This that thrilled Joanne every time she opened a crisp fresh, sharp-smelling copy of the *Gazette*. After nearly two years, she would still nod to herself, smiling softly, as she saw her words, her writing, not quite believing her luck that she worked here as a reporter on the *Highland Gazette*.

The notice: the *late* Robert Bell? When did he die? How did he die? Where? Here? Who was seeking information? His widow? His mother? Why search now, more than six years later?

Joanne hadn't told anyone her idea for the article, and with no story of substance for the next edition, she decided to investigate — anything was better than more recipes.

She went downstairs. "Who placed the notice about the American airman?" she asked Fiona, the *Gazette* receptionist.

"Mrs. Mae Bell," Fiona replied. "She's American, the widow of the man mentioned in the notice. She's paid for it to run three times."

Fiona paused, wondering if she had made a mistake; the notice was so unusual, she had not known where to place it. With Mrs. Bell's approval, it appeared in the Lost and Found section.

"There's been one reply. I left a message

28

at her hotel. Mrs. Bell is coming in later today to collect it."

Probably a waste of time, Joanne thought, *but it might make a wee filler.*

Late on Friday morning, knowing Joanne was alone, Fiona climbed the stairs and stood in the doorway of the newsroom. Fiona had always admired Mrs. Ross. She felt she could and should tell her about the note before Mrs. Bell arrived.

"Mrs. Ross, I found this."

Fiona had found the letter on the reception desk with the other mail that morning. There was no postmark, no stamps on the envelope. She opened it. The writing was in neat capitals, in blue ink. It was almost a plea rather than a threat.

TELL THE AMERICAN WOMAN
TO GO HOME. NO GOOD WILL
COME OF HER POKING AROUND.

When Joanne had read the letter, Fiona asked, "Should I tell the lady about this?" Being new in the job, she was anxious to do the right thing.

"Why did you open the envelope? Isn't this for Mrs. Bell?" Joanne was examining the paper, a lined sheet from a writing pad, probably bought in Woolie's.

"I didn't." Fiona straightened her back; her cheeks went pink. "I don't open correspondence if it's private. There is a separate one for her, but this was addressed to the *Highland Gazette*."

"Sorry, Fiona, I know you wouldn't do anything improper."

"Anyhow, Mrs. Bell will be here later; why don't you talk to her yourself?"

"Call me when she arrives, and I'll come down." Joanne smiled. "By the way, McAllister thinks you are really good at your job." She'd made that up, but she had noticed how efficient Fiona was, especially for a sixteen-year-old. *I'll make sure McAllister tells her himself.*

Joanne was still assigned to the shinty story, but aside from Nurse Urquhart, there were no women or children involved, and Rob was covering the search for the culprit, so once again she was relegated to what the others called the "Wimmin's Page." It rankled. So she was more than ever determined to uncover a news story of her own. That she wanted to impress McAllister, she would admit only to herself, but another part of her wanted to be a real journalist, an investigative journalist, as McAllister called it.

The phone rang. "Mrs. Ross, Mrs. Bell is

in reception."

"I'll be right down."

Rob, who had returned from covering the magistrate's court five minutes since, asked, "What's going on?"

"A story . . . and I'm not sharing." She stuck her tongue out at him and ran down the stairs.

Joanne was watching the stranger from the foot of the stairs. Sideways on, she appeared a strikingly good-looking woman, blond — rich, old-gold blond — and tall for a woman, about the same height as Joanne, who stood five foot nine in her bare feet. Mrs. Bell was reading the letter.

What Joanne noticed next were her clothes: the costume in an expensive wool fabric, well cut, snug fitting — Joanne recognized the design from the *Vogue* magazines her friend Margaret McLean, Rob's mother, passed on to her.

Mrs. Bell's high-heeled shoes were completely unsuitable for February in the highlands of Scotland — unless you took taxis — which Mrs. Bell did. Her nylons, seams perfectly straight, had no runs stopped with nail varnish — something Joanne had to resort to when she couldn't afford a new pair.

Most of all, the beautiful camel hair coat,

in a perfect shade of caramel, draped over her shoulders, and the silk scarf, casually and only semi-concealing the single strand of pearls, made Mrs. Mae Bell the epitome of a fashionable woman in her thirties on her way to have tea with Princess Margaret.

"Hello, you must be Mrs. Bell, I'm Joanne Ross, a reporter on the *Gazette*. I'd like to ask you about the notice you put in the newspaper."

"Well, if it helps me find some of my late husband's friends or colleagues, I'd be happy to talk with you," Mae Bell replied. Her voice, the accent — American but with a hint of somewhere else in it — the way she was cocking her head to one side as though everything a person said was interesting, immediately endeared her to Joanne. *She's a heroine out of an American film.*

"As I'm in your town, I thought I'd have lunch here. Won't you join me? We can talk more easily over a drink." She saw Joanne hesitate. "My treat."

Joanne was about to protest but thought, *Why not?* The woman could obviously afford it.

Mae Bell managed the cobblestones of Castle Wynd with ease, high heels being her usual form of footwear. Joanne felt clumsy as she walked beside her.

"Do you mind if we eat at the Carlton? I enjoyed the lunch there last time I was in your charming town."

Joanne was conscious that she was not dressed for the only smart restaurant and cocktail bar in town; she was wearing slacks — partly because they were so much easier on a bicycle, but also because she had decided newspaper reporters were absolved from the dress code of twinset and pearls, the unofficial uniform of middle-class matrons of Scotland. McAllister had given Joanne a book by Martha Gellhorn, and the American writer and journalist was her new role model. *Martha probably wears slacks,* she reassured herself as they went up the stairs to the first-floor restaurant.

The waiter handed over the menus. Mae Bell said, "Before we choose, I'll have a martini. Mrs. Ross, won't you join me?"

Joanne was staring, her mouth open like the proverbial goldfish; she had never drunk a martini in her life, and never ever had alcohol at lunchtime.

"I . . ."

"Oh, go on . . ." Mae Bell laughed. "A friend of mine owns newspapers; I know all about the afternoon after publication."

Joanne noted the plural, *newspapers,* and said, "I must be one of the few Scots who

33

don't drink. Well, not much anyway . . ."

"Two dry martinis," Mae Bell ordered.

"Oh no, I couldn't possibly drink a martini . . ."

"Go on — let your hair down."

It was Mae Bell's eyes that initially won her over — so dark the brown was almost black, and gleaming like wet coal. It was the way Mae Bell laughed, the gurgle like whisky pouring from the bottle, rich, brown, warming, life-enhancing, which persuaded Joanne she was not being mocked. The drink came, and when they had toasted each other and she had taken her first sip and had managed, just, not to choke, she began to enjoy herself and the conversation. The widow of Robert John Bell was exotic, funny, sophisticated, and clever; Joanne liked the woman immensely. And after the food and the martinis — two for Mae Bell — Joanne was surprised how fast time had vanished; how little time it had taken for Mrs. Bell to endear herself to Joanne.

Joanne Ross knew many people and was liked by many but had only one close friend, Chiara Kowalski — a woman who, like Joanne, was a newcomer to the town. Joanne always thought it was the shame of her violent marriage that made friendships difficult. In moments of introspection, when she considered how small was her circle of true friends, she acknowledged she appeared self-sufficient; her outward image was of a woman in full control, whilst inwardly she had the self-confidence of a caged wild bird.

Mae put a cigarette into a holder, lit it, blew the smoke towards the ceiling, and came to the point of their meeting. "Thank you for agreeing to write about Robert."

Joanne could not recall agreeing to any such thing, but a single martini had made her think she would agree to almost anything on a drink that strong. *And at lunchtime too!*

"When the telegram came, I couldn't open it. I called Charlie, my husband Robert's brother." Mae was speaking as though their conversation had been taking place over a week, not just the last hour, as though Joanne was aware of all the protagonists, the background, the time and place. "He came immediately, read it, and it was as I feared: Robert, my husband, my love, had gone down with his aircraft in the middle of the North Sea. There were no survivors. And the aeroplane was never found. No bits of wreckage surfaced. No explanation ever given. Even after a full inquiry, where the experts had so many theories but no facts,

35

the verdict was 'cause unknown.' Not easy to live with — 'cause unknown.' No body, no funeral, no final farewell . . ." Her voice trailed off. She stubbed her cigarette into the ashtray, causing it to tilt and almost spill onto the whiter-than-white tablecloth. Mae didn't notice.

"But we sure had a wake. In Paris." She closed her eyes. Whether to remember or to hide her emotions, Joanne couldn't tell.

"Yep, three days and nights, and the music . . ." She sighed. "After that — shock, grief, I couldn't sing. For the first time ever . . . since I was a little girl, I've always been singing, humming, but after Robert disappeared, it was nearly three years before I could sing again." Mae recalled the little bird in a gilded cage; one of the Frenchmen who adored Mae Bell bought it at the market and presented it to her and it sang all day long, and before long she was singing with the little bird, to the little bird, harmonies, trills, arpeggios, repetitious phrases where she and the bird competed to outdo each other.

Joanne was quiet, hearing the words and listening between the lines.

"So this is a pilgrimage for me," Mae continued. "I want to visit the places he wrote to me about. See the cathedral in

36

Elgin, the places he described in his letters, and the river there. I want to walk where he walked. To see what he saw. He loved Findhorn, near where he was stationed, thought it an almost perfect place if only the temperature were twenty degrees warmer."

Joanne laughed. "I agree. But ten degrees warmer. Scottish people couldn't survive the heat." She was wondering how to raise the subject of the note, but no need; Mae Bell was ahead of her.

Taking the note from her handbag, Mae smoothed it out on the table. "This is interesting." She touched the paper and traced the writing with a perfectly manicured finger, the polish a sinful shade of red. "A woman wrote this, don't you agree?"

"It's neatly written — the block capitals are elegant — but I couldn't say for sure."

"And it raises the point that the writer must know about my husband's fate . . . don't you agree?" From the coolness of Mae Bell's voice, it was obvious she had thought about the note or, more importantly, the writer, many times.

"Possibly . . ." Joanne looked again at the note.

"A note like that is an invitation for a good journalist to investigate further. Yes?"

Mae Bell's statement and Joanne's need

for a good story that was hers alone collided.

"You're right. And I will. Investigate." A quick glance at her watch and Joanne saw that an hour and a half had passed.

Mae called for the bill, paid, tipped, gathered her bag, her cigarettes, and lighter, and said, "Let's do this again."

As the women made their way out onto the street, Joanne almost walked in to Mal Forbes, who was about to go into the downstairs bar.

"A bit posh for you here, isn't it?" Mal said.

He was friendly. He was joking. Just stating the obvious. Joanne knew that. But was offended just the same.

Then he saw Mae Bell, who was buttoning her coat to be ready for the onslaught of winds funneling down the streets straight from the North Sea.

"Hello, and who have we here?" The voice changed to a purr; the body changed from slightly too short Scotsman to suave lounge lizard. He raised his hat, held out the other hand, and said, "Malcolm Forbes."

Mae Bell ignored the hand — but gracefully, with an I'm-tangled-up-in-coat-and-handbag-and-scarf gesture — said, "I'm a friend of Joanne's . . . Oh my, is that the time? My train is in five minutes . . . Joanne, point me to the station . . . Oh, of course . . . I'll call . . . good to meet you, Mr. Fraser . . . so long, my dear, that was lovely . . . let's do this again . . . soon." And she was gone in a trail of scent and smiles, leaving a beaming Joanne and a curious Mal in her wake.

"Who is that woman?"

Joanne, taking her cue from Mae, said, "A friend," and walked away, but in the wrong direction; the effect of her first-ever martini made her doubt she would make it back to the office. She went for coffee instead and took an hour over two cups, replaying again and again the conversation with the exotic Mae Bell, daring to think that she and Mae Bell might possibly end up friends. *Good friends.*

Next Monday at the news meeting, Joanne said, "I have a story."

She explained about Mae Bell and her search for her husband's friends. Joanne finished outlining the article, but for reasons unknown even to her, she left out the anonymous note. *Wait and see,* she was thinking, *surprise McAllister with a story worthy of the front page.*

"I like the idea," Don said. "I remember

the story of that aeroplane disappearing. There was a huge search-and-rescue operation. Nothing was found. And at the Fatal Accident Enquiry, there was no evidence as to what happened. To this day it's a mystery."

"Human interest stories, that's what a local paper does best," McAllister added.

Joanne smiled. "It may not turn into much but it's a nice story . . ."

"Aye, it's a nice wee story, just right for the Wimmin's Page." Mal smiled at Joanne. She blushed. Her hands were trembling. She put them under the table. And not one of the men in the room noticed anything untowards.

THREE

"Highland Gazette." Rob listened. "Witches did it? Any proof? Your mother-in-law? Name?" The caller hung up. And this was one of the more moderate of the suggestions about how a severed leg had shown up in a local woman's washing.

The story had run in the newspaper for a second week because Don McLeod wanted to string it out as long as possible. Him being a shinty man and the town team the archrival of his beloved Skye team, skullduggery involving rivals he welcomed greatly. The theories as to what had happened were as convoluted as a paperback thriller. And as far-fetched as a faerie story. He loved a story that gave him plenty of opportunities for a good headline.

When the phone went for the fifth time in half an hour, Rob answered, "Highland Hauntings, how may we help?"

"Rob, it's Frankie. Listen. My mother has

gone spare about the story in the paper. So many folk have been teasing her about it, she's likely to strangle Hector. She blames him for all the gossip about her finding the leg."

"Nothing could stop the story getting out. Even in shinty circles, this is bizarre."

"I know, but can you leave her name out o' it if the story runs next week? And warn Hector to hide if she sees him. Thanks, Rob."

Rob remembered Frankie's mother best from his primary-school days. Children and teachers throughout the town knew her as Nurse Urquhart, the Nit Nurse. That she took children's height and weight and checked their general health besides looking for nits was overlooked. And the shame of a letter home pronouncing that you had the wee beasties haunted many a child for the rest of their lives.

It was Joanne who had interviewed her. Mostly Rob interviewed men, Joanne women, though she occasionally thought it should be reversed, Rob being so good with females and her getting on well with men.

"When I saw it, I knew it was no' a fresh leg," Nurse Urquhart told Joanne, "so I knew it had to be a sick joke. Those shinty lads can be a wee bit wild sometimes, and

they're aye joking about Frank — ma husband, how he faints at the sight o' blood.

"No," she said to Joanne, "I've no idea
how the leg came to be in the washing.

"Aye," she continued, "I've racked ma
brains, and all I can think is it was some o'
the lads thinking it would be a laugh.

"No, we've no enemies," she answered.
"Shinty folk are right friendly off the field."

Joanne accepted her story, but there was
something, she thought later, something in
the way Mrs. Urquhart's hands fidgeted
with an invisible piece of knitting as she sat
in the armchair by the fireplace with a cup
of tea untouched on the nest of side tables.

*But finding a severed leg in the washing is
enough to make anyone nervous,* Joanne
reasoned.

Another edition of the *Gazette* came out,
and the story was once more dissected and
discussed, and argued over. Then one bright
spark, a player on the Beauly shinty team,
thinking to stir him up, asked his uncle, a
gravedigger at Tomnahurich cemetery, if he
had lost a body, or a body part.

His uncle was furious, denying that anything had ever gone missing on his watch.
Then Double Donald, as he was known,
remembered the earth on a fresh grave be-

ing disturbed, but not obviously so, when he had come to work the previous Monday morning.

So he, Donald Donaldson, phoned Sergeant Patience and asked him to come over but begged that it be kept quiet. Having made the request *after* he told his story, and *after* he had shown the sergeant the grave in question, he realized there was no chance of the matter being hushed up.

What Double Donald didn't mention was that this funeral on that Thursday afternoon was late, due to some problems with the widow fainting and generally behaving with no decorum.

Hysterics; a sure sign that she didn't give a damn for her husband, Double Donald always thought.

It was getting dark by the time the mourners left, and the pile of earth was almost frozen — the temperature not much above freezing all day. His feet were numb, his hands even colder, and Brian, his fellow gravedigger, was off sick with the flu. Double Donald was afraid of the dark, but never afraid of ghosts; *there's no such thing,* he always said when asked about his job, but still he barely covered the coffin with earth.

He had pulled the tarpaulins over, weighting them with a shovelful of soil at each corner, vowing to get there earlier than usual the next morning, then took off before real dark set in.

Next morning, again the frost was thick, silvering everything in the cemetery, making it look as though ghosts had left their ectoplasm much as a snail leaves traces of its presence. He saw immediately that the grave had been disturbed, but as he was on his own, there was no need to tell anyone. He hurriedly filled it in, doing the job neatly and properly, and tried to think no more about it. Until his nephew reminded him.

"An exhumation order?" McAllister said when Rob, via Sergeant Patience, told him the news.

They were all seated around the reporters' table, except for Mal Forbes, who was seldom in the office.

"You have to sell face-to-face," Mal told Fiona. Often.

"An exhumation? Can I take pictures?" Hector was almost out the door in excitement.

"Only if no one sees you," Don warned, speaking through a mouthful of cold plum duff. "Joanne, if McAllister keeps shilly-shallying around, I'll marry you — this is the best pudding . . ."

"Who's supposed to be in this grave?" Joanne wanted to change the subject. Although she hadn't lied, she had led McAllister to believe she had slaved over a hot stove to test the plum duff recipe. When he asked for a second pudding to share in the office, she had to beg Mrs. Ross Senior to steam another one.

"He was a retired clerk in the county council," Don replied, "married with a grown-up daughter, a man never known to play anything except lawn bowls, and curling when the lochs freeze over. He died of a heart attack and has no connection to any shinty team."

"Joanne, you interview the widow," McAllister decided. "Hec, you go too — and be tactful — better still, say nothing. Rob, any further with finding out why the leg was in the laundry basket?"

"There are more theories floating than on the true identity of the Stone of Destiny," Rob replied.

"Well," Don said, "keep digging," and was rewarded with groans all round.

Double Donald and his workmate, Brian, dug down to the coffin. It was not buried deep. The grave was a communal family plot, with the deceased laid on top of his grandfather; his long-dead sister, who had not survived her fifth birthday; his father; and his mother, with little space left for his wife, who was fortunately extremely healthy for seventy-seven.

Reaching the coffin, the gravediggers stood back. They leaned on their shovels, watching a policeman and two men from the mortuary completing the final task — opening the coffin lid. A representative from the procurator fiscal's office was on one side, noting everything on a clipboard. All that was needed was to check if the deceased had two legs. What state the body would be in was on all their minds.

"Easy does it!" one of the men at the graveside called out to his partner. The earth was wet, and he had a horror of slipping into the hole of the dead, and of putting a foot through the coffin lid.

There was the sound of a crowbar, or a genteel version thereof, echoing through the still air. Hearing the coffin lid crack, the men instinctively stepped back; through the gap a ghost, a vestige of the man's essence, could escape, seek a living, breathing home in one of them, or perhaps remain lingering with the other spirits that inhabited Tomnahurich Cemetery, this home of the dead, this hill of the faeries.

All Double Donald could think was, *Thank goodness it's freezing, I can't stand the smell o' death.* He was a gravedigger because his father had had the job before him, and after the war you took what work you could get.

The policeman nodded, the lid was replaced, the coffin secured. The men returned to the mortuary van and drove away. The policeman followed with no thanks, no explanation, no information offered to the gravediggers — not that they expected any from a policeman.

"So what did they find do you think?"

"Search me," Double Donald replied to. They began to fill in the hole, making it as neat as possible; they took pride in their profession.

No one saw Hector. He was a little up the steep side of the volcanic plug around which the cemetery spread, hiding behind a cyprus. He had a lens that looked like an admiral's telescope. And a roll of fine though gruesome shots.

An exhumation being highly unusual, the story and the speculation ran for a third week. Then the leg was reburied alongside the body of the retired clerk. Double Donald and his assistant were not happy about digging the grave for a third time. Donald helped with the spadework but made his as-

48

sistant open the coffin lid whilst he went for a cigarette some distance away. The smell reached him all the same.

The police, the shinty community, the readers of the *Gazette,* the general population, and Rob McLean and Frankie Urquhart continued to be curious. The event was fast becoming one of the tales shinty lovers and players shared during the after-game drinking sessions and fund-raising events. Some even cut out and framed the front pages of the *Highland Gazette* and hung them in the clubhouse.

March soon came around. Once more there was a lack of good stories to fill the pages, but there was an abundance of advertising. The whole team was around the table discussing the next edition, particularly the ratios.

"We can't continue like this," Don complained. "Soon we'll have more advertising than editorial."

Mal Forbes overheard the remark and said, "What's wrong with that?"

Joanne rolled her eyes and said, "We are a reputable newspaper, here to tell the news — not just sell newspapers."

"And here's me thinking we're a commercial enterprise that delivers information

49

— and that is what advertising is, information," Mal said. "Besides, it's the advertising that pays the wages."

As always, he was right, and as always she found him irritating in his rightness. The conversation continued around her, washing over her like the distant sound of children in the playground. She was looking up through the rain-streaked window. She saw clouds — phantasmagorical creatures, sometimes threatening, sometimes playful, always interesting.

For her, March was cloud-racing season, and these North Sea clouds were superb at the hundred-yard dash. From east to west they would run, down the glens, following the fault line of Loch Ness, Loch Lochie, Loch Oich, to Ben Nevis, where, colliding with the mountain, they dissolved, weeing on the town and surrounding hills. The remnants — the victors — would tear off across the Western Isles to join the big bullyboys of the Atlantic.

"So we're agreed then?" McAllister asked.

"Aye," the others replied.

"Fine," Joanne said. But she had no idea what she was agreeing to and assumed that nothing could be worse than more recipes and no one was interested in a story about clouds.

It was only after the meeting was over and everyone gone that she realized nothing had been said about her article on Mae Bell.

That means it must be boring, she told herself.

When the *Gazette* came out, she saw that Don had put the article on a right-hand page, separate from the Women's Page and with a picture of the missing aircraft culled from the archives. Her first reaction was pleasure; her second, misgiving — wanting to keep Mae Bell and her exoticism all to herself — she dismissed as childish.

That same week, after the third edition featuring the lost leg, and just as Rob decided the story had, in newspaper parlance, lost its legs, he was on the right spot at the right time for the next episode.

Rob picked up the phone, only because Joanne was out. "*Gazette.* Hi, Frankie, what can I do you for? Tomorrow? Can't promise. Okay, but only if it's dry. Hector? Do I have to? Fine. See you then."

Hector came in half an hour later.

"Tomorrow we're covering the shinty match at Bught Park."

"Do I have to?" Hector asked.

"If you want to make amends with Nurse Urquhart by making her husband look good, yes."

That settled, Hector and Rob agreed to meet at two the next afternoon. For once Rob hoped for rain. For once March did not oblige, behaving like June.

The match started well. The locals were playing the team from Beauly, a well-supported, successful, and well-financed team — they had a change of shirts paid for by Lord Lovat, and they had won the Camanachd Cup a few times. Fast, noisy, the crack of stick upon stick, the players running from one goalmouth to the other with good speed, it looked to be a tight game — until halftime.

Rob and Frankie were standing a little away from the huddle of players who were standing, or sitting, or crouching down, sucking on the obligatory halftime quartered oranges. They didn't hear the remark that started the stramach until after Nurse Urquhart had shipped two players off to the infirmary, only a short walk away, saying they needed stitches. Seeing Hector standing near the players, snapping away, Rob suspected, rightly, that Hec had had something to do with the ensuing fight.

"Hello, Mr. Donaldson," Hector had said to Double Donald, "have you recovered from the fright over the leg?"

"What's he got to do with it?" someone in the local team scarf asked.

"He dug the grave the leg came from," Hector said.

"Aye, but it wasn't anything to do wi' him," a man — Double Donald's nephew, wearing a Beauly scarf, said.

It took a moment for the man, a big man with a few whiskies sneaked from a hip flask in him, to work out what had just been said. He turned on Hector.

"You're saying that this manny here" — he jerked his thumb towards Double Donald — "was in charge o' the grave the leg came out o'?"

"Aye." Hector, shielding his camera inside his duffel coat, was not liking the way the man stood over him, leaning forwards as he spoke. Or growled.

"And what's it all to do wi' you?" the man asked the nephew, the Beauly supporter.

"He's ma uncle," the nephew in the rival scarf replied.

"Is he now?"

That was all the man needed. He stepped forwards. Pushing Hec out of the way, he hit the Beauly supporter full on the nose. The spurt of blood was instant and copious and sprayed onto the attacker's jacket, but he didn't care.

53

"Hey lads," he shouted to the team, "this is the manny who dug up the leg."

"No I never, I was the one who buried it." Only after he spoke did Double Donald realize his mistake. *I should have kept ma mouth shut,* he thought as he sat on the damp grass with bright yellow stains on his face where Nurse Urquhart had applied iodine, her remedy for cuts, abrasions, gravel rash, and any ailment imaginary or otherwise.

Although they pretended otherwise, Rob and Frankie enjoyed the stramash — which was off the pitch for once. And Hector, in spite of being told by Coach Frank Urquhart that he was mincemeat if he caught him, took some glorious shots of the game — stramach and all.

"That was great," Rob and Frankie agreed when they had a drink after the game.

"We must go more often," Rob said, knowing they wouldn't because both of them would be pestered to join the team by Frankie's dad.

"This is great," said Don McLeod when he saw Hec's pictures on Monday morning.

"Given Hec started the whole fight, it's a wonder he didn't end up in the infirmary like some of the players," Rob told them.

"You should take him with you more often," Don said.

Once more the shinty team starred in the *Gazette* headlines, and once more Mr. Frank Urquhart and his wife were the talk of the community. And once again Hector was in trouble with Nurse Urquhart.

FOUR

Coach Frank Urquhart was not a man who noticed his wife much. He always assumed his tea would be on the table at six o'clock every evening, the bills paid on time, the washing done and ironed, and that Mrs. Urquhart — Nurse Urquhart, as he frequently thought of her — would, in spite of the incident of the foot in the boot, continue to launder the shinty team shirts. Which she did.

But Nurse Urquhart had other ideas when it came to bringing up her son.

That was another reason Frankie was friends with Rob McLean. Neither minded the washing-up. Both of them spoke with their mothers in words of more than one syllable, and in complete sentences. And both enjoyed their mothers' stories: Rob's mother, Margaret, about her high-society days in Edinburgh; Frankie Urquhart's mother, Nurse Urquhart, of recounting the silly sayings of the pupils at the local schools and the ridiculous prejudices of some of the parents about health and hygiene and inoculations.

"They should know better," was how she put it, " 'specially with the polio scare."

So when the two young men discussed Nurse Urquhart's state of mind, it was with fondness. And concern.

Frankie Urquhart had called asking if Rob had time for a coffee in the Castle Brae café.

Rob asked, "Is it raining?" unable to tell through the only window in the reporters' room, a window set so high, it reminded him of his Victorian primary school, where the architectural principle was never to set windows allowing pupils to see out, in case the view distracted them.

"Not yet."

"I'll see you in two minutes."

From the window table, Frankie watched his friend run down the stairs and across the car park, the collar of his jacket turned up against a blustery wind that set Rob's hair waving like seaweed in an underwater kelp forest.

"Could you do a wee story about my new jazz club?" Frankie asked after the coffee arrived.

"Jazz club?"

Rob knew that his friend's taste ran more to jazz, but he had a fine appreciation of rock, particularly Elvis.

"It's at the top of Castle Street, down a close — but you'll never find it if you don't know," Frankie said.

"Thon place?" Rob laughed. "It's a cellar with no windows burrowed into the hill-side."

"Aye, but I've had it done up, so it's a great place for pulling the birds. My idea is, one night jazz, one night blues, one night rock 'n' roll, but I might have to borrow your Dansette until we're more financial."

Frankie grinned, and not for the first time, Rob saw from the glances of the females in the café that his old school chum and fellow devotee of most things musical from the U S of A was good-looking in a pop star kind of way, with great teeth and a great smile and very carefully chosen casual clothes. *No wonder he's star salesman in Arnotts' gentlemen's department,* Rob thought.

"I'll take a look, but it's a no to the Dansette. It's sure to disappear, and I couldn't survive without my music." Rob tucked the notes of the playbill in his jacket pocket. "How's your dad? Has he recovered from this business with the leg?" Rob asked, grinning at Frankie.

"His pride is sorely battered," Frankie replied. "He's still getting no end of teasing at the shinty." Frankie blew a long blast of cigarette smoke across the table, leaned back in his chair, and said, "No, it's my mother I'm worried about."

Rob sensed there was something serious going on.

"She hasn't been herself the last couple o' months. Then the leg business — it really got to her."

"Doesn't sound like your mother." Mothers were not always people boys noticed — other than as a source of food. And clean clothes. They were not women; they were mothers.

But Mrs. Urquhart was also Nurse Urquhart. Rob remembered the brutal way she would grasp them by the hair and pull at the roots, checking for nits. The no-mercy way she would deal with any poor soul who was found with the wee beasties, the note they were given that said not to come back until the nits were gone. Then back at school, a further inspection, and if one nit, one solitary egg were found, further humiliation would descend on both child and the mother of the offender.

Tough as old boots, had been Rob's mother assessment of Nurse Urquhart the one time when nine-year-old Rob was discovered harboring a bad batch of head lice.

"Your head is alive wi' the beasties," Nurse Urquhart had pronounced, "and you from a good family, too."

"I got them from Frankie," Rob said, and he was supremely satisfied when Mrs. Urquhart checked her son and found that he too had them.

"Most likely he caught them from you," she had said, and banned the boys from playing together until the nits were conquered, to no effect.

They laughed when Rob recounted the story. "I was always terrified of your mum, I can't imagine her scared of anything," he finished.

"Aye, me too. Only . . ." Frankie gestured to the waiter for more coffees. "She had a wee accident two days ago. Fell off her bike, she says. But Mrs. Colquhoun across the road, her lass Jenny said a car hit my mother. It was pouring rain, and the driver, who must have known he hit something, he didn't stop. Mum's knee is bandaged, not much damage, gravel rash and the like on her hands and her knees, but she was really shaken, and the bike's a write-off. Jenny Colquhoun is saying it was deliberate, but she's only thirteen so no one pays her much attention."

"What does your mother say?"

"That's just it, she's saying nothing . . . and you know how normally you can't get her to shut up."

"That's all?" Rob saw his friend's face. "Sorry, I mean, what else happened?"

"Nothing." Frankie stubbed out his cigarette. "But I know something is wrong."

"Her age?" Neither Rob nor Frankie knew much about a woman's life cycle, but they knew there were times when there was nothing you could say or do without being in the wrong.

"Aye. That's likely it," Frankie agreed even though in his bones, he knew there was more to it.

They let the subject rest because out the window and across the street they watched a very unusual person struggle with an umbrella that had turned inside out in the wind, before chucking it into a rubbish bin, then running across the road and straight into the Castle Brae café.

They watched her shake her raincoat at the door then take a table next to theirs. They listened as she ordered coffee and toast and eggs "lightly scrambled."

"I'm not sure we're up to that," the waiter told her. "How about a nice spaghetti bo-

61

lognese?"

"For real?" she asked.

The waiter nodded towards his mother, a large, round woman dressed all in black. "Third-generation Scots and not one drop of her Calabrian blood diluted."

Mae Bell laughed. *"Molto bene,"* she said.

"You speak Italian?" the waiter asked.

"New York Italian . . . only to order food," came the reply.

Rob and Frankie were completely captivated. They were more than captivated when Mae Bell crossed her legs, the sheer nylons shimmering, making that swoosh, that singular sound that made Rob think of sex.

"Can I trouble you for a light?" She had a cigarette, a Lucky Strike, Rob noticed, in a holder, and was leaning towards Frankie. He produced a Zippo. Before he had a chance to open it and strike it up, she clasped a hand around his. "Can I see that?"

The badge of the USAF was engraved on the shiny silver surface.

"Oh my," she drawled, "that was my late husband's squadron."

"You must be Mrs. Bell." Rob was trying not to stare. Unsuccessfully.

"Oh please, I'm not much older than you boys, call me Mae."

A good ten years older, Rob calculated, but he said nothing.

"I got the lighter as a present when I arranged for a dance band to play at the air base," Frankie explained. "I'm Frankie Urquhart, music promoter."

"Pleased to meet you, Frankie." She held out her hand. "And you are?"

"Rob McLean, *Highland Gazette.*"

"Joanne's colleague." The cigarette remained unlit. The pasta arrived. Mae Bell excused herself, and when the waiter had produced a sparkling white napkin, which no one had ever seen in the café before now, Mae tucked it into her cleavage and started to eat.

The young men turned away to allow her the privacy necessary to eat spaghetti, but were too awestruck to leave even though they both had to be back at work.

When Mae Bell pushed aside the plate and reached for a cigarette, they dawdled, taking time to pay the bill, taking time to say cheerio even though they normally would part with nary a word other than "See ya."

"Bye, Mrs. Bell. Nice to meet you."

"Hope to see you again."

"It's been great to meet you."

"Hope you enjoyed your meal."

"See you again."

"Cheerio."

"Bye."

"See you soon I hope."

Falling over each other's sentences, hoping that the other would have the courage to offer a phone number, offer a tour of the town, a suggestion to meet up again, they left, waving through the window, taking in Mae Bell's smile, her wave back. They walked down the brae in a dwam, parting on the high street, neither saying much; Mrs. Mae Bell was like no one they had ever met before — but had dreamed of plenty.

Joanne had written a follow-up story on Robert Bell and the unsolved mystery of the plane that went missing. She found many articles about the accident in the archives, and her interview with Mae read well. Although short and in the Women's Page — human interest, McAllister called it — over the next weeks, it became a second talking point with the *Gazette* readers, reviving memories of the search in the North Sea in atrocious weather, with nothing ever found of the plane or the men on board.

Then, to Joanne's chagrin, Mae Bell became communal property: with McAllister the connection was jazz; with Rob, stories of New York; with Frankie Urquhart it was love — *No,* Joanne corrected herself, lust — *an emotion I know all too well.*

Is lust an emotion? was her next thought. *I must ask Mae.* This thought annoyed her even more. *When do I have a chance to talk to Mae? She's always surrounded by her court of admirers. Court of admirers?*

"Penny for them," McAllister said as he came into the reporters' room.

"Is it a 'court of admirers'?"

He laughed. "Are we talking about you? I hope not. I want you all to myself."

It did not work as either a quip or a compliment. That innocuous phrase, *all to myself,* that inference of ownership, sent Joanne into a panic.

She stood. "I've an interview with a poacher whose defense in the magistrate's court is that all those named Fraser have a divine right to fish the waters of the Conon. The argument has not gone down well with the Fraser clan chief. Must dash."

She was down the stairs and out into Castle Wynd before she remembered that the interview with the defendant was tomorrow. *But I knew that,* she told herself. Her heartbeat was loud; her breathing noticeable. *What's wrong with me?*

A coffee would only increase her agitation, but her feet took her across the bridge and into Gino Corelli's café, coming to a halt at her favorite window table. But she moved to the back. Being on display in front of all the passersby was not what she needed. She took a table beneath the mural of Vesuvius painted in Neapolitan ice-cream colors, a mural her youngest daughter had christened Muriel.

She tasted the espresso, which she was teaching herself to like because it was McAllister's drink, and shuddered.

"Grappa, I put it in the coffee." Gino was standing beside her and saw her face after her first swallow. "It is good for the sadness."

"Sadness? What sadness?"

He said nothing, just patted her on the arm. His look was that of a dog owner saying, *Good puppy, good girl, there, there.*

Panic she had to admit to. But the cause? She would need the emotional equivalent of the Rosetta stone to work that out.

"Finish the coffee. Go an' see your godson." From Gino this was an order. After shooing her out of the café as though she was indeed a lost puppy, he followed her out to the pavement, watched her walk towards the cathedral, made sure she turned towards his daughter's house, that she did as she was told.

Once in her best friend Chiara's kitchen, holding baby Andrew, all did indeed seem right with the world, or at least in this small corner.

She and Chiara chatted, cooed, making small sounds to delight the baby, exchanging all the details of the everyday life of mothers, outsiders, alone in a small circle of friends.

But Chiara wasn't fooled. *She'll tell me when she's ready,* she thought.

As Joanne was unable to identify the cause of her restlessness, she was unable to share with her friend. But sensing herself being examined, Joanne smiled, saying, "Sorry, I'm not good company today."

Chiara smiled back. "Cheerful or not, it's good to see you." Chiara knew not to press Joanne, so she said, "I liked your article about the missing aeroplane."

It took Joanne only a moment to connect this with Mae Bell; so obsessed had she become over the American woman — a woman she hardly knew but whom she had already made into a fantastical creature who represented *not-from-here,* so that the missing aircraft, the missing crewmen, the mystery of the whole accident were the least

67

part of the story to Joanne.

"Thanks. Though I'm not sure it's my story anymore." Joanne sat down again at the kitchen table.

Wee Andrew was back in his pram, fed, changed, and asleep. Chiara rejoined Joanne, stirring sugar into the fresh tea, tasting in, putting it down again in horror. "No matter how much sugar I put in, I don't get the point of tea. Feeding the wee one, it'll be months before I can drink an espresso again." She saw that Joanne was lost in thought, in a dwam. Chiara savored the Scottish word, a favorite of hers. "Daylight dreaming" was the translation Joanne gave her, and she had laughed, clapping her hands in glee. *I love that,* she'd said.

"Mae Bell must have been deeply in love," Joanne said, as though speaking to herself. "Six years on and she is still in love with her husband."

"I can't bear to think how you'd feel if that happened," Chiara added. "Not knowing . . ."

"I'm not sure I could love anyone that much." This time Joanne's voice was so faint, Chiara wondered if she'd heard right. So she let it go.

But when, five minutes later, Joanne said she had to get back to work, and after she

68

had hugged her friend and seen her to the door, and remarked on the weather and asked her to say hello to the girls, Chiara went back into the kitchen. Deciding that one very small coffee would not keep wee Andrew awake all night, she made coffee, sat to savor the three sips of bitter dark sinful liquid and think about Joanne's visit, and knew she had heard right.

I'm not sure I could love anyone that much.

In a straight-out Scottish accent, but with Italian open hands and shoulder shrug, she said to the sleeping baby, "What are we going to do with your auntie Joanne? Eh?"

There was no reply.

FIVE

Maybe, Joanne thought as she cycled across town to work, she was restless because she knew there was no certainty a magistrate would grant her a divorce, no matter how compelling the reasons. Hopefully, her soon-to-be-ex husband would migrate to Australia, hopefully with his new wife, and that would end that chapter of her life.

Maybe it was because McAllister had declared his intent to "court her."

Perhaps it was the appearance of Mae Bell in their small highland town. Or a longing for spring to burst through. Whatever the cause, discontent continued to rumble inside Joanne like distant thunder. So she decided to reinvent herself.

A haircut? Too expensive.

A tight, straight skirt à la Mae Bell from that length of tweed she had been hoarding for the last six months? She would have to take the bus instead of cycling everywhere.

A good story, front page in the *Gazette,* might solve her discontent; then she would be a real news reporter, not a woman relegated to writing up school events and church happenings and plum duff recipes. The attitude of Mal Forbes still rankled. Then again, he was expressing the views of at least ninety-nine percent of the population. Her daydream of becoming the Martha Gellhorn of Scotland was looking highly unlikely.

She pushed her bicycle up the last steep yards of Castle Wynd, then ran up the steps to the office. Mal Forbes was the first person she encountered as she walked into reception.

"You've no right taking that booking, they're my clients." He was leaning over the counter, talking to Fiona, whom Joanne couldn't quite see but could imagine. "I don't care if they phoned the order in, I'm the one who deals with that account, so don't be thinking you'll get commission out of this." He was waving a sheet of paper at Fiona.

Fiona was looking at the floor, miserable, trying to hide behind her fringe of thick dark hair.

Without thinking, Joanne intervened. "Leave her alone, she's only doing her job."

Mal Forbes turned, looked at Joanne, and, as Joanne later told Chiara Kowalski, he snarled.

She also told Chiara she'd never seen anyone who looked and sounded so like a nasty wee dog — a cross-breed, some mixter-maxter of corgi and terrier and collie that's always yapping, going for your ankles, making you want to kick him. (Always a "him" to Joanne.)

"This is my department, Mrs. Ross, so keep your nose out o' it."

"You are bullying a member of staff, Mr. Forbes." She needed a very deep breath to control the itch to slap the man, but Joanne had learned over years of marriage that violence was never an answer.

"Aye, aye, what's going on here?" It took an appearance by Don McLeod to end the standoff, and to get Mal to gather his papers and leave, but not before he passed a little too close to Joanne, making her feel the heat of his anger, even though he didn't actually touch her.

"You all right, lass?" Don asked Fiona.

"Fine, thank you, Mr. McLeod." She gave a half-smile. "Please don't worry on my behalf. Mr. Forbes is a good boss, and I'm learning a lot. His bark is worse than his bite."

72

Joanne stifled a laugh. Her picture of Mal as a wee terrier was obviously shared.

Don made for the stairs; Joanne followed. The reporters' room was empty. Joanne started to speak; she wanted to ask Don more about the disappearance of, and search for, Robert Bell. The sound of Rob's and McAllister's voices made her stop.

"Later," Don said. "Let's get this edition out first."

But later never came; the attack on Nurse Urquhart made them forget "later."

"None o' the shinty boys would do this," Frank Urquhart said when the police asked, at the hospital, who would do such a thing to his wife.

He was shaking; his son, Frankie, was pacing. The cigarette smoke was thick, and both men were finding it hard to comprehend what had happened. "I know the lads joke around . . ." Coach Frank was saying.

"But no one would do this," his son finished.

"It hardly touched her face," the doctor told them. He didn't tell them how badly damaged her throat was, that he privately doubted he could save her larynx, that the acid had run down her chest and etched deep rivulets in her breasts. "Her clothing saved her — and her quick thinking."

Nurse Urquhart had had a few seconds to snatch at her uniform and pull the acid-soaked fabric from her skin before losing consciousness from the pain. Her hands were a mess, the strength of the acid eating into fingertips. Again, the doctor doubted that all of the fingertips could be saved, but as Nurse Urquhart was still in surgery, he couldn't yet say how bad the damage was.

"I'm very sorry about your wife . . . and your mother." He nodded at the Urquhart men. "I'll let you know the results as soon as the operation is over."

It was the lack of reassurance that they could save her that Frankie noticed. He didn't tell his dad. But he knew. Saving her life was what it was about now. *Her throat,* he thought, *how will she breathe? How will she eat? Will she be able to talk?* He knew now was not the time to share his terror with his father. So he took himself and Coach Urquhart outside for fresh air and a cigarette.

Unfortunately, it had been a vital five minutes before Nurse Urquhart had been found. After the school bell released the schoolchildren into the playground, their shrieks alerted the teacher, Miss Rose. By that time the injuries were critical.

74

WPC Ann McPherson had taken the phone call and was on the scene within three minutes. The smell of burnt flesh and acid was revolting, but her main task was to help Miss Rose gather up the children and keep them away from the sight of Nurse Urquhart. Later the policewoman's task was to try to make sense of the children's stories.

At first, clearing the gawping, jittery semicircle of children seemed as hopeless as rounding up a flock of seagulls, and as noisy. Then the headmaster appeared with a brass handbell, and the steady clanging caused a murmuring hush. The ambulance arrived next, bells shrill. Next the uniformed men with the stretcher ran into the playground, and started the children off again, agitation and curiosity running through the crowd like a tsunami.

"In your lines." Miss Rose's voice was as loud as the bell and all the more startling, as she was as sweet and as rounded as her name. "Class monitors, lead your groups back to the classrooms."

The headmaster was watching, along with Detective Inspector Dunne, who had just arrived, had instantly recognized Nurse Urquhart — in spite of her injuries — and was furious. Mostly with himself. *I should have taken this whole incident with the foot*

75

more seriously, he was thinking.

"No," the headmaster told them, "you can't question the children yet. They're in shock." He told the inspector he would deal with the questioning himself, along with Miss Rose.

DI Dunne said nothing. Then, in his usual reasonable, quiet voice: "We need to find whoever did this as soon as possible."

The headmaster relented and allowed that WPC McPherson could assist.

It took nearly an hour and a half of talking to the five classes of children and their teachers before the report came back to the headmaster. "No one saw anyone or anything until they went outside for morning break."

WPC McPherson agreed. "None of the children saw anyone or anything strange."

"Yes," the headmaster told the police officers. "Nurse Urquhart was expected; she was halfway through her annual health inspection — weighing the children, measuring their heights, checking up on their well-being." He held out his hands in a gesture of helplessness. Attacking a woman with acid was beyond his comprehension.

"Hiya, Frankie," Rob answered, receiver under his chin hands, still typing when

Joanne had passed over the receiver. "I wrote up the jazz club but . . . What? When? Where are you now? I'll be right over." He flung the receiver back in the cradle, snatched his jacket, saw his colleagues staring at him. "Someone threw acid at Nurse Urquhart. She's in Raigmore Hospital." He was out the door, shouting over his shoulder, "It's serious."

"Acid?" Joanne asked.

"Here?" Don said.

"Horrible stuff." McAllister shuddered.

"It's no' my fault," Hector wailed.

"I'll call the police station," McAllister told them, and went into his office.

"God love us, thon's a nasty, nasty thing to do to anyone." Don let out a long sigh. "And her such a nice wifie."

"Is it to do with the shinty?" Hector asked. Nurse Urquhart had made it plain to him that his photographs and his "interfering" were very unwelcome. Even though the story of a severed foot was of huge interest in the community, she told Hector she did not thank him for broadcasting the event. That had been three weeks ago; he thought it was over and done with.

"I use acid sometimes. Even a wee drop burns right through your clothes," Hec informed them.

"You have acid?" Don asked.

"Aye, in the studio. I use it for . . ."

"And your so-called studio is next door to the Urquharts'?"

"Next door but one."

"I'd no' be telling anyone that in a hurry," Don told him.

Joanne got it first.

It took longer for Hector to get the implication. "I'd never . . . never ever . . ."

"We know," Joanne said.

"Have you checked the bottle is there?" Don asked.

"I'll go now . . ."

"Better not. Wait until someone can go with you. We don't want . . ."

"What?" McAllister came into the room.

"Hector keeps acid in his shed," Joanne said.

"Ma studio," Hector corrected her.

"And he's next door but one to the Urquharts'," Joanne continued. *And they've had a falling-out,* she didn't say.

"Joanne, go with Hec. Check on it. Take my car." He threw the keys across the table. "I've been told it's touch and go on Nurse Urquhart's life, so . . ."

"We'll be back as soon as we can." She nodded at McAllister. They knew the implications. But Hector didn't. Joanne took the keys and Hector's hand and left.

"Nasty business, acid," Don commented when they were alone. "And there's plenty o' it in this building too. The printers keep some for cleaning the plates." Shaking his head at the savagery of human nature, he spread a new sheet of paper on the desk. He reached for the em ruler and began to draw up the columns. "I'll make up a new front page."

McAllister nodded back. It was not that they were callous. Only realistic. This was front-page news.

That evening Joanne was serving up toad-in-the-hole, the girls' favorite dish, although she suspected Annie loved it for the name as much as the taste.

"Someone was horrible to the Nit Nurse," Jean, her younger daughter, announced.

"We had special assembly," Annie, at eleven, two and a half years older than her sister, continued. "We have to tell our teacher if we saw anyone hurting the nurse."

"Did you see anyone?" Joanne asked.

"We can't see out our classroom windows," Jean said.

Good. No need for them to know the horrors of the world, Joanne thought.

"Even though she's a real nosy parker, no

one hates her," Annie said. "She gives you a sweetie after the doctor gives you a jab."

"An injection," Joanne automatically corrected her.

She ignored her daughter's comments about Nurse Urquhart's being a nosy parker but was disturbed nonetheless at how observant — beyond her years — her elder daughter was. *Surely it's not right she knows these things,* Joanne thought when Annie commented on the world with an adult perspective. But Joanne excused her, always, knowing that the habit of listening in to adult conversations was a habit the child had developed over years of trying to gauge the danger, trying to preempt her father, hoping to protect her mother against the worst of her husband's violence.

"Let's hope Nurse Urquhart gets better soon." Joanne changed the subject; the attack distressed her. "There's custard with Granny's strawberry jam for pudding . . . who wants some?"

The offer did indeed end the conversation, but not Joanne's thoughts; acid aimed at the face — that had been the consensus in the newsroom — images of burnt flesh kept popping up, making her shudder.

"Rob, can we meet up in the dinner break?"

It was Frankie calling from work — a practice frowned on except for emergencies. But his boss allowed that Frankie's mother's situation was indeed an emergency.

This time they met in the bar on Baron Taylor's Lane. Both ordered no more than half a pint of beer.

"They're taking my mother to Aberdeen; she needs a special operation on her throat. They can't do it here."

Rob didn't know what to say; the longer Nurse Urquhart stayed alive, the better. But alive to recover to what?

"The police keep asking if she had any enemies. They keep asking Dad about the shinty team. Stands to reason after the leg and all that, but I don't see it . . ." Frankie stubbed out his third cigarette in fifteen minutes.

"Did you mention the time she was knocked off the bike?"

"I'd forgotten that. I suppose I'd better tell the polis." Here he paused. "I've no idea who would want to hurt her, so . . . So I looked for her handbag, but the police have it. Then I looked in her chest of drawers . . ." This was a huge confession. Boys would no more search through their mother's handbag or chest of drawers than steal the church collection.

"Right at the back, I found these."

Frankie pulled out four envelopes with NURSE URQUHART printed in capital letters on the front. Frankie took out one of the notes, printed in blue ink, from a fountain pen, on lined paper, and showed it to Rob, but half under the table, not wanting to expose the offensive message to a passerby or the light of day.

YOU HAVE BEEN WARNED. NEXT TIME I WILL NOT BE SO FORGIVING.

Rob read it. And whistled.

"The other notes seem from earlier." Frankie was shuffling the order of the notes, trying to make sense. "There's no dates, so I don't know how long this has been going on."

Rob looked at the envelopes. "No postmark. So how did she get them?"

"I don't know. I'm handing them in to the police, but first, I thought maybe we could, you know . . . look into it. But I don't want this in the paper. Not yet."

"I promise not to write this up unless you or your dad agree, but do you mind if I talk to McAllister? . . . He's always good with ideas." Rob stared at the notes again. He

82

thought there was something malicious yet cowardly about anonymous letters. It was the politeness that he found especially creepy.

"All the help I can get . . ." Frankie started. And finished. He was bereft. And helpless. He hated helpless. The notes made him beyond angry. Rob too. And anger helped.

"Let's go to the *Gazette* office now. Show them to McAllister. Then you go to the police station." Rob didn't need to say that the police station was only a short walk from the *Gazette* building, and no one need know that Frankie had shown the notes to Rob and McAllister.

"McAllister, this is my friend Frankie Urquhart. His mother is . . ."

McAllister stood, held out his hand. "I'm really sorry about your mother."

"Thanks." It was all Frankie could manage. Without being asked, he sat in one of the visitors' chairs, leaned forwards, put the three anonymous letters bundled together with an elastic band on McAllister's desk, then lit a cigarette.

McAllister raised his eyebrows at Rob.

"Frankie found these letters . . ."

"This morning." Frankie was leaning

back, blowing smoke upward, doing all he could not to see the offensive notes. "You can read them."

McAllister took off the band, laid them in a row, opened them, shuffled the notes into what he thought might be the sequence.

KEEP YOUR NOSE OUT OF WHAT DOESN'T CONCERN YOU.

This seemed to be the first note.

I HAVE WARNED YOU ONCE. I WILL NOT WARN YOU TWICE.

Then the third note.

YOU HAVE BEEN WARNED. NEXT TIME I WILL NOT BE SO FORGIVING.

The final note gave the impression of regret.

WHY DID YOU NOT HEED MY WARNING? NOW I WILL HAVE TO ACT AGAIN. IT WILL BE MORE SERIOUS THAN THE LAST TIME.

Rob was leaning over the desk, looking at

the notes but not touching them.

"First thoughts?" McAllister asked.

"Old-fashioned English, educated, no spelling mistakes . . ." Rob was rereading them to himself.

"Fountain pen, neat lettering, paper not unusual but not cheap," McAllister continued.

"A woman."

Rob and McAllister looked at Frankie. He had said this louder than he meant to. They both nodded, but McAllister asked, "What makes you think that?"

"Dunno. Maybe the way she put it — polite like. Maybe the way she formed the letters — they're too neat for a man. Maybe it's just the feeling I get . . ." His voice faded away.

McAllister and Rob felt for Frankie, saw how he was struggling to hold himself together, how the bright, cheerful Frankie that Rob knew and McAllister deduced from the smart suit, the good haircut, the polished shoes, was also fading.

"Rob, make a copy of the letters. Use the typewriter in here — it's more private. Then Frankie can give the originals to the police. Frankie, keep in touch through Rob. We can meet anytime you want to talk. And we will do all we can to help."

The decisive way McAllister rattled out orders helped. Frankie stood, thanked him.

McAllister stood and shook Frankie's hand. "Give your father my best."

"Thanks, boss." Rob spoke quietly for both of them, grateful and relieved that McAllister was involved.

McAllister saw that Rob had automatically run in three or four sheets of paper, separated by carbon paper. "Show a copy to Don. Ask his opinion." He was hoping Don the oracle might find some clue in the words.

He took his hat, walked out into a wind that could cut through steel, regretted he'd left his coat at home, and marched up the street to Boots the Chemist, making straight for the stationery department.

Basildon Bond was the label on the writing pads. Matching envelopes were next to them. Parker pens, bottles of blue ink, and black, were on the next shelf.

"Sell many of these?" McAllister asked the woman behind the counter, who was standing, looking bored, and welcomed a chance of a conversation.

"Loads," she said. "Our best line."

"These pens?"

"Aye, they don't sell as well as the new biros, but they sell. Especially after the

86

eleven plus results come out, or when school starts, or after the Highers' results, or for birthdays . . . grannies are always after buying them for birthdays."

"So, mostly sold for high school students." It wasn't a question, more an affirmation, but the woman started off again.

"Aye. Sometimes people buy them for themselves, but . . ."

"Women?"

"Mostly. Men buy black ink and . . ."

It took her a moment to register that McAllister had doffed his hat, muttered thanks, and was walking towards the stairs, leaving her still talking.

A woman, he was thinking as he walked back to the office, *would a woman do this?* He remembered the acid had caught Nurse Urquhart on the throat. *I wonder how tall she is,* was his next thought. *Maybe the attacker was shorter and missed the face?* The very idea of throwing acid was abhorrent — an act of desperation — or revenge. Whatever the motive, it was an act of hate. And hate kills.

Six

Joanne was fascinated by Mae Bell, a woman whom she hardly knew, but an exotic creature in these parts. Mae represented everything Joanne wanted to be — confident, elegant, well-traveled, mysterious. She wanted to keep Mae Bell to herself, but also wanted to show off her fascinating new friend.

Chiara and her father, Gino Corelli, were outsiders, people of the world — coming to this distant highland town from war-ravaged Italy, meeting up when the war was over, and Gino Corelli, released from a prisoner of war camp in northern Scotland, had made the decision to stay. They have no coffee or ice cream, was Gino's simple explanation for the decision. That there was nothing left for him in his birthplace was the real reason; wife killed, home and orchards and olive groves and small café burned to the ground — that was the real reason. That and a chance to make a better life.

Make a better life he did; a new café, an ice cream business, and a fish-and-chips shop were all achieved in the first seven years. His daughter's marrying another émigré, a Polish nobleman who had fled with his air force unit to Scotland, delighted him. The recent birth of his first grandson delighted him even more.

Life is good, Gino Corelli said. Often.

Joanne hoped her friends would find Mae Bell as fascinating as she did, and when Mae Bell said she wanted to thank Joanne for the article on her husband, she agreed to meet in the café on the river.

"Hello, Mr. Corelli."

He looked up, saw Joanne, and smiled with his whole body.

"I'd like to introduce my friend Mrs. Mae Bell." Joanne stood back, gesturing towards Mae as though she were a prize exhibit in an art gallery.

"Mae, please. Hi, Mr. Corelli."

"Gino. Pleased ta meet you." Gino beamed. Mae Bell smiled back, and they both instantly knew they would be friends.

Joanne took her favorite seat by the window with a view over the river and castle and the intersection where traffic slowed down to pass through the narrow stone archways of the suspension bridge.

Joanne asked for a cappuccino, Mae Bell an espresso. Gino himself brought over the order. "I'll leave you lovely ladies to chat," he told them. "An' I hope you stay a long time, Mrs. Mae."

Chiara had mentioned Joanne's friend to her family, and although curious, Gino would not dream of intruding — but he knew a refugee when he saw one.

"So, anything further on finding friends of your late husband?" Joanne asked.

"No. But thanks for the story in the *Gazette.* It seems to have done the trick." She laid out another envelope. Took out another sheet of the same lined notepaper. Joanne looked at another anonymous message.

"It's the same writer as the first one," Mae said.

I HAVE WARNED YOU. NO MORE INTERFERING IF YOU DO NOT WANT TO LOSE YOUR LOOKS.

"That's not nice." Joanne shivered. "And it must mean the writer knows what you look like."

"I agree," Mae said as she exhaled a long stream of cigarette smoke. "I'm losing my looks as it is — don't want to hurry the inevitable." Her laugh sang out across the café, but an edge to it made Gino look across at the pair.

"You're not losing . . ." Joanne started, but was interrupted by Rob walking up to the table.

"I saw you through the window. Hello again." He took a seat without asking, oblivious to the glare from Joanne. "How are you doing? Had any response to the article about your husband?"

"Only this." Mae picked up the letter and passed it to Rob.

Joanne was furious. *This is my story.* But she knew how petty that would sound.

"Bloody hell! Another one."

Both women stared at him. Gino too. "Language, ma boy, there's ladies here."

"Sorry, Mr. Corelli. Sorry, Mae, Joanne."

Joanne shrugged but had caught the use of Mrs. Mae Bell's first name.

"What do you mean?" Mae was watching him, "Another one?"

"I . . ." Rob stopped, unsure if he should explain. "I think we should show this to McAllister." He stood. "Meet you at the office," he called out as he left.

The two women nodded back and, not saying much, not looking at the river and the cold clear rare sunshine reflecting off

91

the water, the castle, the distant hills of the Black Isle, they walked across the bridge, up the steep street, on to the *Gazette* building, not conversing but not uncomfortable, both considering the contents of the letters, both curious as to the writer, and Mae Bell, more than Joanne, worried in a *What? Me? Worried?* way.

Joanne took them straight up to McAllister's office. Rob was already there. When she introduced Mae Bell, she was expecting McAllister to be entranced by the visitor and was not disappointed. Mae Bell sat on the chair and crossed her legs, her nylons making that shimmering sound that normally set Rob a-fantasizing, but this time he managed to ignore.

"Mrs. Bell had a response to her advertisement and the article in this week's paper," was all Joanne said.

Mae Bell laid the envelope on McAllister's desk. He stared at it. Poked it with his pen. Then opened it and read. "Is this the first note?" It was obvious from the wording that it was not the first warning.

"The second. I tore up the first. Never pay attention to anonymous letters," Mae said. "It only encourages them."

"I'm not sure how much I should tell you," McAllister began, "but this has to go to the police."

"Now you're making me nervous."

Mae Bell did not look nervous. Joanne doubted anything could make her nervous.

"You obviously know something. Should I be nervous? At least give me a clue." And that signature Mae Bell send-shivers-down-the-spine laugh filled the editor's poky wee office.

"Are you a singer, Mrs. Bell?" McAllister was staring at her.

"Sure am."

"Don't know why, there's no sun up in the
   sky
Stormy weather . . ."

The sound of her voice was loud; clear — clear as a bell — a phrase Don McLeod would delete if one of them used it in an article.

"Paris, 1948, that wee club on the Left Bank — but you weren't Mae Bell then . . ."

"Oh, my, Mr. McAllister, now you're giving away my secrets . . ."

"I saw you. You were, are, marvelous."

"I took my husband's name. I love the sound of Mae Bell . . ."

"So do I," Rob joined in.

"The anonymous letters." Joanne had

enough of this heroine worship but immediately regretted sounding so churlish. Though no one else had noticed.

"Yes, the letters." McAllister knew he had to call DI Dunne. "I'll ask the inspector if he will come here to talk to you." He thought it better that the inspector come to the *Gazette,* than that the unmistakable Mrs. Bell walk up the steps of the police station, alerting who knows who, maybe even the letter writer.

"Fiona also opened an anonymous letter addressed to the *Gazette.* I think from the same person . . ."

McAllister turned to Joanne. "Why didn't you tell me?" He meant it as a comment, a we-could-have-talked-this-over, but the pink cheeks as she looked at the floor told him he'd upset her.

"My fault," Mae intervened. "I told the young lady always to ignore anonymous communications and chain letters."

Not quite accurate — Mae told Fiona to throw the note away.

But Joanne was grateful for the intervention. Her arms wrapped around herself to hide her shaking hands, she was looking at the floor where a carpet had once lain, leaving a lighter mark on the wood.

"Sorry." Face pink, furious that McAllister should pull her up in front of Mae, she stood. "I have some work to do."

Rob looked at his watch. "Me too. I'll catch you later, Mae . . . Mrs. Bell . . ." He backed out of the room, clearly enchanted.

"Thank you for everything you've done for me," Mae said to Joanne.

Joanne thought Mae must be psychic — the way she seemed to sense the undertow in a conversation, an inflection in a voice, a remark that seemed casual but wasn't. She nodded at Mae. *There goes my story. No one was interested until it got interesting.* Not looking at McAllister, she followed Rob to the reporters' room.

"Did you hear that voice? She's a real jazz singer." Rob spoke as though he'd just had an audience with Phil Everly, his hero.

"I heard," Don McLeod joined the conversation. "So who's the singer?"

"My friend," Joanne said. She sat at the typewriter and began banging on the keys, typing at hurricane force.

Don looked at Rob. Rob shrugged. Ten minutes later, the sound of footsteps on the stairs made Rob look up. Joanne kept on with her work. The footsteps went into McAllister's office. Rob half rose, thinking it might be Detective Inspector Dunne.

"None of our business," Joanne snapped.

95

Rob went back to his notes on the plans to demolish Bridge Street saying, "We'll find out eventually."

"Aye," Don agreed, "and hopefully before deadline."

Joanne was out of sorts, was how she put it when she talked to Chiara later that day.

"Come round after work and hold wee Andrew, that always cheers you up. Bring Jean and Annie. Stay for tea — we've plenty of pasta."

After they had eaten and Chiara had bathed the baby with the help of two besotted girls, and after Andrew was wrapped up tight like baby Jesus in swaddling clothes and delivered to his daddy, who sat with him and the girls watching television, Joanne and Chiara did the dishes — Chiara washing, Joanne drying. The soothing routine and the warm kitchen and the rich food, especially the orange cake they had for pudding, comforted Joanne, melting the cold lump in her chest.

"How's McAllister?" Chiara asked, trying for innocent and failing.

Joanne didn't look at her. "How's McAllister? I don't really know. I've only seen him at work lately."

"Whose fault's that?"

"I've been busy . . . what with the divorce and the girls and . . ."

"It's me you're talking to, Chiara, your best friend . . . or is this wonderful American woman now your best friend?"

"Never! And how do you know she's wonderful? Of course, your dad. She's charmed him too."

"Joanne, I'm only joking. I know we're best friends, and yes, she charmed Papa — he loves blond women, you should hear him go on about Grace Kelly — but you're like a big sister, so I'm allowed to tell you when you're behaving like an idiot."

Joanne said nothing but wiped a large white dinner plate so often it was gleaming.

Chiara was not going to let up. "McAllister is a man. Single. Forty-five. Never been married. You have to train him. You have to —"

The doorbell rang. Peter Kowalski, Chiara's husband, answered.

"Come in, come in. Chiara's in the kitchen with Joanne if you want to say hello." Peter came in carrying his bundle of baby, followed by McAllister.

"We were talking about you," Chiara said as she dried her hands on a tea towel and came forwards for a continental-style double kiss. "Coffee? Tea? Wine?"

"Coffee please," he said. He looked at Joanne. Smiled.

She smiled back, said, "McAllister," then looked away. The large wooden table between them was as wide as a frontier, and as helpful.

When they were alone, the men having taken their coffee into the sitting room, and Chiara had the percolator on the stove for a second round, she felt, then saw, the irritation in Joanne.

"What? What's wrong?"

"You never told me McAllister was coming over."

"I didn't know. But he comes here regularly for a game of chess with Peter. You know that." Chiara was staring. "You, dear friend, have a problem. We will talk later. But first . . ." She was laying the tray with cups and sugar.

"First I have to get the girls home, it's late."

"No, you don't. It's Friday. They can sleep here and we can have a lovely night together, the four of us."

"I can't . . ."

"You have no choice. I've decided."

And a lovely night they had. Then McAllister offered her a lift home. When they were in the car, Joanne remembered Chiara's words. She hadn't liked hearing her friend tell her she had a problem, but she knew she was right. "Can we go to your house? It's ages since we talked alone."

She could feel his reaction. Feel the pleasure emanating from him like the heat from her two-bar electric fire that she practically sat on top of on cold winter's nights.

At his home, they talked. At first the conversation was about Nurse Urquhart. The viciousness of the attack had shaken everyone — especially women who could imagine it happening to them. They talked over the *Why?* They considered motives; an amputated leg in a shinty boot in Nurse Urquhart's washing was a pretty sick joke; acid in the face had no explanation except hate. But shinty, whilst fierce, was not vicious off the field.

McAllister played a soft, haunting piece of music he told her was flamenco. They drank a little wine. He lent her a book. She asked for another, this one a book of poetry, some American woman called Emily whom she'd never heard of.

He kissed her. Once. But a nice kiss, she decided. Then he took her home.

Going to bed in her little prefab and the house empty, she enjoyed the rare solitude.

And regretted she was never able to say to McAllister what she didn't know she wanted to say, which was, *I feel so inadequate. Naïve. Uneducated. Unsophisticated. Untraveled. Is that a word? Mae Bell is much more your style than me.*

Thoughts kept gushing out, unstoppable, like a burst water main. She gave in, got up, went to the kitchen, made cocoa, sipped it in bed. When sleep finally came, the thoughts transformed into dreams, where, in a running race with McAllister, Mae Bell, her girls, and her mother-in-law, she lagged far behind, watching the others disappear across the hill into bright sunshine, leaving her behind in the rain.

SEVEN

The following evening Joanne had a little more sleep — marginally.

"We need Nurse Urquhart and her warning notes," Joanne muttered to herself when she finally finished remaking Annie's bed and had the sheets soaking in the boiler. The thought of Nurse Urquhart sent a shudder down her spine.

The evening had started with Annie's announcement — said with a whiff of superiority that irritated Joanne: "Maureen Forbes got sent home from school yesterday."

Joanne had made cinnamon toast, her favorite, and she was busy fishing the skin off the cocoa, her pet hate.

Joanne knew what was expected of her — Annie would make these statements, then dribble out the information one sentence, one paragraph, one chapter at a time. Joanne blamed Enid Blyton for the way her daughter perceived the world.

"Nits." The child was aware of the re-action the word would cause, and sure enough, Joanne stood, reached for Jean, who was cutting off the crusts from her toast. Her mother did not say "Eat your crusts, they're good for your teeth" — she was too busy lifting the hair above her daughter's ear searching for eggs and hopefully no hatched nits.

"Maureen says her wee brother, the one that's always sick, is riddled with them."

"She doesn't have a brother," her sister said, munching on toast whilst her mum parted her hair an inch at a time, examining each section as carefully as a mother chim-panzee searching her baby for fleas.

"Does." Annie had never seen this brother but would not be contradicted by a sister two and a half years younger.

"You're fine." Joanne went around the table and stood over Annie, who flinched and tried to move her head out of reach.

"Sit still." Joanne had a hold of a thick strand of hair crinkled from the pigtails she insisted Annie kept her hair in for school and which Annie hated and often threatened to cut off but was too afraid of what Granny Ross would say, or do, it being her belief that as well as jam making and chutney making and crunchy toffee cooking, her grandmother could brew up witch's potions and cast spells.

Joanne couldn't see any nits, but they were there, the telltale eggs dotted around the hairline and up in the nest of hair at the back of the head.

"Have you been scratching?" The colony above the ears was particularly thick, and on one side, where the scalp was inflamed, Joanne was certain she saw something move.

"It's only dandruff." Annie knew, from the way her mother stood back, trying to search without her hair coming anywhere near her daughter's, that it wasn't.

"It's nits."

"I'll have to stay off school."

The obvious satisfaction in her daughter's voice made Joanne want to shout at her. But nits were no person's fault, no respecters of family or fortune — a fact Nurse Urquhart agreed on.

"Into the bathroom," Joanne ordered Annie. "Jean, you sleep in my bed tonight; this is going to take a long time."

She was looking at the thick hair, the same chestnut brown as hers but with more red in it, thinking how many nights she would have to soak it with olive oil and comb out every nit, every egg, and even then with no guarantee she would get them all. She would never inflict on her daughters the method used by her mother from the one time she had caught them. Her eight-year-old self shuddered at the dire warnings about playing with the village children, and the loneliness she had to endure that summer, and the memory of paraffin rubbed into the scalp — a memory so strong that filling the paraffin heater in the winter still made her queasy.

"Give me a haircut like Nurse Urquhart makes the boys get."

"That's this short." Jean held her fingers half an inch apart.

Annie felt rather than saw her mother consider the idea, before saying, "Into the bathroom. Now. I'll bring the olive oil."

"It'll take forever and I want short hair and if I don't get rid of them, I'll be off school for ages and" — she was calculating what else would tip the battle in her favor — "and maybe Jean will get them, and you too."

"You sit down, Mum; I'll have a look." The sweetness of her younger daughter's offer, the girls' assumption that Joanne might have them, her fear of losing her mane of beautiful hair she treasured so much that she always gathered rainwater for the final rinse . . . The argument was won.

"I can make it shorter."

"No. Really, really short so the eggs don't cling." Annie's pronouncement sounded like the quote it was. "Then the olive oil, then the comb, then wrap the head tight and do the same again in the morning for . . ." Weeks, Nurse Urquhart had said, but that sounded too long.

"I'll use the dressmaking shears." Joanne went to fetch her sewing basket.

Annie had enough sense not to cheer; she scratched more vigorously instead.

The haircut took place in the bathroom, the hair first cut in big chunks and dropped into a paper bag. Joanne wanted to burn the hair, burn the beasts alive. The rest of the haircut was traumatic for Joanne. She shuddered at one point, when holding up the scissors to examine the progress of the style — a pixie look was what she was trying for — and she saw something moving along the blades. She almost shrieked, before turning on the tap until it ran as hot as possible. She rinsed the scissors, and continued the cut, now moving more quickly. When she'd finished, Annie stared in the mirror. Joanne had to admit that her daughter looked more than good with a shorn head; she looked elegant and older and stronger, and the unfashionably short

105

hair seemed to suit her daughter's personality.

"This is better than a real hairdresser."

Joanne knew the back was not even, but Annie couldn't see that. She took the olive oil, rubbed it in, and began the tedious process of combing every section of the head, over and over, rinsing the steel comb under the tap until the hot water ran out and until all the eggs she could find were gone, but knowing there were more, there were always more, lurking. It was well after nine o'clock before Annie finally went to bed — she even helped her mother strip her bed and put the sheets and pillowcases in the washing machine and the quilt outside in the washhouse.

"Thanks, Mum, I love my new haircut," Annie said.

"Wait until your granny sees it."

"I'll tell her I chopped my pigtails off 'cos of the nits, then you tidied it up."

Joanne smiled and didn't contradict her daughter. Granny Ross would believe the story, and Joanne would be saved that long look of disappointment she often received from her mother-in-law, along with the famous phrase, which summed up her relationship with her husband's mother, "Whatever next?"

Next morning Joanne took Jean to school on the back of her bicycle, telling Annie to do some schoolwork, not to turn on the gas cooker, to leave the washing to soak, and to stay indoors — or at least not leave the garden.

"And don't let anyone in the house," was her parting shot.

Joanne was the first into the office. Rob next.

"Do me a favor, would you?" Joanne asked him.

"If I can."

She turned her back to the window. "Would you check me for nits?"

"It's easier if you sit down."

This was one of the many reasons Joanne was friends with Rob; she could ask him almost anything. There might be a jokey comment or two, but with him, she didn't feel awkward, she felt herself.

"I had to cut off all Annie's hair."

He was now examining the hair and scalp behind her left ear. "I bet she liked that."

"She did."

"Turn round a wee bit."

"It's as though the nits know Nurse Urquhart isn't here and are taking revenge." Joanne was joking, but the injuries, the sheer nastiness and pain of them, the thought how a face would look after an acid attack, were never far from her mind — nor were the threatening letters. And the why of it all that no one could work out.

"Frankie went to Aberdeen yesterday to see his mum. She was flown there by the Air Ambulance for an operation. He said his dad is falling apart without her."

"Was it someone from the shinty?"

"I can't see it. I know how fiercely they hate each other on field, but it's a wee community. They're mostly pals off the field. Naw, sick joke, probably after three too many drams is my theory on the leg in the laundry."

"Am I interrupting?" McAllister stood in the doorway.

"No," Rob told him before ruffling Joanne's hair back into place. "No nits."

"Rob!" she swatted his arm.

"Have you heard how Nurse Urquhart is?" McAllister started.

"Better, but she may never speak again. She'll also have a lot of trouble swallowing." Rob left out the worry about how Nurse Urquhart would breathe, which Frankie didn't mention but which was implicit in his description of his mother's injuries. "DI Dunne told Frankie and his dad they are doing all they can, but so far" — Rob shrugged — "no news."

Joanne and McAllister were silent, absorbing the information.

"So what are *we* going to do?" Hector as usual had appeared in the room as though by magic. He still believed that his pictures of the leg, although not published in the newspaper, had started the whole catastrophe. He had said this to his granny, who told him not to be stupid, and to Fiona, who said it was not his fault. But the guilt would not go away.

"We?" Rob looked down at him. "Who's we?"

"You, me." He wanted to add Joanne and McAllister but didn't dare.

"He's right," Joanne told them. "Rob should concentrate on helping Frankie find out who did this." *Then you can leave me to dig into the Robert Bell story,* she was thinking.

"Why not?" McAllister said. "First we'll start a shinty column. That gives us an excuse to hang around teams and supporters. Rob, you report on the games, Hec takes pictures, see if you come up with anything . . ."

"And make sure you get the names and teams right." This came from Don McLeod, who had come in in a current of rain, his coat and hat wet, and the turn-ups of his trousers a distinct shade darker than the legs. "There're an awful lot o' McLeods and Macleods and MacLeods, to say nothing o' the Alisters and Alastairs. If two are the same, ask their father's name, I'll work it out from that."

Rob really liked Frankie Urquhart; he was one of the few in the town who shared Rob's twin enthusiasms — music and girls, but not girlfriends, for Rob was a recovering lover — and they had known each other forever. Frankie understood Rob when he said he was getting out of here one day, and he believed him.

Rob said, "There go my Saturday afternoons." But he was secretly pleased that he might help the Urquhart family, secretly pleased that he was once more on the hunt for a scoop.

Mal Forbes came in with a tentative layout for the next edition.

"We're starting a shinty column," McAllister said as he looked at the advertising blocked out on the sports pages. "We'll need space for it."

"Why? There's no money in shinty, only football."

"Do you think of nothing else?" The

remark was out before Joanne could stop herself.

Mal smiled. "Aye, you're right. I do tend to be a wee bit single-minded."

Joanne squirmed. "Sorry."

Mal Forbes ignored her. Not nastily. His only concern was the newspaper. *Obsessive,* his wife, Moira, called him. He agreed. *If a job's worth doing . . .* he always said to his wife and family. He asked Don how many column inches were needed for "this shinty lark." Don told him. He left.

No one said anything, just went on with the morning's work. It was as though Mal was part of the team but separate. McAllister, being the only newspaperman to have worked out in the real world, saw this as normal; advertising and editorial seldom mixed. Don, who had only ever worked with the late office manager, Mrs. Smart, missed her and her no-nonsense approach to the job. Every day. Joanne thought everyone should be friends. Rob didn't care. Hec never noticed.

Much later Rob asked, "Jo, come with me to Arnotts. I need your help with a present for my mother's birthday."

"Only if we don't take too long. I need to go home to make lunch for Annie." She saw Don look up. "Nits."

"Aye, come the Apocalypse, the nits will survive."

"Not in my household." She stood, smiled at McAllister. He winked. And the day suddenly became much better.

She and Rob were at the cosmetics counter. Joanne had pointed out Margaret McLean's favorite perfume. As they were waiting for it to be wrapped, Rob said, "You should ignore Mal Forbes, he's not deliberately trying to annoy you." Rob was counting out what seemed like an enormous sum of money.

"I know. But he is so . . ." She didn't know a word for men who treated women as wee fluffy creatures that should be kept on the mantelshelf and cuddled every so often.

"He's good at his job."

"I'm sure he's a nice man. Fiona likes him. So do his clients. All he says is no more than most men say and think . . . Ouch, what was that for?"

Rob had nudged her with his elbow. Accidentally hard. "I'm not most men."

"That's because you're still a boy at heart." She ran off up the street, a thirty-one-year-old woman giggling and running, and giggling some more as Rob shouted out, "I'm not most boys."

When he caught up with her she said, "Feels like I haven't laughed in ages."

Rob drove them to her house in McAllister's car, the unofficial office car.

Rob admired Annie's hair. Joanne reheated the potato soup and buttered rolls.

"Nurse Urquhart, is she going to be all right?" Annie asked Rob, knowing Uncle Rob would tell the truth.

"Not really. She'll live, so Frankie says, but she may never be able to speak again." *Eating, drinking, and breathing will be almost impossible too,* but Rob didn't want to share that.

"You don't have to speak to tell someone they have nits," Annie pointed out. "You just jump back . . . that's what everyone does when you tell them you have nits."

"Like this?" Rob leaned towards Annie, then jumped back, holding his hands up in mock horror, and Joanne agreed with Rob's certainty that he would one day make it big in television.

Rob was right. Nurse Urquhart would never be able to talk again.

Frankie and his father had taken the train to Aberdeen. Neither of them knew the city and neither of them could understand the accent until a bus conductor took pity on them and told them which bus to catch and where to get off. Coach Frank Urquhart had spent most of the train journey in silence, his only real comment on the strangeness of his wife being taken to Aberdeen by air ambulance.

"It's more gentle than the road or train," Frankie explained, not wanting to say it was for serious cases only.

"Aye, but she's so far away."

Now, a few days and another two operations later, Frankie was hoping his mother was over the worst, hoping the longer she lived, the better her chances. Just plain hoping.

Nurse Urquhart — like his father, Frankie thought of as a nurse first, mother second, and as a wife never. In his picture of her she was always in uniform with the upside-down watch pinned to her chest, sleeves rolled up, hair short and tucked into her cap. In winter she wore a navy blue trench coat, tightly belted, and until last year went everywhere by bicycle. The health authority gave her a car, dark blue, to match her uniform, she said. She treated it like a cherished offspring — keeping the polish sparkling, patting it on the bonnet as she went around to the driver's side, proud she needed no man to ferry her . . .

"Mr. Urquhart?"

"Ma dad's outside." There was no need to say that in this situation and in this hard, driving rain, he was outside only because smoking was forbidden in the hospital.

"You are Nurse Urquhart's son?"

Frankie nodded. "Frankie Urquhart. Mr. Urquhart's my dad."

The man held out his hand. "I'm Mr. Beattie, the surgeon . . ."

"Pleased to meet you . . . are you all right?" The man was looking tired, uncomfortable, unable to look directly at Frankie. Frankie worried he might be unwell. He didn't want the surgeon to be unwell.

"Mr. Urquhart, Frankie — can we go into my office? I'd like to talk to you and your father together."

"You can tell me, I'll tell Dad. She will be fine, won't she? My mother, Nurse Urquhart, she's as strong as a Clydesdale. Big feet like a Clydesdale too, she always jokes, she'll be fine . . ." He knew he was blethering. He didn't want to hear. He told himself that if he kept talking, the man wouldn't say what he feared he was going to say.

He looked at the doctor. He could see the man was no good at this. He then knew that he would have to say the words. *Always get a nurse to give the bad news,* his mother told

115

him, *doctors is a' useless at the right words.*

"My mother didn't make it."

"I'm so sorry." It was all the surgeon could say. He offered his hand again. Frankie took it. It was cold. He caught a glimpse of whiteness and short clean nails. Smelt a whiff of antiseptic. *Carbolic soap,* he was thinking, *Mum uses that.*

"Thank you for everything," Frankie was comforting the surgeon, feeling his distress. "And don't worry, I'll tell my father."

The relief was obvious, and Frankie felt sorry for him. "Don't worry," he repeated, "I'll tell Dad."

When they walked into the reporters' room, they knew immediately it was bad.

Don and McAllister were sitting together, smoking and saying nothing. McAllister looked at Don. Don looked away. He had had enough of death in the past months.

"Nurse Urquhart died this morning." McAllister came straight out with it; there was no way to lessen the shock.

"No," was all Rob could say. He was shaking his head from side to side, "No." Joanne had her hand on his arm. Rob was blocking the horror for both of them.

"Frankie and his father are still at the hospital in Aberdeen. I don't know much

116

more." McAllister put out his cigarette.

"Someone should tell Hector." It was only Joanne who guessed how guilty Hector must feel.

"He's at home printing this week's pictures; I'll go round and tell him. And his granny." Rob wanted to do something, anything, for the Urquharts. They would need their neighbor and friend Granny Bain in the months to come. And Hector and his granny needed to hear of the death of Nurse Urquhart from a friend. Who would tell Morag, Frankie's sister; he didn't know but hoped it wouldn't be him. "See you later."

McAllister looked across at Joanne. She looked back.

"I know. We're a newspaper. We've work to do."

He nodded. Don sighed. McAllister rolled a piece of paper into the typewriter, then sat for a moment, thinking.

"I'd like to write the obituary." Joanne had never written one before, but she knew this was right.

"Thank you." He wanted to touch her, but didn't.

"I need a drink," Don said, but didn't move.

So they did what they did best, turned out a newspaper that honored Nurse Urquhart.

Joanne's obituary reminded the community — mothers and fathers, grandparents and colleagues, the shinty community, the schoolteachers, the health workers, the children — all reminded what a good woman, what a straightforward, old-fashioned yet progressive, efficient, funny, and caring woman she was. Some remembered her prowess at Scottish country dancing; some remembered how she always rubbed her hands together to warm them before examining the unborn in *Mummy's tummy,* as she would say. A shinty player who received a particularly painful bash on the shins shared his story of the medicinal flask of whisky handed out with a smile and *This'll make it go away.*

"We'll no' see her likes again." That old Scottish phrase was said often, before and after the funeral and for many a year after that.

The church was full, with many more standing outside — friends, acquaintances; parents, headmasters, and teachers from all the schools Nurse Urquhart had ever worked in; the shinty teams and the mothers and wives who did the washing; neighbors and families. Along the streets, as the funeral cortege passed en route to Tomnahurich Cemetery, people gathered outside their homes, silent, the curtains of the houses closed in the traditional mark of respect.

Frankie, his sister, Morag, and his dad, Coach Frank Urquhart, felt supported by the sheer number of mourners, the wreaths, the bouquets, the small bunches of garden flowers from children who liked the school nurse because she told the truth.

Yes, she would say, *the needle hurts a wee bit but it'll soon be over.* Or, *Nits is awful wee beasties, but they don't bite.* Or she'd say that the cold or the flu or the measles or the mumps or the whooping cough is nasty, *But soon you'll be all better.*

They all knew what had happened but couldn't comprehend such a crime. *Who would want to hurt her?* was one question. *Who would do such a thing?* was the other. *Acid — that's so horrible, so vicious, so . . .* this observation was often followed by a shudder and a loss of words; it was beyond them to fathom out the evil behind such an act. Above all hung one question — why?

"Oil of vitriol is the old name for acid," McAllister said as he and Joanne walked from the cemetery.

"Vitriol, vitriolic, that certainly sums up the attack." Again, as she pictured it, she recoiled. Although she had never seen an acid burn, or been around acid outside the school science laboratory, she could imagine what Nurse Urquhart had endured, and feel it, to the point of her skin burning.

McAllister took her hand and linked it through his arm. "Let's take the Infirmary Bridge."

They were quiet, just walking side by side, occasionally mentioning a trivial work matter, commenting on the weather, Joanne saying she was glad they had the excuse of work to avoid the funeral feast of sandwiches and whisky. His sense that the wind and the river and the occasional shaft of sunshine would wash the image from their minds didn't completely rid them of the sadness, the waste of a life, the loss of a vibrant, cheery woman who never harmed, always helping the children, the families of the town. And although Joanne did not appreciate this until much later, in the company of McAllister, there was no need to say anything; his quietness was his strength, in turn giving her strength.

As they came up the steps into the office, they saw that Fiona was back in her usual place behind the front desk, Hector having given her a lift back from the funeral. She had been crying, but now seemed anxious.

"Mr. McLeod is waiting for you upstairs; he said it was urgent I find you but you were . . ."

"Thanks," was all McAllister said.

Don didn't bother to greet them or wait for them to take off their hats or sit. "A bottle of sulfuric acid is missing from the print room. I left a message for DI Dunne."

"He was at the funeral." McAllister was standing, but Joanne now had to sit, had to put her elbows on the desk, had to hide her face in her hands; the mention of acid, the thought of burning flesh, made the horror return.

"The inspector'll be here soon enough." Don said no more. He hadn't been at the funeral. He couldn't bear the thought of standing at the graveside of another woman he had known for decades, murdered. Nurse Urquhart was buried in the ground, never again to be seen at the shinty with her first aid kit, shouting at "ma boys," cheering every pass, every corner, booing at every penalty awarded against them, jumping up at every goalmouth stramash that brought her team closer to the Camanachd Cup.

McAllister lit a cigarette. They waited, in silence. When the sound of footsteps carried

121

up the stone steps, the steps where the middle had been worn into a bow curve, all three of them knew that the investigation — perhaps involving someone in the *Gazette,* someone they knew, worked with — was not going to be pleasant.

Eight

Mae Bell said she had been in Edinburgh for a week. When she returned, the first person she contacted was Joanne.

"I read the newspaper. The nurse was Frankie Urquhart's mother, right?"

"She was. It's a terrible story."

"Let's meet."

They met in Gino Corelli's café, as Mae Bell loved the place, its warmth and the steam and the noise. And she liked Gino. *Old friends at first sight* was how she described him to Joanne.

"I've moved in to the hotel along the river from here." She removed a silk scarf in a print of many colors. "This side of the river reminds me of Paris, and I love looking across at the castle." They were sitting in the window, and Mae gestured across the river that today was a dark blended-whisky tone.

"Paris?" Joanne thought the comparison

very far-fetched.

"Didn't I tell you I live in Paris? I sing in a club in Saint-Germain, with some old friends."

"That's where McAllister saw you."

"Ten years ago. Don't remind me, it makes me feel old."

Mae's laugh was the same. She was as elegant as ever. But there was a weariness around the eyes and a slowness in the way she stirred her coffee that made Joanne examine her. Mae was tired. And Mae was looking, almost, her age. Delicate lines ran down from nose to mouth that could be laughter lines but were not. Furrows above the nose were only obvious when the dark magnetism of her eyes did not distract with the fatal attraction of a deep, dark well. But her hair was freshly gold, her nail polish red, the same dark red as her mouth, and her coat, a wool from some baby animal unknown in these parts, was black, showing no stray hairs, nor flecks, nor imprint of child.

"First," Mae said, "tell me about Mrs. Urquhart."

For an American, she says the name right, Joanne thought, *she gets the Scottish* ch *sound.*

"Nurse Urquhart, she was flown to a

hospital in Aberdeen but . . ."

"She passed away."

"Aye. Nothing could be done. And now it's a murder inquiry. But so far . . ." Joanne didn't know how much to tell. The wide-open eyes, the quiet way Mae Bell sat, her legs tucked under the table, her hands resting crossed on her lap, made Joanne want to tell her all. So she did.

Gino was watching from behind the counter, and he did not interrupt. Customers came and went. A waitress, a new woman Joanne did not know, was clearing the lunchtime dishes from tables around them, but at a shake of the head from Gino left Joanne and Mae to their conversation.

When Joanne finished, Mae said, "Poor Nurse Urquhart." She said it simply, the voice, the emotion coming from a dark place inside her; she knew what it was to be physically assaulted. They dipped their heads simultaneously, an acknowledgment of the death of a fine woman.

"Is the death of the nurse connected to the anonymous letters?" Mae asked.

"I don't know." Once more they were quiet, once more thinking the same thought: *Why?* And, though neither said it, there was also the fear that Mae Bell might be next.

The bells, from different church steeples

around the town, struck two o'clock.

"I must get back," Joanne said, even though Mae had not had a chance to tell her of the Edinburgh trip. "Look, this evening, after deadline, I usually have a drink with McAllister. Why don't you join us?" She knew that McAllister would be more than delighted to have Mae Bell visit his home. "Eight o'clock suit you?"

Mae smiled, nodded, saying she would love to. Joanne scribbled down the address, and Mae watched her run across the street and onto the bridge, hair and coat flying, and she smiled. She liked Joanne, was sorry she was deceiving her, but *needs must.* It was a phrase her Scottish grandmother used to use. It made her smile again. Only Gino, watching like a bird on a branch, saw the melancholy in the smile. *Triste,* he would say. *Blue,* she would say. Or sing.

Leaving the café, she buttoned up her coat against a wind straight from the North Sea. *Oh my love, you hated the cold.* Talking to Robert was still a habit even after six years. *Your Mayday Maeday, I know you made an enemy, and I will find out what happened to you — six years too late maybe, but I'll find out what happened to you — no matter how long it takes.*

She made the short walk to her hotel just

126

in time. Back in her room, the papers still in the envelope unopened on the dressing table seemed to brood with a malevolent presence. She took a deep breath. The feeling of imminent tears she had felt outside the café, the pain when the wind blasted her ears making her fear for her hearing, all had vanished at the thought of rereading the report.

Printed and bound, making it all the more real, was the full report from the Fatal Accident Enquiry: the final report from the air force, the police, the investigating officer on the loss of the aircraft over the North Sea; the long and frustrating report, months in the making; a report that reported nothing; a report thick on theories but light on hard facts; a statement that recorded that no sighting, no evidence, no leads had been found. The conclusion left the inquiry open. And six years later, still nothing, except more speculation. All that was certain was that the aircraft set off over the North Sea and did not return.

The taxi driver wished Mae Bell good night. She walked down the path to McAllister's front porch and was about to ring the bell when the opening piano riff, faint but clear, from the record player in the sitting room, hit her with such force that she had to hold on to the door frame.

The voice started. Her own. The lyrics undid her now as much as they had when she had first sung the song in Paris. *Blue Moon . . .*

She could feel him holding her, dancing slowly, the hum of him singing vibrated through her, the words he would say, whisper, again and again, *Please adore me.* She did, she always would.

Robert. His name, as so often before, came out in a sob. She clutched her bag with the two unsent letters to her chest; she had the final two unsent letters; she had finally tracked them down. The letters, his passport, his dog tags had been kept in Edinburgh with the rest of his belongings — not returned to her as promised.

Sorry, madam, the officer at RAF Kinloss had said. *The police didn't return your late husband's property and we hadn't an address for you.*

Now she had Robert's notebook — doodles, half-written melodies and song lyrics, and his binoculars. His clothes she couldn't bear to touch and had left behind. The unposted letters she kept with her. She slept with them next to her pillow; she read them and reread them. In among his descriptions of his work, his colleagues, the weather, there was an anxiety, and a mention that he had made a stupid mistake, upsetting someone. Nothing more. She needed company. Was glad to be on McAllister's doorstep. She rang the doorbell.

The door opened. Joanne was startled to see Mae looking half a foot smaller. Joanne would have noticed the tears if Mae hadn't quickly turned away and fumbled in her handbag, saying, "Darn, I think I left my cigarettes in the taxi." Mae took out a packet. "No, here they are."

"I've been telling McAllister for ages he needs a new bulb in the outside light." Joanne was aware she was blethering, and didn't know why. "Come into the sitting room, and here, I'll take your coat. McAllister will get us a drink . . ."

"I thought you might like this." McAllister grinned at Mae and put the recording on again. This time Mae was prepared. This time, when the piano trilled the opening notes, she could smile. And when the saxophone came in, she could see him, Robert, and smile. At him. At Robert.

"One of my favorites." She raised the whisky glass he handed her. "Thanks." She took too large a gulp and almost choked. Not from the whisky — she couldn't bear

129

hearing that song again. "I hear things have gotten worse since I left."

"It's hard to credit how someone could do such a thing, especially up here." As opposed to Glasgow, he meant. "Have you heard any more from the anonymous letter writer?"

"No. Then again, maybe the person thought the threat was successful. I did leave town not long after I received it." Mae shrugged. The anonymous letters were not her only concern. What she had discovered in Edinburgh superceded everything else — not that she was sharing.

Joanne was enjoying the ease of the conversation between Mae and McAllister. Like old friends, she thought. It felt important that Mae like McAllister. That Mae validate Joanne's choice of maybe future husband.

"How would the person who wrote the letter know you left?" she asked. The thought came that the letter writer might know of Mae's return and threaten her again. "I'm really glad you're back. It's dull without you . . ."

"Let's hope the letter writer feels the same." Mae Bell laughed.

"I hope you're not including me in 'dull.' " McAllister gave a grin, loving the way Joanne could no more hide her emotions than stop the tide turning.

He stood. "Any requests?"

"Basie?" Mae Bell asked. She did not want to risk anything associated with Paris.

And as the night wore on, as the clock struck late, and the wine and whisky sank and the music did its magic, the conversation, the laughter, the stories, flowed and floated, as various as a highland cloudscape, and Joanne never did find the chance to ask about Mae's trip to Edinburgh. Which was good; it saved Mae from lying.

When it was time to leave, Joanne said she'd share a taxi with Mae. McAllister suddenly looked bereft. Mae raised an eyebrow. McAllister saw her watching him. He looked away. Joanne didn't notice — too busy with the books she was borrowing. *So that's how it is,* Mae was thinking.

The taxi crossed a deserted town, the women sitting in the back, thinking on the same subject, thinking from such opposing viewpoints that it would startle them if they shared.

Why doesn't she stay the night with that fascinating man? He's pretty attractive in a world-weary way, Mae was thinking. *She must know how much he wants her and tries to fool herself he doesn't. But it is a small town. It is 1958.* Mae knew how hard it was for the amorous of the community who were not married. *Nowhere to go, nowhere to hide, trysts consummated in the backs of cars, down cold, lonely lanes. Even a hay barn is out in this climate.* She remembered a hay barn in France with Robert. They were grown-up adults, and married, but it was irresistible — *and itchy.*

She stood on the steps of the hotel, waving good-bye to Joanne, before knocking on the door with her lighter, waiting for the night porter to open the door. Seeing him look at her, then ostentatiously look at his watch before letting her in, the word *suffocate* came to mind as she remembered that all small towns were the same.

Joanne too was wondering why she didn't stay with McAllister. It was not the fear for her reputation — half the town had them already bedded but not wedded. It was not that she was not attracted to him. And, given half a signal, she knew he would love her to stay, to sleep in his huge bed, which she had looked at when staying once before in the spare bedroom, the bed that one day might be the marital bed — if only she could stop prevaricating, stop holding back, stop . . . She paused. *Stop being so scared?*

She sighed as she stepped out of the taxi.

Opening the garden gate, she looked up at the stars, contemplating the heavens, finding solace in the beauty of a bright Milky Way, dreading the cold waiting in her little house, knowing that inside the thin walls, in her tiny bedroom with the narrow bed, and no fire, it was often colder inside than out.

McAllister's bed would be warm, she was thinking as she filled the hot-water bottle. Again the fear and doubts crept up on her as steadily as a dose of the flu. *I'm not yet divorced and I'm thinking of marrying again? Glutton for punishment you are.*

The next morning, a banging on her door awakened Joanne. Suddenly. She hated that, preferring to come into a new day slowly. She looked at the time: Twenty-five past eight. She'd slept in.

The banging started again.

The girls were at their grandparents'; perhaps something had happened.

"I'm coming." She did what she never did, what she was brought up to believe was "common": she answered the door in her dressing gown.

The man was holding a large envelope and a clipboard. He and the envelope had an official look.

"This is from the court," he said. "Sign here." He knew what the letter was. Look-

133

ing at her, with her hair uncombed, her eyes tired, and an aura of stale alcohol about her, he decided he now knew why the documents were being served on her.

She signed. Glancing at his freshly shaven chin and his smartly pressed suit and white shirt and blue regimental tie, she could see on his face, as he handed over the documents, what he thought of her.

"Thank you." She pulled her dressing gown tight, stepped back, shut the door, and without opening the summons said, loudly enough for the man to hear from halfway down the path, "About time."

She was shaking the envelope above her head as triumphantly as a winner with all the correct lines in the football pools. "About blooming time."

It was only when she was on her second cup of tea that the thought struck her, hard. She knew, because she had typed up the reports often enough, that the *Gazette* reported all Sheriff Court proceedings, including divorce. The fact of the case, details of the proceedings, all would be there for all to see. No wonder Betsy Buchanan, her husband's girlfriend, wanted to flee to Australia. But she, Joanne Ross, she would be here to face the gossips, the curious, the outright malicious. Her children too, her girls . . . someone somewhere sometime would bring up their parents' divorce. The elation evaporated, leaving a stale scent of defeat that Joanne Ross was familiar with and accepted.

And the fantasy, the dreaming of what she would call herself after the divorce, came back — as anxiety. Joanne Ross, I will no longer be Joanne Ross.

Joanne McAllister was not in her thinking.

Chiara Kowalski née Corelli had been Joanne's closest friend for five years. The had met over ice cream; the Sunday ritual cone of ice cream, the one treat she could afford for her girls before she took the part-time job as typist at the *Gazette.*

Chiara and her family had been true friends through the disintegration of Joanne's marriage, but divorce? Joanne sensed — she did not include Chiara's husband in this, as she knew he lost his faith when he lost his homeland — that for the Corelli family, a separation was acceptable, divorce not.

Joanne did not confide in her sister, nor her brother-in-law — a minister in the Church of Scotland — for the same reason. "Till death do us part." She felt it hypocritical, the Church's attitude to marriage. She had been subjected to physical and mental abuse. It had been accepted, although gossiped upon, that she could set up a separate household. Her husband already had another woman pregnant. But when it came to a divorce, it was she who would wear the mark of Cain, not her husband.

McAllister; she knew she could, should talk to him. He would listen. He would smile. He would be sympathetic, encouraging even. But he found it hard to see why she was so ambivalent about a divorce, about marrying again.

She needed to talk. She needed someone who would know that a divorce was more than a civil matter before the Sheriff Court, more than a matter of gossip and innuendo and losing your good name; it was the end of who she was and the beginning of — *of what?*

"Gazette."

"Hello, Mae Bell here. You left a note at my hotel."

"It's just . . ." Joanne didn't want to explain; the newsroom was busy, and McAllister, Don, Rob, Hec, and Mal Forbes were all there.

"I get it, you can't talk," Mae said, "Twelve thirty at Gino's café?"

136

"How about the tearoom in Arnotts? You know it?" she did not want Gino Corelli to guess at their conversation.

"I'll find it."

"As I was saying," Mal Forbes continued, "we can make this page more profitable if we add advertising editorial — which I know you all think is not good newspaper ethics, but if it's clearly marked . . . and paid for . . ."

"Let's see it again." Don pulled the mock-up towards him. It was a cartoon-like drawing, lines of copy squiggled in, clear black borders around the quarter-page, and *Advertisement* in a small font at the top.

"Up the font on the top heading and I see no problem."

McAllister shrugged. The proposed advertisement was a six-month contract, not something he could dismiss.

"So we're agreed then," Mal continued. "The copy will change regularly, but we need someone to write it, and being women's interest stories . . ."

"No." The word was out of her mouth before she thought.

"I'm thinking that as you're the only woman writer on the *Gazette* . . ." Mal's point was reasonable.

Oh so reasonable, Joanne acknowledged

137

to herself. "I'm fed up with being given all the so-called 'women's business.' "

"This page is the women's page. You're the only woman reporter." Mal was looking straight at her. She could see that he genuinely couldn't see her point.

"Sorry, Joanne. I don't get your objection."

She wanted to yell, *Stop patronizing me,* but she could see that underneath the neat, horizontal eyebrows, there was no malice, only bewilderment.

Don interrupted. "Children . . ." He meant it as a joke. It offended Joanne nonetheless.

They continued on the small matters that needed writing up, filing, discarding, dealing with — the everyday business of producing a weekly newspaper.

When the meeting was over, she ignored McAllister's smile and went on with typing, and the noise of the machine, which Joanne complained was as ancient as a claymore from Culloden, drowned out any further conversation.

Once more it was an observer who noticed McAllister's little shrug of hurt at being shut out. Don thought courtship as complicated as an eightsome reel, and not nearly as much fun. He cared deeply for Joanne, and for McAllister. They were the only family he had. His life had been devoted to the *Highland Gazette,* to a woman who had been murdered, to betting on the horses, and to reaching the end of a bottle of whisky in as short a time as possible.

Love was not an easy word for him. But if it came to defining the many varieties of love, he would have to admit — but only when well inebriated — that love would include how he felt for Joanne. Maybe stretching the definition would include McAllister, a man he was old enough to father. And Joanne, *dear lass,* as he called her privately, could easily be the mother of his never-to-be-grandchildren. Though even a spell on the rack in the Tower of London would never make him admit this.

Only at lunchtime, when he and Joanne were alone, did Rob say anything. "Don't let him get to you; he thinks women are a delicate species in need of a man's protection. He obviously doesn't know you."

Joanne shrugged, pretending she didn't know who "he" was. She stood to take her coat off the rack.

"I sneaked a look at Mal's references from the paper in Elgin. Excellent at his job, the letter said, honest, reliable, hardworking. But . . ." Rob grinned making Joanne wait.

"I phoned one of the reporters and —"

"Nosy parker," Joanne teased.

"— she told me that Mal has 'communication problems' with women. Believes they should be at home 'minding the bairns,' even though his own wife had a job."

She burst out laughing. "Ninety-nine percent of the population including my mother-in-law would agree."

Rob agreed. "And if you tell anyone I've been checking on Mal Forbes, I'll give you a Chinese burn."

"I never reveal my sources." Smiling to herself, she ran down the stairs, across the street, off to meet Mae Bell. She was still grinning when she walked into the lunchtime crowd of housewives from out of town on a shopping spree, locals from the banks and solicitors' office, the courts, the town and county offices, and all the various businesses that a capital town catered for. *Communication problems.*

Joanne could hear that she had made a mistake suggesting the tearoom. The buzz of conversation drowned out any privacy she had hoped for. The furtive looks she and Mae received from the town's matrons were worse. After a sandwich and tea, Joanne suggested to Mae they walk to her thinking spot, the castle foreground.

"Just as well I bought these." Mae lifted a leg to show off her new shoes. "Your town has so many cobbled streets, I had to buy flat shoes."

Joanne had a feeling that Mae Bell was aware that she was lifting her leg just a little too high, that the glances from assorted males were noted and the frowns from the females unheeded.

"Only you, Mae, could make a pair of lace-up brogues look glamorous." Joanne smiled, glad to be and be seen in the company of such a woman.

"Oh my," Mae said as they went towards the railings on the river side of the forecourt, "what a view." She pointed to the turreted hotel along from the cathedral where she was staying. "There's my room, second on the left, second floor, great to see the view from the other side."

Joanne looked, saw the room, knew the hotel, fleetingly wondered how Mae could afford a hotel bill for the weeks she had been in the Highlands, but with fifteen minutes before she was due back at work, she needed to hear Mae's opinion.

"I've been served with the court papers for my divorce."

"Why, honey, that's great news." She saw Joanne was waiting for more. "It really is

141

good news, isn't it?"

"Aye. But . . ."

"I know, it's a small town. A divorce — so tough for the woman."

"I knew you would know."

"Believe me, I know." Mae pulled out her cigarettes, felt the wind, put them back. "I really do know how prejudice can destroy you."

Her eyes seemed bright, but Joanne put it down to the wind.

"I'll tell you one day," Mae said. "It's a story for a long night and a glass or two of wine. But you, dear friend, you stick to your guns. Don't let anyone get to you. And keep your eye on McAllister — he's quite a catch. Might even take him up myself if you don't watch out."

She was teasing and Joanne didn't mind. She knew she should be jealous, but somehow Mae Bell's fancying him, even in jest, only put McAllister up in her estimation.

They were smiling and chatting about shoes and weather as they made their way back down the steep slope of Castle Wynd.

Mae Bell may or may not have known, but her approval of McAllister made Joanne reexamine the man who was courting her. *Mae Bell finds him attractive,* she was thinking, *and Mae Bell should know, she's from*

New York and Paris. So why do I hesitate?

She was back on the same seesaw of emotion. Perhaps fear. And it frustrated her almost as much as it frustrated McAllister.

NINE

Rob McLean was a good friend to Frankie Urquhart, especially in the days and weeks following the death of Nurse Urquhart. He had liked Frankie's mum. He thought her funny and kind and always ready to laugh at the boys' shenanigans — even the memorable nit outbreak, she would laugh about later. He wanted to find whoever had done this to her. He also wanted a front-page scoop.

Rob knew he would one day leave the Highlands. He was certain that one day he would be somebody in the world, and television was the world he would star in. He applied twice to Scottish Television for a position as news reporter. He was turned down, but not left without hope. The rejection letter advised him to finish his cadetship on the newspaper and then reapply. By this summer, after five years training, he would be a fully qualified journalist. Next stop, stardom.

But the coming of McAllister to the *Highland Gazette* had not only changed the newspaper, it had changed Rob. The role of bright young investigative reporter and lead singer in a small-town rock 'n' roll band was alluring, flattering even. He was the proverbial golden fish in a pond of sticklebacks.

His mother, Margaret McLean, saw this. And she was worried.

It was not that she wanted her son to leave home; it was that she did not want him to accept second best. She could see how entrenched he was becoming at the *Gazette.* She could see him being appointed senior reporter, deputy editor, editor, accepting life — a good life, here in the Highlands, marrying, having children — all of which she knew she and her husband, Angus, would love, but there was more to her only child than that.

Margaret McLean believed that everyone was born with wings but only a few knew how to unfurl them, stand on the edge of the precipice, and fly — or crash; but to die without trying, that was sad. She encouraged Joanne to find her wings and she wanted Rob to unfurl his. She saw in Joanne's daughter Annie a child she felt would need little encouragement; and she herself had flown and tasted the rarefied air and had made a choice, out of love, to settle, to have a child, her wings folded — temporarily. Now it was her son's turn. And in the article she was reading in *The Scotsman,* she believed she might have found the solution.

"Do you know who, apart from printers, would need sulfuric acid?" Rob asked, breaking into his mother's bubble of dreams for her son.

Margaret thought for a second. "Ask your old chemistry master at the academy." She had a horror of acid. She knew what simple drain cleaner could do to the skin. "And try to think why someone would choose acid . . ."

"As opposed to . . ."

"An axe, a shotgun, a motorcar . . ."

"Poison?"

"Ah . . ." Margaret paused here. "Throwing acid, combined with writing anonymous letters — it all feels female to me."

"Maybe." Rob bounced out of his chair and was across the Persian rug and kissing his mother's cheek in one bound. "Thanks." He stood back, saw her fair hair had now more silver than gold, and with a flash of sadness, he knew she was right; their time

146

together was coming to an end.

The eye contact between them lasted perhaps two seconds before she had to look away.

"I'll be late tonight," was all Rob said before leaving.

She heard the kitchen door close. Then the gate shut. Then the motorbike start. She shook open the newspaper to the article she'd been reading, folded the pages back, took it to the writing bureau, copied out the information. Rob was never annoyed when she tried to organize his life, his career, and this was a perfect way for him to gain a foothold in the world of television. *No harm in sending for the prospectus,* she thought as she started to write the letter.

"My mother feels it could be a woman who threw the acid," Rob said.

"Never." Joanne was indignant at the thought. "A woman knows how disfiguring acid is, how painful, how . . . Never."

"I'm off to ask my old chemistry teacher the places sulfuric acid can be found. Catch you later." Rob was gone. He didn't feel like arguing the point. Whoever threw it, male or female, it was a shocking thing to do, in Rob's opinion; it showed a viciousness, yes, but was cowardly too.

McAllister stopped typing. He was thinking about Margaret McLean's idea. He
looked across at Don, who shrugged. Since
the death of his wife six months previously,
Don McLeod worked, lived quietly, chatted
and joked, but with no real interest: he was
living a surface life; without love he was half
a man — a cliché he would strike out with
his wee red pencil if presented to him in an
article, but true nonetheless.

"I'm not much help," Don said to Mc-
Allister, not bothered that Joanne was listen-
ing. "Since I've all but given up the drink,
I'm no good at thinking."

"Maybe, but you're much more hand-
some," Joanne said.

"Better stake your claim, McAllister, she's
almost divorced . . ." Don saw her blush.
"Thanks all the same, it does an old man
good to flirt wi' a bonnie lass." He gave her
a pat on the arm, slid off his stool, and went
down to the print room with a sheaf of copy
to be set.

She watched him. She worried about him.
Since the death of his wife, he seemed so
much older. And since he was the nearest
she had come to a real father, his well-being
mattered to her. Greatly. She shook her
head. Beneath this news story, she sensed
an undercurrent. The intent may not have

been murder. It may have been to disfigure only. *Only?* She thought. *Evil,* she felt. *But why? Why throw acid?*

"Is that what you think? That a woman could have done this?" Joanne asked McAllister. As all at the *Gazette* were writing about, thinking on, and investigating the attack, there was never a need to explain what "this" referred to.

"I think a woman could have written the letters," he began. "But the little I know of that particular crime — revenge, wanting to destroy them by disfiguring them — is that it's usually men against women. A woman doing this? I couldn't say."

"I'm not sure I'd want to live if I was that disfigured — not being able to speak; breathing and eating really difficult. Someone must have really hated her."

Joanne had been brought up in the hell and damnation version of Christianity. She knew that if there was love, which she believed there was, there surely must be its opposite. Hate. She thought she knew love. And dislike — occasionally intense dislike. But hate?

She sighed. "McAllister, I've had enough of miserable news. Let's go to the pictures. Something cheerful." She reached for the *Gazette.* "Doris Day? She sings that song

'Que Sera, Sera.' You know the one . . ."
The one you love, she was going to say,
knowing he hated it. *One o' those songs that
get stuck in your head and drives you to drink,*
he told her when the song had blasted out
of the wireless for the umpteenth time.

McAllister was saved by the phone. Joanne
answered. "Yes, he's here. DI Dunne," she
said as she handed over the receiver.

"Yes, they're all here." McAllister was
nodding and doodling the chemical equa-
tion for sulfuric acid on a sheet of copy
paper. "Aye. Right. Use my office." He put
down the phone, "Sorry, Joanne, we'll have
to make the pictures some other night. The
police want to interview the printers, so it's
best I stay here."

"Liar. You're not in the least sorry." She
laughed. He grinned back. "McAllister, I
was teasing. I would never put you through
a Doris Day film."

It was the last cheerful moment in what
turned into a long and fractious day.

Later in the morning, Rob came in, talking
as he stripped off the layers of protection
needed to drive a motorbike in March in
the Highlands. "Mr. George, at the academy, he says finding sulfuric is not hard if
you know where to look."

150

"Including here." Joanne knew that acid was kept in the *Gazette* typesetting room. "And in Hector's studio," she added, "but I made him get rid of it and told him never to mention he kept acid. You know how bad that would look to Sergeant Patience."

"Good thinking." McAllister knew this may not be strictly legal but was glad of Joanne's decision. He had also warned Don, whose job it was, laid down in union rules, to liaise between journalists and printers, to be careful not to upset the printers. *A temperamental lot, printers,* he'd said after DI Dunne had explained to him, "We're only here to find out about the missing bottle." His tone had been that of a curious archaeologist trying to identify a rune.

"None in the print room are happy," Don said. "They're offended anyone should think one of them guilty of throwing acid." *That's a right cowardly act . . . none o' us would do such a thing,* the father of the chapel told him, affronted at any interference in his bailiwick.

Midafternoon, McAllister was in the reporters' room. He had asked everyone to attend, so, along with Don, Joanne, Rob, and Hector, Mal Forbes was there with Fiona.

"The police don't know if the acid came

from here," McAllister started. "The bottle was smashed to bits. Our men have had their fingerprints taken, including the father of the chapel. DI Dunne asked if we would volunteer to have our prints . . ."

"Gazette," Joanne answered. "A moment please." She handed the receiver to McAllister.

"Aye. Right. I see." McAllister was doodling naughts and crosses on a piece of copy paper as he listened. "Never!" His pencil stabbed through the paper and broke. "Have you arrested them? Aye, I know . . . helping with inquiries. Aye. Thanks for letting me know." He hung up the receiver. The others were watching him, waiting, as he lit a cigarette. "The bottle came from here."

Rob was indignant that the printers should be suspected. "None of our people —"

"DI Dunne has taken Alan Fordyce, the apprentice compositor, in for questioning. His thumbprint is on a piece of glass from the bottle found at the scene." McAllister blew out a long stream of smoke towards heaven.

"Never." Don was indignant. "He'd never . . ." The others saw a thought as obvious as a cloud crossing the sun at midday. "He plays for Glen Achilty."

Joanne took a moment longer than the others to work this out. "Shinty?"

"Aye, lass, shinty." Don climbed down from his stool. "I'd better go and speak to the father of the chapel."

"Too late. Another print matches his." McAllister was partly horrified at the thought someone at the *Gazette* might be involved, partly concerned that the printers would not be released in time to print the next edition, and mostly confused. The father of the chapel was the epitome of respectability.

"So, no need for us to give our fingerprints then," Mal Forbes said.

Joanne ignored Mal. "What will we do?" she asked McAllister.

He shrugged. "Wait." He saw she was waiting for more.

Don was beginning to take an interest. "Mislead, confuse, confound — all and more of the above — then cobble together an article . . ." This was his territory — the print room, shinty, the men he worked with, some he had known for twenty years and more.

"Send the readers off in different directions," Joanne continued.

"Anywhere but the print-shop of the *Highland Gazette,*" McAllister finished.

153

Forty minutes later, Don remembered. He waited another hour until everyone had left, then asked McAllister did he fancy a drink. "Only a pint," he said, "that doesn't count as alcohol."

Don didn't want to talk in his usual haunts, so they walked across the river to a pub on Glen Urquhart Road. It was mid-week quiet. They found a corner where only the observers on the top deck of the buses stopping outside could see them, and only if they squinted through unwashed windows into the shadows of the nineteenth-century bar lit with 40-watt bulbs filtered through lampshades as old as the pub.

"The father of the chapel lives on Plane-field Road," Don started, and then remembered that even after two years, McAllister did not know every street, lane, and vennel in the town. "Planefield Road runs along at the back of the school. That's the entrance to the playgrounds where Nurse Urquhart was attacked."

"A coincidence surely." McAllister leaned forwards, staring at Don. "It has to be."

"Aye, probably. But let me think on it, and I'll ask around." He didn't say, but Don had heard something about Nurse Urquhart and the printer's wife. He couldn't remember what; recent or past he couldn't recall, either.

McAllister knew that if there was anything to be found out about the vendettas of the town, Don would find it. "DI Dunne will know this?" he asked.

"Maybe."

"So what do we do?"

"Make sure we get the paper out." Don was not being heartless, just realistic. "That's the best way to help the Urquharts — keeping the story in the news, maybe jogging someone's memory. You know."

McAllister did indeed know. What he also knew was that if this evil originated in the *Highland Gazette,* their rivals would love to splash the news with front-page, heavy-type, large-font headlines.

"And the father of the chapel, you'll talk to him?"

Don nodded. It was not a meeting he was looking forwards to. The man was obstinate, and more negative than one of Hector's contact sheets. "Aye, I'll speak to him. Just pray he doesn't call a strike over some wee procedural error . . ." He saw McAllister's eyebrows shoot up. "Revenge for being questioned like a criminal."

The chip shop was a few doors away from the pub. They ended the evening walking back across the bridge, not saying much, eating, scalding their fingers on the hot chips and fish batter, glad of the company. And for once, neither of them stumbled home to their respective beds drunk or hungry.

The same evening, Rob met up with Frankie Urquhart for a game of billiards. Thinking to take Frankie's mind off his mother's death, he had invited him for a game. The first game Rob won by a large margin. And the second.

"Sorry, I can't concentrate." Frankie was setting up for another, then changed his mind. They took a seat to watch a game on a neighboring table — a tight game between a local and a man from Elgin, who was good, very good. As the balls clacked and spun, Frankie, speaking quietly so as not to disturb the players, said again, "Have you heard any more about — you know?"

Rob's silence before attempting a casual "Not much" alerted him.

"Tell me what you heard. I have a right to know who killed my mother."

"It's ridiculous." Rob was tossing a cube of chalk, worn to almost a hole in the middle, from hand to hand. He had a feeling he shouldn't be telling Frankie this.

"So you *have* heard something?"

"Not really, it's just that the bottle of . . . the bottle might have come from the *Gazette* print room."

Rob knew he was right when Frankie burst out, "Alan Fordyce!"

The yell put the Elgin player off his shot. He turned and growled, "You! Shut yer bloody trap!" He turned back to his opponent. "I'm taking that shot again."

"No, you're no'," his opponent replied, and his pals — for this was their town, their billiard hall — rose from their seats.

Rob grabbed Frankie's arm and pulled him towards the steps, keeping hold of him as they came out into the dark and damp of a desolate Thursday night where only the drunk could withstand the wind and rain.

"Back to my house."

Margaret McLean was still up though it was past ten o'clock. She went into the kitchen; saw the state of the "boys," as she always called them. They were wet and cold and shaken. She handed each of them a towel. "Whisky, Frankie? Gin?"

"Cocoa for me," Rob answered, "and I'll make it."

"Frankie, telephone your father. Tell him where you are." Margaret was giving an order, not a request. Even though Frankie was twenty-three and hadn't had to inform his father of his whereabouts in seven years, he did as he was told.

When they were by the fire in the sitting room, it seemed natural for Margaret to join them. It was a good move, Rob thought later. His mother had a way of calming people. And her contribution to the conversation made sense.

Rob told them both about the bottle coming from the print room. He told them of the fingerprints and whose they were, found on the broken pieces. He managed throughout the telling to avoid the word *acid*. He ended with the question, "So why did you get so het up over Alan Fordyce?"

"He used to be in our team, but ma dad sacked him for dirty play."

Rob considered this. To be thrown off the team for dirty play in a game as rough as shinty would be hard.

Frankie continued, "He swore revenge on Dad. Then he joined the Glen Achilty team. Every game we've met since, he's been right vicious."

"Do I know him?" Rob asked. He couldn't put a face to the name.

"He's thon skinny wee runt, the one they call 'Ferret.' "

"He's short, nearly as wee as Hector."

"It didn't take height or strength for the attack on Nurse Urquhart," Margaret pointed out. "Sorry, Frankie — I shouldn't have mentioned that."

"No, I prefer people to speak to me normally. Many people can't even look me in the eye. My mother's death is embarrassing enough, but to be a victim of . . ."

"It's not that people don't care," Margaret said. "It's because they're scared of death." At their age, and having missed the war, the young men had little experience of death.

Frankie left shortly after. Margaret insisted Rob give him a lift in his father's car. When Rob returned, his mother was still up.

"Do you believe it could be this lad from the *Gazette*?" she asked.

"Not really." Rob was having a hard time accepting that anyone would throw acid, especially over a shinty competition.

"The acid hit Nurse Urquhart in the throat, but it was probably meant for her face. If this fellow is as small as you say, it makes sense." They knew the nurse had been a tall woman, perhaps five foot eight.

"I know, Mum, but it's all so . . ."

"Horrible, nasty, vicious . . ."

"Deadly." Rob said what he had not wanted to say. "It killed her."

It took three days — and one day after the *Gazette* came out with the information about sulfuric acid, but nothing about a bottle being missing from the print room — before another anonymous letter was delivered to the *Gazette.* This time the letter came in the post. A similar letter was posted to the police.

The accusation was enigmatic but grammatical, the vocabulary and spelling correct.

ASK THAT SELF-RIGHTEOUS MAN ON THE GAZETTE ABOUT HIS WIFE AND THE NURSE.

Joanne was in the reporters' room when she opened the letter. It was in among the other letters addressed to the *Gazette* — letters usually to the editor complaining about anything from the council to the obituaries to the state of the Commonwealth, and usually innocuous, occasionally funny or libelous.

This letter was on cheap white unlined paper, in a brown envelope, posted, not hand delivered. The message she read once to herself. She shuddered. She loathed anonymous messages of any kind.

She read it a second time — out loud to the others.

"All we need to work out is who is 'self-righteous,' " Rob said.

"There's more than one self-righteous man on the *Gazette*," Don pointed out.

Mal Forbes was Joanne's candidate. Then she felt her cheeks warm. *Me too, I can be a wee bit self-righteous — though goodness knows I've no reason to be.* Joanne's prejudice was women who wore too much makeup or who started sentences with "I'm no gossip but . . ." She would also admit to being self-righteous about people who never read and never took an interest in anything outside small-town life.

"It's nothing like the other letters," Joanne pointed out. "Different notepaper, posted — not hand delivered."

"Who is married and self-righteous?" Rob asked.

"Mal Forbes," Joanne muttered. Only Rob heard and nudged her with his elbow, whispering, "Meow."

"The father of the chapel lives across the street from where the attack on Nurse Urquhart took place," Don told them, not sharing his thought that the man was the most self-righteous person he'd ever worked with. "His fingerprint is also on the bottle . . ."

"Never." McAllister thought the man too much of a worthy Dickensian character to be a suspect.

"Two suspects and both from the *Gazette,*" Rob said. "Unbelievable."

"No, laddie, for many only too believable." Don knew how many loved to hate their local paper. He knew how many believed they could do the job much better than the professionals, because so many over the years had told him so.

"Someone threw the acid. Why couldn't that someone be one of us?" Joanne's observation was correct. And depressing — much like the low-level cloud that came up that morning, enveloping the east coast; hanging over the firths, moors, and mountains; enveloping the town in shades of pewter for the next three days.

With both printers released without charge, the matter did not go away. Theories as to the culprit abounded, theories involving strangers, neighbors, family, and friends. Even a visiting missionary seconded to the Dalneigh Church was suspected, but only because he was a foreigner from Nigeria and different. All the speculation was accompanied by an awareness of horror: the knowl-

162

edge of how damaging, indeed fatal, acid could be; images of the scarred and the maimed and the dying haunting many — mostly women; the smell of burnt flesh haunting others — mostly survivors from two world wars. This was a death that touched all.

TEN

Frankie Urquhart didn't realize his anger was actually grief.

"Thon apprentice. Him on the *Gazette.* Alan Fordyce. What's the police saying?" He was not yelling at Rob, but the way he spoke with a full stop every few words made his bitterness clear.

Rob had the phone under his chin, trying both to give Frankie his attention and to ignore Don, who was pointing to the clock with his forefinger.

"I don't know, Frankie. The police talked to him, they talked to all of us on the *Gazette,* but there's no evidence, only his print on a piece of glass, and part of his job is to clean the metal print . . ."

"Five minutes." Don was loud enough for Frankie to hear.

"I'll have to go, we're on deadline. Talk later."

Frankie hung up.

Rob didn't call back, knowing he was winging it — to make the edition he needed to write a story about the formation of a local Ban the Bomb branch in seven minutes.

"Frankie Urquhart," was all he said to Don.

"Aye. Poor man." Don was referring to the father. As a recent widower himself, he felt for the man.

One of the main jobs of the chief and only sub editor on a small newspaper job was to stay until the first of the newspapers rolled off the presses. Don loved the evenings when he put the newspaper to bed. Forty-odd years — even he would have to stop and count exactly how many years he had been at the *Gazette* — and still there was that moment of excitement when he was handed the first newspaper off the rollers. He would open it carefully, feel the warmth, smell the ink, see his layout, his headings, and feel the pride.

He knew that Rob grabbed the newspaper, glanced at the front page, searched for his own articles, then moved on to the sports pages. When he finished, he was off and planning the next edition. He knew Joanne would read the paper from cover to cover, including the classifieds, the births deaths and marriages, and all the wee community events and council planning notices. He suspected she even read the God Spot.

McAllister . . . you can't count on what McAllister will do, Don was thinking as he left the building.

The evening was unseasonably mild for the end of March. Still and quiet too, no wind, no rain, no gales, no sleet. *Unusual,* Don was thinking, when he heard a groan echoing down the tunnel of the close that ran between the *Gazette* building and the neighboring office.

He looked in. It was too dark to see anything. A fainter lowing like a cow in distress made him reach for his matches. He struck one. He could see a shape farther down. He went in. Lit another match. He saw the blood.

"Alan? Is that you? Alan?" He could see the young man was far from right.

"Hang on, I'll be back wi' help." He hurried back inside — running was beyond a forty-cigarettes-a-day man — but he went as fast as he could to the loading bay. The noise was deafening; bundles of newspapers coming off the conveyer belt, being tied and covered and tossed onto the loading bay, ready for the delivery vans to take them to the trains. He gestured to the father of the chapel to come outside. The man was in his coat and cap, about to leave. Don took his arm and hurried him into the street so they could hear each other talk.

"It's young Alan Fordyce. He's in the close. He's injured. I'm phoning an ambulance."

The father of the chapel grabbed the senior compositor as he came out of the building buttoning up his jacket for the short walk down Church Street to the Market Bar.

Don left them to care for the lad and made the call from the *Gazette* switchboard in reception. Wednesday night was a slow night, so the ambulance was there in seven minutes. The yell from Alan as they carried him out told the men bones were probably broken.

"Who did it? Did he say?" Don asked as the men lit their cigarettes, waiting for the police to arrive.

"No, not a word." This came from the head compositor. But not until after he looked at the boss, the father of the chapel.

Don didn't believe him. But he knew he would hear no more tonight.

Sergeant Patience arrived with a young constable who seemed more a schoolboy playing dress-up in his dad's uniform.

"Do you want to give me statements here

or at the station?" the sergeant asked.

"Inside." Don jerked his head towards the *Gazette* building. "I don't know about you" — he was speaking to the men but knew the sergeant would have a quick one with them — "but I could use a drink."

The sergeant glanced at the boy policeman, told him to guard the close, then followed the men up to the reporters' room. But despite all his questioning, all he found out for certain was that Don McLeod kept a good whisky. The printers and the deputy editor said they knew nothing about the attack. He suspected they knew more. He was certain they would not tell him. He put away his notebook, telling them he would talk to them more in the morning, and bade them good night.

Don did the same, saying, "We'll sort this out in the morning."

The morning brought no more news other than that Alan had three broken ribs, broken bones in his foot, and a great deal of bruising. Rob was the reporter on the case. When, having charmed the nurses into letting him see Alan out of visiting hours, all he got was *Dunno. No. Didney see their faces. No. No idea.*

A very sorry Alan had a purple-green bruise and a scrape from the flagstones in the close on one side of his face, and his leg was in plaster, hoisted up on a pulley. The exposed part of his foot, toes mostly, were in Technicolor purple, yellow, red, black — Rob had to look away.

The doctor told him more when Rob explained he was Alan's colleague and friend — although friend was stretching it a bit far, as they were only on nodding terms.

"He said he plays shinty," the doctor began. "I haven't told him, but I fear his playing days are over. The bones in the foot . . . it seems like the stomping, mostly on one foot, the right one, was deliberate."

"His foot was the target?" Rob was beginning to feel queasy about the foot connection and couldn't remember if the other foot, the foot in the boot, was the right or the left.

"It looks like it."

On the drive back to the office, Rob began to piece together the sequence.

First, Don McLeod had reported the bottle of sulfuric acid missing from the print room. The printers and *Gazette* staff questioned. The printers and compositors fingerprinted. Fingerprint matches for Alan Fordyce and the father of the chapel. What was his name? He was always known as only the "father of the chapel" or occasionally as

169

Auld Bugger-lugs — Don's name for him when the union official was being particularly obstreperous. A Welsh name — William? Williams? Evans? That was it, Mr. Evans. Then what? The questioning of the printers was not reported in the *Gazette.* So who knew? *Silly question, Rob,* he told himself, *this is a small town.*

"Who knew the police questioned the printers?" Rob asked as he came into the reporters' room to a silent McAllister, Don, Joanne, and Hector.

"Frankie's dad called." It was Hector who spoke. "DI Dunne came round for Frankie before breakfast. He's no' home yet."

"Alan Fordyce is saying nothing, so how could Frankie . . . ?" Rob stopped. He remembered.

"How do the police think it was Frankie who gave the lad a hiding?" Don asked.

"I never said . . ." But Rob couldn't look at him.

"I heard you on the phone telling Frankie about the fingerprints." Don had him there.

"Alan had most of the bones in his right foot broken, looks like he'll never play again. Frankie would never do that." Rob was trying to convince himself.

The others could hear it. They said nothing.

The phone went. Joanne answered. It was a call about the fire brigade chasing a pig that escaped from the slaughterhouse and was last seen running towards the Black Isle ferry, making a break for home. She made a note. Hung up.

Still no one spoke. No one typed. No one threw paper darts. Phoned the bookie. Went for coffee. None of the usual Friday-day-after-publication-not-doing-very-much-day stuff.

The phone went again. Joanne answered, "Yes. Hmm. Uh-huh." Wrote down a number.

"Are you covering tomorrow's match?" McAllister asked Rob, trying to keep the question casual. Failing. There was little need to ask which match.

"I am," Hector replied. "It's us versus Lochaber. But without Coach Urquhart, we haven't a chance."

"And without Nurse Urquhart," Joanne added, then wished she hadn't.

"I'll be there," Don said.

"Me too," Rob added.

McAllister looked up at the clock. "Right. The Criterion Bar. My shout."

Mr. Evans, the father of the chapel, rarely came into the reporters' room. When, later that afternoon, he did, everyone stopped working.

"I have some information."

"Let's get McAllister in here too," Don told him.

Rob yelled, "McAllister!" It worked.

McAllister stood. Joanne waited, saying nothing. Mr. Evans addressed Don, as the deputy editor was the one he always dealt with.

"A group o' young lads, four or five o' them, were seen coming away down the Wynd last night."

Joanne thought Mr. Evans sounded like a policeman in the witness box.

"One o' the delivery drivers saw them as he was turning in to the loading dock. He had no idea where they were coming from. He wouldn't recognize them again. The dock was lit bright, an' the opposite side where they were passed by is in shadow. He thought nothing of it. Until he heard. Then he came in to tell us."

Don was quiet, waiting for the rest of what he decided was a rehearsed speech.

"This manny is no' from around here, Tain man he is. He wouldn't know lads from the town." The father of the chapel was almost reciting his speech.

"Have you told the police?" McAllister asked.

"Not yet."

"Use the phone in my office."

The father of the chapel nodded and left. Don and McAllister looked at each other. And waited. When the footsteps receded down the stairs, they lit up. McAllister was the first to put the question.

"Do we believe him?"

Don scratched his chin and said nothing. Joanne stretched her shoulders. Rob was flicking a pencil back and forth between his fingers.

"Do we believe what the father of the chapel just said?" Hector asked.

No one replied. So Hec squeezed his eyes tight shut. "It's late," he started. "Most places are shut. There's what, four vans? Three? They're parked in the lane and the loading bay. So there's the drivers, and the man that loads the papers onto the vans, maybe some others from the print room having a fag. Four or five lads come past. No one sees anything?" He opened his eyes. "Naw, I can't picture it."

"How did the delivery driver know what happened to Alan Fordyce?" Joanne asked.

"When did he come in to talk to Mr. Evans?" Rob asked.

"Why would anyone do such a thing to Alan?" Hector asked.

"There's trouble on the way," Don finished.

"Aye," McAllister agreed.

That one word, the Scottish positive — or negative — that could be used to fill silence, to release tension, to punctuate, summed it up. Aye. Agree. It's how it is. Bad. And could get worse.

Saturday had rain bursts, sunbursts, cloud-scudding, wind-cutting-to-the-bone weather. Bught Park, where the shinty was played, was a wide-open space on the north side of the river next to the Royal Northern Infirmary.

Rob and Hec were walking there. Don walked too, taking the Greig Street Bridge then following the river westward to the playing fields. Although Lochaber was not his team, it was of the Gaeltacht. He knew some of the players' grandfathers — although he told Rob it was their fathers he remembered.

Just as well it's close, Don thought as he passed the sign indicting the emergency entrance to the hospital. He knew this could turn into a grudge match. He'd heard the rumor that some in other shinty clubs were taking sides.

When he arrived he saw clusters of spectators stood around the sidelines, gathered in groups of team loyalty. Lochaber Camanachd Club colors were red and white stripes.

And they're as good as I remember, Don thought after the first forty-five minutes, particularly thon wee fellow on the right wing.

It was a low-scoring match, 1–0, but fast and furious nonetheless, with many shots on goal. The clash of sticks, then some very skillful passing, started the game, but hacking led to three penalties. There were far too many offsides, the players were watching their markers rather than the whole game. From the yells of the players, all twenty-four of them, the shouts from the referee and the coaches, and the cheers and groans of the supporters, Don appreciated how much more seriously than usual they were all taking this game.

"Nurse Urquhart would have been proud," Don told Rob when the match was over. "It was hard to hold Lochaber to only one goal up."

"We still lost." Rob had his hands in his pockets, kicking at the grass, looking the epitome of glum. Hec was over the other

175

side of the field taking snaps of the winning team.

No one expected the fight to come from where it did.

"You're liars, the lot of you!" the voice shrieked — the sound of someone in pain. Someone female. "And you're ma father's team. Why aren't you . . ." The rest of the shrieks were blown upriver by the fiercesome wind that had come up in the last half of the match.

Rob could see Hec running towards the kerfuffle. And it was not to take pictures. He put his arm around a girl and walked her rapidly towards them. It was Morag, Frankie's sister. She was sobbing as though her heart would burst.

"They're, saying, it was, our Frankie . . ." She was coughing and spluttering between the words, "He never, he wouldney, he . . ."

"Who said what?" Rob asked.

Don could see Rob's hands clench into fists and took over. "Take her home," he told Rob and Hector.

Rob stepped forwards. Don grabbed his sleeve. "Home. Now."

When he saw Rob and Hec walk off, Morag between them, he looked over at the bunch of supporters milling around the edge of the stadium. Then he was in among them, his anger propelling him across the pitch with surprising speed.

"Which fine laddie has upset a wee girl that's just lost her mother?" he yelled out in Gaelic to a group of Lochaber supporters.

"Which brave man, or wifie, has made Nurse Urquhart's lass cry?" This time in English to the town supporters. "Can you no see this family has had enough?" to both groups.

He stood his ground, arms out from his sides, a small, round, tight-as-a-bow-ready-to-shoot old Highlander, glaring, shouting, "Which one o' you upset the lassie? Which one?"

No answer. Only a shuffling, a murmuring, most looking away or gathering their coats tight around them, ready to leave.

"I'm no' having it. If you've anything to say, say it at me." Don was poking his chest with his forefinger, hurting himself.

There were mutters. Some in the back started to walk away. Some of the women, more than the usual one or two, who had come today to support Nurse Urquhart's team, looked at Don McLeod, nodding thanks as they passed. Within a few minutes there were hardly any spectators left on the field and the Lochaber team had retreated to their bus.

When Don looked back, Hector and Rob had disappeared with Morag. Probably taken her back to Granny Bain's.

He buttoned up his coat, pulled his cap low. Might as well join them. He trudged over to the far-northeast corner of the field, walked through the prewar housing scheme in the shadow of Tomnahurich Cemetery, and went around the back of the house, knowing front doors were only for policemen, ministers, bad news, and strangers.

The back door was open onto a wee porch. He knocked.

Hector's sister Marie answered. "We're in the front room, Mr. McLeod," she said. "Can I take your coat and fetch you some tea?" She showed him into the sitting room.

"Thank you." As he came into the room, a fire blazing even though it wasn't that cold, he nodded at Morag and said to Granny Bain, sitting on the couch with her, "A fine-mannered lass you have there, Maraidh."

The old woman didn't look up. "Sit yerself down, Donal."

Rob was gone. Hector was there but excused himself saying he had film to develop. Eleven-year-old Maraidh served the tea. After Granny Bain had added a drop of whisky to their cups and after she suggested Morag go with Maraidh up to the bedroom for "a wee lie-down," she and Don talked. In Gaelic.

In English or in Gaelic, the sentiment was the same. "What is the world coming to?" Granny Bain sighed. "Some troublemaker in the crowd was saying Frankie Urquhart put Alan Fordyce in the hospital to get back at him for killing his mother. But that can't be."

Don told her it was a possibility. He told her about the acid bottle, everyone on the *Gazette* being questioned by the police. He said fingerprints were found on broken bits of glass, and that one of them belonged to the father of the chapel.

"Thon too-big-for-his-boots wee manny?" she said. "His wife is more likely to have a go at someone . . . but acid? I can't see her throwing acid — even though she's a right meddlesome piece o' work."

They chased and teased the story round and around until Maraidh came down and said Morag was sleeping.

"Run round to Mr. Urquhart's, tell him his Morag is here . . . and ask him if he wants his supper wi' us." She rose from her chair. Don could see it took her an effort. *Her back, is it?*

"You'll be staying for supper," she said. It

was a statement, not a question, and he was glad of it. It had been a long time since he'd eaten a home-cooked meal.

"Here, make yourself useful." She handed him a pencil and the forms. "Check my footba' pools." She switched on the wireless in time for the six-o'clock news and left to cook or brew potions or charm a frog.

Neither Frank nor Frankie Urquhart accepted the invitation to supper; in spite of the temptation of a home-cooked meal, company was not what they wanted.

Don stayed until late, reminiscing with his old friend until he saw her eyes closing and the trace of a smile linger at the corners of her mouth, even in sleep. It was an intimate picture, a reminder that she was his first love, his possible wife — until WWI, an almost fatal injury, and the appearance of Joyce Mackenzie, his late wife, intervened.

Morag Urquhart slept the night in the Bain household, sharing the bed with Maraidh. She stayed with them all day Sunday. There was nothing at home for her, only a father and a brother who, in their grief, were as lost to her as her mother.

Eleven

When another anonymous letter arrived at the *Gazette,* Fiona knew immediately what it was. She shivered when she picked it out of the other correspondence with her thumb and forefinger, laid it aside, and called upstairs to the reporters' room. As usual, Joanne answered.

"You'd better give it to McAllister," she told Fiona.

"It's addressed to you."

Joanne was down the stairs in a lightning strike. She looked at Fiona. She looked at the letter. She too shivered. This one was from no copycat. "Do you know where McAllister is?" she asked.

"I think he went out for cigarettes."

Joanne waited. She couldn't touch the letter.

"Mrs. Ross . . ." Fiona hesitated, "do you know Morag Urquhart?" She didn't wait for a reply. "We were in the same shorthand

and typing class at school; she's worried about her brother . . ."

McAllister came in, removed his hat. "Ladies." He smiled. Joanne didn't notice. Fiona did.

"McAllister" — Joanne pointed to the letter — "another one."

He picked up the envelope, told Fiona to call DI Dunne, took Joanne's arm, and steered her up the stairs to his office. He felt her tremble before he saw her face. "Don't worry," he started.

"What a useless piece of advice! Don't worry. When anyone says that, you know to worry." She slumped onto her chair. "Sorry. It's just the thought of acid . . . poor Nurse Urquhart. Sorry." She was staring at the envelope with her name on it, sitting on the table like unexploded ordinance.

"We should wait for the inspector before opening it." McAllister was trying to shield her.

"Open it."

He did. He read it twice. Then read it aloud.

I SAW YOU WITH THE AMERICAN WOMAN KEEP AWAY FROM HER OR FACE THE CONSEQUENCES.

"That makes it clear the anonymous letter writer is the person who attacked Nurse Urquhart," Joanne said.

There was a knock on the open door. DI Dunne stood, hands clasped as though he was about to deliver a eulogy.

"There's no evidence to link the writer to the attack on Nurse Urquhart." He had overheard Joanne's remark.

"And nothing to connect Nurse Urquhart with Mrs. Mae Bell?" Joanne asked, as she had been desperately trying to find a link other than the letters.

"Not that we can find."

McAllister stood. "Inspector, have a seat." He pushed the letter across the desk.

"You opened it."

The reprimand was slight, but Joanne rushed in. "It was addressed to me, I asked McAllister . . . sorry." Once again a shudder made her shoulders clench. Acid. It burned a woman's throat beyond repair. "Sorry."

"My fault." McAllister was watching her, longing to reach over and take her hand. He didn't. He smiled instead. She looked away. *Wrong move,* he told himself.

The inspector finished reading the letter. He put it back in the envelope. Told them not to open any further communications from the writer. Stood. Looked at Joanne, said, "We will investigate this — and please, don't worry," and then left.

"If one more person tells me not to worry, I'll scream."

"As the letter mentions her, I think you should tell Mae Bell. Invite her to the house if you want," McAllister said.

She noticed he didn't say *my* house. She would have liked him to say *our* house. She knew she was being silly, especially as she was far from certain what she really wanted. She did not see that all he wanted was to gather her and her children up, and hide them, protect them, in his house, in their house.

"I'll leave a note at her hotel." Joanne stood. "Thanks, McAllister." She smiled and shrugged her shoulders. When he came towards her, she put a hand on his arm in an I'll-be-fine gesture. "Don't worry," she said, and they both smiled. "We'll talk later." She sighed knowing she must get back to the reporters' desk, to the fascinating task of collating the monthly Women's Institute reports.

Once more Joanne and Mae Bell were sitting in the window of Gino's café and ice cream shop overlooking the river.

As soon as they were seated, Joanne rose again. "Sorry," she said to the waitress, this time an elderly woman who was slow but, Chiara told her, a relative of some distant cousin who had begged her father for a job. "We'll take a table at the back."

Mae Bell raised an eyebrow, but followed. "You sound serious," she said when they had resettled themselves and ordered.

"I had an anonymous letter warning me to keep away from you."

"It's not the first time that threat has been made." Mae laughed. "The last time it was someone's father."

"This is serious, Mae. What if the writer is the same person who threw the acid at Nurse Urquhart?"

"I know it's serious — but never let bullies know they upset you." She winked. She knew, much more than Joanne would ever realize, how serious this was. Her life with Robert was one long escape from prejudice. Even though they met when they were part of a big band entertaining the troops in postwar Germany, there was nowhere in her own country that she could avoid the disdain, the stares, the outright hostility that her love of Robert brought.

Except in Paris, she was thinking. Even there, they were accepted only in a particularly small milieu of left-wing thinkers and jazz lovers on the Left Bank. *Never in the countryside* — she remembered a trip to a small town on the Riviera. *The hotel refused us a room together even after we showed them our marriage certificate.*

She had given up family, friends, reputation for love.

Mae Bell didn't want to remember past troubles. And most of all she did not want anyone to discover why she was here in the Highlands. Being with Joanne and McAllister she could find out much. But she hadn't allowed for a real affection to develop with these once strangers, now friends.

She veered the conversation slightly off target. "I heard one of your printers attacked the nurse."

"Who told you that?" Joanne sat back, her neck stretched in righteous indignation.

"It's all the talk amongst the staff at the hotel."

"Oh, Mae, I've no idea what's going on, but an acid attack, that vicious . . ."

"Cowardly . . ."

"Horrible . . ."

"But we must never live in fear." Mae lit a cigarette, blew out a long stream of smoke, and said so softly that Joanne had to lean forwards to catch her words, "If I've learned one thing, it's that you must never give way to fear or they win." She didn't explain exactly who "they" were. But Joanne took her meaning.

Around them the café was quiet except for a crashing of cutlery and dishes and Gino shouting in Italian what Joanne took to be "careful," or maybe stronger. The St. Valerie Avenue double-decker bus stopped outside, and the top-deck passengers peered down into the café. Joanne was nervous for herself, and for Mae, hoping the steamed-up windows would hide them.

"Don't go anywhere on your own at night, will you?" she asked Mae.

"Here? In this town? Is there anywhere to go at night? Do tell!" The way she said it, her hands and her eyebrows acting out her remarks, made Joanne laugh.

"Honey, I'm all grown up, I can take care of myself. And changing the subject, have you gotten rid of your rat of a husband yet? Are you and McAllister now ready for a bit of loving — real loving? Do you have anyone else dangling around? Tell me all — I love a steamy story."

"I'll tell you mine if you tell me yours."

Joanne's laughter made Mae smile and say, "Steamy stories, no, but I will tell you about my true love."

187

It only took about twenty minutes. Joanne had never heard anyone talk so truthfully, so tenderly about love and loss and the deep, raw pain of grief. Later she would remember not the words but the sensation of being touched, a sensation almost physical, as Mae Bell recounted the day she met Robert Bell, the day she received the telegram, the days and weeks of waiting for confirmation, each hour the hope draining away, and the day Mae knew, a sensation like ice water running down the spine, she said, that Robert, her love, was never coming back.

"We first met in Germany. Nineteen forty-seven. His brother was a good friend of mine; he played piano in a big band. I was the singer — we were entertaining the troops. Robert and I caught up again in Paris two years later."

"That was when McAllister heard you sing."

"Must have been. I was with that band for five years. Robert played saxophone and sat in with us a few times, but flying was his love. Until he met me, he always said, it was his way to touch the sky, he said, same as you reach heaven when you sing. And love, I told him. You touch heaven when you love," Mae Bell said.

Joanne felt a stab of envy. She once, maybe twice, thought she was in love. But she had mistaken destructive attraction for real deep-down unconditional love — of the lasting kind. Now she was not sure she knew what real love was.

"He never had enough schooling to be a pilot," she continued, "but he was clever, good at math and at reading maps, and had this amazing homing instinct. Towards the end of the war, his captain recommended him to stay on and retrain. His lucky charm, he called Robert. So Bobby signed up and went from rear gunner to navigator."

"Bobby?"

"Everyone called him Bobby except me."

"Bobby Bell." Joanne said it slowly, making Mae smile.

"He called me Mae Bell, always. He told me how proud he was that I was his wife, so it was always Mae Bell, never plain Mae." Again that laugh, the sound a song of a laugh, a song that made Joanne glad.

"We had a joke between us." The way Mae Bell said it, Joanne knew it was no joke. "He said if he was ever in trouble, he would send out a Maeday. You know, Mayday, the distress call?"

Joanne nodded.

"Only he said it would be M-A-E day,

189

Maeday, because if anyone could rescue him, it was me. In the end, of course . . ."

That he had left a message with a waiter at the club two days before the fatal flight, she never told anyone, not even his brother. That one call, barely understood by the Frenchman, but written down at Robert's insistence on a scrap of paper . . . and even after Robert spelled it out, it didn't make sense to anyone except to Mae. The written message read: Maeday.

Repeating Robert's words, the waiter said "Maeday" clearly, plainly, no interpretation necessary. Mae tried to contact Robert. Telephoned every number she could find. She'd spent a small fortune talking to operators in local Scottish exchanges who all said the same thing; they could only connect to the base switchboard number.

Mae spoke to commanders who knew nothing except Robert had been on a training mission. Trying to contact his closest friends, who were on the same exercise, she spent days of tears and frustration. There was nothing, no contact, no news — until an officer from the U.S. embassy tracked her down at the club. The moment she saw his uniform she knew.

Now she had the unposted letters. Two of them. Found in that box of his effects, kept by the police and forgotten about, with very little there except a lighter, a notebook, a music score for *Porgy and Bess,* and a dictionary — she smiled when she held it, remembering his aim to learn five new words a day.

"So that's why I'm here, why I visited Elgin and Kinloss and Findhorn. I wanted to meet some of the local guys he worked with, to talk, to remember him, maybe find some kinda . . . when someone goes missing, no wreckage found, no funeral, you keep hoping . . ." She sighed, smiled, chuckled. "We sure did have a huge wake in that club in Paris though. Robert's brother Charlie composed a piece for him, *North Sea Requiem* — a hymn to his brother, a hymn of joy as well as pain." And the smile and the laugh were through eyes that still shed tears, though not as frequently as before, for her lost husband.

"I don't know that area," Joanne said, just for something to say.

"Beautiful in a bleak kinda way." Mae reached for another cigarette. "I'd love to see it in summer."

"Wouldn't make much difference." Joanne smiled, wanting to lighten the conversation. "Scottish winters, Scottish summers, all beautiful — in a bleak kinda way." They

191

laughed at Joanne's attempt at an American accent.

"That's what a lady in the hotel there told me."

The woman in the hotel had also told Mae Bell of the great times the local lassies had with the American air force men. *Great fun they were. And the dancing, we loved that. Mind you, there was many a person who disapproved. But no, we had fun.*

Mae Bell did not doubt it for a second. The end of a war, a distant location, the long winter nights, a recipe for fun, she thought.

"So" — she winked at Joanne — "on a more cheerful note, how's the divorce coming along?"

"Cheerful? Mae Bell!"

"Honey, from what you *haven't* told me, this is your liberation."

Joanne thought of divorce as a defeat. This was the first time she had heard her well-suppressed dreams said out loud. Free. Freedom. Liberation. It was true. Mostly she dwelt on the consequences of being a divorced mother in a small town in the Scottish Highlands. Dwelt on the scandal, the gossip, the consequences for her and her children. But liberation? This was a notion not new, but longed for.

"Thank you. I will work on seeing it that way."

"And don't let that McAllister escape or I might be tempted to snatch him up for myself." Mae said this not because it was true — she was not ready for another man in her life — but because she saw Joanne's hesitation, and McAllister's need, and felt her new friend needed a push.

"I really like him, he fascinating, he's . . . I'm not sure I'm ready."

"He may not be the love of your life, Joanne Ross, but you need someone to care for you and your children, and good men are hard to find." Mae Bell was nothing if not practical. "And love can grow."

"You really believe that?"

"I do."

When they parted — Joanne back to work, Mae Bell back to planning her next move, Mae took her time walking along the river, watching the rush of water, watching the angler in high rubber leggings cast his rod, remembering her last visit to Findhorn, remembering another time, another walk, a sea, not a river.

Watching the North Sea, where lay the bones of Robert Bell, horizon fused with sea, forming one vast, heaving expanse of grey, one limitless sense of melancholy, Mae

Bell had turned away, pulling her coat tighter. Tasting the salt from the wind and the tears. Walked back along the shoreline. Sand in her shoes, she thought of calling into the local hotel for a drink and the warmth. Instead she walked on past the caravan park, on to where the river met the sea. Once more she looked out at the heaving pewter and gunmetal, shades of shining grey, now flecked with white, and said, "I'll be back, honey."

Without a quiver of self-consciousness she waved to the sea, to her husband. She waved not farewell but *au revoir.* "Bye, Bobby, talk soon."

Two days later and another deadline over, Joanne went back to McAllister's for supper. *We're like an old married couple,* she thought, as she served the shepherd's pie she had made that morning at home and carried carefully in the basket of her bicycle.

They were doing the dishes, she washing and he drying, when the doorbell rang. Someone opened it and came in.

"Are you decent, you two?" Don McLeod's voice echoed down the hallway.

Joanne was giggling at his ridiculous insinuation when the look on his face stopped the smiles.

"Someone held up the delivery van taking the papers down the Great Glen. They were wearing balaclavas, so the driver can't identify them. He's fine, but the papers were dumped in Loch Ness."

Don sat down at the kitchen table. "Any chance of a brew, lass?" Since he had cut back on drinking, he was an eight-or-ten-or-more cups a day man.

McAllister sat down with him, and they both lit up.

"There's more." Don said through a haze of Capstan Full Strength. "The Glen Achilty Clubhouse was burnt to the ground early this morning. No one phoned it in. It seems they want to extract revenge in their own way."

"Shinty clubhouse?" Joanne asked.

"Aye. A shinty vendetta has begun, it seems like," Don replied.

McAllister ended the conversation saying, "I've heard of blood feuds. But a shinty vendetta is a new one on me." He was shaking his head wondering what to do. "Do we print more papers? How about distribution?"

"Nothing can be done until morning," Don advised.

But next morning the news was worse. Dozens of bundles of the newspaper were not delivered, or missing, or had been stolen from the doorsteps of local shops and newsagents. Some had been set alight; some were soaked in water, and, in one village, pig manure.

The father of the chapel was livid. He was standing in McAllister's office shouting.

"You have to do something."

McAllister said, "The police . . ."

"Forget the polis, Frank Urquhart's team is behind this. Aye, the man has a right to be upset, but this is no fair."

"Do you know this for sure? The other teams could be responsible. Or are you accusing Coach Urquhart?"

"No, I'm no' accusing him directly, but the lads from his team . . . I knew running a shinty column would lead to trouble."

He welcomed the new column when it started, McAllister remembered.

But there was no placating the man. He took the loss of the newspapers as sorely as if he had lost his own precious possessions.

The police are investigating, a policeman said when McAllister phoned for information.

Don McLeod had his network of moles, spies, and barroom pals looking.

Rob McLean and Frankie Urquhart were asking around the billiard hall, the shinty teams, their old school pals, and their old school enemies.

"*No one knows nothing,* that's a quote," Don said at the end of a long day when they were all gathered in McAllister's office, Hector included. But not the father of the chapel; he had gone home, where his wife, who feared he might have a heart attack he was so angry, had the good sense to say nothing. For once. Nor was Mal Forbes there. *He's never here,* Joanne thought. She knew he would be equally upset. No matter how much he condescended to her, Mal Forbes was a dedicated newspaperman.

The loss of the newspapers, the letters, the death of Nurse Urquhart, the leg in the laundry hamper — round and around the conversation went. Getting nowhere.

"I was wondering . . ." Joanne started, again with that hesitation that annoyed McAllister. Again he told himself, *Bite your tongue.*

"The letters are hand delivered to the *Gazette* reception. But how?"

"Good point," McAllister said, but wanting to say, *Listen to yourself, your ideas are good.* "DI Dunne asked me that, and I can't think how."

"Does Fiona have any suggestions?"

"No. She was interviewed but said she saw

no one suspicious."

Joanne accepted that, but decided to have a talk with Fiona, preferably outside the office. *I want to know about persons above suspicion.*

It was Rob who remembered — but only because Frankie Urquhart had phoned to remind him. "This Saturday, we have an away game against Glen Achilty."

There was no need to say who "we" were, no need to say "shinty." And no need to say that a game against Glen Achilty was played in Glen Achilty, on a field that no longer had a clubhouse, only a blacked wreck with one and a half walls standing, the roof a twisted torment of corrugated metal.

"I'll take extra film." As ever, it was Hector who said the unsayable.

"I'll join you." Don McLeod was upset that the shinty community was upset.

"Might as well come too," McAllister said. They all looked at him — his idea of sport was wrestling with a book in a language he barely knew with the aid of a dictionary. "It's our town team, so our newspaper is involved; let's show a united front."

"In that case, count me in," Joanne added.

Frank Urquhart attended the game. Frankie stood at his side. Morag had the first aid kit. The teams' supporters were out in force and lining along the pitch, the remnants of the Urquhart family in the center.

Glen Achilty supporters faced them across the field. There seemed to be more female supporters than usual.

On each side of the narrow glen, the hills stood sharp and clear, smelling of spring green and heather and emptiness. Inhabitants mostly clung to the narrow valley floor. Few wanted to live along the northern loch edge, fearful of the darkness of that body of water, the fault line of legends. And monsters.

The game was started and was unusually subdued. The game finished with the score nil-all. As the opposition players were leaving the field, they formed a queue to shake Coach Urquhart's hand. And Frankie's.

Joanne looked at Don for an explanation. Then she realized that many of the supporters from both teams were coming up to Don, shaking his hand, or glancing his way as though seeking approval. Not much was said beyond the occasional *Aye* or *Fine day* or *Bad business this.*

Joanne also noticed glances and nods and nudges coming from the wives, the mothers, the keepers of the first aid kits, the washers of shirts and shorts, the makers of tea and cakes and shortbread for the fund-raising sales. Some came up saying, "Thank you, Mr. McLeod." Others just smiling or nodding. Don McLeod was emerging into the world again. His bereavement fresh, he knew the state Frank Urquhart was in.

Joanne saw and understood and was moved. As was he. She tucked her arm into his. "Tell me, Don McLeod. Nil-nil. Is it always this boring?"

McAllister laughed a loud hearty guffaw. It felt good to laugh. Joanne joined in. Don shook his head. But was smiling.

"Aye," he said, "we sore need a good laugh . . . and maybe a dram." He had foresworn drinking, so he added, "My feet are frozen."

TWELVE

The court case was simple. William Stanley
Ross of Laurel Avenue admitted being
resident at that address with Mrs. Elizabeth
Mary Buchanan, widow. He further admit-
ted being the father of Mrs. Buchanan's
child, delivery expected in four weeks' time.
No one attended the hearing except Bill
Ross.

There was a great deal of shuffling of
papers and documents handed from one
court official to the next to the magistrate,
and time taken up with frowning and reading and more shuffling, all of which Bill assumed was meant to shame him. But he'd
been through worse. He'd survived the
battle for Monte Cassino.

He had to endure a lecture from the
magistrate about abandoning one family to
make another. It almost made him speak
out. But the pain of a too-tight collar
stopped him; Betsy Buchanan fed him really

well, never leaving him to make his own tea — one of his many complaints about Joanne.

The divorce application was granted. When Bill told Betsy, she was delighted, but more than anything relieved.

"We can't get married until the decree is final," Bill reminded her. He was surprised at himself; the thought of marrying Betsy pleased him.

"It will say on the baby's birth certificate we're not married." She knew it unlikely the divorce would come through before a marriage. "Unless . . ."

Bill Ross was used to his future wife's scheming.

"All it takes is the right word in the right ear," she told him. As she was usually right, and as she was the one who arranged everything in their lives — paid the bills, did the washing, the ironing, the shopping, the cooking, knew when it was a birthday, an anniversary, a wedding, a funeral — all as a good wife should, he thought no more about it.

Bill Ross waited a week before telling his parents the news, adding that he and Betsy would marry as soon as possible. He said nothing of Australia; one scandal was enough. He had seen the sense of Betsy's argument and wanted to leave, to "start over." Leaving this wee place *to be somebody* — his words to Betsy — appealed to him.

Next he visited Joanne's prefab bungalow in Ballifeary Lane, one of many houses built for returning WWII heroes, constructed to last a few years, now feeling so permanent that it was hard for the planners to knock them down.

She was not there. Not only was she not there, he knew the girls were not with his parents.

The house looked empty. The curtains were drawn. The garden seemed neglected. Her bicycle was gone. Then he remembered. The girls now had bicycles. He had paid for them — at his father's insistence. He didn't see why he should, but as he had never been asked for money by Joanne, he decided, in front of his parents and children, to be magnanimous.

Then he had an idea. He drove across the bridge and up the hill past the castle and around the terraces, reaching McAllister's house just as it was turning dark. The lights were on, the curtains open. Annie was sitting on a sofa reading. Not a sight that surprised her father, as he had always thought his elder child preferred books to real life.

There was no sign of Joanne.

He caught a movement; a small figure crossed the room also holding a book. It was then he saw McAllister half hidden by the high back of the wing chair on one side of the fireplace, kneeling down, perhaps lighting the fire, where now a flicker of flame flared blue-red, as when newspapers were used for kindling.

Bill Ross watched as his younger daughter, the one he liked, handed the book to McAllister. He saw the man, *Joanne's fancy man,* take his daughter's hand, squeeze her into his wide armchair beside him, and open the book.

Still no sign of Joanne.

I bet she's in the kitchen cooking. That thought, and the substantial house he'd heard McAllister had paid for in cash, enraged Bill Ross even further.

When she heard the back door slam enough to rattle a windowpane, Betsy went for the whisky, poured him a dram, and put the water on the side in a small jug in the shape of a West Highland terrier.

She heard Bill out. She didn't question what he was doing keeking through McAllister's window. She could make no sense of his rage, only calm him the only other way

204

she knew, her being eight and a bit months pregnant — whisky.

In the morning she considered Joanne and McAllister and Bill and herself and the baby, who, she was sure, would be good at any sport involving kicking. No clear thought emerged, only a conviction that she had to talk to Joanne.

She called the *Gazette* office. Fiona surprised her.

"Mrs. Buchanan, it's good to hear from you. We all miss you, especially the clients." Fiona was certain it was mostly the male clients who missed Betsy, or Busty Betsy, as the men in the print room had christened her. But Betsy was kind in a ruthless, used-to-getting-her-own-way way. Fiona appreciated that.

"You too — I really miss all of you." She meant it. "Fiona, can I speak to Joanne?"

"I'm putting you through to Mrs. Ross now."

Betsy Buchanan barely made the last few yards of the climb up Castle Wynd.

"Mind you don't drop it here and now," a woman coming down from the library said to a heavily peching Betsy.

They smiled at each other, as Betsy didn't have the breath to reply. Once inside the of-

205

fice, Fiona made her sit down in her old chair in her former office and made her a cup of tea.

"Is Mrs. Ross expecting you?" Fiona asked as she handed the tea to Betsy in her same old cup, the one with painted primroses she had donated to Fiona when she left.

"It's you I wanted a word with."

Now Fiona was wary. No one ever wanted just "a word."

"How's the new man, Mr. Forbes?" Betsy asked.

That was enough to set Fiona off.

"He's nice enough in his own way. But he's never here. Has his own home office, he calls it. Leaving me to do all the boring stuff . . ." She talked, saying all the things she had been keeping in, and it came out in a tidal wave, a flotsam and jetsam of complaints, observations, worries, and comments, even on his wife delivering the man's sandwiches to the office.

"Why can't you bring them in with you in the morning?" Fiona had asked.

"Oh no," Fiona was repeating Mal Forbes's words, " 'I need fresh bread from the baker on Eastgate,' he said, 'not day-old bread for sandwiches.' "

Fiona's mum worked in the bakery and said Mrs. Forbes was there most mornings at ten to eight, before the bakery shop even opened properly.

"You'll no' catch me running around after a man like that," Fiona told her mother, and her mother had laughed. Fiona couldn't be too harsh on Mal Forbes, though; she had seen, almost every time she came to the office, that Mr. Forbes had kissed his wife on the cheek, his eyes bright, her eyes adoring. *They're in love so they are,* she told her mum, who laughed, saying *Fi-o-naa* in that long-drawn-out way she had when dismissing her daughter's opinions.

When Fiona had wound down, and when they were on their second cup of tea, Betsy said between the pauses as Fiona darted in and out to answer the phone, "I'm meeting Joanne later — just like old times. She's not at all bothered about me anymore. Especially since Bill is now her ex-husband."

Although Betsy said this, she was never sure if her new relationship with Joanne was genuine. She couldn't see why Joanne didn't care about her and Bill. As for the stories of Bill hitting Joanne, she chose to ignore that. *He would never hit me.*

Fiona nodded. She knew as much as everyone about the Rosses' divorce and Betsy's pregnancy, and although it was interesting, she wasn't really interested. But

Betsy knew Fiona would tell her mother and her mother would tell everyone and Betsy would once more be a respectable woman of the town. *Almost respectable,* Betsy hoped.

"I admire Joanne for moving in with McAllister before they're married. Goodness knows I realize what courage that takes." Betsy was moving her head in that budgerigar-preening-itself-in-a-mirror habit of hers.

"I don't know about that." Fiona stood, trying to invent a reason to be at the front desk, remembering what a gossip Mrs. Buchanan was, and fearing for her own secret, not Joanne's. "If you'll excuse me, Mrs. Buchanan . . ." She lifted an accounts book.

"Of course," Betsy had accomplished what she came for. Fiona might not gossip, but her mother certainly did. Time was short. Maybe the baby would be late. Three weeks, the hospital said. Four weeks, four weeks, Betsy kept repeating to her unborn baby.

Betsy Buchanan waited three days before continuing with her plan.

"Joanne, nice to see you." Betsy was waiting for Joanne in the tearooms on Church Street.

"You're looking really well, Betsy." It was

true. Busty Betsy, the *Gazette*'s very own pinup girl, had that flush, that bloom that expectant mothers or those in love have: a pinkness to the skin, shining eyes, a tiredness — yes, and a smugness. And in spite of past enmities, Joanne was happy that Betsy Buchanan had taken over her ex-husband. *Gonna wash that man right out of my hair.* Joanne wanted to hum the song in triumph.

"We can't wait for the birth; Bill is convinced it's a boy."

Betsy was blethering away. Joanne knew it was from nervousness. She had been unable to give Bill Ross a son, one of the many faults he had flung at her, and Joanne wished, with fingers crossed and touching wood, that Betsy would have a son and they would migrate to Australia. It was through this fog of wishful wishing, inventing a future yet to happen, that she heard Betsy say, "So we thought McAllister might have a word."

"With whom?"

"Whoever can hurry up the papers." She saw Joanne's blank look. "The divorce papers." As she said this she leaned towards Joanne and whispered the word *divorce* as though it was the dirtiest swear word in the world.

"But why?" Joanne was not being deliberately obtuse, just not thinking clearly, wary as to what Betsy wanted from her; she understood well what a stain it was to be *born out of wedlock* — another phrase Joanne could remember her father uttering from his pulpit.

"Look, Joanne . . ."

Joanne recognized the tone; she had heard Betsy Buchanan in full warrior-in-marshmallow-coating mode before.

"Bill stood up in court and admitted living with me. He took full responsibility for the end of your marriage, even though it wasn't his fault, and you're living with McAllister — Bill could easily have brought that up . . ."

"I am not!" But Joanne was blushing.

"That's not what everyone's saying . . . ask Fiona, she'll tell you the gossip . . . not that that girl gossips . . ."

Joanne never quite understood how Betsy, with her limited education, her never-having-left-a-small-town life, could and did come out the victor in almost every encounter between them. She knew Betsy needed a favor and she was surprised to find that she didn't mind. More than that, she admitted to herself later, Betsy was her protection against Bill's rages. *He won't be bothering me again,* she thought.

"Betsy, what do you want?"

"Your help."

Betsy explained. Joanne listened. Joanne agreed to help. Betsy was delighted.

"McAllister, let's take sandwiches to the Islands." It was twelve thirty. Joanne had parted with Betsy an hour earlier and needed to tell McAllister about the conversation.

As they crossed the first bridge, Joanne watched rays of sunshine, filtered through the green of budding beech leaves, dance on the swaying suspension bridge. Upward reflections coming off the river collided with the flickering above. The water was high, the weir unsuccessful in holding back spring as it flooded towards the firth and the fish and the dolphins and freedom. Joanne felt she was suspended in an impermanence of light.

They took a bench in the heart of the cathedral of trees. They didn't speak for minutes, letting the susurrus of wind and water and leaves envelope them.

Calm her. Enrapture him.

He had never had much time for nature before courting Joanne. A city, any city, Glasgow, Paris, London, Barcelona, Madrid, was his natural habitat. But the majesty of mature beech and oak and elm and ash and sycamore worked a magic he now appreciated. His nearly three years in the Highlands was changing him.

When Joanne explained Betsy's mission, he laughed. "I'm only a small-town editor, not God." But he was delighted the divorce was finally happening.

Joanne sighed. "I know. I told her we couldn't help."

She opened the greaseproof paper and handed McAllister a sandwich of wholemeal bread, homemade potted hough, and the last of last year's apple chutney.

"This is bliss."

She thought he was speaking of their refuge under the trees in the middle of a tree cave in the middle of the river at lunchtime with no passersby. But he was speaking of the sandwich, holding it in the air, his other hand holding tea in a cup from the top of a thermos flask. A drip of chutney splattered onto his trousers.

She laughed. "You're worse than the children." She leaned forwards to rub the mark on his trouser leg. Her hair parted at the back of her neck, revealing white skin that seldom saw sun. He thought this the most erotic sight he'd ever seen.

"Betsy's dilemma." The solution came to

him as he was trying to think of something, anything, to distract himself. "I'll call Angus McLean. Surely the town's foremost solicitor can hurry the paperwork along."

"That will cost. Bill won't like that," she pointed out.

"I'll pay the solicitor's fee." He considered it worth it to be rid of Bill Ross and married to Joanne as soon as possible.

Joanne guessed what he was thinking. It wasn't hard. A small cloud passed over the Islands. She shivered. And it wasn't from cold.

Out of the frying pan into the fire, she'd joked to McAllister once when, without asking, he'd assumed a wedding would follow a divorce. She'd meant it in a positive way. She liked fires. She liked being warm and loved. But still she felt a chill.

He loves me. I love him. He will look after me and Annie and Jean. So no second thoughts, my girl.

Once again it was Fiona's face that told them the news.

"Someone tried to attack Mrs. Bell at her hotel. But she wasn't there."

"No," Joanne cried out. "Why would . . . The letters!" Now she was scared for Mae Bell.

"Damn and blast him — the miserable coward." McAllister was furious.

They could hear the sound of fire engines from across the river the moment they stepped back out into Castle Wynd.

"Come on." He took Joanne's arm. "Quicker to walk." As they hurried across the bridge, they could see the red of engines and men in uniform. A ladder was reaching up to a top bedroom window.

"That's Mae's room," Joanne told him when they arrived at the scene of controlled chaos. There were firemen, policemen, and onlookers, but Joanne could see no sign of Mae Bell. "Thank goodness she's not here." She spotted Rob in full reporter mode, notebook out, questioning the porter.

"Hiya." He waved when he saw them. "Someone threw acid on Mae's bed." He sounded almost cheerful; he had a story and no one was hurt.

"Where's Mae Bell?" Joanne asked.

"No idea."

Rob went to join Hector, who was taking shots of the upper floor, where a fireman atop the ladder was half in, half out of the smashed window.

"It never caught fire," Hec explained, "thon mess is the fire brigade's doing." He was pointing to drips and runnels of foam

214

and water staining the stonework.

"But no one will let me inside." Hector was quivering like a wasp in the raspberry jam, a sight Rob knew well. He agreed with Hec. A shot of the inside of the room would make a great front page.

The woman who managed the hotel was in the foyer with the police. No way past them. The porter? Looking at the man, who was obviously ex-army and a "more than my job's worth" type, Rob rejected that idea.

"Hector, there's bound to be a back stairs. If I keep everyone busy, why don't you saunter —" He stopped — that might be too difficult a concept for Hector. "Why don't you sneak round the back and in through the kitchen and upstairs and take a picture of the damage?"

"What if anyone catches me?" Hector liked the idea but was afraid his archenemy Sergeant Patience might catch him.

"The police are taking statements from the owners." Rob pointed through the reception doors, and sure enough, the bulk of the sergeant filled up most of the space. "If it all goes wrong, we can blame McAllister." He pointed back towards the river, where McAllister was leaning against the railings, talking to Joanne.

The plan worked.

The *Gazette* published a spectacular front-page photograph of a bed where the acid had burnt through to the mattress in an imprint not unlike that of a body — if one had been lying there. Sergeant Patience was furious.

On Thursday morning, with three copies of the paper spread on the reporters' table, they all — Don, Rob, McAllister, Joanne, and Hector — discussed and admired their work.

Mal Forbes was in the office briefly. He poked his head in the door of the reporters' room, said, "Brilliant front page. Great for circulation." And was gone before anyone could say anything. Which was just as well because Joanne thought the remark insensitive, and was about to say so.

"I never found out what the last letter threatened, but I agree with Mr. Forbes. This is brilliant." Rob was pointing at the shot of destruction.

"Rob, that's a horrible thing to say," Joanne said. "You're as bad as Mal."

"It was a right mess," Hector told them, pointing an index finger at one of the prints.

"Mrs. Bell's clothes, her other things . . ." He meant underwear, a word he couldn't say in company. "They were scattered everywhere. There was broken lipsticks, and pots of face-cream opened, and talcum powder over everything . . ." He pushed another outtake at Joanne. "Someone was feeling very mean."

Joanne listened to Don and McAllister and Rob sending the ideas back and forth. "They must have known she wasn't there," she said.

"Where is Mae Bell?" Rob asked, but no one knew.

"A warning, you think?" Don hoped the intent was no more than that.

"How did the person get past reception?" McAllister asked.

"The same way as Hec?" Rob remembered how easy it was for the photographer to sneak in.

Joanne was shuffling through the photos again. It was like a children's' comic-book game, Spot the Odd One Out. There was something off that she couldn't identify.

Rob was the one to voice the obvious.

"Anonymous letters sent to Nurse Urquhart. Then, anonymous letters sent to the *Gazette* addressed to Mae Bell . . . now this."

Joanne said nothing about the letter addressed to her.

"Don't forget the leg." Hector was the only one who had seen the leg and was not likely to forget it.

"Who's telling the story?" Rob nudged him.

"A list." McAllister was about to write on a sheet of foolscap when Joanne took it from him.

"Here, I'll do it; no one can read your writing."

They're definitely like an old married couple, Don thought.

The list when completed, fifty minutes and a lot of bickering later, read:

Boot with foot in a shinty sock found by Nurse Urquhart
Letters to Nurse Urquhart (dates unknown)
Letters to Mae Bell
Attack on Nurse Urquhart
Nurse Urquhart dies
More letters to Mae Bell and *Gazette*

Here Joanne paused. The letter addressed to her she had told no one about and didn't add to the list. She continued writing: Mae Bell's hotel room attacked.

218

When the list was passed around, Don said, "We know the writing on the notes was neat and grammatical. This list tells us the sequence. There's not much else we know for sure . . ." He remembered. "The other note, the one that was posted?"

"Nothing to do with this." McAllister put that note down to a personal feud, and DI Dunne agreed.

"We know one thing for sure. Nurse Urquhart is dead." Joanne was speaking more to herself. But everyone heard.

The meeting broke up. They all were pre-occupied by the list, could see it as clearly as a photograph, and no one had any ideas, bright or otherwise. What was clear was that Nurse Urquhart's death was only a mile-stone in the ongoing drama, and Mae Bell was now the target; the connection between the women was still a frustrating, frighten-ing mystery.

Where is she? Joanne was thinking. *Is she safe?*

I hope she's safe, McAllister was thinking, *I like that woman — and what a voice.*

What's she doing here? Don thought for not the first time. *Why is she in this town when her husband was stationed in Moray-shire?*

This is a great story — as long as Mae

doesn't get hurt. Maybe I'll make the national papers with it, Rob was thinking.

Smashing picture — that was all Hec ever considered.

On Friday night, in McAllister's kitchen, the photos in the *Gazette* office so she couldn't check, Joanne realized what she hadn't seen through the initial haze of fear. Plimsolls. Black school plimsolls.

"I've thought of something." She walked into the sitting room, a dish towel in her hand.

"So have I," McAllister said.

"You first." She was unsure of her ideas and wanted to hear him out.

"The story you wrote about Mae Bell's search for her husband, Robert. Did the anonymous letters start before or after the article was published?"

"Mae Bell's letters came after. And I think Nurse Urquhart's letters came before the article."

"That's that theory shot down."

"The ads were published. The first letter addressed to Mae came in answer to the ad."

"Makes no sense." McAllister was shaking his head and drumming with his fingers in frustration.

Joanne sat down.

"Your idea?" he asked.

"It's nothing." She blew her hair out of her eyes. "What?"

"Your ideas are never nothing."

"Don't lecture me." She heard the sigh he couldn't hold back. "All right. In the photos of the room, there was a pair of school plimsolls. Why would Mae Bell have them? As far as I know she doesn't do running or sport."

At first he silently agreed that the idea was nothing. But he knew her judgment was good.

She took his silence to mean he thought her observation silly. She stood. "Do you want tea?"

He read her well. "No. This requires a glass of wine." As he was taking the glasses out of the cabinet he said, "Plimsolls, did you know they are named after Samuel Plimsoll, him of the Plimsoll line?"

"Yes, Mr. McAllister. I did it in school. But how they came to name shoes after him . . ." She saw he was about to get up. *To get the encyclopedia, no doubt.* "Later. Look it up and tell the girls." She was laughing at him. He grinned back, thinking, *She knows me so well.*

"Don't you think Mae Bell and plimsolls

seem incongruous?" Joanne asked.

"I agree it's out of character for Mae Bell to have school gym shoes . . ."

"Right. Well." Now she needed to work out what only a passing thought could mean. She sat down on the arm of McAllister's chair and took his wine, sipped it, then began, "From the beginning I was interested in the story of Robert Bell. His plane disappearing in the North Sea. Bodies never recovered. It's like a John Buchan novel . . ."

"Or a thriller film . . ."

"It's fascinating."

And so are you, he was thinking, *so are you.*

"But Mae Bell said the Fatal Accident Enquiry found nothing, no explanation, nothing to indicate what happened, so I can't for the life of me see how it all connects."

"Unless someone somewhere knows different." It was only a thought. McAllister had nothing tangible. Joanne considered the thought.

"If she knows something, or has discovered new information about the accident, it would explain why Mae Bell is staying on for so long. Explain her absences."

The enigma remained with them all evening. Putting the girls to their separate beds. Putting themselves to bed. Awake. In their dreams. Robert Bell. The North Sea. Acid. A requiem — for a husband, a brother, a man lost forever in a cold, cold grave.

Yet in their hearts, neither of them able to say it aloud, they both felt that grief, loss, the end of love, could bring about a state of hope, and illusion, and fantasy. The accident inquiry had taken months, every aspect of the loss examined in minute detail. Nothing had been found. No plane part recovered. No bodies found. Five men had gone missing. Five families grieved. Mae Bell was asking what they all were asking. Still. Asking for a resolution. For an end of uncertainty. And pain.

Thirteen

Mae Bell did not turn up until the day after the fire. She went straight to her hotel, not looking up to the second floor, so did not notice any change on the outside. She certainly noticed a change in the reception.

"You're back," the owner, Mrs. Hardie, said.

"I am." Mae smiled, knowing any small kindness would not work; the owner had disapproved of her from the instant she saw Mae Bell, but she needed the custom. "My key?"

"Oh, it's a key you're wanting. That's fine then. A key. But don't be expecting a bed. There is none. And we need to have a wee talk about the damage you caused. Beds are not cheap, you know."

Mae Bell had had enough of the woman.

"Explain," was all she said.

"Your room was attacked with acid. The mattress was burnt beyond saving and your stuff was ruined by the firemen."

"Glad I wasn't there," Mae said.

She sat down on the sofa that was even harder than the train seats, crossed her legs, lit a cigarette, and blew the smoke at the No Smoking sign, glad to see Mrs. Hardie looking as though she would combust at any minute.

Smoking with harder, longer draws, the tobacco calmed her. Her normally pale skin had now a corpselike grey tinge. Her eyes, although carefully made up, were betraying her age. She uncrossed her legs, not wanting to give Mrs. Hardie the satisfaction of seeing the tremble in her knees. All she could think was, *I need a drink.*

"As I said, your things are beyond rescue, and we need to settle the bill for the damage . . ."

"Always take all I need with me." Mae pointed to the substantial suitcase the porter had taken from the taxi. "Never know when you might need a ball gown, don't you agree?" She waggled her head in perfect imitation of an Indian sage. "As for the compensation for the damage to my *things,* it's very kind of you but I can't accept *damages.*" She knew full well that was not Mrs. Hardie's meaning. Mae Bell had endured much worse when she married Robert; the disapproval of a Highland landlady was not anywhere in the same league.

The porter cum doorman cum factotum coughed and said in a sweet deep Scottish Louis Armstrong growl, "The police said for you to call the minute you showed up."

He liked Mae Bell and thought the news should have been broken gently. It was a vicious attack, no getting away from that. "Maybe your friend Mrs. Ross can explain more."

Mrs. Hardie was standing with her ample arms crossed, furious that her moment of revenge hadn't materialized.

"I'll keep your bag for you," said the porter, who was Mr. Hardie but always known — even by his wife — as *the porter.* "You go and see your friends." He took her elbow and led her out the door.

When Mae Bell left he turned to his wife, saying, "Where's your Christian charity?" There was no reply; he hadn't expected one.

Mae went as far as Gino's café only fifty yards down the street. She took a seat near the counter, keeping the cheerful Gino in sight.

"Espresso?"

"Do you have anything stronger?"

"Sì." He saw what he recognized as shell shock, a word his son-in-law had taught

him. He poured grappa into the coffee and prepared a second cup just in case. He took it to Mae. She downed it in one. The second cup was indeed needed. She took her time over that one.

Gino phoned Joanne. It took four minutes for Joanne to come over, McAllister with her. Gino served the same drink to McAllister, but a cappuccino for Joanne. Then he served the same grappa-charged coffee for himself.

McAllister explained to Mae Bell what had happened. She chain-smoked three cigarettes after she understood exactly what was meant to have happened, calming down only after Joanne told her her opinion.

"It was a warning, Mae." Joanne chose to believe that. McAllister disagreed but didn't say so. Mae was on McAllister's side.

DI Dunne arrived. Tea for him; he regarded coffee as an abomination. "Mrs. Hardie at the hotel called to say you were here."

"I bet she did." Mae laughed through the smoke, her voice as smoky as ever, but now with an edge.

She could be fierce if she needed to, Joanne thought.

"You were saying, Mr. McAllister?" DI Dunne asked.

"I was saying that I don't feel the attack was meant on Mae personally, only as a warning — as with the letters — only more graphic." McAllister decided to go along with Joanne's more optimistic view of the attack.

"Reassuring." Mae stubbed out a cigarette.

"I agree with Mr. McAllister." DI Dunne sipped his tea, surprised it was real Scottish tea, having suspected they did not do tea in Italy. "The question remains, why you? What have you done to invoke such anger?"

"And how does this connect with Nurse Urquhart?" Joanne asked.

"Would you please excuse me?" Mae rose and made for the ladies' room, quickly. She was there some time.

When she came back, Joanne asked, "Are you all right?"

"I'm tired," Mae said. She was looking as glamorous as ever, but the fresh lipstick, the eye makeup added, not quite hiding the redness of the rims, gave Joanne the true answer. "I need to rest," Mae said. She needed to think. "First a long train journey, then this."

"Ah, there might be a wee problem — Mrs. Hardie is not keen . . ." DI Dunne shifted from one buttock to the other.

"Inspector, she was never keen, as you put it. Loathed me on sight, but not my money."

"You must stay at my house," McAllister said. "There's a spare key under the doormat. We can call a taxi from the hotel."

"I can find another hotel," Mae Bell said. But she meant differently. The shelter of a real home with good people after weeks in hotels, after strange discomforting news, after an attack she knew was meant to maim her, perhaps worse, made the offer hard to turn down. "And I have to talk with the police," she added.

"You're staying with us," McAllister said. "I'm sure the inspector can wait till later." It was not a suggestion, and the inspector only nodded. He had heard the "us," a confirmation of the rumors he'd heard. He did not disapprove. Nor approve. But years as a policeman had taught him to suspend moral judgments.

"Later today," DI Dunne said, "I'll call round to Mr. McAllister's house. You can give me a statement then." Neither was this a suggestion. Nurse Urquhart had died from an acid attack, so the case was manslaughter, a particularly nasty manslaughter that, in Inspector Dunne's opinion, was murder. He had no leads. This latest incident gave him hope of solving the case. Less than twenty-four hours later he was as confused as ever.

It took Rob to scare Joanne with what should have been obvious.

"Mae Bell at McAllister's house? Aren't you scared whoever's after her will try to attack her there?" he asked when the editor explained what had happened.

Rob hadn't meant to scare anyone and didn't know Joanne and her girls stayed at McAllister's regularly. He saw the attack at Mae Bell's hotel as a warning and only half believed the attacker would strike again. "Anyhow, I don't suppose anyone will know Mae is at your place," he added.

"There's no way anyone can find out," McAllister said, more confidently than he believed. *Everyone knows everything in this town.*

"What did Mrs. Bell say about the attack?" Don asked.

"Not much. She wasn't feeling well," Joanne told him.

"Two reporters — in the same room as the would-be victim — and you didn't ask?" Don asked McAllister — only half joking. "Young Robert. Jump on thon red chariot o' yours and get round to McAllister's and interview Mrs. Bell. I want a story with suitable quotes in . . ." He looked up at the eye of a clock. "In two hours — subbed and retyped — two and a half hours. Now, what's next?"

He knew what was next — choosing which of Hec's seventeen pictures of gamboling lambs to use in "Spring Is Here," a maudlin pre-Easter story to placate the traditional readers of the *Gazette*.

The worry of an attack stayed with Joanne. That night, she was at home, enjoying her own house with her own books and her own night noises, not missing the company, knowing McAllister and Mae Bell would be prattling on about Paris and music and life in the city now that the war and occupation was a memory. "A bitter memory," Mae told him, "but you know . . . it's still Paris."

The lilac was early. The scent had greeted Joanne as she pushed open the garden gate. The girls were already home. Annie had a key and although Joanne didn't like it, she had no choice but to allow them to come home to an empty house. *They're nine and eleven now,* she reminded herself, often.

"Hiya, Mum. Look, Snowy is happy we're back. And I think Mrs. Murdoch" — this was the next-door neighbor — "she's been feeding her too much, she's right fat."

231

Jean gave the cat to Joanne. She was examining it and discovering fat was not the problem when she saw the envelope on the table.

"Where did that come from?" she asked Annie, trying to keep her voice steady.

"It was on the doormat." Annie took the cat from her mum and she too was examining it. "It's no' fat, silly, it's kittens."

"Really? Really and truly?" For once Jean wasn't offended at her sister's calling her silly. "Mum, Mum, we're going to have kittens."

Joanne didn't answer until Annie dumped the cat back on her lap. She automatically rubbed her hand over the cat's belly. She could feel the little wriggling creatures inside. "So she is," she said.

"Who's the letter from?" Annie asked.

"Ask no questions, tell no lies." Joanne tried to make nothing of it. "It's only something to do with work." She forced her voice to a bright, cheery, joking tone, trying to keep everything normal.

Annie didn't believe her. She knew of the divorce and was convinced that was what the letter was about. It wasn't. The contents of the letter were beyond even her imagination.

232

YOU ARE NEXT.

Joanne wanted to grab her girls and run. Run all across town to McAllister. *No. I need to show him I can look after myself.*

She was wishing she could afford a phone. Wishing the wind would stop shaking the huge oak, throwing shadows across the curtains so it felt like Halloween, not springtime.

Never before, alone with her children, had she felt this nervous about the unknown. Now every crack and groan and shudder the wind whipped up scared her.

When the yowls started at twenty to four in the morning, for a few seconds she was so terrified she froze. Then she recognized the noise.

"I'm coming, wee Snowy, I'm coming."

Across town the wind was no less, but the house was built to contain weather. It was late and McAllister and Mae were reminiscing.

"Springtime in Paris," she said smiling; a cigarette in a long holder in one hand, a glass of wine in the other, sitting sideways in the chair, her legs tucked in in an elegant swanlike pose. "It's time I got back there, spring is almost over."

"In Paris, not here," McAllister pointed out. April in the Highlands, and May, were spring to him. "You'll go back to Paris even though you didn't find what you came for?"

"It's my home. I'm the proverbial American in Paris." Again he thrilled to hear her laugh, a sound coming from deep within her singer's diaphragm. "And I've walked where Robert walked, I saw the sea, the river, the sand dunes at Findhorn, his favorite place — high and empty, and when the wind blows it whips up the sand, stinging your face and hands. I found sand in my bed the next morning. It took two washings to get it out of my hair."

She took a sip of wine. Needing it.

" 'It's cold,' he wrote, 'really cold, and wild, but beautiful.' And it is." She shivered. "I took my shoes off, put my feet in the sea. Boy, it was icy — in ten seconds my feet were blue . . ." She took another sip of wine to warm her. "Robert, he hated the cold. Hated it."

McAllister topped up her glass before adding another log to the fire and putting on some music. Not jazz, this time Bach, an elegy for Robert, a man he would never know but was sure he would like.

"I met people who didn't know him but remembered the American airmen as fun."

Mae needed to keep talking. McAllister was happy to be her audience.

" 'Right polite,' the lady in the pub said." Mae almost had the accent. "I read the newspaper stories, I saw the fatal accident report, I talked to some of the people on the base who were around at the time, and the local policemen. They all said the same. It was an accident. Bird strike was the theory. No sign of the aircraft, nor of Robert and the pilot and crew, so," Mae finished, "nothing new. No more information. But I've seen what Robert saw, and it is beautiful." She was almost telling the truth. But not the whole truth.

McAllister had had one glass too many to notice.

FOURTEEN

The next morning when Joanne was about to drag herself up the stairs to work, she met Rob in reception talking to Fiona.

"You look terrible."

She started weeping.

He was appalled. "I'm sorry, I'm so sorry, I was only joking . . ."

"I didn't get much sleep. The cat had seven kittens and . . ." She held up her hands and shoulders in the universal gesture of helplessness. "What am I going to do with seven kittens?"

"Let's get out of here."

They met McAllister on the steps outside the office. He too looked as though he hadn't had much sleep.

"We'll be back in half an hour," Rob told him, shielding Joanne from the editor, in case it was her love-life that was upsetting her.

"What's happened?" McAllister shouted

after them, but they were halfway down the Wynd and didn't hear.

"What happened?" he asked Fiona.

"Mrs. Ross's cat had seven kittens," she explained.

When the waitress left the coffees on the table — the one in the far corner, half hidden by the jukebox — Rob said, "What's really wrong?"

"I had a letter."

He knew instantly what kind of letter. "What did it say?"

She handed it over. "This is the second. I didn't tell anyone about the first one — it came to the *Gazette.* This one was delivered to my house. Annie found it. They know where I live . . ." She was no longer crying, but her hand was unsteady as she lifted the cup.

"This is horrible." He did not question her fear. Did not try to reassure her. *She's right to be scared.* "These letters are getting more frequent." *And attacks,* he had the sense not to add.

"Thanks a bunch, Rob." She gave him a half-smile. She needed Rob to go straight for the jugular.

"That's when people make mistakes."

"Really?"

237

"I've no idea, but isn't that what detectives say?"

She laughed even though she was terrified. She asked him, all in a rush, *What am I going to do? Will my girls be safe? Why is someone after me? Would your mother take a kitten?*

Then he was the one laughing. "My mother? Take a kitten? Only if you abandon one in the garage so she has no choice. Tell you what, I'll put on a disguise, stand outside a school, and give kittens to little girls. They take them home, and the mothers have no choice but to keep them."

"I was thinking of an ad in the paper, but your solution would work better." She smiled at him. He smiled back. They were close to deadline, so they left, walking back arm in arm.

Disguise, she was thinking. *I wonder.* She didn't have time to discuss it with Rob, and after that she forgot. Handing the letter — the warning — over to McAllister and seeing his face take on the look of the Grim Reaper, fear returned.

"I've bloody had enough of this." He was shouting.

Don picked up the note, dropped it. "Cowardly, nasty, revolting . . ."

"So what are you going to do?" Hector

238

asked. He didn't say "we" because he still believed it was partly his fault for taking the pictures of the leg in the shinty boot.

Rob heard him. "It all started with the bloody foot."

Once again, they were stuck. No connections, no ideas, nothing.

Joanne was remembering that the foot and Mae Bell's appearance in town happened in the same week. "No, they didn't," she said suddenly, not realizing she had spoken aloud.

"What?" McAllister asked.

"Hold on, I need back copies of the paper. No. Dates. Don, help me. What date was the foot found? Right. The ad went in . . . right. Found it."

For once she was grateful that recent copies of the *Gazette* were sitting in a big pile in the corner, waiting to be filed. She put the newspapers on the desk and turned to Lost and Found. Next she opened the week before's newspaper.

"No. Not there," she muttered. Then, "This is it." She looked up at four pairs of eyes watching her with varying degrees of puzzlement — or rather three, because Hector was permanently puzzled.

"The first ad appeared in the *Gazette* two weeks before the foot was found: 'Seeking friends and colleagues of the late Robert John Bell, USAF, based at RAF Kinloss 1951 to 1952.' "

"So what does that tell us?" McAllister asked.

"I don't know." The adrenaline flooded out of her. She sat down. She looked at the ads again. "I don't know." The timing bothered Joanne like an ever-so-slightly-off-key note from a single singer in a choir — not obvious to everyone, but discordant all the same.

"I don't know either." McAllister was considering her idea. "But however tenuous, it's the only link we can find."

With a wink at Joanne and a nod to McAllister, Don said, "Good luck telling your not-at-all-clear theory to DI Dunne."

"McAllister, fancy a trip to Elgin after we get the edition out?" Joanne asked.

"A picnic? An Easter outing? A roll in the sand dunes?" He couldn't resist teasing her; he loved the way her cheeks flushed, her eyes brightened.

"Behave. You're too old to roll in sand dunes. No, just a wee journey . . ." She had thought of taking the girls, but this needed to happen on a weekday.

"Who's too old for sand dunes?" He

reached over and brushed her hair aside for her.

"McAllister. Behave. No, I'm thinking this investigation needs a visit to Elgin — to the local newspaper, the library, the local registry office. We need to find out more about Robert Bell. Find out more about his life at RAF Kinloss before the accident."

Don was enjoying the skirmishes between Joanne and the editor. He smiled and said, "I'm sure DI Dunne will have checked. And Mrs. Bell. But there's nothing like the personal touch, one newspaper person to another. I'll call the editor at the *Northern Scot*." Don remembered Mal Forbes. "Mal Forbes worked there. He was there at the time of the accident."

"You can ask him," Joanne suggested. Lately she had begun to appreciate Mal Forbes. Possibly because he was seldom in the office but mostly because she saw how smoothly the advertising side of the *Gazette* was running. She had once tried to run the advertising department along with Betsy Buchanan. Never again, was her attitude about that side of the newspaper.

"Let's go at the end of the week. Early. We should be back by late afternoon. I'll make a picnic."

"A picnic, then a roll in the dunes." Don

looked at both of them, nodded, and smiled a benediction.

She leaned across the table and tried to swat at his precious wee red pencil.

"No smutty talk in front of the juniors. McAllister and I are going to try to find a connection between Robert Bell and Nurse Urquhart." Joanne loved it when Don teased her. Don McLeod, a man who should have been a father, a grandfather, but never was.

"Aye" — Don winked — "that too."

Joanne found Mae's presence in McAllister's house comforting. Rob had given her one of his looks, the one that said, *Really? Are you sure?* when she told him.

She thought about the question, examined her feelings, and was certain.

"She livens the place up," she said.

"Good, it needs it," Rob replied.

He took to dropping in after work to have a glass of wine with them. Sometimes he brought his guitar. He and Mae sang. Not jazz. She said she needed a piano for that. They sang all the silly love songs and pop songs and war songs. Joanne joined in her voice clear and true and Scottish. Once, only once, after at least half a bottle of a decent burgundy, McAllister joined them on comb and tissue paper in an extended version of "Bye, Bye, Blackbird," which Joanne was certain would have the neighbors knocking at the door it was so late.

Mae Bell being there meant Joanne could stay the night when the girls were at their father's or grandparents'. Not with McAllister. But in the single bed in one of the three guest rooms — the one originally meant for the maid, on the attic floor. From up there, on clear mornings, she could look northwards to the ridge above town, the dark pine woods on either side framing the dairy farms that supplied much of the town with milk so rich that she kept the four inches of cream at the top of the bottles for her apple pies. McAllister once remarked that her apple pie was so delicious he would have to marry her, until he saw his mistake and again backed off.

Mae Bell was finding living in McAllister's house peaceful. There was enough music to keep her entertained, books by the hundreds — although she was not a reader and would have preferred magazines — but most of all she found the British wireless programs fascinating.

When McAllister was at work she kept the wireless on for company, tuned in to the

Home Service.

"Really? You have a show called the *Home Service*?" she asked when Joanne recommended the channel.

She discovered *Woman's Hour,* a program that relaxed her with the comfortable stories of everyday life. She loved the chapter a day of a novel reading. She found something called *Mrs Dale's Diary,* a short daily show based on the life of a doctor's wife. And the news, and the news analysis and the quizzes, the dialect of Wilfred Pickles with his quiz show, *Have a Go,* and the comedies — though what *The Goon Show* was about she had no idea. Most of all, the reassuring voices of the announcers, the slow, solemn news readers, the posh tones of the British Broadcasting Corporation were a world far removed from hers. The news from Britain and America and Europe about the atomic bomb and the arms race she ignored, not needing any more bad news, and she switched the wireless off every time it was mentioned.

This is another country, another planet, from my life, she thought. The Highlands were very far from the clubs, the crowding, the harsh life of an orphaned jazz singer. Yes, her father was alive, or so she believed, but she was an orphan. Her life choices had made her so, and she did not regret it for a moment.

Still, she missed her Robert. Still, she talked to him.

"You'd really like this guy McAllister," she told Robert. "Clever, but not arrogant. He knows his music. He's known hard times. He's funny. You don't need to worry, hon; he's not my type. Besides, he has the love of his life beside him — only she can't see that they are made for each other. Yep, I know, not like us. We knew."

She'd voice these thoughts as she wandered from sitting room to kitchen, a cup of tea in her hand. *Hey, Robert, would you believe I'm addicted to tea? Sure, I can find coffee, there's this little Italian place — you'd love it.*

So the conversations with herself went, all the while the wireless playing, all the while her hurting, thinking, wondering if she had the strength — and the money — to continue her search.

She had planned the confrontation for this week. She thought she now knew enough, and needed her theories confirmed. She was still unsure it was wise. It might even be dangerous. She kept thinking of skin-melting acid. Dying did not scare her; she believed she would join Robert in some great smoky place with good music. Abandoning her mission was not possible, not now that she had read Robert's last letters to her.

"You're quite a guy, aren't you?" she whispered one particularly dark and wet and windy and cold day. "But Robert, you need to help me. I'm really close, but I don't know what to do next." She lit a cigarette. *If only he'd posted those letters,* she was thinking, she'd have started her search long ago. She let herself cry. Then she turned up the volume and danced a completely inappropriate sexy twisting jiving boogie to Jimmy Shand and his Band playing an eightsome reel.

That's better, she thought as she collapsed on the armchair trying to catch her breath. *Now it's time to move. But this time, no disguise, no hideous school sports shoes.*

She didn't hear McAllister come in. She didn't see him standing in the doorway. She felt his presence, was grateful he didn't interrupt her reverie, only walked to the kitchen, where, she was certain, he would put on the kettle and make a cup of tea.

McAllister and Joanne didn't take their trip to Elgin that week. A notice in the newspaper was the first distraction from their plans.

Don blamed himself for not spotting it. Fiona was distressed because she was the one to set the classified advertisements, the notices, and the court reports. This week, she hadn't run a final check, too distracted by events and by Hector's grin.

"Who let this through?" Joanne's voice was at shriek pitch, and McAllister almost ran from his office to the reporters' room.

"Who authorized this?" She was pointing at the newspaper.

Don bent over the page at the court proceedings notices and saw what she was pointing at. "I'll find out." From the speed of Don's departure, Joanne was glad it was not her in his sights.

"I'm sorry," was all McAllister could say.

"The divorce decree published for all to read! My mother-in-law will be mortified." She blew her hair out of her eyes in frustration. Then another shriek — this time like a puppy someone tripped over. "*The girls!* Someone's sure to tell them."

"I'm sorry, I . . ." McAllister saw the notice further down the page in the Lost and Found section. He grabbed the paper again. "What the hell is this?"

Seeking friends and colleagues of the late

"Why the hell did Mae put this in again . . . we agreed to keep quiet, to not stir up the letter writer." He grabbed the phone. Dialed an outside line. Dialed his house. Talked to Mae. Put the phone down. He looked as though he would throttle someone.

"Mae didn't place that advert. Someone else did."

"Mal Forbes." Don came in with the pages from the compositors. "He's the one to make up the dummy with the classifieds. I never checked. I seldom do."

"Why would he put these in?" Joanne was pink. She was hot. She was ready to slap the man. But the morning after press was a half day off for him.

"It's probably a simple case of having a space at the bottom of a column," Don said. "I've done it myself. You reach for the nearest bit o' copy, or rerun an ad at no cost to the customer, or make up a house ad, anything to fill the gap." Don knew they needed to be able to work together. And Don was sure there was no malice in the insertion of the notices. "McAllister?"

"Oh really? He put in those *particular*

notices without checking?" Joanne was furious, her face pink; she was standing, then sitting, trying hard not to run down the stairs and confront the man.

"It was last minute. Mal filled up the space at the request of the typesetters." Don was trying to assuage her. Not succeeding.

"I agree. It was a mistake. I'll talk to Mal Forbes." McAllister neither raised his voice nor showed any shade of anger. Yes, he could see how upsetting it was for Joanne but her marital affairs were no secret. It was unfortunate the notices had been published, but Mal was only doing his job.

Joanne was even more furious than before, this time a steel cold anger. She looked at the editor. She looked at Don, who had the grace to shrug. She reached for her coat. "I'm off. Don't expect me back anytime soon."

McAllister sighed. Problems in the newspaper, he knew how to deal with them; with Joanne he was lost.

Joanne did not stay out for long. She came back within the hour and went straight to his office, where McAllister was sitting talking with Don.

"I'm sorry," McAllister said to Joanne.

"No, I'm sorry. If you say it was a mistake, then it was a mistake." *But I'd still like to slap*

Mal Forbes, she didn't say.

"Sit down." Don pushed the other chair towards her. She sat close to him. A dear, dear man was what she called him.

"We need your . . . intuition, it's about . . ." McAllister started.

"You were going to say women's intuition." She smiled.

"I'm trying to treat you as an equal." He smiled back.

"Oh for heaven's sake, you two." Don lit up again.

There was a knock on the half-open door. McAllister thought it might be Mae Bell. Don thought it might be Mal Forbes. All three were surprised to see the Reverend Duncan Macdonald, Joanne's brother-in-law.

"Joanne . . ."

"Is it the girls?"

"They're fine. It's . . ."

McAllister stood. Don too. "We'll leave you alone."

"No." Joanne suddenly needed them there.

When he spoke in his clear calm sympathetic voice, all were reminded why the minister was a loved man and a respected preacher. "Joanne, your father suffered a heart attack. He did not survive. I'm sorry."

She would never forget how hard she had to bite back the instinct to say, *I'm not.* What did come out was trite, all she could think of. "Thank you for telling me. I'll call round later. You can tell me more then."

There was an immense stillness within her. A void. She was waiting, waiting for feelings to emerge but there was only emptiness. She knew herself well enough to know reactions would set in later but for the moment all she could think was, *I feel free. First Bill is out of my life, now my father. I'm free.*

Different reactions to death were part of a minister's lot. He knew not to say more. And as Joanne's brother-in-law, Reverend MacDonald knew it took her awhile to absorb information — good and bad.

"I'll collect you and the girls when they are home from school. We'll have supper together."

"Yes."

He left. Don went with him, leaving them alone, and he would guard the stairs and make certain they were left alone.

McAllister was unsure what to do, so he offered her a whisky.

"It's eleven thirty in the morning, McAllister." She started laughing. She couldn't stop. He came over to her, pulled her to her feet. Held her.

"I'm rid of my husband. Now my father. All in one week." It was a strange laugh, a choking sound more than real laughter, a sound forced up from within, a sound from on the precipice of panic.

McAllister held her, saying nothing.

He knew she didn't mean to be callous. He knew she was only saying the truth. The two men who had tried in vain to mold her to their idea of a daughter, a wife, were gone.

Joanne might not yet know how she feels, he was thinking, *but me, I'm relieved they're gone.*

FIFTEEN

Two days later, McAllister drove her south to Stirlingshire for the funeral.

They set out at dawn. They did not talk much on the seven-hour journey. Joanne had been quiet since hearing the news, waiting for a reaction to set in. The emptiness she was feeling she mistook for not feeling, not knowing this void was too an emotion.

When they were close to her childhood village, she made him wait until five minutes before the funeral was due to start. Then she directed him to the church.

As she walked up the steps and through the stone archway into the churchyard, she felt the familiar dread; she was about to attend another service in her father's church, certain his voice, his eyes, his gestures, would be as censorious as ever. Except he was dead.

McAllister kept a respectable distance. Half a step behind, he walked with her on the winding path between tombstones that had fallen, or were laid flat, or, with the more recent, standing erect and lichen free. He noticed the grass, brighter than grass on lawns or bowling greens or golf tees, and not for the first time pondered on the source of the fecund lushness.

Pausing on the church steps, he felt rather than saw her disquiet. She was not looking at anything or anyone, but the rise of her head, the slow, deep in-breath, the slow out-breath, the stiff set of her shoulders as she gathered her courage in a protective cloak around her, reassured him.

He longed to reach out and touch her, support her, but knew every eye was turned from the gloom of the interior to her silhouette framed in a beam of spring sunshine that penetrated like a spotlight through high arched windows towards the coffin lying horizontally across the nave, only just falling short of the coffin of the Reverend John Innes, her late father, minister of the church, shepherd to his flock, bar one black sheep, his daughter Joanne.

The pews were full, mostly with parishioners and villagers there out of duty, and perhaps relief. They were gathered together to bury a disciple of John Knox, a man whose attitudes were firmly set in the seventeenth century — proven by his casting out of his child and his steadfast refusal to forgive her.

Joanne had accepted McAllister's offer to accompany her, to be at her side in front of family, parishioners, and the plain curious. He welcomed the comments and gossip his presence would bring. He welcomed the unsaid announcement that he, her boss, was now more than that.

The service was conducted by the Reverend Duncan Macdonald, son-in-law, brother-in-law, minister of the loving and forgiving Jesus of Nazareth, carpenter and fisher of men, branch of Presbyterianism.

The hymns, the sermon, the lifting of the coffin on the shoulders of six men of the parish, out to the open grave, all went by in a blur for Joanne. But the sound of earth on the coffin lid brought reality back with a clatter. She glanced across at their mother and, for the first time in over eleven years, looked her in the eye. What she saw surprised her — a nod, a brief pursing of the lips. Joanne knew this was all the acknowledgment she would get, an acceptance that she and McAllister had a right to be there.

Joanne kept telling herself, *It's over, he's gone.* The constant repetition was to reassure her, that he, her father, would never again make her feel unwanted. Unloved.

She did not acknowledge that it was she herself who allowed her father — and her former husband — to doubt the one good man who valued her for who she was.

They took the Loch Lomond road home. It was the one McAllister knew best and loved: the narrow twists followed the shoreline of the loch, Ben Lomond to the left. The wait for the Balachulish ferry; the drive up to Glencoe; the lone piper at the head of the glen where many a car would stop to cool the engine, hear a tune, or drop a sixpence into the tinker man's hat and look down to the desolation of a never-forgotten massacre, before climbing back in and taking the turn for the east coast and more rivers and burns and glens and slivers of silvered loch and lochans glinting in the breaks between gatherings of clouds — all familiar, all magic, all ignored by Joanne.

Again, as often over the years, she rehashed that scene with her father, the one where he cast her out because she was pregnant and not yet married. In these versions she came out triumphant. She mentally wrote and rewrote her words, hearing herself respond with dignity and strength as opposed to the weeping sniffing trembling wreck she had been when he had made her stand in front of his desk, beating her with his words, the Old Testament unloving unyielding words — his weapons.

She had been in the kitchen when he summonsed her to the study. She had looked at her mother, but her mother had gone to the kitchen sink to polish already dry dishes before putting them back in the dresser, not once turning around, only showing her younger daughter her stiff stern back in the habitual grey cardigan, hand-knitted in itchy Shetland wool.

She had followed him into the cold study — his version of a hair shirt, cold in temperature and in atmosphere, a room that as a child she thought he kept deliberately chilly so as to imbue his bleak Sunday sermons with dread. Starring a bleak God, a God who was yet to become a father of a loving son, a God who belonged in high echoing enclosed spaces built in unforgiving stone and worshipped by unforgiving people, mainly men, he preached the gospel according to John Knox.

"Your mother tells me you are pregnant." Straight to the heart of the matter, she remembered.

"I want to marry Bill Ross," she said.

"And you always do what *you* want."

This was the injustice that had blighted

her life, not what followed; not his disgust, his shame, his cold rage, not his forbidding any contact with her mother — not relenting even when the girls were born. It was this accusation, implanted in her from before she could remember, one she did not doubt, that she, his daughter, did exactly what she wanted to do, with no thought of others, that she was considering in the silence of McAllister's car on the long drive back to the Highlands.

It was on the final descent into town with the familiar swelling of Ben Wyvis on the evening horizon that she asked, "Do you think I'm selfish?"

Her voice was so earnest he had to stop himself from smiling. "Who says you're selfish?"

"My father said I always do exactly what I want to do." *Implying no thought for others,* she didn't say.

He wanted to slam on the brakes, take her head in his hands, kiss her eyes and lips, and tell her not to be foolish, but another man telling her what not to do wasn't what she needed. He shifted down a gear for the steepness of the hill into town.

"Joanne, I have never met a less selfish person than you." He was unconsciously shaking his head at her father's accusation, angry that this false thought had been planted in her and encouraged to grow — that she was selfish — willful even. He now knew that the accusations had continued — seamlessly — from father to husband. *But no more,* McAllister vowed.

"Joanne," he started again, "you are never a person who does whatever you want; you think of others . . ." He did not know how to tell her, or whether to tell her, that her habit of putting others first, of holding back her ideas, her opinions, her needs, how she looked to others — himself, Mae Bell, even Rob — to seek approval, to validate herself, drove him crazy.

He knew that what he said now, in the cocoon of the car on the last miles through the dark tunnel of trees, around the bends and turns down to the firth shore and the railway tracks and the beginning of town, would stay with them.

He began slowly. "Your father is gone. Bill will be leaving soon. You are free to be whoever you want to be. All I hope is that there is a place for me in your life."

She reached over, squeezed his left arm. Her palm felt like a flamethrower sending fire through the tweed and the cotton, directly to his skin, his body. She moved her hand to his wrist, touched the skin where the jacket rose up from his hand resting on the steering wheel. They were looking straight ahead, driving towards the remembered light of the river, seeing the evening dim as the streetlights came on.

"Is Mae still staying with you?" she asked.

"No, she's in Glasgow for a few days — looking up long-lost relatives, she said."

Joanne was too lost in her own little deaths to query yet another absence from Mae Bell.

McAllister turned left after crossing the bridge. The lights were out in Gino's café. He was driving past the cathedral towards Chiara's house, where her girls were staying. Chiara and the children were not expecting them until the next morning.

"Turn around," she said as he slowed the car down, to park. "I want to stay with you tonight."

She did not know it, but he did. He had been in battle. He had lived close to death, in the hills above Barcelona, in the suburbs of Madrid, in the aftermath of the liberation of Paris; the proximity of death brought a lust for life. And for sex.

He remembered something from the Bible about lust, sin, death. *No doubt her father knew the quotation.*

"Are you sure?" He was looking at her, unable to see her eyes in the dark, unable to put the question more directly, but the meaning was clear to both of them.

"You mean you want to wait until we're married?" She was incapable of saying more, flippancy hiding fear, concealing emotion. The air in the car was stifling. She needed to roll down the window.

He turned the car around outside the cricket ground. He drove back across the bridge and up the hill to home. All in silence.

They went into the house. He went towards the kitchen.

"No," she said, and took his hand. She walked up the stairs, him following, straight to his room. She did not switch on any lights, leaving the curtains open, allowing starlight to be their only illumination. She undressed, slid into his bed. And waited.

"What's happening?"

McAllister walked into the reporters' room to find Don alone, fiddling with a portable wireless, the whine and hiss and occasional faraway voices in Russian and German and English and Scots English beaming into the *Gazette* from outer space.

"Not much," Don said. "How's Joanne?" He asked out of interest, believing she was much better off without a father who would cast his daughter out over an error of human frailty.

"She's fine."

McAllister's voice made Don look up. He was not hearing the horse race caller; although he said it was to listen to the national news, the reason he bought the secondhand wireless was to listen to the races from Musselburgh, Ayr, and occasionally from England. He heard a calibration in McAllister's tone, an attempt at casual in the "She's fine" — which McAllister might have carried off with anyone other than Don. *Something has happened,* he guessed from the nothing-is-happening attempt at nonchalance, and he tightened his lips to keep in the smile, saying nothing but thinking, *Good luck to them, we could be doing with a wedding instead of death.*

"Nothing's happening. But that may be something it itself," Don told him.

McAllister lit up, waited until Don had done the same, and then waited some more.

Don was blowing smoke towards the ceiling, watching it coil and spiral like a genie escaped from Aladdin's lamp.

"Does this mean the end of it? The death of Nurse Urquhart solved the problem? Or the person has given up? What about the warnings sent to Mae Bell? Has she heeded them?" McAllister was impatient to see an end to the saga. He knew Joanne would not consent to a wedding whilst an anonymous letter writer was still on the loose. And an acid-throwing maniac — unless they were one and the same.

"Mrs. Bell is still looking for information about her late husband." Don had never been certain that was all Mae Bell was looking for. The longer she stayed, the less he believed her. However, he knew McAllister was mesmerized by the American and would not welcome criticism.

"The police?" McAllister asked.

"There's no evidence the printers were involved, except the bottle of acid came from the *Gazette* and the letters were delivered here."

"Any ideas?"

"Aye an' no. Joanne's idea that we look again at how the letters were delivered makes sense."

"Is Fiona still here?" It was Saturday morning, eleven thirty, a half day. Fiona worked until noon.

Don was never one for using the phone when he could shout.

"Fiona. Up here."

She reminds me of Joanne, was McAllister's first thought as the young woman came

263

in — the look on her face that of the Scottish red-haired queen being led to her execution.

"We're not going to fire you," he joked, "you're doing too good a job."

"Aye, McAllister might have to answer a phone if you weren't here," Don agreed.

He had on his Nice Highland Granddad persona — much better than McAllister's scary Glaswegian — so Fiona took one step farther into the room.

"Any more letters?" Don asked.

"No, I'd have told you . . ."

"I know you would." Don shifted his weight on the stool. The wireless continued to hiss in the background but with no noise resembling a horse race commentary coming through the ether. "We're trying to work out how the letters were delivered." His smile, the way his face crinkled up, reminded her of the walnuts in her Christmas stocking her mother still insisted she hang up — even though she was sixteen, nearly seventeen, made her relax. Marginally.

"I've been thinking about it, too, but I can't see how . . ." She did have an idea, but it was so preposterous, she would never tell Mr. McLeod and especially not Mr. McAllister — she was only the office junior. "Maybe someone gets in after the cleaner

264

gets here."

"The police talked to the cleaner. She says she locks the front door after she gets in." McAllister had already asked DI Dunne about that.

"Maybe through the printers' back door?" Fiona was hoping that was the solution.

"Only the father of the chapel had the keys to that door," Don told them, remembering that even he, after repeated requests, could not get hold of a spare key. "You're not suggesting *he* could have left the anonymous letters?"

"No. I don't know anything about the man." *Except that he scares me,* she didn't add. "My mum's in the Woman's Guild with his wife . . ." Again, she didn't add that the woman had a notorious tongue on her, that she hated Nurse Urquhart, or that Mum said it was because Nurse Urquhart had married her sweetheart, but Fiona couldn't imagine Mr. Frank Urquhart being anyone's sweetheart, him being so old.

"Come on, lass." Don clambered down from his stool. "You and me are going out." He saw the panic in her eyes. "Don't worry" — he patted her arm — "Mr. McAllister will answer the phone."

She stiffed a giggle and followed the deputy editor down the stairs. They walked across the bridge to Gino's café.

Don bought a double chocolate cone for her and a strawberry and vanilla for himself. They walked along the river towards the Islands, where, finding a bench, he told her he had to rest his legs. She believed him because her granddad was the same. Twenty minutes later, they decided someone could have posted the letters in the outside boxes, but how did the letters find their way onto her desk after she had emptied the mailboxes? That would mean someone inside the building put them there.

"Lots of people pass the *Gazette* on their way to the library," she added when they had discussed the possibilities. "So it's not as though the Wynd isn't busy."

"Right enough. And the anonymous letters were in the box for the classifieds?"

"I don't know. I don't always clear that box, and I can't really remember if the letters came on the days someone else did."

"Mr. Forbes?"

"Aye. He has another key an' all." Her English was deteriorating, and Don had dropped into dialect to encourage her. He had heard her say "really remember." In a dialect of double negatives, the *really* was telling.

"So Mr. Forbes *could,* not that I'm saying

266

he did, but he *could* have put letters in with the advertising?"

"Aye," Fiona said. "Then again so could lots o' people."

Don groaned faintly, and Fiona took it as a sign he'd been sitting too long on a bench in the wind, not wrapped up properly as old people were meant to be.

"If you don't mind me saying so, Mr. McLeod, I don't think it was Mr. Forbes. The two times he saw the letters, he was really shocked. Aye" — she was picturing him leaving the building — "he was right upset."

Don didn't say more, not wanting to gossip with the office junior. But he listened. And heard her.

He glanced backwards at the Royal Infirmary clock, "Would you look at the time? McAllister will be having kittens if he's had to answer more than two phone calls. He's probably unplugged the switchboard by now." He stood shaking the crumbly flakes of ice cream cone from his trousers. "When we get back, you take off early. Surprise your boyfriend." It was a granddad joke. He was surprised when she gripped his arm.

"You won't tell, will you?"

She was looking so alarmed, he smiled. "Don't worry, lass, Mr. Forbes will hear nothing from . . ."

267

"It's no' Mr. Forbes. I'm not seventeen till next month and . . ."

"Your mother? She wouldn't approve?"

"No. Ma father. He says no boyfriends till I'm eighteen."

"I'll no' say a word."

They were walking away from the spot, mid-bridge, where sixteen-soon-to-be-seventeen Fiona told him, her boss, a man older than her real granddad, of the first and, she was convinced, the only love of her life, the man she hoped to marry. She couldn't believe she had shared her secret with him.

She never said his name. Don never guessed; he put it down to a first-love-young-lassie infatuation, not for a minute imagining he would soon be dancing at her wedding in an old-man kind of shuffle, at a wedding where the bride didn't *have to* get married, the wedding that would make everyone in the *Gazette* glad.

"I knew it — that creep Mal Forbes."

McAllister smiled, not so much at her description of Mal Forbes but more at her daughter-of-the-manse inability to use words higher up on the scale of nastiness.

"That creep, as you put it, left a condolence card for you at the office." He handed her the plain black-bordered card printed with a Bible verse from the Twenty-third Psalm and a brief handwritten note in small left-leaning writing, Mal Forbes's handwriting, McAllister knew — because he had checked.

Condolences on your sad loss from
Moira and myself.
Malcolm Forbes

Joanne flushed and looked away. *The man means well, only he gets me all het up with his attitude to women.* She knew it was not just Mal but most of the population of the United Kingdom who disapproved of women working. *She should be at home wi' the bairns,* was the cry to any woman other than a widow who dared work. Never mind that his own wife had a part-time job, never mind the hundreds of thousands of women who had contributed to the war effort in factories, on the farms, in the police, and, like Joanne, in the army.

"As Don said, there's absolutely no proof it was Mal Forbes, other than he has a key to the mailboxes." McAllister was not defending Mal Forbes; he was being realistic. "The key is hanging in plain sight in the downstairs office, and it's labeled 'mailbox.'

Plus, the police have questioned him and say he knows nothing."

"They believe him?"

He shrugged. He did not want this discussion. Did not want to say he thought her unreasonable when it came to Mal Forbes.

They were at home, McAllister's house, and the girls were watching early-Saturday-evening television.

Joanne was picturing the front of the *Gazette* building. There were two mailboxes on each side of the heavy glass doors, one marked Mail, the other Advertising and Notices. They had been introduced by the late Mrs. Donal McLeod. McAllister had a key to the mailbox that he had long since lost, the advertising manager had a key to both boxes, and Fiona was given a key to the Advertising box, but had somehow acquired the other as well.

Part of her job was to sort out what went to McAllister and what went to Mr. McLeod or the other reporters. Many went to Hector, who received a surprising amount of mail, mainly asking for copies of pictures, along with invitations to events far and wide, from sports meetings to children's gatherings to golden wedding anniversaries to large holes in the roads neglected by the council.

"So the letters were in with advertising, not mail?" Joanne mused. "And all we have is Mal's word he didn't put them there?"

"And Fiona's assertion that the letters appeared after she'd sorted through the mail."

"Aye, that'll be right." Joanne had seen how much work Mal Forbes left to Fiona, preferring instead to be "out on the road chasing clients." In a bar chasing drinks, more like. Although not a real drinker, frequenting hotel bars rather than pubs, Mal Forbes had become a well-known character in the short time he had been in town. To Joanne's surprise, he was well liked. But not by people she had time for. His wife was in her church, his daughter in Annie's class. There seemed to be some tragedy associated with their son, whom no one had seen, the rumor being he was disabled — physically or mentally, Joanne hadn't heard.

She so wanted it to be Mal Forbes that she dismissed all other possibilities — Fiona, the cleaner, others in the office slipping the envelope into the box as they came in to work, or when they passed reception or . . . "Blast the man." She was shaking her head.

"Dad?" Annie had walked into the kitchen, scared she was missing out on something.

Joanne said *Mal Forbes* without thinking, so horrified that her child thought of her father in that way.

"Maureen Forbes told me her dad's a good dad, he smacks her an' her brother only when they're really bad. And Maureen's dad never hits her mum."

Joanne was upset by the thought of Annie comparing dads with her friends. "I never knew there was a brother."

"He's mental." She saw her mother's frown. "I mean, he's no' right in the head." That wasn't the phrase either. Annie sighed. "He's disabled. Only a wee bit, so Maureen says. But I've never seen him."

It was not for want of trying. She had tried to bribe Maureen with *Bunty* comics — preloved — and with sherbet dabs, but Maureen had been too afraid to take Annie to her house, afraid of her mother finding out, which was a pity, as Annie wanted to see what a boy who was *mental* looked like.

Joanne said no more but again, she felt guilty; she too now believed she was being unreasonable when it came to Mal Forbes.

On and off all evening they discussed it, in between getting the girls to bed, McAllister reading them a story, them dancing to a slow meandering song from Edith Piaf, a singer new to Joanne and whom she now loved.

When the conversations, observations, speculations ran out and they could put off the decision no longer, once again it was Joanne who took his hand and led him upstairs to his bedroom, making the decision for both of them.

She never knew how to tell him, but it happened at her father's graveside, when he was there, out of sight, just a step or two behind her, when her mother had looked across and through not one drop of tears, had nodded to her. Then to him. He had moved imperceptibly forwards, so she could feel his presence; he put a reassuring hand on her arm when she turned to walk once again through the tombstones, this time back to the manse where she had endured her childhood of little light and little love, and he was there with her, her support, her rock, her future husband. For it was then that she knew this was the man she could perhaps share her life with.

Sixteen

Mae Bell chose her outfit carefully. It was hard for her not to be noticed, especially her hair.

Ever since a child she had dressed with care and looked after herself. She did not have much else. No books, no toys, clothes handmade, often cut down from dresses and coats her mother was given by whatever household she was working in, for her mother never stayed long in a job, eighteen months being the longest she had ever stayed sober. Sober, what a delightful woman she was. Drunk, she was quiet, and it was hard to tell how far gone she was. But Mae always knew — from the cigarette to the lips; the cup, glass, spoon to the mouth as though the film had been slowed down; the too-careful placing of the feet; the odd angle her hat sat at when she came home from work, late — *they kept me back to clean up for a late guest,* or some other excuse she would offer — relieved when her daughter smiled and said, *You must be tired,* and she could take to her bed, the remains of a half bottle hidden in plain view by her pillow.

Her father was a traveling salesman specializing in sheet music. Seldom at home when she was a young child, often at home when she was in high school, when the work became less and less. When home, he joined in the "fun." Fun meaning drink. He had a fine voice, about the only fine thing about him that she remembered, and in spite of, or because of, his love of the bottle, he became a fierce, but to her fake, evangelist in ʼhis middle age. A drunk or a puritan, Mae was never sure what was worse.

She examined herself in the mirror and was momentarily horrified by what she saw. She pulled off her transformation by dressing as her mother had for work. *Scary.* Her hair was no problem; she made a turban out of a scarf, one with pink and purple roses printed on synthetic silk. The only real problem had been shoes. Then she remembered sand shoes; her mother had worn them because she had a bunion.

"Plimsolls," the shop assistant in Woolworth's called them when she pointed out the school sports shoes lying in bundles, black or white.

The dress didn't matter, but she added the floral cotton tabard cum apron, the uniform of housewives, in a clashing print to the head scarf, this time with pansies and another indeterminate flower in a lemony shade of orange. The coat, a war-era utility label raincoat, martini-olive green, she had found in a fundraising bring-and-buy sale held in the Northern Meeting Rooms for the Liberal Party. A shopping basket in wicker, rescued from a dustbin, the edges broken, with stray strands poking out at just the right angle to catch on clothes, completed the disguise.

What she hadn't thought of was buying the bus ticket. First, she didn't know the price; second, she didn't know which bus to take, plus she did not want the bus conductor to remember her, especially her voice. So she walked. She hadn't walked more than a hundred yards for many years. The plimsolls were no help; she had been walking standing stumbling wearing high heels for two decades, calf muscles atrophied in a tiptoe position.

When she arrived at the street, she once more reconnoitered the house, the garden, the neighbors, the hiding places. When satisfied, she saw a bus coming towards her and was about to take it, but decided it was safer to wait for the next one and get on around the corner. *Take no chance of being recognized,* she told herself.

The journey back to town was short — only four stops. She changed out of her disguise in the ladies' toilets in the train station; she had donned her disguise in the bus station toilets, but they were disgusting.

As Mae Bell once more, she walked across the station square towards the covered Victorian arcade. Halfway across the street, she discovered she was still carrying the basket. Dressed again in her usual garb of cashmere and silks, the basket smelled of poverty, of her childhood, of her mother, and she wanted to throw it in the nearest bin but couldn't see one. It was a bus driver blowing his horn, making her jump, that brought her back to where she was — back to the place she should not be.

Would Robert want me to do this? She hid the basket behind a parked car. *Of course he would.*

She walked towards Eastgate, heading for McAllister's house, not noticing Rob McLean, even though he was in clear view in the window of the café at the entrance to the arcade, observing her. He was smiling. He thought nothing odd of her behavior and saw nothing odd about the basket. It was his habit to notice strangers. He thought, *She's a fine-looking woman, but very different from us.* He couldn't say why he thought that, but knew it was not because she was American. There were depths to Mae Bell that an older person might, or might not, recognize as scarring.

Rob ordered a second cup of tea. Then called the waitress back. "And another bacon roll, please."

As he waited he wondered if he should once more attempt smoking — it seemed a useful habit for passing the time of day. He looked across at the station clock. Fifteen minutes to spare. He paid and went across Union Street to Arnotts department store, up to the men's department, and saw Frankie shake a man's hand, then give the customer what was obviously a suit neatly wrapped in brown paper and tied with string with a loop for a handle. The parcel looked substantial.

"Heavy tweed. Three-piece. It'll see him to his coffin." Frankie was still new to the bereavement scenario, making remarks that some would call in bad taste, refusing to be anyone other than Frankie Urquhart. It was only when Rob asked him where he had been hiding these last ten days that he became a furtive Frankie Urquhart.

"What do you mean? I've been around." Frankie started tidying up, putting discarded choices back on their hangers, then back on the rails, then moving them so the spaces were exactly equidistant.

"Friday night, you coming to the Strath? There's this band from London playing; they're meant to be great."

"No, I can't make it. Family — you know."

Rob couldn't believe Frankie wouldn't come to the dancing in Strathpeffer with a London rock band top of the bill. He saw how Frankie couldn't look at him, busying himself doing very little with scissors and pens and string. "Oh, I get it." Rob laughed. "You've found a girlfriend."

"Naw. I just don't feel like going out." Frankie couldn't bring himself to say that he was worried about his father, who seemed to have aged twenty years in two weeks, plus a sister who hid in her room saying she was doing her homework — hours upon hours of homework.

"Sorry. I'm being insensitive." Rob felt so helpless, unable to comfort his friend. "Your mother wouldn't mind you getting on with your life . . ."

"Can I help you, sir?" The manager had moved in as though on silent wheels.

"I'm fine, thanks. Must be getting back to work. Thank you, Mr. Urquhart." Rob was joking, but there was no humor in the manager's eyes.

Frankie didn't look up as Rob left, saying, "Catch you later."

It was not only his father and his wee sister who were lost; after the blessed numbness of the funeral, life without their mother was empty and, without their mother to cook and shop and do the washing, chaotic. Frankie would never dare tell his best pal that many nights he set up the ironing board to see to his work shirts and his sister's school uniform. His father worked in the foundry, and his blue boiler suit went unironed. Frankie hadn't the time to iron them as well as everything else. Mr. Urquhart's workmates noticed. But no one commented.

What with Joanne going to Stirlingshire to bury her father, and McAllister with her, and with Frankie avoiding him, and no fresh leads in the investigations, it turned into a week when Rob had no real friends to talk to or go out with.

In desperation he'd asked Hector, "Do you want to come to the dancing in the Strath? I've got my father's car and . . ."

"No thanks, I'm busy." Hec grabbed his

school satchel and beetled down the stairs.

When Hec was gone, Rob realized Hec hadn't even asked what night the dancing was.

Don came in.

"I think I have a bad case of psychic stink," Rob declared. "No one wants to come out with me."

"I've no idea what you're blethering about, but it won't get these pages done." Don shoved two heaving marked articles at Rob and said, "See if you can fix these. They're from a man from Daviot who thinks he's a poet when he's supposed to be writing an article on sheepdog trials."

They worked away.

"No progress on who left the letters?" Rob asked.

"None. But I hear Mrs. Bell received another one."

It took Rob a moment to register who Mrs. Bell was. "What did it say?"

"I don't know; Fiona gave it straight to DI Dunne." Don was aggrieved because he did not get to read the letter. Fiona told him, "I have to follow the detective inspector's orders."

"Leave it to me," Rob said, "I'll find out."

Mae Bell was not expecting Rob. But from

281

the way she was dressed, the way she was sitting in the Station Hotel foyer, on the edge of a hard leather sofa, legs together and at a slight but studied angle, it was clear she was expecting someone.

"How good to see you, Rob. How did you find me?" The tone was honey, the intent the opposite.

Rob saw it, was hurt, but recovered. He couldn't tell her he had spent an hour running from one place to the next — bar, café, hotel — looking for her. "I can see you're busy, so can I ask a quick question?" He didn't wait for an answer. "Another anonymous letter came for you at the *Gazette*. What did it say?" He saw her eyes widen slightly. Assumed it was at the thought of the letter.

Mae could see the hotel receptionist, listening, not missing one word, including *the* and *letter.*

"Say, why don't we discuss this someplace else?"

Mae Bell steered them towards the Carlton's cocktail bar, a short walk away. Rob was worried he wouldn't have enough money to pay for a martini, as he was severely broke. As usual, most of his wages went on buying records.

"The anonymous letter was more of the

same," she began to explain. "So I'm choosing to ignore the unpleasant." She smiled and looked up at the chandelier, blowing smoke towards the glistening crystal drops. He noticed the darkness under her eyes. He observed how the smoking was now constant. He saw her nail polish was chipped. He felt for her and was all the more determined to find the letter writer.

"What did the letter say exactly?" Rob was persistent. He wanted a story, if not to publish, then to share with Don.

Mae pursed her lips, gave a tiny shake of her head. "It was unpleasant. Definitely the same writer and" — she leaned forwards, her eyes meeting Rob's with an intensity that made him look away — "I will not be frightened off by some cowardly rat of a . . ." She was about to say *bitch*, but stopped. That was crude, and might give too much away. There had been much speculation that the writer was a woman — *No need to confirm it*, she told herself.

Rob stayed for one glass of wine, then said he had some work to do.

Mae said she too had to leave.

When the bill came, Mae said, "My treat."

"Thank you. And Mrs. Bell, Mae, I want you to know I am doing everything I can to

283

find out who is sending these horrible letters."

"Don't." She put a hand on his arm. "It's not important. Please leave it."

She was gone, off down the street, before he could reply.

On the drive home, Rob was not thinking about the letters but about Mae's request. *Why shouldn't I look for the letter writer? Why is she warning me off?*

He wheeled the bike through the garden gate and into the garage, taking care not to scratch his father's car. It puzzled him but eventually he put it down to an older woman concerned for a young man's safety; *Mae worries about me, the same as my mother.* Just how wrong he was he would never know.

That night Mae Bell resumed her watch.

Four times now she had checked out the house and the garden and come to the conclusion it was the shed that mattered. She had seen the woman, and occasionally the man, unlock the door, stay for only a few minutes, then lock the largish, concrete, tin-roofed, obviously home-built structure with, from what she could deduce, at least two padlocks. The small window, facing a garden wall that was at least six feet high, she could only see from a narrow angle.

"So late for here," she muttered, a half-smile stretching her lips, for once without the deep red lipstick, "but about the time I usually go onstage."

Sure enough, a church bell started chiming. She counted eleven. As the last bell sounded, she thought she heard a cry. Or crying. Then it died.

"Very soon now," she whispered to the night. "Back in Paris very soon now."

Seventeen

Fiona was young. She was bright. She qualified top of her year at school. She could have gone to the academy but chose the technical high school because she was good at sports, and they had much the better facilities.

Besides, she told her mother, *I want to learn shorthand and typing, not Latin.* Her mother was slightly put out — she'd have loved to impress the neighbors with her lass in an academy uniform. But her husband disagreed.

"Academy brats," was what he called the few pupils in their royal blue blazers who came from their council estate.

Fiona never regretted the decision. *I have a great job here. I'm saving money. I'm seventeen in three weeks. I don't go out with the wild bunch. Why can't I have a boyfriend?*

She had rehearsed her lines over and over, was now word-perfect and ready to tell her mother — but not her father.

"Hiya." Hector had come in to reception without her noticing.

He knows what I'm thinking . . . she was frantic for a safe topic of conversation, anything to banish her dreams of a white wedding dress and a piper in full dress kilt playing the music as she entered the church.

"Hiya." They had picked up the greeting from Rob. It was hard to have a conversation in the office; Fiona was terrified her father would hear and make her leave the *Gazette.* It was not that her father had an opinion on Hector, but he certainly had an opinion on his granny. "Witch" was one of the kinder things he said when describing Granny Bain.

Hec wanted to tell everyone, especially Rob, and Hector was incapable of hiding anything; even an untruth would make him blush "beetroot," as Fiona put it.

"I'm taking photos in Kiltarlity on Saturday afternoon. Do you want to come?"

"The shinty?" she asked.

"Aye."

Mal Forbes came in. "Shinty is for teuchtars." He winked at her as he said it, then leaned over the desk, rifling through the mail. Finding nothing of interest, he asked, "Where's McAllister?"

Hector answered. "He's gone to Elgin."

Mal Forbes went as still as the proverbial statue, back rigid. "And his bidie-in, is she here? Or with him?"

Hector took a step backwards. *Bidie-in,* the colloquial term for a woman living in sin, shocked him. He knew McAllister and Joanne Ross were friendly; it was the first time he had considered they were more than that.

"We know nothing of Mr. McAllister's personal life." Fiona, suddenly ten years older, glared at Mal Forbes.

"Aye. I'm sorry. That was right rude o' me."

The phone rang. "*Gazette,* how may I help you?" She started writing. "That'll be fine. Bring it in this afternoon and it will make the next edition. Thank you." When she hung up, Mal Forbes was gone, but not Hector.

"Jings, you stood up to him — an' he's your boss an' all." His eyes were shiny, his grin megawatt.

"Mrs. Ross is great. She's always kind to me. Maybe we can have a double wedding with them . . ." It was out before she knew it. Her hand over her mouth, she was furious with herself.

"Joanne is already married."

"Oh, Hector." She was giggling. "Hector."

"What? What have I got wrong this time?"

Joanne knew of Elgin but had never visited it. An ancient cathedral town, with a hill reputed to be the realm of the faeries not far from the town center, it was a bonnie and prosperous place.

Joanne was interested in history, in ruins, and towns with character — some of the many reasons she was looking forwards to Elgin.

She had a book borrowed from the library. "It says here, Elgin has a rich and ancient history. The cathedral was built in 1224. It was burnt down later, then . . . hmmm . . . various battles and . . . this looks interesting, the Bishop's Palace, early thirteenth century as well . . ."

"I researched Elgin and Morayshire. More distilleries than you can poke a stick at."

"Trust you!"

They parted in the town. McAllister left the car in the square, walking to his appointment with the newspaper editor.

Joanne went to the library, her point of reference in every town. There she found the notice board with all the parish happenings. One of the librarians also provided information on the best café, with toilets, for it had been a long journey. Walking around, she was struck by how prosperous the town seemed, then she remembered the air force base. And the distilleries.

The farmland they had driven through was prosperous too. Rolling, tree-studded hills, a castle or three, substantial stone steadings and farmhouses, dairy cattle, Aberdeen Angus beef herds, crops showing through in green shoots from dark earth, with frequent rivers and burns falling from a horizon of hills and the distant Monadhliath Mountains. The rivers Nairn and Findhorn had sweet water with trout and salmon abundant and water that gave the whisky its distinct peaty color and flavor.

Findhorn Bay, at the mouth of the river, was a renowned beauty spot. Joanne remembered Don's teasing. *Roll in the dunes indeed;* she was smiling to herself when the waitress came up and asked if she would like more tea.

"I'd love some."

When the tea arrived, Joanne went straight to the point.

"I don't live here, but I'm trying to help my American friend. Her husband was lost in that air crash in the North Sea a few years back . . ." She didn't need to say more. The woman was out of the starter's block faster than a greyhound.

"Thon was terrible. Nice young men like them, what a waste."

"You knew them?"

"No, but you can't grow up hereabouts an' no' meet the airmen. They come to town to the dancing and the pubs, most o' them are right nice. Aye, we had some fun."

"This is the notice my friend put in the newspaper."

The woman took the notice Joanne had cut out, held it at some distance, and squinted. "Bell. Bell. I remember the name from the accident, but I didn't know him. Aggie!" she screeched. "Come away out here."

The only other customer ignored the shriek. *Probably deaf,* Joanne thought. *A shepherd,* she guessed, seeing a crook leaning against the wall. *Maybe not, maybe he's part of the historic decorations — who walks around town with a crook?*

A younger, shorter, thinner, fairer version of the waitress appeared, shaking Joanne out of her dwam.

"This is Agnes, ma wee sister, and I'm Effie Forbes; it's ma teashop," the older, chattier woman said.

"I know a man called Forbes from here, Malcolm Forbes." Joanne saw the woman's cheery face turn wary.

"His daughter is in the same class at school as my daughter." She didn't know why, but for once Joanne was not eager to say she worked on a newspaper.

"*She's* no blood relative," Effie Forbes continued, "but Mal, he's good to his wife right enough."

"Aye," her sister agreed, shaking her head as though baffled by their cousin's choice of wife. "She's not from here you know; she's from the Highlands." Aggie Forbes said this as though she shared the view of the English that Highlanders, although a mere seventy miles away in distance, were another race, an uncouth, unwashed, uneducable rabble.

"Anyhow, show Aggie your wee bit o' paper." Effie Forbes wanted the subject dropped.

"Oh, him . . ." Aggie smiled. "He was a nice man, really tall. I didn't really know him, just to smile to . . ."

"Those Americans, they have nice manners," her sister interrupted, and Aggie went quiet.

Joanne knew that lassies who went out with foreign airmen risked their reputations for "a bit of fun." "My friend put the same ad in your local newspaper but didn't get a response; that's why I'm here," she explained.

"Really? I never saw it an' I read the paper cover to cover," Effie Forbes said.

"So do I," Joanne said, "I even read all the classifieds . . ."

"Best bit," Effie was now looking at the ad again. "I'd have seen this if it was in our paper, I'm sure o' it." She handed the ad back to Joanne. "You can check in the library; they keep back copies."

"I was there earlier. The lady recommended your café."

"Aye, she's ma sister an' all."

Joanne paid for the tea, told them their scones were delicious, which they were, and walked back to the library. It took an hour, but after searching through all the classifieds for a six-month period, there was nothing. Even with the help of Jessie, the sister, there was nothing, no advertisement seeking information on Robert John Bell.

Maybe we have it wrong, Joanne was thinking as she went towards the car, *maybe Mae Bell meant another newspaper.* She saw McAllister leaning on the bonnet, long legs stretched out to the pavement, hat on the back of his head and in profile; she saw what a good-looking, interesting man he was.

He's mine, she wanted to say. Then told herself, *Don't. Not yet. Too soon. Wait a bit.*

293

Don't take risks. Don't get trapped again.

"Hello, lady." He stood, taking her hand. "Come into my shiny car so I can have my wicked way with you." He loved the way she would drift off into a dwam, her eyes unfocused, so obviously thinking over whatever it was she was thinking over.

"Let's go somewhere out of town, somewhere we can talk," she said, smiling at him.

"Findhorn. I was told there's a small . . ."

"Pub."

"Hostelry."

"Same thing."

The turnoff for Findhorn was also the turning for RAF Kinloss. They passed the base, but there was not much to see, just flat land, runways, windsocks horizontal in the North Sea wind.

But on the north side, the estuary was spectacular — wide, flat calm, and protected by sand dunes at the river mouth; every cloud, every tree shimmered in mirror image.

She was still oohing and aahing at the scenery when they arrived at the small hotel bar. After a beer for him and a shandy for her, they went for a walk. In early-afternoon sun they headed along the foreshore towards the rolling dunes that protected the land from the often fierce winds that cut through clothing, forming dancing white foam horses on the choppy water. The sandbar across the river mouth set up a string of breaking waves, making the passage from river to sea an exacting and sometimes dangerous undertaking for the small inshore fishing boats.

"So, what did you discover?" she asked.

"Later." He took her hand. "We'll talk in the car on the journey home. For now, let's enjoy this." He gestured around to the sea, the estuary, the woodlands reaching the edges of the dunes, and the afternoon sun.

"What was the editor like?" Joanne asked as they drove home following the curve of the river back to the main road.

"He's nearly bald and he can't be over fifty . . ." McAllister's single point of vanity was his thick, black Celtic hair, greying at the temples but plentiful and shiny in an almost Oriental way. "Like all newspaper editors — smokes too much, likes a dram, calm under pressure."

"How do you know that?"

"I'm guessing he's like me and every other editor I've known." He signaled right. Northwards. "I liked him. He said he's missing Mal Forbes, as the newspaper's revenue is down since Mal moved north to join the *Gazette*."

Joanne had wondered how Mal Forbes could be so successful, until she overheard him on the telephone.

"I know everyone knows your bakery," Mal was saying, "but you have rivals — Morrison's, for example. So what an advertisement does is show the others how well you're doing, showing you can afford a weekly space in the newspaper."

She could see him even now, licking his lips in that strange gesture he had, writing it down, talking all the while. "A quarter page? I could do a discount for three months. That's right kind o' you, the bairns really likes the jam donuts. I'll get ma wife to collect some."

It took Joanne a moment to realize they were no longer on the subject of Mal Forbes.

"Mr. Murray, the editor, knew nothing of the advertisement. He asked everyone in the office; no one knew anything about it. They all knew about the aircraft going missing in the North Sea. It was a big story. Most remembered Robert Bell's name. Mr. Murray then telephoned around the most likely hotels and B&Bs. No one has seen or heard of Mae Bell. My feeling is that if she *had* been in town, someone would have noticed her."

"Is there another local newspaper?"

"No. The *Northern Scot* covers the whole area."

They were silent for a mile, thinking over the implications of the information.

"I spoke to sisters who run a tea shop in town," Joanne told him. "The towns in Morayshire are dependent on the bases, and would be much the poorer without RAF Kinloss. I got the feeling the airmen are also a source of potential husbands. The plane going missing was a major catastrophe, everyone would remember it."

"According to the editor, there were not many Americans stationed at RAF Kinloss."

"So, what does this all tell us?" Joanne was speaking more to herself than him. She was upset. Mae Bell was her heroine, a role model of a self-sufficient woman, and she was fun.

"We'll ask her when we get home."

They passed through Nairn. Joanne saw a white milestone marking seventeen miles to town and home.

As they were approaching the town McAllister made a left turn towards his house. *The girls are with Chiara and Mae is at McAllister's.* She suddenly didn't feel like talking to Mae Bell just yet, so she asked,

297

"Could you drop me off at Chiara and Peter's house?"

If he was disappointed, he didn't show it.

She leaned over and gave him a peck on the cheek. "I'll see you in the morning. We can talk then."

Half an hour later, there was a ring on the Kowalskis' doorbell.

"Aunty Chiara, can I get it?" Annie, ever the curious, loved answering the door.

"Your uncle Peter would be delighted."

Peter had baby Andrew in the crook of his arm, a glass of wine in the other hand, and was leaning over a picture book Jean had on the table explaining to her what glaciers were.

"McAllister is here," Annie announced as she came back into the kitchen, the editor in tow.

"Mr. McAllister to you," Joanne told her and stood. "What are you doing here? I thought . . ."

"Mae Bell has gone. Left town. There was a letter for me, and one for you." He handed it to her. Then, without being invited, he took a chair — not that anyone was standing on manners. Peter and Chiara could see how shocked McAllister was looking, how fearful Joanne seemed as she stared at the letter in front of her. Plain envelope. Familiar ink. Familiar block capital letters. JO-ANNE ROSS — no "Mrs."

Without asking, Chiara poured a glass of wine and put it in front of McAllister. She then reached over to her husband and took baby Andrew. "Who wants to help me give Andrew his bath?"

"Me. Me," both girls shouted, startling the baby, who gave a cry then quieted as his mother put him over her shoulder, patting his back and whispering in his ear. The girls followed mother and baby, making funny faces at the wee boy as he watched them follow behind, up the stairs to the nursery.

"Peter knows all about it." Joanne still didn't touch the envelope.

Peter got up, took the bottle of burgundy, and even though she'd refused earlier, poured Joanne a glass.

"McAllister . . ." Joanne started.

He produced his envelope, took out the note, laid it on the table. This time no capital letters, only a scrawl, elegant as Mae herself, as enigmatic.

I love Paris in the springtime.

Joanne opened hers. The note was equally brief, equally mystifying.

Paris is perfect for a honeymoon.

She pushed the letter over to McAllister. He looked at it. He smiled. Joanne was furi-

299

ous. "What are you smiling at? That woman deceived us — the newspaper, friendship . . . Maybe she even . . ." She stopped herself. That was unthinkable.

"I think Mae might be saying we should come and find her in Paris."

"Then why doesn't she say so? And why these envelopes, this paper?" She was furious at his calm.

"Every stationery place in town sells this brand."

"Aye. But the printing on the envelope is the same as on the others. I can't believe . . ."

"You two should go home. Talk." Peter's words were gentle. Wise. "The girls are happy here."

McAllister nodded, picked up the notes, took Joanne's arm, and waited in the hallway as she put on her coat and hat. She was in the car when she remembered she hadn't said good night to the girls. Then she remembered the sound of their laughter coming down the staircase. *I'll telephone from McAllister's,* she thought.

When they arrived there, the house felt emptier than usual, the sitting room colder. McAllister put a match to the fire he had laid before leaving — a habit from his childhood when it was his job to set the fire

300

before going to school.

"A glass of wine?"

"A cup of tea. I'm not used to your sophisticated habits." She said this without bitterness, only as a matter of fact.

When he came back with the tray, she noticed the teapot in a cozy she'd knitted and left for him, and was pleased.

"I can't think straight." She was exhausted.

He poured tea for her, a whisky for himself. "Tomorrow is soon enough."

As he raised his glass, she suddenly said, "Can you take me home?" She didn't give him an explanation because she didn't have one. All she knew was that everything was going too fast.

I'm not even properly divorced, and now it's as though we're man and wife. I haven't even thought about my father — not properly.

He said nothing. Just put down his glass. She was grateful he didn't drink it.

When they arrived outside her prefab, he leaned towards her, brushed her hair behind her ear, then touched her arm. "I'll see you in the morning. And Joanne . . ."

She looked at him, waiting for disapproval, displeasure, perhaps resentment at her capriciousness.

"I had a great day. We should do that more

301

often. But next time, let's leave all discussions about work behind."

She almost changed her mind. But didn't, grateful he didn't try to kiss her, and grateful he didn't try to change her mind. *If he's disappointed, he's not showing it,* she thought, not knowing how much it hurt him, not knowing it took all his patience not to shout, *For heaven's sakes, make up your mind!*

In her solitary bed, if she dreamed, she was not aware of it. If Mae Bell was to disenchant her, it would not be tonight. If her father was to haunt her, it did not happen. Yet. Her fear, her nightmares were of burning, dissolving flesh.

What did stay with her, in that stage between waking and finally sleeping, was McAllister. *A rare man — a good man, so why do I push him away?* She was asleep before she could answer her own question.

EIGHTEEN

The same morning McAllister and Joanne were in Elgin, Mae met Frankie in Arnotts' tearooms. It was early, not yet ten o'clock, and the usual array of women and parcels had not arrived for the tea and scones or buttered gingerbread the only department store in the Highlands was famous for.

Frankie had five minutes at most. Even that was risking another row with his manager.

She said what she came to say.

"How soon?" was his immediate question when she said she was going back to Paris.

"Oh, another week or so," she answered, "I have to get back to work. It's expensive here and I have to earn my living."

Frankie did not notice the shadows under her eyes. Only a woman would see the pallor of her skin under the makeup that was now a shade too dark, stopping in a faint but discernible line around the jaw. He did not see the constant cigarette smoke, the way she played with her spoon, unable to drink the coffee, made from a glutinous mixture out of a bottle, more spiced treacle than coffee.

He tried not to beg — *Marry me; I'll look after you.* He did not understand, so besotted he was with Mae Bell, so lost in his fantasies, that he ignored her age, her profession, and the impossibility of her becoming a housewife of the Highlands. He was also unaware that he had yet to properly mourn his mother's death.

"I can save up, come to Paris to visit you, maybe work in a bar . . ."

"That would be wonderful, Frankie. But right now, your father and sister need you." She thought him sweet in a kid-brother way, but Mae was used to men fantasizing over her and never took them seriously. Even after six years, Robert was her man.

A waitress who looked as though she should be in a school, not working, paused at their table and muttered at Frankie, "Your manager's looking for you. You'd better not let him catch you with a customer." She sniffed at Mae Bell and, holding a laden tray as steadily as she could, she hurried off in case her manager caught her talking to her secret crush — Frankie Urquhart

— something she had been warned about before Mae came on the scene.

Frankie stood, and could feel all the eyes on them, so he didn't touch her; he didn't shake her hand, put a hand on her arm, touch her hair, anything, and he regretted it ever after.

"I'll see you soon."

"Bye, Frankie."

He left.

She stayed. For a moment, staring at the white tablecloth, not moving, ignoring the glare from the waitress, who started to clear the table, she felt immensely sad and knew that what she was about to do was difficult, illegal, and she was terrified she would fail. *Only one chance, so it had better succeed.*

"I'll get you the bill," the waitress said.

Mae stood, leaving far too much money on the table.

She walked to the station, once more hating the cobbles on the street, which caught her high heels if she was not careful. She bought a train ticket, making a fuss about the price of a day trip to Elgin. Next she left the station and went to the ladies' room in the hotel.

Ten minutes later the doorman was put out when he saw a decidedly unsuitable person leaving by the main doors. He thought, from her coat and sand shoes, that she must be a cleaner. He did not tip his hat to her. As his wife had left him years since for a neighbor, he had no one to share with; the oddity of such a person being in a smart hotel and then climbing into a taxi was puzzling. *How can the likes o' her afford a taxi,* he was thinking, and he did not go to open the taxi door.

Saturday mornings at the *Gazette* were a time for filing reports and expenses and catching up on the boring tasks, with the phone mercifully quiet.

Don didn't always appear on a Saturday, so this morning McAllister drove to Don's to pick him up from the tiny terraced house where he lived and which he hated, it being in sight of the scene of his late wife's murder.

When Rob wandered in to the reporters' room, trying to remember where he had put his petrol receipts so he could write up his expenses claim, the editor was there with Joanne and Don and Hec. When McAllister announced he wanted to talk about the anonymous letters again, Hector surprised them by insisting Fiona join in the discussion.

No one expected Hector to be part of the

discussion, far less Fiona but, as he pointed out, she had been the one to receive the letters, the first one to talk to Mae Bell, albeit on the telephone.

"The lad's right," Don said.

Silently thrilled to be asked to join in the discussion, Fiona came upstairs to the reporters' room.

"Is Mr. Forbes in?" McAllister asked her.

"He said he's away to Beauly." Fiona doubted it was true; there was always somewhere Mal Forbes was "away to" on Saturday mornings.

"The anonymous letters. Mae Bell," McAllister began.

"Nurse Urquhart," Joanne added.

The leg. Hector hoped no one would mention the leg.

McAllister laid the notes he and Joanne received on the table.

Fiona noticed immediately. "That's the same paper and envelopes as the others. The printing on the envelopes is the same an' all." She blushed as soon as she said it, not sure she should have spoken up.

"Thanks, Fiona, you've confirmed what Joanne and I thought."

She blushed again. Hector nudged her with his elbow.

"Does that mean . . ." Fiona couldn't finish.

"So you've no' mentioned these to the polis." Don stated the obvious.

Like Fiona, Rob saw the similarity. "Mae Bell has written these" — he was tapping the notes with a forefinger — "but I'm certain she didn't write the anonymous letters." He stopped. Looked around at the silent faces. "Did she?"

Joanne and McAllister had had time to digest the idea. Neither of them could quite bring themselves to believe it. Not the writing of the letters, there could be an explanation for that, but the next step, that the letter writer threw the acid, *that* they could not countenance.

It took Don to sum it up. "The envelopes and notepaper are the same brand as the anonymous letters. Maybe Mae Bell wrote the letters. But why would she?"

"Why was she here in the Highlands for so long?" Joanne was puzzled as to why Mae should stay when the advertisements were bringing no results. "But the main mystery is Mae saying she'd placed an advertisement in the local Elgin newspaper. There was no advertisement. No sign of Mae Bell. Nothing."

More silence.

McAllister sighed. "I'll have to pass these on to the police."

"Aye," Don agreed.

"Hector, do you have the photos of Mae Bell's room, the ones you took after the acid was thrown?" Joanne was asking because the strangeness of the plimsolls still bothered her.

"Here." Hector reached into his schoolbag. "I've only a couple; the rest are in ma studio."

For once Rob did not correct him on "ma studio" but pulled the pictures towards him, looking for what Joanne was seeing and not succeeding.

"That coat. And that apron, it's hideous." She hadn't seen this particular shot before, and it more than ever confirmed her confusion. Joanne hated the pattern of cabbage roses and hollyhocks, even in black and white. "Mae Bell would never wear clothes like that."

"We don't know they're hers." Rob was still finding it hard to contemplate Mae Bell involved in a crime.

"There's no link between the letters and the acid attack," Don reminded them all. "I was found with a bloody knife and I didn't kill anyone."

The others well remembered how Don

had been locked up in a prison cell, with the threat of a life sentence hanging over him, for a murder he did not commit.

The next hour was taken up with "what if" and "maybe" and "perhaps" until McAllister told them he would have to phone DI Dunne.

Although Joanne joined in the speculation intermittently, she was hurt. *I can't believe Mae has left without saying good-bye. I thought we were friends. What's so important she couldn't tell me she was leaving?*

"Aye, and when you see the inspector, prepare for a right bollocking for no' taking these notes to the polis sooner . . ." Don finished.

Sundays were a day of deadly boredom for the young men and women of the town — unless they were courting. Rob called round to Frankie's house in the late morning, knowing that without Nurse Urquhart to make them, none of the family would be at church. Rob didn't want to, but he knew he should be the one to tell Frankie the news.

"Do you fancy going out?" Rob didn't go in, staying on the doorstep of the Urquharts' semi-detached house.

"Where?"

"Drumnadrochit?"

"As good as anywhere."

Church services finished, there would soon be the usual convoy of Sunday drivers out for the afternoon, driving at twenty-five miles an hour as they peered at the loch, hoping to catch sight of the monster. With Frankie on the back, Rob threw the Triumph into the bends, passing cars, perilously close to oncoming traffic at times, enjoying every moment of the road.

The Clansman Motel was a new construction of stone and glass and tartan carpets, and, being a motel, the bar was open. The view from the first floor was spectacular. "We can keep a lookout for the monster," Rob joked as he returned with beers for Frankie and himself. The joke didn't work. He noticed Frankie was looking more suave than usual, not so much his former Teddy boy self. A new haircut, that's it. And jeans.

"How did you get hold of a real pair of jeans?" Rob was postponing the conversation, although he really did covet the denim jeans, knowing they were impossible to find in the Highlands.

"Mae bought them for me."

Rob was about to say, *I bet she never bought those in Elgin,* before he remembered yesterday's meeting in the *Gazette* office.

"Mae said she's leaving soon." Frankie

311

was staring into his pint.

"Ah. Mae." Rob hesitated how to put it, then went for honesty. "I heard she's already gone."

"Never." Frankie's glass spilled onto the coaster — tartan, naturally. "Mae would never go without saying cheerio."

Rob shrugged. "She was staying at Mc-Allister's house . . ."

"Because she was scared."

"She left a note for him and another note for Joanne . . ."

"Was there one for me?"

"Frankie, she's gone." He too was upset Mae Bell had not said good-bye to anyone. "All her things are gone, even her lipstick . . ." Rob didn't know this. He meant to lighten the dark surrounding Frankie. *He doesn't need any more misery,* Rob was thinking, *he's obsessed with her, it's completely unrealistic, it hurts.* He was remembering how he'd felt when he split with his last girlfriend, Eilidh. She turned out to be a nasty piece of work, yet he was still hurt.

Remembering the envelopes and notes lying on the reporters' table yesterday morning, he started again. "Frankie." But he couldn't say it. He couldn't say, *Mae Bell may have written the letters.* He couldn't think, far less say, *Mae Bell may have at-*

tacked your mother.

Rob could see from the way Frankie, eyes glazed, was staring out the window, that speculating on Mae Bell's possible involvement would devastate Frankie. He took a sip of flat beer. *I wish the Loch Ness Monster would appear.* Even that, Rob decided, would not take Frankie's mind off Mae Bell. *And I haven't the heart, or the courage, to tell him there's worse to come.*

Although Rob did not know this absolutely, he was certain there was much worse to come.

After dropping Frankie off at his house, Rob went home. His parents were out. He was glad. He didn't feel like talking.

He was in his bedroom, the wireless on low, a big band playing not Rob's favorite music but he couldn't think clearly without some noise in the background. A notepad and pencil beside him, he was lying on the bed, remembering yesterday's gathering, trying to come up with some ideas, ideas that would make sense of the information and give him a killer of a story.

Sunday afternoon was the ritual walk through the Islands for Joanne and family. Granddad Ross was with them but not Granny Ross. She had terrible pains in her stomach and was pretending it was the flu, but knowing it was the worry about her only son leaving to go to Australia. She was also terrified that Joanne would be estranged from them; she knew her daughter-in-law was more than friendly with her boss, Mr. McAllister. Bill had made sure she knew.

What if Joanne marries and they leave for the south with the bairns? She put more Epsom salts in a glass, stirred, swallowed, waited. Half an hour later there was no relief.

"How's Mr. McAllister?" Granddad Ross asked as he and Joanne walked together, the girls running ahead, desperate for their Sunday ice cream. From Granddad Ross this was a genuine inquiry. He was ashamed his son was a wife beater.

"He's fine," Joanne replied. She waited to hear if there was more to the question.

"He's a right fine man, so I hear." He said no more as they had arrived at the café in the middle of the Islands.

The girls thanked their granddad for the sixpences and ran off to queue. Joanne and her father-in-law sat on a bench in a warm patch of sun shining through a gap in the canopy of beech trees. The sounds of water and the constantly shifting green light made Joanne feel they were underwater.

"I hope you and Bill splitting up won't make us strangers." He couldn't use the word *divorce*.

What he said, so plain, so simple, so heartfelt, made Joanne reach out, pat his arm, noticing the dark spots on the wrinkled hands resting on the walking stick, hands that had wielded a bayonet in an earlier war that he, unlike his son later, had survived mostly intact. The hands were trembling.

"Dad, I think of you as the father I always wanted." She was shocked to feel the tears start to fall. "I . . . I mean I haven't seen him, my father in ten, no, eleven years. He was a hard man . . . not like you, he . . . I don't miss him. But . . ."

"He was your father."

She took the neatly folded, worn but newly bleached white hankie from him, and shook it open. She wiped her eyes. "I don't know why I'm crying . . ." She saw that the girls had reached the head of the queue and told herself to behave, they've seen enough tears in the past.

Her father. Her husband. Mae Bell. Who else is going to let me down?

"Your mother and me, we're right glad you'll be staying. Thon wee girls mean the world to us. And you."

"Not so wee anymore, Dad. Annie will be

315

doing her eleven plus and then off to the academy." They agreed it was certain Annie would make the academy.

"Mum, Granddad, Mr. McAllister was taking a walk too." Jean had a strawberry ice cream in one hand and McAllister in the other.

"What a coincidence." Granddad Ross said standing, holding out his hand. There was no cynicism in the remark and the greeting was glad.

"Aye, a real coincidence." Although peeved at his assumption that she would be here and he could join them, Joanne had the grace to smile.

As they walked back homewards along the riverbank, her with the girls, McAllister asking Granddad about the start of the bowling season, the state of the greens, who was on the lawn bowling committee this season, Joanne was watching McAllister, seeing him as others saw him — a man of substance. With his substantial house, his standing in the community as editor of the newspaper, his acceptance of her girls, her family, she knew he truly cared for her, and knew she loved him in a quiet way. *So why do I hesitate?*

They reached the Infirmary footbridge. Granddad Ross turned back to Joanne.

"You young things go off and enjoy your-
selves. The girls are coming home with me."

Joanne had to put her hand over her
mouth at "young things."

"Granny's made a treacle tart and she'll
be waiting." He lifted his hat. "Mr. McAllister, it's been good meeting wi' you." Without
waiting he walked onto the bridge, the girls
following like faithful puppies.

Annie turned to wave. "See you later,
Mum." Her grin was for McAllister. "Mc-
Allister, don't forget you owe me a book."

Joanne was about to say, *Mr. McAllister,*
then shook her head. She was wondering if
she might end up marrying McAllister to
please her daughters and her in-laws and
everyone on the *Gazette.*

"Joanne, sorry to break up the family
afternoon. I wouldn't have if it wasn't important."

She stood. The wind blew her hair in her
face, catching in the corner of her eye, stinging.

"Mae Bell?"

"Aye." He pointed back to the triangle of
park next to the war memorial. "My car is
up there."

She couldn't wait. "Tell me now."

"The police are looking for Mae Bell.
Nothing more at this stage. But she has dis-

appeared."

"And you think . . ."

"Joanne, I don't know what to think. I went into her room and found her makeup bag. Her suitcase is under the bed. And no one has seen or heard from her since Friday morning, when she bought a ticket to Elgin."

"Really? Elgin?"

"Inspector Dunne said the ticket inspector swears she wasn't on the train."

"So where is she?" Joanne was looking at him, the anxiety clear in her eyes.

"I wish I knew."

NINETEEN

It's quiet for a Monday, Joanne was thinking as she sat at the reporters' table, making notes for her page. When the sound of a commotion rang up the stairs, she smiled. *I knew it was too good to last.*

"Don't you treat my fiancée like that," Hector was shouting, "it's no' her fault your stupid copy has gone missing."

"It's the silly wee girl's job to find it. So where is it?" This sentence Joanne heard as she was running down the stairs.

"Would you all keep your voices down? They can hear you as far as the high street."

Mal Forbes turned. He pointed his finger at Joanne instead of Fiona. Aiming squarely at the sternum, the extended digit finger and the wild eyes made him look as though he was about to cast a curse.

"This is all your fault, you and your nosy parker friends." From his voice, from the poking gesture, finger trembling, Joanne wouldn't have been surprised if lightning came out of the fingertip to emphasize his anger.

"Mr. Forbes, I don't know what you've lost, but can I help you find it?" Her tone was gentle, soothing, as though trying to calm a terrified child.

He looked into her eyes to see if she was being sarcastic. Saw the offer was genuine. All the anger drained out of the man. Looking at his shoes, he shook his head, saying, "No, I'll ask the client if he has the original." He went towards the door, and with his back turned to Joanne said, "Thanks all the same."

She would have sworn he had tears in his eyes, but no one would believe her, least of all Rob, who came in saying, "What's up with cheerful face?" tossing his head in the direction of Mal Forbes, who could be seen disappearing down Castle Wynd, hands in his pockets, hat pulled down.

Mal's smaller than I remember, Joanne thought.

Rob said, "Let's go upstairs, I need to talk to you."

Hector stayed with Fiona.

"Fiancée?" Fiona asked. "Since when?"

She was trying to be casual about it, but she was thrilled. Marrying Hector Bain was all she wanted — that and a job for life on the *Gazette*. She appreciated Hec's standing up for her but had Mal Forbes's measure. *All the same,* she was thinking, *it shows Hector really cares.*

"I want to marry you — if you'll have me."

"Of course I'll marry you, Hector, but we might have to elope to Gretna Green — my father, he'd kill me, or you, if he found out we're engaged."

"I *think* ma granny's car would make it that far," he said but wasn't at all certain the old jalopy would manage the climb up the Pass of Drumochter.

When Hector left to take pictures of a woman's one hundredth birthday party, Fiona was too thrilled by the unofficial engagement to wonder too much about Mal Forbes.

A few days previously — she'd come in a quarter of an hour early to tidy up the accounts — she'd seen Mal Forbes in their office, but from behind. She saw his shoulders shaking, him sniffing. He didn't turn around, but blew his nose on his hankie, and she backed out of the room to leave him alone. When he came out, he walked quickly past her and as he was going out the door he'd said, *Sorry, I've a terrible cold,* and she had accepted his explanation.

Almost. *No, I must be mistaken,* she was thinking, *he couldn't have been crying. Men don't cry.*

Rob and Joanne's conversation was less cheerful.

"Frankie Urquhart called me. He's taken a day off work. Told them he has the flu. He doesn't. He's heartsick."

Joanne thought it all through: the leg in the shinty boot; the acid attack; his mother's death; an infatuation with Mae Bell; Mae Bell leaving. For a small-town young man whose height of excitement was dancing in the Caledonian Ballroom to the Harry Shore Big Band, this had been a momentous two months.

"Frankie says he's off to Paris as soon as possible, but he can't leave his dad and wee sister yet. I never mentioned Mae might have had an accident — or something."

"Mae Bell is off on one of her mysterious jaunts. She wants to find out all she can about her late husband. Grief takes us all differently." That she was wrestling over her own lack of grief at her father's death she didn't share. "I don't know what all the fuss is about." Joanne almost believed this.

DI Dunne had said the same. "She's a grown woman," the detective had told McAllister after examining Mae's room. "I know she left her things here, but women always have more than one lipstick."

"I want to help Frankie, but I don't know how." Rob was finding it hard to explain to Joanne that he was lost when it came to dealing with his friend's grief. He felt clumsy. His usual mode of confronting unpleasant situations — jokes, quips, avoiding the topic — weren't working. The raw grief on Frankie's face, in his voice, the way Frankie couldn't line up a snooker shot without fluffing it or gouging the green of the cloth, told him how deep Frankie's pain was.

"Rob, the best way to help Frankie is to find his mother's killer." Joanne's own frustrations were more than enough for her; her divorce, the death of her father, McAllister's need for her; although she felt for Frankie, she had little space left to worry about someone else.

Rob knew this and knew he was losing sight of finding Nurse Urquhart's killer. *Mae Bell,* he thought, *she so enchanted us we've forgotten Nurse Urquhart.*

"Nurse Urquhart, I've run out of ideas," he said.

"Nurse Urquhart." Don came into the room. "The woman deserves justice." The deputy editor sat down, pulled out a copy of the racing guide to mark off the horses that had won or lost. He was transferring the information into his wee black book, his personal form guide. Finished, he looked at Rob. "Nurse Urquhart? You were saying?"

"I'm out of ideas," Rob replied.

"Me too," Joanne added, but quietly; she was out of ideas on many fronts.

"Get hold of thon editor of ours; it's time to convene a kitchen cabinet."

They met that evening in McAllister's kitchen. Joanne brought the girls over on the bus, leaving their bicycles at home. They were delighted. From the front seat of the top deck, Annie announced loudly that she wanted to live in McAllister's house so she didn't have to keep books in two places. Mercifully, Joanne thought, there were only three young lads on their way to the bus station, off to hang out with their friends from other housing estates, kick litter and beer cans, and generally look fiercesome. Joanne knew it was all bravado and knew they were not interested in a housewife in a Fair Isle beret with an overloud schoolgirl daughter.

"Are you going to solve Nurse Urquhart's murder?" Annie asked when she saw the four musketeers from the *Gazette* sitting around the kitchen table. She knew nothing of Mae Bell's disappearance.

"Annie!" Joanne scolded. Then, shaking her head, smiled with her lips closed.

"We're going to do our best," McAllister told her.

"Good enough." That Highland phrase, covering everything from grudging approval to outright praise, sufficed. They would do their best; in Annie's opinion, that meant they would succeed.

She returned to the sitting room, to her sister, her homework, to the essay on "What I Want to Be." *I am going to be an editor of a newspaper in Edinburgh,* she wrote, *or I will write books.*

"Right, here's the old list." McAllister said. "I'll add any new information."

Don was nursing a cup of tea, saying nothing.

McAllister was staring at the list.

When there were no further ideas, Don asked, "Do we know how all yon connects?" He tapped the sheet of foolscap. "Do we know for sure there *is* a connection?"

McAllister stretched his back and sighed. Joanne leaned forwards, cupping her head in her hands. Rob tapped a light nonrhythmic pattern on the underside of the table.

They took Don's point. And it was disheartening.

"Right. Let's play What If?. I'll start." Don lit a cigarette before beginning, "What if this has nothing to do with the shinty?"

McAllister was next. "What if this is all to do with the American Robert Bell?"

"What if this has nothing to do with Robert Bell?" Rob countered.

"What if . . ." Joanne hesitated, afraid she would seem spiteful. She looked at Rob. He always listened to the outrageous. "What if this is all to do with Mal Forbes?"

"Explain." Don was curious, not dismissive of the suggestion.

"Elgin. I can't think why Mae Bell would say she put an ad in the Elgin paper when she didn't. The one time she met Mal Forbes, she was really rude to him . . ." She remembered the incident more clearly because it was her first and, she'd decided, last taste of martini. "Mind you, he was as sleekit as a stoat towards her." She saw the skepticism on the faces of the others. "He comes from Elgin. Robert Bell was stationed near there, Robert Bell's plane . . ." Her voice faded. She could hear how ridiculous it sounded.

McAllister stood. "Anyone for a dram?"

"Sit." Don's voice startled them. "You

can't avoid it, McAllister. Get it out, then you can have a dram." Joanne noticed he didn't say "we."

He did as he was told. He said, staring out the window at the darkening from the north dimming the black outline of Ben Wyvis, "Mae Bell. She *could* have written the anonymous letters . . ." His voice trailed away.

"Why?" Don challenged.

"What if she knew or found out something connecting her husband to Mal Forbes?" Rob asked.

"Why would she throw the acid at Nurse Urquhart?" Don said it. Said what they all had speculated on, dared not say, in case the saying of it named it and made it true.

"That can't be right." Joanne refused to believe Mae Bell capable of such a cowardly attack. "Someone threw acid at her room."

"What if she staged the attack on her own hotel room to put everyone off the scent?" Don again. He was not so involved with Mae Bell that he felt he couldn't stand back and say the unthinkable.

Joanne remembered that her suggestion that Mal Forbes might be involved had become lost in the speculation about Mae Bell. She didn't mind too much, but there was that familiar feeling that anything she contributed was sometimes seen as of little significance.

"Joanne." McAllister had his pencil back in his hand, the sheet of paper in front of him, and this time a dram at his elbow. "Mal Forbes? What made you suggest him?"

He surprised her. He'd listened. "Why did he leave Elgin? He had a good job. He's from there."

"He also had a good house inherited from his father, so the editor told me," McAllister said.

"This is a much bigger wee town. He makes more money here?" Rob asked.

"Not necessarily. He's on commission and he had the County of Moray to himself on his last job. There's money in Moray." Don would know this.

"Mal could easily deliver the letters to the *Gazette*," Joanne said.

"Sorry, I just don't get it. Mal Forbes comes from Elgin. You're not overfond o' him . . ." Don directed this at Joanne, and she had the grace to look away, somewhat ashamed after Mal Forbes's emotional breakdown early in the day. "There's nothing else against the man. Joanne, you asked why Mrs. Bell has been in Scotland for three months. You're right, it's a gey long time to be searching for her husbands' friends."

"And expensive," Rob said. "But she looks as though money is not a problem."

McAllister said nothing, but he was surprised that a nightclub singer was seemingly so wealthy.

"We keep going over the same questions and getting nowhere," Don summed up the meeting. No one wanted to hear this. And all agreed they were no further on.

The clock in the hallway struck ten. Rob stood.

"Radio Luxembourg is on, I have to go." It was not why he was leaving, it was the discussion — he couldn't bear to think about Mae Bell one minute more. "Don, can I give you a lift?"

He was as amazed as everyone, including Don, when Don said, "Why not? If I'm to die tonight, it might as well be in style."

As the sound of the motorbike faded, the house was once more quiet, and to Joanne it seemed to be listening. She said, almost in a whisper, "Mae Bell. I can't believe she'd do anything wicked."

"Then don't." McAllister stood to empty the ashtrays. "Don't unless you have incontrovertible proof."

They washed up together, went to bed. Like an old married couple, Joanne thought as McAllister was in the bathroom brushing his teeth. Here we are, like we're already married. But I'm not even finally divorced. *Fornication, my father would have called it. My father was certain about everything, had a name for every sin.* The thought made her sad. *I suppose I'll be married in a registry office, like the first time.* She told herself she didn't care, but she wasn't certain she was certain about anything anymore.

The decision to arrive separately to work was not something they discussed; it had just evolved. Joanne would leave early to take the children to the bus stop down the hill on Eastgate. McAllister would walk, leaving ten minutes later. They met when they met. Today it was on the doorstep.

"Good morning, Mrs. Ross. Morning, Fiona," McAllister said, winking at Joanne.

"Morning, Mr. McAllister, Mrs. Ross." Fiona replied. "Mrs. Forbes phoned and left a message for you. Mr. Forbes had the flu and won't be in for a day or so."

"Right. Show me the advertising bookings this afternoon so I can make up the dummy."

"Can I do it with you?" She immediately went bright red, mortified at her boldness.

"Great idea," Joanne said. "I'd like to be involved too."

"I can see you two doing it without me."
McAllister smiled. Joanne knew he was only
half joking; like all journalists, he hated
advertising, seeing it as a necessary evil.
"And ask Mr. McLeod if you have any
problems."

Five o'clock and the dummy finished, Don
made a final check of the pages. "A fine job
the lassies have done," Don said as he ap-
proved the layout. "It's a wee bit different.
They didn't need me or you at all." He nodded at McAllister.

"How different?" Joanne wanted to know.

"It's somehow more . . ." He was searching for a word, rare for him. "It's elegant."

That was what Joanne had been hoping
for.

"Can we do it again next week?" Fiona
asked.

"Anytime," McAllister said.

"I'm not sure Mr. Forbes would like that."
Joanne was smiling at Fiona. But the answering smile, so small, so fake, made her
ask, "Fiona, is there something you're not
telling us?"

"I don't know anything." The emphasis
was on *know*.

"I'm away out. Men's business," McAllister said.

"And I have to get home to my girls."

331

Joanne looked at Fiona. "You live not far from me; would you like to come over this evening? Once the girls are in bed we can have a good blether."

"I'd love to."

Fiona was thrilled. She'd always wanted to see inside Mrs. Ross's house. She'd been by on her way to the Islands to meet Hector. She'd walked slowly, peering at the gingham curtains, which she thought unusual, gingham being for wee girls' dresses or the aprons and bags you made in primary-school sewing class where you did cross-stitch edges using the squares to make sure the stitches were even.

The girls were not shy with Fiona.

"You're Hector's girlfriend," Annie said, and Fiona said, "I am."

When Annie continued, *McAllister is Mum's boyfriend,* and Fiona said *I know,* everyone relaxed, secrets out in the open.

"How do you know about Hector and Fiona?" Joanne asked Annie, not wanting to admit that she hadn't noticed.

" 'Cos Maraidh told me. She really likes Fiona and wants her to be Hec's girlfriend and for them all to live together with Granny Bain."

Fiona didn't look so sure but she smiled and said, "We'll see."

And again, Joanne was reminded what a small town she lived in.

Fiona was happy to have cocoa with Annie and Jean, happy to read Jean a story whilst Annie struggled through *Jane Eyre* by herself, and when they were alone, she was happy to discuss events with Joanne.

Mrs. Ross treated her like a grown-up, so her natural caution melted. It was not that Fiona didn't love her mother, but she'd never thought about it. If asked, she would have been astonished. Of course you love your parents. That didn't mean she was unaware of her mother's faults; *could talk the hind legs off a donkey* was her father's phrase. *An auld fishwife* was her granny's (on her father's side) less charitable phrase.

It's working in the baker's shop with all the other women, Fiona decided when as a thirteen-year-old she became aware of her mother's insatiable appetite for the minutiae of everyone's business, customers, neighbors, strangers alike. She determined then she would not be a gossip.

Joanne was saying, "I'm not asking you to spy or to tell tales, but we — McAllister, myself, and Mr. McLeod and Rob — we want to help find whoever threw the acid at Nurse Urquhart."

"Aye, Hector told me you were trying to

333

help the Urquharts." Since she was friends with Morag Urquhart, she wanted to help too.

"The letters, we're trying to work out how they were delivered."

"And you want to know who wrote them," Fiona corrected her, "and if the same person killed Nurse Urquhart."

Joanne jerked back. It was like talking to Rob at his most direct, something she hadn't expected from Fiona. As the conversation went on, it was also obvious that Fiona had thought hard, analyzed the events, and had some clear ideas of her own.

No wonder she's good at accounting, Joanne decided.

"Mrs. Bell might have written the letters and put them in the *Gazette* post box." Fiona was sitting differently. Her voice was not louder, but clearer, her accent less, the thoughts logically organized. "Hector showed me the photos of Mrs. Bell's room again. I see what you're saying. Them clothes is all wrong. Plus she took a wee suitcase with all her good stuff with her. Why? Then I remembered."

It was barely perceptible, but Joanne noticed Fiona nodding to herself as she told the next part of her story.

"I can see clearly the people coming and

going from the library through the glass in our doors, so I don't take heed o' them anymore, except if it's a stranger. I'd seen this woman a couple of times and there was something about her. I said that to Hector, and he said it's not the clothes you look at, it's the way people walk, hold their heads, you know . . ."

Joanne did know. It was one of Hec's pet theories that you tell more about a person by their walk than their face.

"She was wearing a head scarf, I couldn't make out her hair, and wearing a horrible old coat, but the sand shoes were brand-new and she had on nylons, not socks. It was right cold, and wet, so you'd think she'd have on wellies — anyone can afford well-ies. I didn't know why I thought I knew her until Hector said *watch her walk.*" She took a deep breath. This was the longest she'd talked to anyone apart from Hector, and Joanne was listening to every word.

"So this one morning, I saw her heading for the stairs that go under the castle walls down to the river. I thought, she's not been visiting the library 'cos it's not open for another hour."

She looked at Joanne, her young face free of pimples for this week, telling her earnestly, "Many of the older people, they've

335

nowhere to go 'specially in the rain, and they stay in the library for hours. Sometimes they call in for an old copy of the *Gazette* and I give it to them for free — I hope that's all right?"

"Of course it is." Joanne toes started to twitch. *Get on with the story, Fiona.*

"I think the person I saw was Mrs. Bell."

Joanne was about to ask, how can you be sure?

"The clothes were the same as in Hector's picture, the coat, the shoes — that's what bothered me as I couldn't see Mrs. Bell wearing plimsolls. I'm pretty sure it was her, and that same morning, there was another o' them letters."

After Fiona left, Joanne wanted, needed, to talk to McAllister. *I wish we had a telephone,* she was thinking, then remembered that McAllister hated talking on the telephone.

As she was reading in bed, she put the book down, thinking, *This is when I need McAllister; I can talk to, talk at, him, and he listens whilst I ramble on, letting the thoughts out, the ideas, and the replies — or not — but when needed, he says just the right phrase, or word, and then I can sleep, my brain emptied out, nothing left to bother or worry me. I wish I were with him right now.*

TWENTY

Mal Forbes was off work all week. McAllister checked and there were no cancellations in the advertising bookings, and with the help of the part-time bookkeeper, Fiona was working well.

He decided to pay Mal a visit. *Flu can be bad, but the worst should be over,* he was thinking, and as editor, he needed to know if other plans should be made. He was also curious about Mal's home circumstances, as the man had never shared his personal life with his *Gazette* colleagues.

Face it, McAllister, you're hopelessly inquisitive, he told himself, knowing *suspicious* was the more accurate word.

He didn't know this part of town. The single-story granite-block houses with bay windows were set back from the road, some with high hedges, others with low walls, most with smart gravel pathways, all showing a stolid, respectable exterior. He was surprised how secluded the Forbeses' house was. It was the tall, abundant, wild cherry tree with pink blossoms and new rusty-green leaves, the privet hedge long overdue a good clipping, the overhanging elder and lilac bushes, the windows with curtains tight shut as though a death had occurred in the family, that made McAllister wonder if sun ever reached into the lives of the Forbeses.

Stepping onto the front porch with black and white checkerboard tiles and a coconut mat, he rang the doorbell. A girl about Annie's age answered.

"Hello, I'm Mr. McAllister from the *Gazette*. I'd like to speak to your father." He wondered why she was not at school.

"He's not here. Mum's not here either." The child was nervous, her story instantly betrayed by the sound of clashing metal from the back of the house and the voice shouting, "Maureen, come and help me."

The voice was muffled but unmistakable; Mal Forbes hadn't heard the doorbell.

Maureen was examining McAllister, taking in his appearance. She knew who he was — not from her father but from Annie Ross, who was maybe not her best friend, but one of the few she was friendly with, and who, like herself, was an outsider in the school-playground popularity stakes.

338

"Glad to see you're better," McAllister said when Mal appeared. He held out his hand; Mal Forbes shook it, but didn't ask him in.

"I'm wondering will you be back at work next week?"

"Dad, I can stay home and look after Mum," Maureen said.

"It's fine, Maureen, you go off and check the oven, the gingerbread is smelling ready." He smiled at the editor, a rare sight. "Ma wee hobby, I like baking cakes. Look, I'm sorry, Mr. McAllister, a wee bit o' a white lie; it's ma wife who's poorly. But don't you worry about the advertisers; when Moira's sleeping I make ma phone calls. Checking up on the customers and the like."

McAllister doubted it was only Mrs. Forbes who was ill. Mal himself was looking distinctly pale. "Of course. Give your wife my regards, and if there's anything we can do to help . . ."

"Not at all. We're managing just fine. I'll see you at the Monday morning meeting."

The front door was closed before McAllister was one step down the path. He walked past the narrow flower borders on either side, fading daffodils still in brown melting clumps, smelling of decay. He knew nothing about flowers but had a vague idea these should have been tidied up by now. Wild-cherry blossoms covered one corner of a bare, straggly lawn, reminding McAllister of grass that had been decimated by numerous games of football.

As he turned to latch the garden gate, he saw a lace curtain fall back into place. As he looked again at the house and garden, he wondered at the height of the side fence, new-looking, a larchwood construction of parallel strips in a solid frame. The back garden seemed entirely enclosed, as though the Forbes family kept a ferocious dog. *Wasn't there a rumor his son is disabled? That must be why they want privacy,* he thought.

On the walk back to the office, he was re-assured by the ordinariness of Mal Forbes and his daughter and particularly by the gingerbread but was thinking, *Why didn't he admit his wife is unwell? And his son, why hide his condition? He could tell me privately so we can make better working arrangements.* He realized that was unnecessary; Mal Forbes had already arranged his work around his family and McAllister thought better of the man for that. He also knew what stopped people, particularly men, from admitting there was anything wrong in their family life — pride.

Pride, the worst of the seven deadly sins,

according to Descartes. After the visit, McAllister felt sorry for Mal Forbes, forgiving him his oddness, his rudeness.

Ever since he became a manager in newspapers, Mal Forbes kept an office in his house. He liked calm. He liked order. He worked better without interruptions. The house was exactly right for them: set back from the road, private, three bedrooms plus a wee cubby of a room he'd turned into an office by installing a wide shelf the length of the room, a filing cabinet, and a lock on the door. He'd had the phone put in there. *Keeps it out of the boy's hearing,* he'd told Moira. The boy loved sounds. Distant fire engines, church bells, any music, the boy would set up a discordant wail that made the neighbors think the Forbes family kept a dog.

When they first came to the town, Moira was healthier than she had been for a long time. Although he didn't like her working, the part-time job in the county council — which she loved — meant they could afford this perfect family home. But lately Moira had been off work so many times, they might lose the house that Mal had found through the *Gazette,* him being able to read the classifieds before anyone else. Lately

Moira had been having more and more of her "spells," as she put it, that he was worried she would have a full-blown episode and end up committed to the mental hospital. The boy's physical health he never worried about; a strong boy, never a day's illness, only his brain was a bit *scrambled* — Moira's phrase.

Mal was not unhappy working at the *Gazette,* but thought McAllister much too modern. *What's wrong with the advertisements on the front page?* he'd asked his wife, knowing no one on the newspaper would answer his question. *That's the way it's always been done,* he told her. For him a newspaper was the advertising — news taking up too much space.

He didn't mind Don McLeod; *Good at his job but he's getting past it, he should retire.*

Rob he thought too big for his boots. Hector a necessary evil, as he needed him for the football photos, the sports pages being prime advertising spots. He thought Joanne flighty but had nothing against her.

Moira Forbes thought differently. Even though she had only met Joanne in passing, she'd complained to her husband, *It's not right, Mrs. Ross leaving her husband, taking up with the editor, and her still married. She's probably with him because Mr. McAllister has money and a big house.*

Mal Forbes preferred Elgin. He was from there, but his wife was from Daviot, a tiny place a few miles outside town, only notable because there was a station where the trains stopped for water. He accepted they had to leave their home. He knew there were too many prying eyes in Elgin and no hiding Moira's condition from his nosy cousin Effie.

Thank goodness Mother and Father aren't alive, he thought as he saw Moira through another bout of screaming and crying and pulling out her hair. At first he'd enjoyed the times when Moira was so full of energy she would literally dance on the kitchen table. The following bouts of sadness were bearable; all she did was lie on her bed and stare at the ceiling, playing with the corner of a pillow slip, chewing it, sucking it, until the thin cotton fabric gave way. As the years went by, the long periods when she was stable became shorter. The cycle of crying and sleeping and doing nothing, followed by hysterical laughter, cleaning the house from attic to coal shed, and hardly sleeping were becoming more frequent.

More than once the doctor in Elgin had tried to persuade him to commit Moira to an asylum for treatment.

"The place in Aberdeen is excellent," the doctor said. "Think of it as a rest from the illness, not an asylum for the insane."

"Insane? Who's insane? I'm not insane," Moira was so angry, he had to hold her back from attacking the doctor. He held her arms as she shouted, "I'm not insane. Mal, tell him, tell the doctor, I'm never insane."

He knew that the people waiting in the doctor's reception had heard. He wouldn't have been surprised if passersby on the street heard. Sure enough, the rumor ran around town, and he witnessed the sly looks, the shakes of the head, when they walked to church the following Sunday.

That had been bad enough, but his cousin Effie coming to visit regularly, more to stare than offer real help, wringing her hands, saying "The poor soul," over and over . . .

"Honest to God," Effie had said, "it's a right shame. There's never been any loonies in the family before now."

He'd thought he might have an episode himself, and smack the interfering cow across the face.

And now this. He didn't think he could cope. There was no one they could tell. No one to turn to. Once Mal Forbes had broken down and cried real, deep sobs, deep howling crying. No one comforted him. No one heard, so he thought. He didn't know the sound had carried through to his daughter's bedroom and terrified her.

He was not a real drinker. But one time, at twelve o'clock midday, he had poured a substantial dram and drunk it down, and the rest of the day paid for it. So drinking as solace was not an option.

His wife blamed everything on Joanne Ross. *If she hadn't interfered, we wouldn't be in this predicament. It's all her fault, Joanne high-and-mighty Ross.* Quite how his wife had come to this conclusion, Mal had no idea; it was completely illogical, but he knew that once she took against someone, Moira was unshakable.

He heard a slight murmuring from the bedroom. Moira was asleep, knocked out by the extra strong medicine he saved for emergencies, medicine he had great difficulty making her swallow. He knew it was Maureen reading to her wee brother.

"A good lass," he said to himself. "I don't know how I'd cope without her."

Effie, the woman from the teashop in Elgin, that's who it is, Joanne reminded herself as she was walking past Station Square deciding where to go to buy a tie for Don, a present for no particular occasion just that she was horrified at the state of the one he had worn every day for the last six months, and it was so disgusting she thought it might harbor a new strain of flora or faunae. The woman, who was walking whilst reading a bus timetable, stepped to one side, Joanne did the same, and then they stopped, looked at each other, smiling.

"Sorry," Joanne said.

"No, I'm sorry, it's this timetable, I canny figure out which bus to take." She flapped the booklet in the air. "Oh, hello, you're . . ."

"Joanne Ross, we met in your teashop in Elgin. You're Effie Forbes, the same as Mal Forbes."

"He's ma cousin." The reply was automatic. "I'm here to visit."

"But I thought . . ." Joanne was certain the woman had disowned Mal Forbes — or was it Moira Forbes — when last they spoke. "I work with Mr. Forbes."

"You never told me you're on the newspaper," Effie Forbes gave her a look, lips in a thin line, as if to say, *You lied to me.*

"It never came up." Joanne was searching for an excuse to question the woman. "Can I help you with the buses?"

That simple offer of help did it.

Honest, and, *Honestly,* and *To be honest,*

— the conversation lasted four minutes and forty-five seconds by the station clock over the woman's left shoulder. Joanne lost count of the number of times she used the word *honest* or variations thereof, but by the fifth time, she was certain the woman was lying. That and the way she rushed her words, patted Joanne on the arm, and kept staring directly into Joanne's eyes to emphasize her honesty.

"To be honest, we're not really close. I mean, honestly, what with his work, and me in the teashop, we hardly ever see each other, and honest to God, when he married Moira, well, we thought . . . she's not the friendliest of souls."

Joanne didn't know Moira Forbes, but she thought that would be her description of Mal — when she was being charitable.

"Aye, to be honest, we've no idea why he would want to move here." Effie gestured around Station Square. "My mother honestly thinks they were mad to leave, but you know, with the way things are wi' Moira's nerves . . ." Her hand had a life of its own; much like a spring on a mousetrap, it snapped across her mouth to stop the flow of words. Too late. Whatever she was hiding had partially escaped.

Her eyes searched around. Rescued by the

clock, she gave a shrill cry of "Is that the time? Honest to goodness, I'm that late they'll think I'm no' coming. The Laurel Avenue bus goes from over there, does it no? To be honest, I've never been here much, so I'm all at sixes and sevens. Nice to meet you again. Bye for now."

She was off in a fuss of scarves and basket and handbag and umbrella and what looked like a Red Cross emergency parcel tied neatly with brown twine, clearly addressed to Mrs. Malcolm Forbes, which bulged out of the basket. A box, possibly a shoe box, where the wrapping paper didn't quite meet, also tied with twine, dangled from her fingers. There was no address, only the name *Maureen* in huge capital letters.

Joanne watched Effie Forbes running, or rather lumbering, as the Laurel Avenue bus swung around the corner into Queensgate. She jumped on board; the bus was delayed by a woman with a baby and two small children and the week's shopping, then took off, leaving Joanne staring after it, wondering what on earth Effie Forbes had been so panicked about.

As ever, when it was important, it was the unimportant little words, thoughts, memories that put the pieces in place.

"I thought you said it was Mal Forbes who is sick," Joanne said to McAllister as they sat in his kitchen reading the Sunday newspapers.

"I thought so too, but when I called round to his house, their daughter answered the door saying her dad was sick, then he appeared and said he was fine, that his wife is sick. He's taking time off to look after her. Fair enough, as long as the work's done, I don't mind where he does it from."

"Aye, I heard she has trouble with her nerves."

McAllister laughed, "Oh, what it is to be Scottish." He saw her smile, but she was smiling at his laughter. "Why can't people say she has a mental illness? It's nothing to be ashamed of . . . it's as natural as . . ."

"Appendicitis? Scarlet fever . . . no, not that, that's catching . . ."

"Maybe a broken bone. I've always thought of it as an illness where something snaps . . ."

"But from a reason?"

"Maybe, maybe for no reason, just that a person's mind is stretched to the limit . . . I've seen that more than once." He was quiet when he said this; he had seen it many times during the war.

"The war is fourteen years over, and still

some minds are damaged." She was think-ing of her former husband.

"Moira Forbes, have you met her?" Mc-Allister had never seen the woman and was curious.

"I've seen her at the school but I don't know her. Fiona's met her. She sometimes comes in with a flask and sandwiches for Mal, so Fiona says. Remember I told you about the woman from the teashop in Elgin? Mal's cousin? I almost literally bumped into her in town yesterday. She was carrying a parcel addressed to Moira Forbes and one for Maureen. But in Elgin, she said she hardly knows them."

"Hardly knows — another Scottish way of saying definitely knows but is not friendly."

"You should write a dictionary." Joanne was flicking through the *Sunday Post* and as ever had to stop and read *The Broons,* her favorite cartoon strip of everyday life in an everyday Scottish family. Ma Broon and the adventures of her brood of assorted children, who were drawn as though they all had different fathers, always made her smile and occasionally had her laughing out loud.

McAllister had taken out his pen and was writing down the side of the newspaper. He stopped, got up, and went to the kitchen dresser, where he kept the copy paper he used to make lists of messages needed for the week. *Messages,* Joanne was thinking, *another Scottish word that confounds the English.*

"Messages means shopping," she'd explained to a girl at school.

"No, it doesn't," the English girl had replied, "it's the plural of message." They never did agree on that word — or much else, as Joanne recalled.

Elgin. Mal Forbes. Came to Highlands. Why? Mae Bell comes to Highlands. Why? Nurse Urquhart attacked. Why? Anonymous letters, why? Mae Bell leaves without a farewell. Why? Time frame? All close. Events linked? Maybe. But how?

"Questions, questions, all there is is questions," Joanne said as she looked over the lists.

"Fine, I'll start another list," and he headed a paper *What We Know.*

"Not much of anything at all, McAllister," Joanne said.

They began laughing, and Annie came into the kitchen to check if she was missing out on something adult. The girl saw her mother was happy, and that was enough. "I want to read, so I'm going to bed here tonight."

McAllister liked the way Annie treated the house as though it was her home.

"Jean's asleep," she informed her mother. "McAllister better lift her up the stairs to bed. Night-night."

Joanne looked at McAllister and said, "So that's us told."

He looked at her and decided he wanted the rest of his life to be like tonight.

On Monday, Mal Forbes came in for the morning meeting, didn't say much, and then left.

Early Monday afternoon, Joanne had an hour or so to spare, and checking with Fiona, she learned that Mal Forbes was meeting the manager at McGruther & Marshall, the coal and timber company. She decided to call on Moira Forbes.

She couldn't think of what to take, so she bought grapes and was horrified at the price. She caught the bus, leaving her bike at work. She walked up the path and rang the doorbell, thinking she had an hour before the children came out of school, which meant an hour to talk to Mrs. Forbes, see if she could help, and be back in time to finish an article on new traffic lights in Eastgate.

She rang the doorbell. It took a long time

for an answer.

"Hello, I'm Joanne Ross, I work with Mal. I heard you're not feeling well so I brought you some grapes." As she said it she realized how lame it sounded, how much of a busybody she must appear.

The small woman in front of her had an odd shape, short but wiry, reminding Joanne of a circus acrobat she had once admired. Dressed in a glittering leotard, it was the acrobat's muscular legs and arms and thick torso Joanne had noticed. *I bet she could lift a heifer,* she'd thought, and was proved correct when the woman bore the weight of her male partner on the high trapeze.

Moira Forbes had the same body shape, but her unwashed fair hair, the darkness around the light grey eyes, skin that resembled a garment that had been washed so often it no longer had an identifiable color, all showed she had been ill for some time. *This is more than flu,* Joanne thought, *this is a long-term illness.* She thought it might be the unsayable, cancer, and her heart went out to Mal Forbes and her family.

"I know about you," Moira said in a tired voice, but there was a hint of malevolence in the whine.

Joanne thought she must be mistaken. *The*

poor woman's ill.

Moira's hand reached out, a surprisingly large hand for such a wee woman, and again Joanne was reminded of the trapeze artist. The eyes looking every way except at Joanne, she took the brown paper bag with the grapes, and without another word shut the door, leaving Joanne ashamed at her audacity in visiting a woman she'd never met, for reasons she couldn't quite fathom.

Joanne took a deep breath, her shoulders dropping as she blew the air out, telling herself, *Think how offended you would be if a complete stranger turned up on your doorstep . . .*

The voice was too faint to give a name to, but not the tune.

Stormy weather, since my man and I ain't
    together . . .

It was coming from the back of the house. Joanne went to the high fence that cut the front garden from the back.

"Da da daaa, da dah da da, dada daa . . . stormy weather . . . hmm hmm hmm hmm hmmhumm, keeps rainin' . . ."

A shiver ran through Joanne. Mae! She wanted to call out "Mae Bell!" but knew she shouldn't. She went to the side of the

354

house, to a gate, padlocked, and saw the fence continued three yards before joining with a high stone wall, with meager, child-sized footholds in the crumbling mortar.

Putting her handbag in an azalea shrub, Joanne clambered up, losing the skin from two knuckles before she was over and in a long back garden of mostly lawn. An old air raid shelter was at the far end. She moved quickly. Another two padlocks locked the door, and the single window was sealed up with corrugated iron that was not quite big enough, allowing gaps at the sides for thin shafts of light.

"Mae, Mae Bell, it's me, Joanne," she was trying to shout in a whisper.

"Joanne! Oh, Joanne! Get me out of here. Please get me out!" Her voice was weak; her singing had been stronger.

Joanne could hear the tears. The panic. "The door's padlocked, I'll see if I can pull this off the window." She had her fingers in the lower gap, was pulling as hard as she could when she felt rather than heard the person behind her — then a crashing, a thunderbolt of pain on the side of her head. Then no more.

"McAllister, it's Annie, I'm at Granny and Granddad's house because Mum didn't come home. Granny is really cross. Can you tell Mum to come and get us?"

"Your mother isn't here." He knew Joanne hated leaving her children for that hour and a half between school ending and her arrival home from work. He knew she would never leave them longer unless something had happened.

"Where is she then?" Annie sounded scared. "Where's Mum?"

"Annie, what's your grandparents' address?" He tried to keep his voice calm but Annie could hear his fear.

"Come quickly." She hung up the phone.

He ran to his car. He didn't have time to lock his front door. He drove so fast over the bridge he almost hit the sandstone pillars on the south side. Annie was watching out the window and had the front door open as he was halfway up the garden path.

"I think you should talk to Granddad," she said. "Granny's in the kitchen with Jean and I don't want Jean to know."

McAllister could see how pale the girl was, every freckle clear, in spite of the steady, I-can-cope-with-anything voice.

"Maybe you should join them," he replied.

"No." She was eleven years old yet she was aged; or no age; perhaps the universal age of a female worried to death about a loved one — husband, child, sister, brother, fading parent; a female whose role was to sit and wait; to knit; to make tea, a role all too familiar in the twentieth century, a century of not-too-distant wars. "No." Annie was certain. "I want to know what's happened to Mum." She showed him into the sitting room.

Granddad Ross rose to meet McAllister, held out his hand, and thanked him for coming, saying, "I'm sure it's nothing," and not meaning it.

Granny Ross looked in to see who the visitor was, nodded at McAllister, and said, "I'll put the kettle on."

Annie began, "Mum didn't come home. She's sometimes late, but not as late as this." It was twenty to eight — almost Jean's bedtime. "She wouldn't do that without telling someone."

This time it was McAllister's face that said it all. He was terrified.

"Not five minutes since, we called the Royal Infirmary and Raigmore Hospital and she's not there," Granddad said. "Then I phoned the police and they've heard nothing."

There was a knock on the front door. Granny Ross answered. "Come away into

357

the sitting room," she was saying. It was DI Dunne.

"McAllister. Mr. Ross. Mrs. Ross." He looked at Annie, wondering if he should speak in front of her. As no one dismissed the child, he continued, "My sergeant called me to say you were asking after Mrs. Joanne Ross. Is there a problem?"

From looking at them he could see there was a problem. He would not normally be concerned so soon after a person was missing — it being a matter of only hours, not days — but the phone call worried him. And with the anonymous letters, and the death of Nurse Urquhart, he was taking the nonappearance of Joanne Ross seriously.

"I'm going to phone Rob, just in case she's there," Annie said, and left the room.

"Does the child know?" DI Dunne asked.

"It was Annie who had the presence of mind to come over to her grandparents' when Joanne didn't come home. Annie also called me to ask if her mother . . ." McAllister sat down.

Granny Ross came in and handed him a mug of tea.

Annie came back, saying, "Mum's not there and Uncle Rob's coming over." This time she looked close to tears.

Her granny took her hand, saying quietly,

"We mustn't let Jean see there's anything wrong," and led her into the kitchen.

The roar of a motorbike shattered the quiet of Dochfour Drive. Rob ran down the path and came in through the back door.

"Where's Joanne?" He was looking as distraught as McAllister, but had not aged the ten years McAllister had in the past half hour. "What's happened to her?"

"Joanne's late home. She probably had an accident on her bike or . . ."

"No, she leaves her bike next to my motorbike. It was still at the office when I left," Rob said. "When did you last see her?"

DI Dunne was about to ask the same but Rob got in first.

"Late this morning, around eleven." McAllister couldn't remember if she had phoned anyone on the *Gazette* after that. *I must check.*

"It's too early to worry." DI Dunne took control. "In case she turns up at home, someone should leave a note for her."

Rob nodded. "I'll do that."

"Mr. McAllister, you'd best wait at your house." McAllister nodded, relieved DI Dunne was taking charge. "We will check the hospitals, check around town. Please give me a list of her friends . . ."

"Her father died recently, maybe . . ."

Granddad Ross was clutching at the proverbial straw.

"I'll call her brother-in-law — the Reverend Duncan Macdonald," McAllister explained to the policeman.

"I'm off to Joanne's house," Rob told McAllister. "Then I'm going to call in on Don, see if she's there. Then I'll come over to your place." He wanted to do something, anything, to find Joanne. He was chilled with fear, and the memory of Nurse Urquhart, her fate, her funeral, kept surfacing as fast as he tried to block it out.

Annie came in. "Uncle Rob, I think you should tell Hector. He sees things other people don't notice."

"You're right." As Hector lived nearby, Rob volunteered to do that first.

"Everyone should call me at the police station if you hear anything, or think of anywhere Mrs. Ross might be." The inspector was readying to leave, his request more a command. Despite his initial thought that it was too early to worry, he felt a great unease at the absence of Joanne Ross. "No matter how insignificant it may seem, if you have any information, call the police station."

DI Dunne shook McAllister's hand, then Granddad Ross's, and left to organize a search. It was clear the detective was taking Joanne's absence seriously, and for that McAllister was eternally grateful.

When he walked into his own kitchen, McAllister found the letter on the table.

SO WILL YOU STILL MARRY THAT
MEDDLING BITCH WITH HER
FACE BURNED OFF AND HER
EYES BURNED OUT AND
HER DAUGHTERS THE SAME?

There was no need to wonder how someone got in — the door was unlocked, the key under the doormat. McAllister made straight for the phone to tell DI Dunne.

When Rob arrived, he said, "Sorry, Joanne is not with Don."

Don came in behind him. McAllister pushed the note towards them. It was Don who said what Rob and McAllister were avoiding.

"This is from the same person as wrote the first letters."

McAllister slumped in his chair, his head in his hands. "For God's sake, man, I can see that!"

DI Dunne first rang the doorbell, then walked straight to the kitchen. After a bustle of questions, the answers being "No," "I don't know," and "No idea," and with neither McAllister nor Rob nor Don McLeod having anything useful to tell him, the policeman left with a sense of fresh urgency, taking the note with him.

McAllister was glad of the absence of the malignant piece of paper. He sat at the table smoking, replying to questions only in grunts.

Don waited out the night with McAllister, saying little, making tea, keeping the whisky consumption to a minimum, knowing they needed to think straight, returning the kindness the editor had shown him in his time of troubles.

Rob had no idea what to do with himself, so, finding the wireless in the kitchen wasn't working, he spread an old *Gazette* on the table and proceeded to take it apart. When he had put the wireless back together again, but before returning it to its Bakelite casing, he tuned it in, and was pleased to hear the shipping forecast. Less pleased when he realized a cold storm front was making its way across from Norwegian waters straight to Cromarty and the Moray Firth — their waters, their region.

McAllister thought that night the longest of his life. He knew it was a cliché, and he was a wordsmith who hated clichés, but the night and the clock stretched towards dawn with a reluctance that made him ache, physically hurt.

DI Dunne called around at seven in the morning with no news. He found Don asleep on the sofa, Rob asleep in a chair, and McAllister awake in the kitchen.

"I'm sorry, Mr. McAllister, there's no news . . ." The inspector saw the life force drain out of the editor, from his face, his shoulders, his legs — so much so that McAllister had to sit again at the table.

"We're doing all we can . . ." the inspector added.

"No news?" Don came in and saw McAllister's face. "Right. McAllister, me and the boy are away to the office. We'll keep in touch." Don motioned to Rob saying, "We've a newspaper to put out," leaving McAllister to maintain the vigil.

Fiona came in to work at her usual eight o'clock and was amazed to hear sounds from the reporters' room so early in the morning. Hector came in half a minute later and explained. Fiona burst into tears.

Bill Ross called McAllister and asked if he could help. It was the first real, albeit brief, conversation they'd had, and McAllister was grateful for the offer. "Better to call DI Dunne," he'd said.

Joanne's sister, Elizabeth, visited, bringing McAllister bread and bacon and eggs, and she cooked him breakfast. Mortimer Beauchamp Carlyle, one of the *Gazette* directors, called round and brought a bottle of the Glenlivet, offering help and feeling helpless, knowing all he could do was keep McAllister company as they waited out the hours for Joanne's return.

Then the gale hit. And the rain. It didn't let up. It rained and rained and the gutters flowed and the river rose and the trees waved and wept, and McAllister waited, along with everyone else.

But no one knew anything, except Mae Bell and whoever had locked her in the air raid shelter.

They were in a double-bricked-up space at one end of the small shelter. Not much wider than a coffin, their gaol was six feet long and completely dark; the door was invisible from the outside, hidden behind a cupboard. There was a draft coming from somewhere, although Mae Bell was yet to identify the source. There was also a puddle of rainwater creeping into the semi-underground cellar. From where, again Mae couldn't tell.

It had taken hours of patient cajoling, but the boy now let Mae touch him. In this space, which he seemed familiar with, he leaned into her as they lay on the tarpaulin and blankets that the madwoman, as Mae called her, had thrown in after them. Then she and her husband — *Equally mad!* Mae had shouted at him — had padlocked the door before moving the cupboard back.

Mae was now seriously worried. Joanne had been unconscious for far too long. She bathed her friend's head from the pail of drinking water. The bleeding had stopped, but even in the impenetrable black, she knew Joanne's injury was bad. Perhaps, without help, fatal.

When the door was once more unlocked — in the morning, Mae thought, as she had lost track of time — she shouted, "Get Joanne out of here. She'll die if she doesn't get help."

Moira Forbes whispered, "Shoosh. I told you, any sound an' I'll kill you."

Mae could feel the child tremble. She hugged him and forced herself to slow her breathing.

Moira laid a tray with a cake tin of porridge and three spoons and a bottle of milk on the floor at Joanne's feet.

"Now that Joanne is missing, they will come here looking for her," Mae said. *Keep calm. Always sound bored,* she told herself, *for the boy's sake show no fear.*

"Maybe, but if they do, I'll throw the acid, and I don't care which one of you it catches."

"Moira," Mae Bell deliberately used her name, "with Nurse Urquhart, I'm sure it was an accident. If Joanne dies, it will be murder. Please call the ambulance, a doctor, someone. Please" — she was pleading, but she couldn't help it — "I'll leave, I'll never bother you again . . . please get help for Joanne."

"And have them steal my boy? Never." Moira stepped back, holding out the small, flat blue bottle as though warding off evil.

With the final sound of the door shutting, then the padlocks, Mae had to dig her overlong fingernails into her palms, almost breaking the skin to stop herself shuddering. And crying. The sound felt like the final closing of a coffin lid.

"Eat," the boy said. So they did. And still Joanne had not stirred.

TWENTY-ONE

"I will interview Mr. Forbes again, and if I find good cause, I will get a search warrant, but so far, there's not enough evidence for one," DI Dunne repeated for the third time.

"It's a day and a half — nearly two nights. Joanne would never abandon her children." McAllister was pacing in the narrow gap between table and wall, pulling at his hair, thumping the table, reaching the other end in a few paces, glowering at DI Dunne, who stood, coat on, hat in his hands, immobile, immovable. "Mal Forbes had the opportunity to steal the acid from the *Gazette*. He could easily have left the anonymous letters, he and Joanne are on bad terms . . ."

"Excuse me, Mr. McAllister . . ." It was Mal Forbes. "I couldn't help overhearing . . ."

"The whole town probably overheard." This came from Don, who was sitting at the far end of the reporters' table watching the exchange.

"It's not that I don't get on with Mrs. Ross, we just see things differently." Fortunately for Mal Forbes, he was standing on the other side of the table from McAllister; even with his long arms, the editor couldn't reach him.

"Where is she?" His voice as harsh as a raven's. "What have you done with her?" This time pleading, his voice lowing like a bull at the slaughterhouse gate.

"I'm sorry, Mr. McAllister, I haven't done anything to Mrs. Ross."

Don thought from the way Mal Forbes spoke and the way he held his head — the brilliantined hair, the gleam of his false teeth, the unconscious way he tugged at his equally gleaming shirt cuffs with regimental cuff links — he might be telling the truth. *But he's a salesman,* Don thought, *deceit comes naturally.*

"You're from Elgin." McAllister was clutching at the proverbial straw, knowing there was nothing to connect Mal Forbes to Joanne's disappearance, to Nurse Urquhart, nothing.

"I don't see what that has to do with anything." Mal Forbes cocked his head to one side — the embodiment of puzzlement.

He is *hiding something,* Don decided,

368

watching Mal's every move, every blink, catching a twitch in the left corner of the man's mouth.

"Mr. Forbes," DI Dunne intervened, "would you mind coming to the police station and making a statement?" It was not a request. He needed to separate the two men.

"Not at all." Mal went down the stairs with not a word more.

The inspector was buttoning his coat. The wind was still fierce. "McAllister, I'll keep in touch, but as I said, you're best off at home. Maybe Mrs. Ross will come back there, or call you, or . . . Good morning, gentlemen."

The inspector, now he's definitely lying, Don thought.

"What do we do?" McAllister slumped onto a chair, elbows on the table, head in hands.

"Is someone at your house in case Joanne turns up there?"

"Mrs. Ross Senior. She's there until I get back."

Granny and Granddad Ross had the girls staying at their house but had made them go to school.

"No one will harm the bairns now they have Joanne," Granny Ross told her husband. "So no sense in worrying them by doing things different." She was convinced Joanne had been kidnapped. Why, she couldn't say. Worse she forced herself not to think about.

That morning, after leaving the girls at the school gates, Granny Ross continued on her bicycle to McAllister's house. With only a *Good morning, Mr. McAllister,* she went straight to the kitchen, put the kettle on, and started to cook breakfast. She knew there was no news. He'd have said if there was.

Whilst he was eating, she started on the dishes. When he'd finished, she said, "Go to work, you're worse than useless here. I'll mind the phone. Dad is staying home in case she rings there." She was in her usual flowery housewives' cover-all apron, her hat she kept on, held to her scalp with the usual array of lethal hairpins. She spoke matter-of-factly — keeping busy was her solution to all dramas.

As he was making for the front door and work, she asked, "Where do you keep the hoover?"

He wanted to rush over to her and hug her but knew he might break down; the ordinariness of Joanne's mother-in-law's words concealed her emotions — and he had no doubts they were legion. And he knew that when he came home, his house would be scrubbed from top to bottom and the front step and the brass doorknob and knocker gleaming.

"McAllister, we have to get a newspaper out," Don had told him when he arrived at work. As with Mrs. Ross, work was what McAllister needs, Don thought, *else the wait will break him.*

They took the layout Fiona had prepared, both too tense to notice how professional it was.

Hector came in. He said little; Fiona had told him there was no news. He handed over a larger-than-usual sports section, bigger pictures taking up most of the space. He was guessing, rightly, that without Joanne, and with McAllister in a mess, the *Gazette* would need filling with something, anything.

"I've added an article and a picture of the ladies' hockey team as well as the usual football reports," Hector said, giving the photo to Don.

"Thanks, lad." Don sized it up, filled another page.

"I was wondering how I can help." Hec looked as miserable as the rest of them.

"Leave it to the police. We're best getting the paper out."

Hector walked down to reception. He was

exhausted. And scared. He'd been out until late in the night, joining in the search party of friends, neighbors, Joanne's brother-in-law, and many of his parishioners.

He knew Bill Ross was helping coordinate the search for the mother of his children. He had taken his van, and with three comrades from his old regiment, volunteered to search the Islands, knowing it was one of Joanne's favorite places to sit and think — something he had never understood.

Hec was hoping against reason that she might have fallen, was hurt, *But please, not fallen into the river.* If she had, he knew well enough there was little chance of her being alive; although not deep, the river was wide and swift, impossible even for a strong swimmer.

He had seen police frogmen preparing to check the canal at Muirton. He knew the harbor had been searched and fishing boats in the firth were asked to keep a lookout. He knew the army would be called in next to search the outlying woods and hills and other likely places. He knew that meant they were searching for a body.

Hec also well knew that the town and countryside and glens and hills were easy places to lose a body; a swift-flowing river, deep, dark lochs and empty moorland, woods and wells and quarries all within easy reach of the town. And in the town itself, there were many places a person, or a body, could disappear.

"Still no word?" he asked Fiona.

"Nothing." She was as scared as him and knew that publishing the newspaper was essential. "I wonder if the *Gazette* will run an appeal for information . . ."

"That's two days off — they have to find her before then." Hec leaned over and took her hand.

She let him, even though she had vowed to never show affection in public. "Hector, I've never been this scared in my whole life."

"Me neither."

Upstairs, Don was thinking the same thing; he didn't voice the thought in front of the others, but he was mentally preparing a front page appealing for information on Joanne's disappearance. He daren't contemplate worse.

Rob came in. "Here, some copy for page five, and the article on the town dogs worrying the sheep at the Leachkin farms." He didn't take off his jacket. He was dangling an old aviator's leather hat with sheepskin-lined earmuffs in one hand and the bike keys in the other. "Elgin," he said. "Joanne was convinced Mae's search for information about her husband was the cause of all" — he gestured to thin air — "all this. So, Elgin, or the air force base at Kinloss, is where it started. I'm thinking of driving there."

McAllister said, "I don't see how that will help find her."

"I'll be back tonight, and it's better than doing nothing."

They all understood, and McAllister envied Rob his freedom to escape, to drive fast, to burn up the frustrations on his red motorbike.

"Aye. But drive carefully. We need you." He coughed, looked away, knowing Joanne's disappearance meant almost as much to Rob — and Don — as to him.

He told Rob, "When we were in Elgin searching for information on Mae and Robert Bell, Joanne said the woman in the tea shop, who turned out to be Mal Forbes's cousin . . ." He got up, tried to shut the door, but as it had been open for a century, it wouldn't move. He went into his office. Rob followed. Then Don, who shut the editor's door.

"Joanne thought the woman in the tea shop was hiding something about the Forbes family. I also got the feeling the editor of the newspaper knew something but didn't want to gossip."

"First time I've heard of a journalist who doesn't gossip," Don said.

"I could go and see him," Rob offered.

"No, you're too young. I'll give him a call — one old journalist to another. But you talk to the women, that you can do right well, so . . ." Don looked at the clock, looked at Rob.

"I'm off," Rob said. "The tearoom in the town square, you said?"

McAllister only nodded. He was lighting a new cigarette from the previous one, his mouth felt foul and his bones were hurting and his eyes were gritty and his brain had all but seized up.

"Don't drive too fast, it's no' worth it." Don patted his reporter on the back "We don't need to . . ." *lose another reporter* he was about to say, and caught himself just in time.

When they were alone, McAllister, needing to fill in the silence, started, "I used to think that when you love someone and you were parted, you'd know if they were alive or dead," speaking to himself more than to Don. "But I don't believe that anymore. I have no idea where she is, or why she's missing. I'm terrified."

Don knew that terror better than anyone

at the *Gazette*. "She's not dead yet. Until you know, you should always hope." Don's voice, his words, were firm. And he didn't believe a word of it. "Back to work, McAllister."

This was the day for McAllister to compose the editorial. Don decided to pass the task on to Mortimer Beauchamp Carlyle, chairman of the *Gazette* board and sometime correspondent on matters rural, who could be relied on to conjure up the right tone, the right topic for such times. When it arrived, the editorial was on spring in the glens, and the moors and the farms and foreshores, an innocuous piece on the rhythm of life. More a poem, it was beautiful and right and full of hope; no one wanted to anticipate the worst.

Rob arrived at Nairn so fast he scared himself. He overtook the Aberdeen train rattling along on the track that ran parallel to the road. He passed a convoy of army lorries. A steam-road roller, as massive as a leviathan, he overtook on a sharp corner.

He drove the next twenty-five miles less fast, the countryside no longer a green blur; the horns of cars, lorries, and buses, from drivers he had scared the wits out of, no longer a long, fading moan of fear accompanying him out of every bend, every blind corner.

He drove into Elgin Town Square. He looked around at the stone façades of offices and shop fronts with rooflines of crow-stepped gables, the fountain, the menacing church filling one side of the square with heavy columns reaching skyward to impress the faithful and intimidate the unbeliever. Amid the architecture of old and ancient and no discernible modern, he spotted the tearoom; half curtains of lace, the obligatory strip of faded tartan on the window ledge, an assortment of decorative plates on stands interspersed with china ladies and figurines of cute wee bairns of the maudlin variety, posed with lambs, or dogs.

A bell clanged as he opened the door. He introduced himself to the woman he assumed was Effie Forbes and ordered tea.

She covered her surprise well. She asked after Mrs. Ross. When he explained she was missing, she said, "That's terrible. Honest to God, what's the world coming to?" But he knew she knew. He could tell by the way she moved her hands, the way she said "honest."

He sat listening to Effie warble on. He was drinking tea and demolishing three scones with lashings of butter and homemade raspberry jam; he was certain she was prevaricating, and was waiting for her to give herself away.

After half an hour, just he was despairing of finding out anything at all, the bell above the door clanged. Five women came in. By the hats and coats and sturdy walking shoes, Rob knew they were town worthies. *Some sort of committee,* Rob thought.

Effie Forbes rushed forwards to seat and serve them, then stood chatting as though she were having an audience with some relatives back from visiting the queen at Balmoral.

The young woman who came from the kitchen with a fresh batch of scones, piled high on a plate covered by a glass dome, was a younger, more attractive version of Effie.

She asked Rob, "Are you wanting a fresh pot o' tea?"

"No thanks, I'm full." He grinned at her. "Did you make the scones? They're terrific."

She smiled back and leaned just that little bit too close, clearing the crockery and knife and empty teapot. "Meet me outside the Assembly Rooms at six," she murmured.

"We're needing fresh scones at this table," her sister called across the tearoom. She'd glimpsed the hurried exchange and was not at all pleased.

"Don't you be talking to strangers now," Effie said to Aggie, the younger sister, who was putting on her coat.

"There's no one else interesting to talk to in this place," her sister said, but was out the door quick smart before Effie could comment.

Rob had an hour and a half to kill before the meeting, and as he wasn't into visiting ancient monuments — of which the town had plenty — he went to the library to read the local newspaper. The *Gazette* looks good compared to this, he thought. At five to five, he was asked to leave by a woman who so resembled Effie Forbes that he thought Elgin must be populated with women from the same clan — or close cousins thereof.

He was leaning against his bike, keeping an eye on the high street, when Aggie Forbes came up from behind and said, "Hello stranger." She giggled. "I came up the back way," she explained, looking around in case Effie was lurking behind some column or monument or statue. "Can we go somewhere out of town?"

"Where?"

"I'll show you." Aggie knew Rob was look-ing for information, and if it meant she would see more of this exciting, good-looking stranger with a dangerous motor-bike, she would help all she could. She swung a stocking leg over the pillion seat. An old boy on the pavement watching them caught the white flash of thigh above her stocking tops, sending him halfway to a heart attack.

Rob and Aggie ended up at a café on the main road north, frequented by long-distance lorry drivers and Teddy boys.

Rob ordered bacon, eggs, sausage, black pudding, and tattie scones, plus a work-man's mug of tar-black tea — breakfast at half past five in the evening.

"Did you hear about the woman who works with me on the *Highland Gazette* who's gone missing?" he asked Aggie when he'd finished.

"Mrs. Ross? Aye, I heard about it on the wireless. Effie said she was the woman who came into the tearoom a couple of weeks ago." Effie hadn't mentioned to Aggie her visit to Moira Forbes, or running into Joanne again. "Is Mrs. Ross your friend?"

"Aye. We work together and she's my friend." He told Aggie about Annie and Jean and babysitting them. He told her about McAllister and Don and Hector, and Mal Forbes now working with them, and how everyone was terrified that something had happened to Joanne. "She'd never leave her girls," he finished.

That decided Aggie.

"Mal Forbes is our cousin. He met Moira when he was working as a clerk at the air force base — you know, RAF Kinloss. Moira was working in the same office when they were first walking out. Granny Forbes told him she was flighty, but he never listened, he was right crazy about her." She shook her head. "It turns out she was the one that was crazy."

"Really?" Rob had on his best I-want-to-hold-your-hand smile.

She explained to Rob about Maureen, Moira and Mal's first child. "Before she was married she was good fun — so ma sisters say. After the birth of their Maureen, Moira went a wee bit funny and Mal looked after her, really good to her he was. Then she got better. Then she insisted on going back to work. Mal hated that, but ma granny took care of the wee one. When she was expecting again, and when she had the boy, she was sick for at least a year after. And they say the boy's no' quite right." The child Aggie had never seen, but she didn't tell Rob that. She looked at him, saying, "There's no loonies on our side o' the family." She had been terrified it might be catching.

"That's all really sad." *Get on with it,* Rob was thinking, but knew not to hurry her.

"When Mal told my mother they were moving north, he said it was because there's better doctors there."

The asylum maybe, Rob thought, *but for his wife or his son or both*? He asked, "Do you think Moira Forbes is still ill? Ill enough to do something silly?" He was thinking, *Kill someone? No,* he told himself, *Joanne's alive, she has to be.*

"Oh, aye." Aggie was delighted to dissect her cousin's wife, divulge family secrets to a stranger. Talking about Moira Forbes was almost a sport among the Forbes sisters. "Moira takes some queer turns and there's no knowing what she'll do. One time she went to Aberdeen and bought a shopful of clothes — not for herself, mind, for Mal and wee Maureen. But none of them fitted so he had to take them back and . . ."

"How does Mal cope?"

"As I said, he's crazy about her. He can't see how much worse she is since she had the boy. If you had a child who's not quite right, plus a bampot for a wife, it's no wonder he needed to live where no one knows them." She said this kindly; the idea of keeping family troubles away from prying

382

eyes seemed reasonable, especially in a small town like theirs where gossipmongering was as much a sport as the football.

"Would Moira Forbes harm someone?" Rob persisted. He needed some facts if he was to persuade the inspector to search the Forbes house for Joanne.

"Naw. Never. She's only a wee thing. All she does is cry a lot, then laugh a lot. She's great fun most o' the time, really good to go out wi' to the dancing and the like." Aggie didn't know this for certain, had only overheard her two elder sisters talking. "Mind you, she's strong — hauling sacks o' tatties on the farm when she was young," she said.

"What about Mal, would he hurt anyone . . . to defend his wife?"

"Oh, aye, he'd have a right go at anyone who said anything nasty about his wife. As I was saying, he's absolutely besotted wi' her." She couldn't think why. Then again, she couldn't understand why everyone didn't want to leave their small town like she did.

"It's late, I have to get home," Rob said. "Thanks for your help, Aggie, but I'm no further on finding Joanne."

"Aye, but you found me." That was when Aggie Forbes started kissing him as though her escape from the small town depended on it. And before long, they were on a bench by the river kissing and cuddling. At first Rob was kissing her because she had helped him and he needed to charm her as a potential witness. Although she had been the one to start the kissing, he was never one to say no to a bonnie lass.

It took half an hour and many promises to meet again before he could escape Elgin. The drive back was cold and hard. He stopped twice to relieve himself. *I've drunk gallons of tea, but found out very little.* He stopped again when he was ten miles from town to clap his hands, as he had forgotten his gloves and his fingers were dead.

Arriving back in the late evening, he decided it was too late to call on McAllister. *And there's not much to tell.*

He now knew Moira Forbes was ill. *Nutty as a fruitcake,* as Aggie Forbes put it. *But is Moira Forbes capable of . . . ?* Here he stopped. He had been thinking, *killing Joanne.* But had to forcibly change to — harming Joanne. Kidnapping her. Hiding her. Anything but killing her. That Moira Forbes had attacked Nurse Urquhart Rob considered a strong possibility. That she would attack Joanne was what he was terrified of. *But still there's no real information that will force the procurator fiscal to sign a warrant to search the Forbes home.*

He slept five hours. He came into the office early, hardly showing the lack of sleep. Today was deadline day. He was needed. He reported his findings to McAllister and Don. Then he telephoned DI Dunne. Then got on with the ordinary task of the newspaper.

Two hours later, DI Dunne called McAllister. "I spoke to Mal Forbes. Their son was committed to an institution in Aberdeen before they came to the Highlands. That was the main reason they came here — for a new start. The boy has been diagnosed as mildly" — and here DI Dunne had to consult his notes — "autistic." He hesitated before saying more, then relented, knowing how distressed McAllister was. "I was also told that although Moira Forbes is sometimes unwell, she is stable. She is on some new drugs and is not a danger."

He didn't tell him that Moira Forbes had received a course of electric shock therapy. This was confidential information even he was not entitled to, but he had persuaded the doctor in Elgin to divulge, saying it was a matter of life and death. Which the inspector believed it was.

When DI Dunne repeated that there was no news of Joanne, McAllister dropped the receiver into the cradle. Lifting his head to the high window, where rain was streaming down like water from a hosepipe, he let out a roar of pain. Everyone who heard it felt the hurt, the wound, the despair.

TWENTY-TWO

Mae thought it must be late afternoon or early evening. She knew Moira Forbes would be bringing supper soon, and this time, she was determined she would escape. *Have to,* she was telling herself, *I have to. Joanne is getting worse by the hour.*

"McAllister?"

"It's Mae Bell. Here, honey, drink some water." Mae felt for Joanne's lips, held the plastic cup to her mouth. Joanne spluttered. Then asked, "Where am I?"

The words were slurred, the voice so low, Mae only heard because for once the boy had stopped his background humming. Since Mae Bell had been locked up with him, first in the big room and then, when Joanne was captured, in this cellar, his repertoire had expanded from one traditional Scottish lullaby, two nursery rhymes, and what Mae recognized as "Frère Jacques, Frère Jacques, Dormez-vous? Dormez-vous?" Though how the boy would know that song she had no idea.

"Moira Forbes has us locked up in an outhouse. The woman's as mad as a hatter." She tipped the plastic cup up to Joanne's lips. "Drink a little more."

"I thought you'd left." It came out as though a full stop was after every word.

"Without saying good-bye? My dear friend, I'd never do that." Mae was putting into her voice all her experience singing love songs from the heart; she was giving Joanne the warmth and love they needed to stay strong. The despair she kept for the long hours when Joanne lapsed back into unconsciousness.

"I can't see," Joanne murmured.

"It's nighttime." Mae knew it was day because Moira was due to deliver the clean bucket and the water and the sandwiches for their evening meal — never anything at lunchtime. Mae lied because she couldn't tell Joanne they were locked up in a narrow, semi-underground sarcophagus in the darkest dark.

When the noise of padlock and chain and scraping furniture awoke Mae Bell from her more and more frequent spells where nothing penetrated, not even the boy's humming, this time she was prepared to attack the woman; Joanne's head wound was dangerous, perhaps fatal if they were not rescued soon. And her friend's condition gave Mae an added incentive to attack — if only she didn't feel so lethargic, if only her legs would move when she told them to, her arms lift without effort, her fingers not fumble with simple knots. Most of all she wanted her eyes to clear, the red clouds, the clear film swimming over the eyeballs, to disappear.

The door opened. Moira Forbes was illuminated in the fingers of light coming from the gaps in the sheeting over the window in the main part of the shelter. One hand was holding the small bottle out to one side. With the other she was putting a small brown cardboard box inside the door.

Moira, her voice kind, almost apologetic, speaking as though it was a completely normal conversation, was saying, "There's sandwiches in the box but stay in the corner please till I've gone or I'll have to throw the acid in your face." It was as though she was warning a child not to go too near the fire.

Mae knew Moira would throw the acid without hesitation. She could still see the wild, staring eyes, the saliva leaking from a corner of her mouth as the woman had held up the bottle, when Mae was first captured, saying, "You'll get the acid in the eyes, not in the throat like the nurse. That shut thon busybody up, didn't it?"

Mae would never forget how Moira held out the blue glass bottle, saying, "It will make a fine mess of your face. Burn your hair off, too."

That day — Mae thought it was ten days or perhaps two weeks ago — Moira Forbes had come home from her doctor's appointment early, the queue being long, the wait an hour, so the receptionist had told her.

Mae knew that Moira was part of the clique who went to the dances held in the air base canteen. Mae now knew that Moira had known Robert. She knew Moira was already married to Mal Forbes, with a daughter, but that didn't stop her flirting with the airmen. She had found out that both Mal and Moira were working at the air base at the time of the plane's disappearance. Mae was convinced something had happened.

Then Moira had caught Mae Bell trying to pry the metal off the air raid shelter window. Mae Bell was trying frantically to reach whoever was crying bitterly, from pain or from fear. Moira had come up behind her, unheard because of the sobbing from the shelter, and grabbed Mae Bell by the hair, yanking her backwards onto the grass.

Moira was sitting on top of Mae Bell, straddling her. She started pounding up and down on Mae's torso like a frenzied perversion of sex, knocking the wind from Mae's lungs.

"What are you doing in my garden?" she'd said, the voice direct into Mae Bell's ear, not loud, more a hissing noise. And spitting. Mae felt the saliva running down her neck and longed to wipe the evil off her skin, but with both arms pinned to the ground, she could barely move. She was kicking, squirming, trying to bite, then decided on calm. She went slack. She would use her voice. Moira was too strong; she had the strength of a gymnast — or a woman possessed.

"You know what's in here." She took a bottle from her pocket, and without taking off the lid, she terrified Mae. She was waving it in Mae's face. "I'll pour it into yer eyes, see if that stops you being so nosy."

"Hey. Let's talk about this. I'm sorry. If you let me up . . ." Mae tried to talk to Moira the way she would talk to the old horse that lived out the back of her late grandmother's place in the country. "I'm sorry," but Mae found it hard to say more than "sorry."

The continuous keening of the voice in the shed was disturbing, heartbreaking. Mae couldn't compete. She went stiff. The terror in her eyes was clear to Moira.

"That's better. Now I'm going to get up and you're going to go into the shed. Then I'll bring us all a nice cup o' tea."

Mae had done as she was told. She went into the shed. At first she did not see whoever was in there with her. She sat on the floor, handed over her handbag; she had done everything Moira Forbes told her to do — the flat blue bottle hypnotizing her.

Mae waited first for Moira to return with the cup of tea. That didn't happen. She waited for the person whom she could hear breathing noisily through mucus-filled nostrils to calm down and speak.

Mae met the boy in the dark, dank shelter. Immediately she saw him in a chink of light; when she saw him, she knew he was Robert's child. For days and nights he cowered in the corner and wouldn't speak. It was like taming a wild animal. Moira must have put something in his food, because at night the boy slept for twelve hours, barely moving. In the daytime he was restless, lethargic.

It was after hearing the distant voices of strangers in the house that Mae and the boy were moved to the underground part of the former air raid shelter; from a dark, damp, but not pitch-black room to the semi-basement of a dirt-floored, narrow, coffin-shaped space at the end of the original shelter. Normally the boy was in the house during the day, but after whoever it was had visited, no more daylight for the lad.

It's like those atom bomb shelters people in the States are being told to dig, Mae joked to herself.

Her sense of humor was now exhausted along with every part of her body. It was Mal Forbes who had dragged Joanne in. Mae had been hoping, praying, he didn't know of his wife's madness and would release her when he found out she was being held prisoner. The sight of Mal holding Joanne by the arms, ignoring the blood from her head, ignoring the obvious — that she was injured, unconscious, in need of a doctor — made all hope vanish.

Mae Bell had tried to reason with Mal Forbes. "Help me. Help Joanne." He didn't answer. *It's as if he can't see or hear me,* she thought. *As if he's hypnotized.*

Moira was now removing the empty food containers. Then she took out the bucket that was near the door. Next she passed in a pail of fresh water — all the while holding out the bottle of vitriol.

"You must get help for Joanne." Mae was trying to keep her voice calm. "No one will miss me, but you can be sure the police and everyone else will be looking for Joanne."

"No one cares about Mrs. Joanne Ross." Moira put in an empty toilet bucket before taking out the full one, as calm and organized as a farmer cleaning out the pigpen. "That woman's nothing but a hoor, living wi' a man she's no' married to."

The boy was moving, swaying, muttering, not words, only sounds but increasing in volume. "Muuum. Reeen." He hated the smaller room, the one he was always locked up in when he tried to get out into the garden and the light. He hated having to share with two big people, the space so tight he couldn't move around. He tried to stand.

"Get back!" Moira shrieked.

He moaned. Mae tried to grab his leg but missed. His moans became louder. Mae was horrified that even in these wretched, torturous conditions, he was reaching out to the woman saying, moaning, *Mum. Muum.* Reaching out for a touch from this monster. This demon he called Mum.

"Go on, get in there. I promise I'll be back for you soon, ma wee man. Just wait till we're rid o' them two, then you 'n' me'll be thegether again."

That phrase sounded like a death sentence — *just wait till we're rid o' them;* it paralyzed Mae Bell. She knew what she'd said was true; there would be a major search for Joanne. Apart from the police, and her colleagues, she was absolutely certain McAllister would never give up until he found Joanne. *The man is in love. He is intelligent. He will do all that it takes to find her. But will he be in time?*

"Let us out or you'll be the one locked up!" Mae Bell had summoned all the strength she could to threaten the woman, but Moira Forbes shut the door and all Mae could hear was the rattle of chain and padlock, the moving of furniture, and silence.

She felt across Joanne's body and held her fingers lightly against her temple. The pulse was faint. She tried the wrist. Very faint. The bleeding had stopped. Externally anyhow. Internal bleeding was another matter she tried not to think about. Her hearing was keen, and the lightness of Joanne's breathing, the shallow in-and-out, worried her most of all.

Joanne spoke — or rather breathed, single words, minutes, half hours, hours apart, throughout the day; consciously or unconscious Mae could not be sure. *McAllister.*

Water. Father. Nits. Water.

Mae was unsure of the last word but the boy said, *nits,* and scratched his head with both hands, saying, *nits, nits.*

Mae told him, "We don't need nits right now."

The boy smiled, the whiteness of his teeth creating a flash in the pitch black. "No nits. All gone." He reached out and touched her lightly, and the touch of his wee hand on her leg made her almost weep; but she didn't. Knew she mustn't, knew if she started she would not be able to stop.

No nits, she was thinking, but the itching, the crawling sensation on her skin revolted her. She tried rubbing her hands and arms and legs with cold water and the edge of the filthy sheets she had lain in for . . . *How long? Two weeks? Less? More?* She rubbed the dirt off in small granules, pellets, making her feel slightly cleaner. She stank but could no longer smell herself.

She was so hungry she was no longer hungry. *Don't need to use the bucket as much,* she said to herself, taking comfort from small mercies. It was the clumps of hair coming out in fistfuls when she scratched her head that upset her the most. *Robert loved my hair.*

"A real blonde," he said when they first

spent the night together.

Not so much anymore, she thought.

"Nits." Joanne spoke clearly this time. "Nurse Urquhart . . ." she faded again.

Next night when the door opened, it was dim outside, northern long gloaming dim. With the toilet bucket removed, and the water bucket full, Moira put a tray with bread, cold potatoes, digestive biscuits, and a lump of cheese inside the door. The cheese, although tasty, with bread and biscuits and not enough water, made Mae Bell thirsty. But the boy liked it. He also had extra rations.

"Some nice ham sandwiches for you, ma wee lamb," Moira crooned at the boy. "Thank you, Mummy," he said. He'd learned good manners meant treats. "Good boy, Mummy. Can I play with Maureen?"

"Maureeen," Joanne echoed in a voice so low it came out as an elongated keening.

"Get her a doctor, you bloody madwoman." Mae was struggling to stand. "Throw your dammed acid but get her a doctor." She fell backwards, landing on Joanne's foot. Joanne jerked, gave a cry, then passed out.

This time, when Moira Forbes once again dragged the cupboard across the door and they were left in the dark so black that the air itself felt heavy like a woolen wartime blanket, this time, Mae started to sob.

She shook. Her body convulsed with sobs so deep, she felt she would never have the strength to take the next breath. The little hand patting her, small regular pats on her back, slowed the sobs.

"There, there, dinny cry." His accent an exact echo of his sister's, the gesture the same. He patted Mae Bell, his father's wife, his father's love, until her breathing became regular. Then she slept.

And when both women were deep asleep, he pressed up against the door and whispered, *Maureen, Maureeen.* He whispered at irregular intervals for almost an hour. He breathed the chant, *Maureen, Maureen, Reen, Reeen, Reeeen.* He stopped. Listened.

He heard movement but not the moving of the cupboard. It was too heavy for Maureen to shift, but she could whisper to him. The old door her dad had used, when he blocked off the space at the end of the shed with the two leftover sections of timber from the fence, did not fit. There was a good four inches at the bottom, wide enough for Maureen to pass a banana, a packet of short-bread, three gobstoppers, and a comic through. It never occurred to her that he could not read. Nor see in the complete dark.

"Crying," he said. "She's crying."

"Don't worry. She'll be gone soon."

"New lady's sick."

This puzzled her. She knew Annie's mother had disappeared. She had heard her father shouting at her mother: "Moira, I can't protect you this time. The police are already suspicious."

Could it be . . . ? No. Why would Mum . . . ? She tried desperately to work out what was going on. She had heard her father make odd noises. He sounded like he was crying.

"Moira, Moira. What were you thinking?" he'd asked.

For Maureen, this was the worst part — her father crying. She felt helpless. She felt lonely. And really scared.

"I have to go," she whispered through the gap in the door. "Night-night, Charlie, see you tomorrow."

"Nigh-nigh, Reen."

As she crept back to the house, taking care to keep to the shadow of the fence so her mother would not see her, she thought about it. *The lady would be gone soon; her dad said so. But what about Annie's mother? Is she in there too? And how will the other lady leave? Will she catch the train? Will she keep the secret about Charlie? Will the welfare come and get him like Nurse Urquhart threatened?*

Maureen knew it was all her fault. Her mother had told her after Nurse Urquhart came to visit that it was all her fault.

"Why did you tell her you have a brother?" Moira shouted. "We've told you never to mention him. Now they'll take him away."

"The nurse asked if we had brothers and sisters 'cos they might have nits too." Maureen was terrified. And confused. *Maybe Charlie would be better off somewhere else. Somewhere he could run and sing and sleep in a real bed.*

That night before going to sleep, she knelt down beside her bed, clasped her hands like her mother taught her, and said her prayers.

"God bless Mum. God bless Dad. God bless Charlie. God make me a good girl." She opened her eyes. Then quickly closed them. "God bless Annie Ross's mum and help her come home."

Her mother came in to kiss her good night.

"Said your prayers?"

"Yes, Mum."

"Good girl." Her mum ruffled her hair in that way Maureen didn't like.

When the lights were out, and the wind

still, and the night dark but bright with stars, Maureen was almost asleep when she heard it. Not the song, but the tune. The one she had taught Charlie. He didn't know all the words, but he remembered most of them. He learned the tune even after her singing it only two times. It was a song she learned in school choir. She listened again. Yes, it was Charlie. Singing the song she had taught him, his voice was high and sweet and true. And the woman, the lady as Maureen thought of her, she was joining in. Faintly, but singing along with her brother —

Dreams to sell, fine dreams to sell,
Angus is here wi' dreams to sell . . .

Throughout the town, there was a sense of busyness. More police walking the streets, and many volunteers, going into shops and cafés and bars, into the Victorian market, the bus station, the train station, the petrol stations, distributing the poster that Don had the printers make up, headed MISS-ING.

Underneath was a picture of Joanne. Hector volunteered the photograph, one he had taken of Joanne leaning against the guardrail on the riverbank. She had been joking with

Rob, unaware Hec had his camera out. Her hair flying in the wind, her head slightly to one side, her eyes bright even in black and white — you could see that if you met this woman, she would light up your life.

Most of the phone calls to the police station were people asking *for* information. And the sightings — they were for days and times before the disappearance. One person thought she had seen Joanne on the Dochfour Drive bus, but she couldn't remember the day, only that it was early afternoon. That being the bus that passed her parents-in-law's house, it was dismissed.

Annie Ross went into the newsagents on Glen Urquhart Road near her school. She had stopped the home delivery of the *Girl* comic. As they now regularly stayed at McAllister's house, she preferred to collect it herself and pick up the *Bunty* for Jean. When she saw the poster with her mum smiling out at her, she ran outside to grab her sister. She always complained Jean was a slow coach, always hated waiting for her sister to catch up; this time she was grateful.

"The comics aren't in yet." She surprised Jean by taking her hand, saying, "I have a sixpence, let's catch the bus." She could see one in the distance. She was desperately hoping it wouldn't have the picture of their mum. There was no picture. It had fallen down and the conductress hadn't put it back up, as she had no sticky tape.

"Two halves to Dochfour Drive, please." Annie held out the money, then took her sister's hand again. That was what scared Jean.

"What's happened to Mum?" she asked quietly, knowing Annie might answer, knowing no grown-up would.

"I don't know." Annie was staring straight ahead, kicking the seat in front as though she were six, not eleven. "She's gone off somewhere and forgot to tell anyone." That was what she was trying to believe, but failing. She knew their mother would never leave them.

"Let's say a prayer." Jean closed her eyes tight. Still holding Annie's hand, she started, "Dear God, please tell Mum to come home. Amen." That was it. No more.

Annie was close to crying. She opened her eyes. They'd missed their stop. She rang the bell. They hurried down the stairs. Hand in hand they walked back to their grandparents' house. Granny Ross was waiting for them. Desperate for something to do, she was in the garden weeding the rockery. She looked up. Seeing her granddaughters

403

walking towards her, holding hands, she could not stop the tears. She rushed into the house, calling out to the girls, "I think I left the gas on."

Maureen Forbes saw the poster taped to the inside of the phone box on the corner of her street. The border of the pane of glass cut off the words, but she recognized Joanne Ross; she had seen her dropping Jean and Annie off at Sunday school and thought she looked happy, not like her own mum. She knew Mrs. Ross was missing — everyone in their class was talking about it. And she was scared. She didn't know why she was scared, but why had the police come to their house, twice that she knew of, to ask about Mrs. Ross?

She was in a hurry to get home. She was eleven and a half and only her mother knew she had started her periods three months ago. She had been terrified, no idea what was wrong. She thought she was really ill.

She ran into the house. Her mother was in the sitting room, sleeping with the curtains closed. Maureen could tell from the way she was breathing and the small bubbles of spittle coming out of the side of her mouth that Mum had taken too much of her medicine. Nothing would wake her for a long time.

She went into her parents' bedroom, to the double wardrobe. Mum left the pads in a brown paper bag in the back, behind her shoes. It was dim in the bedroom. Mum always kept the curtains shut. Maureen felt around for the bag. Her hand caught something unfamiliar, something leather. A bag, it felt like. She took it out. It was not new; it was not her mother's. She put it back. She had what she came for, went to the bathroom, went back to her bedroom. But curiosity about the bag made her check her mother. Moira Forbes was snoring lightly; it was safe.

She opened the wardrobe again and took the handbag to her bedroom. It was brown, not very big, closed with a clasp in silver, and had a shoulder strap as well as handles. Inside was a purse, a hankie, a wee spiral-bound notebook full of what looked like scribbles, a pencil, and a fountain pen — a blue-marbled Conway Stewart that looked old.

Maureen took out the family allowance book. Her mother had one, so she knew what it was. She opened it. She read *Mrs. Joanne Ross.* Underneath, it had *Annie Elsie Ross* and *Jean Joanne Ross* and their dates of birth. She was so shocked, she

405

didn't even register Annie's middle name — Elsie — a name that in better times she would have teased her almost friend about.

The back door opened. "Hello. Where's my girls?"

She shoved the bag under her bed. But she kept the family allowance book, putting it under her pillow. "I'm doing ma homework," she called out.

"Good girl." Her father went into the sitting room. She knew she would be left in peace, as Dad would be busy cooking. Then he would waken Mum.

That night, as she often did, she wanted to talk to Charlie, but she was scared, terrified her dad would find out. She was absolutely forbidden to visit Charlie when he was in his wee room out the back. The one time her dad had discovered her secret was because Charlie had nits — caught them from her. It was the first and only time he spanked her.

"Never ever go out there again. You only play with him when we are all together," he told her. "I'm only thinking of you, Maureen love — you might catch his disease. How could I cope with three of you sick?" It was the only time he admitted that Mum is sick, she remembered. *Charlie isn't sick,* she told herself, *he's just different.*

406

Tonight was not a night to risk going down to the shelter. Tonight, when Dad woke Mum up for her tea, her mother started sobbing loudly and long. "It's no' my fault, I'm so sorry, Malkie, but it's no' ma fault."

Maureen thought she would put in the little balls of cotton wool she sometimes used to block out her mother's crying.

In the night, when her mother had quieted, and after her father had come in to say night-night, and she had heard him shut their bedroom door, she felt under the pillow for the small cardboard-covered book, making sure it was safe. She was scared but did not know why. She was trying to forget the shelter in the garden, the strange woman, Charlie, her mother, her dad, who was trying his best to pretend everything was normal, but Maureen could see how worried he was. Most of all she was trying to ignore the poster with Mrs. Ross's face, looking out of the telephone box, smiling saying, *Hello, Maureen.*

Next morning Moira Forbes was coming in the back door and heard someone ringing the doorbell. It was barely light, but to her nothing and no one was strange.

Mal answered. He was in pajamas and

dressing gown. "Good morning." He looked at his watch, his gesture and the look of surprise as exaggerated as a mime artist. "Nothing wrong, I hope?"

His pallor, the way he tried to brighten his voice but the voice coming across as too bright, too controlled, his arms protruding from his pajamas, stick thin, worried the policeman, making him think there was more than one person unwell in the house.

"Good morning, Mr. Forbes," DI Dunne said. "We'd like another word with you, and I'd like your wife to join us."

"My wife is not well enough to talk to anyone. I'm right worried about her . . . woman's troubles, I'm afraid. She might need an operation. The doctor will be around later." He hadn't called a doctor. *But the policeman will never know that,* he was thinking. "Come in, come in."

In the sitting room, Mal Forbes sat down without inviting the detective and constable to sit, making the policemen stand over him. In his despair, Mal Forbes had forgotten his manners — and betrayed his anxiety.

He shot up out of the chair. "Sit down, sit down, do you want tea? Can I get you a drink? I'm so sorry. My manners. Sorry. It's just the wife, she's not at all well."

Moira Forbes was listening in the kitchen,

hearing what she thought of as her husband's working voice. The sitting room was at the front of the house, the bedrooms in between, so from the kitchen she could not hear the conversation. Not that that bothered her; she was sublimely unaware that their situation was critical. But she knew that her Malkie was upset at her.

What were you thinking? He'd said again and again. *Moira, this has to stop. You have to let her go.* Then he said, *We'll be in real trouble when she tells everyone what you've done.* He'd even cried a wee bit before shaking his head and washing his eyes and face and telling her he'd look after her. Take her to the doctor for help. That had really frightened her; she was certain that doctors were looking for an excuse to put her in the asylum along with all the loonies.

Mae Bell she hated. *Coming here, asking all those questions about Bobby and the accident.* "What accident?" she'd asked. But the American woman said Robert had told her he was worried someone was out to get him.

Moira vowed that the woman would never be found. *Not wi' all my pills inside her to keep her quiet.* Moira was particularly proud that she'd thought of giving the woman her medicine inside the gingerbread. The woman had eaten a slice, *said it was delicious but you could see in her face she tasted something strange — too late*! Moira smiled, remembering the way the woman wrinkled her nose and took a sip of tea to take away the taste. *But there was medicine in the tea, too!* Moira laughed out loud at that recollection.

Says she's Bobby's wife, indeed, Moira fumed. *He loved me. Besides, all that happened years ago, the aeroplane disappearing, all that. What's the point in looking for answers now? There aren't any. They're all gone.*

She was listening for the conversation with the police to end. Often she was certain she could hear through walls, but not this time. She went back to quietly stoking her rage.

It's her, thon woman, she's the one made me put the wee lad in the cellar again. He should be out in the garden these evenings; he loves the flowers and the birds. Sings back at them so he does. Note-perfect.

She started drumming her fingers on her thighs. *Mal says we have to let her go. Give her answers, then she'll go back to wherever she came from. Hah! I'll make sure she goes back to where she came from — in a coffin — just like thon nurse.*

410

The boy had to be put in the cellar along with the American woman and Joanne. Normally he slept in the nice part of the shed. She remembered making lace curtains and cushions — when she could still operate the sewing machine — lately she couldn't figure out how on earth the machine threaded. She bought him toys and made sure the bed was nice, but as he grew older he was less and less happy to be shut in a shed for long periods of time. That was when she had to threaten him with the cellar. She used the cellar more and more to hide him away. *But that's because I'm right tired.*

Moira told herself she had to hide the boy. *In case someone sees him and takes him away. We look after him; we keep him safe and warm. We wouldn't give him away to strangers,* that was her logic.

Although Maureen was curious about her little brother, she accepted her mother's wisdom. "We don't want him taken away, do we?" her mother had said. "He can't help it he's different — it's the Lord's judgment on his sins." What sins a wee baby could commit was as yet beyond Maureen's capacity to argue.

"Yer dad, he's a good job, brings in good money so we can have a nice house an' nice clothes, an' a wee holiday or two, and mind you never let your dad know you and Charlie is friends."

Moira Forbes used her daughter to help with the more difficult tasks of looking after the boy. Maureen could quiet him when he started shrieking, banging the doors to be let out. When Charlie was particularly difficult — kicking and pushing to get out into the garden, Moira would say to Maureen, "Keep him happy, talk to him. Don't let the neighbors hear. We don't want the shame o' a backwards boy, do we? Think what your friends would say."

The time Nurse Urquhart had come to visit, asking about the boy, had been horrible and set her mum off on a bout of crying and screaming that lasted days if not weeks.

"Mr. Forbes, the records show your wife had a boy five and a half years ago. You say he was committed to the hospital in Aberdeen, but I can find no record of that. If you won't give me more information, I will have to tell the police."

Her mum tried to attack Nurse Urquhart at that visit, but her dad stopped her in time, saying Mum had forgotten to take her pills.

No, Maureen decided, she didn't want the

shame of a loony brother, she didn't want teasing at school. There was a girl in her class whose brother had polio. Some of the children tormented this girl, saying she couldn't join their games; they would refuse to have her on their team or refuse to sit next to her on the bus in case they caught polio. Maureen hated the thought of what would happen if they found out about Charlie. It had been bad enough being a new girl from Elgin with a different way of talking — one girl asked if she was from the moon. Another asked if she was a loony. They laughed at that.

Now that she was eleven and a half, Maureen found it hard when she and Mum and Dad went on their "wee holidays" — mostly on the train to Aberdeen, where her mum went to see a doctor. Not a normal doctor but a doctor in this huge, dark hospital outside the city. It's because your mum's delicate, Dad explained, she needs medicine for her nerves.

"Why can't Mum go to the hospital here?" Maureen had once asked.

"We don't want anyone knowing, do we?" Mal Forbes replied.

When they arrived in Aberdeen on the train, they then had to catch a bus to the hospital, which was way out in the countryside up on a hill, and could be seen for miles. A man in a uniform had to let you in, as the doors were locked. When Mum was with the doctor and she and her dad waited outside, they would watch the strange people wandering around, some talking to themselves, others saying nothing, just looking at the ground and shuffling their feet. If she walked like that, her dad would say, *You're walking like your slippers are too big.*

The times when Maureen begged them not to leave her brother alone, her mother insisted, *It's only two or three days, he'll be fine.* But Maureen knew how he hated being left alone with cold food, mainly biscuits, and only water. *Milk goes off,* her mother said, *and lemonade is bad for your teeth.*

When her brother saw the biscuit tins he'd start this wailing noise that her dad said sounded like a wolf. Even though she did not know what a wolf sounded like, Maureen became upset; there was something haunting, scary even, about the boy's cries; it was like being at the pictures watching *Snow White,* waiting for something bad to happen, knowing it was not all *fine,* like Dad said it was.

Most of all, when they went away, Maureen was upset because her brother would have no one to empty his bucket for days. Her mum told her that as he was backwards, he wouldn't notice. She doubted that; when they returned, the stink was so horrible, you could smell it all the way across the garden and in the kitchen — even with the door shut. Her mother told her not to be ridiculous, but Maureen remembered Mum wrapping a scarf around her mouth and nose when she went in to clean after a holiday.

Maureen could hear the policeman in the hallway. He was leaving. She knew it was the policeman who came before from his voice. Maureen was ironing her school uniform. Dad said Mum always forgot to switch the iron off. She didn't mind, she liked ironing. She heard the front door shut. She came into the sitting room and asked, "Who was that?"

"Just something to do wi' work," her dad said, but she looked out the window and could see a policeman in uniform open the door for another man, who had a hat on and a raincoat. She thought he looked like the detective who came to the school after Nurse Urquhart was attacked.

Her mum and dad were now arguing in a soft, half kind of way. She didn't mind arguing; it was the crying she hated. Especially her dad crying. She went to the kitchen.

She ate a spoonful of the porridge her mum had put out. Cold. Salty. Lumpy. She took the porridge and flushed it down the toilet. One time she had put it in the bin, but her dad found it and shouted at her for wasting good food.

What's good about watery salty porridge? she wanted to ask but didn't. Her dad would slap her, but not hard, just a wee slap on her hand or arm. He wasn't like Annie Ross's dad, who, another girl had told her, hit hard enough to leave marks.

Her parents were still arguing, shouting now, so she went out the back door, looked at the sky. No rain on yet. She wheeled her bicycle to the side gate, heard a noise from the shed, and ran to say bye-bye to her wee brother.

"Help." Followed by a banging on what sounded like a bucket. "Help, please help." The voice was faint, and normally Mum had the wireless on loud so you couldn't hear anything from the shed. *She's forgotten to switch it on,* Maureen thought.

"Help!"

It wasn't her brother. It was that woman Mum said was staying in the shed to help her brother with music lessons. It seemed strange to Maureen that a woman would stay in a shed, but then, her mother had been getting stranger and stranger these past months.

"Charlie?" The boy had no name. He was just "the boy." But Maureen had named him Charlie after Bonnie Prince Charles, who came from over the water to rescue Scotland. "Charlie, I have to go to school, but . . ."

"Please help us. She'll die if you don't get help." The woman no longer shouted. Her voice sounded funny, *like when you forgot to wind up the old gramophone,* Maureen thought.

"Maureen! Get away from there!" Her mother was screeching in that voice that meant she was about to go "berserk," as Dad put it. She ran back and grabbed her bike.

Who the woman was, Maureen didn't want to know. And why she had been there two weeks, she didn't want to think about either. There was a lot Maureen didn't want to think about — things like her mother, her brother, nits.

Her father came out, shooed her mother back into the house, unlocked the side gate, saying, "Your mum's not feeling great today." Before he locked the gate after her, he said, "You're a good girl, Maureen, but mind and keep quiet about . . ." He looked

417

towards the shed. "You know." He nodded. "And we don't want them taking your mum away, do we?"

"I'll never tell no one."

He patted her shoulder and gave her half a crown. She put it in her coat pocket. *It must be bad if Dad's given me a whole half a crown,* she thought as she cycled to school.

Mal then made his wife a cup of tea and gave her an extra one of the extra-strong pills, enough to knock her out whilst he decided what to do to get them out of this disaster. He shook the brown glass bottle. The pills were nearly finished. He knew Moira was feeding them to Mrs. Bell and he went along with the scheme. *Until I can work out a way to send her back to America or Paris or wherever.* That had been before this latest disaster.

Moira was weeping, quietly this time, weeping as easily and as naturally as breathing. Mal understood that she truly loved the boy; she was his mother after all, but she didn't love him the same way he did. He loved the boy in ways he didn't understand. He had given up so much — a job, his home, and his friends — for the boy. He had done something wicked to preserve their family. And now this.

Even Maureen suffered for the boy's sake,

never having friends round to play, never having a wee birthday party in case anyone saw him. They'd all suffered. But he was worth it, their boy. One smile from him and everything was forgotten, forgiven.

Mal looked out at the dying daffodils along the flower borders beneath the high timber fence. The boy loved daffodils. He would clap his hands and shout, *dancing, dancing,* whilst the daffodils and jonquils and narcissus did indeed dance in the wind.

And now this. Mal was looking out of the kitchen window, staring at the shelter at the bottom of the garden, half hidden by a lilac bush and a rank of parallel rows of raspberry canes. Moira had calmed down, the medication taking effect, sipping her tea, totally unaware that disaster waited — whichever way this finished. But Mal knew. He was repeating to himself, *How on earth are we going to get out of the mess? What on earth can I do to save us?*

"Does Malkie still love his precious wee Moira?" Her voice was that of a seven-year-old.

"Always," he replied. And he meant it. "You know I'd do anything for you."

He took her cup, took her arm, led her into the bedroom where the bed was still unmade. He took off her slippers, he held her hand until she fell asleep.

He went back into the kitchen and turned on the wireless. He caught the news bulletin in the midst of a statement about a missing person. He heard the name, Mrs. Joanne Ross. He jumped up to switch the wireless off. He sat again at the table, his head in his hands, the tears dripping onto the tablecloth. He sat there for a long time. Nothing, no solution came to him. So he made another cup of tea.

It never occurred to him to take tea to the shelter. That was Moira's job. He seldom went there — except when he had to help Moira move Joanne Ross.

He didn't go there because he did not believe it was his business. *She's not right in the head,* he reasoned, *she can't help what she does, but it's nothing to do with me.*

He'd done his part to save their family years ago. Moira and Maureen — keeping his family together was all he cared about. Then the boy came along. The calamity of their situation he refused to face. *If the women die,* he was thinking, *there will be no witnesses against us.*

Imprisoning a child, letting him out in the dark of night, letting him sleep in the house the few days in the year when the neighbors were on holiday, was, he believed, kind, not wicked. *People are cruel,* he told himself. *If they see him, they'll laugh, say nasty things about him, about all of us.*

He was angry no longer, only tired; everything that had happened was because Joanne Ross and Nurse Urquhart could not stop interfering. He was scared yet accepting; Moira was ill, she was not to blame. Through the prism of distorted love he could deny his own past guilt and present complicity in acts so evil they could cost lives.

He got up, put the kettle on, then decided to bake a gingerbread. *Moira loves gingerbread.* Everything vanished in the ordinariness of beating the butter and sugar, adding the treacle, the ground ginger. The smell: everything hung suspended with the smell of baking filling the house. For two whole hours he could deny his complicity. Then Moira woke up.

TWENTY-THREE

Mae was praying for Maureen to visit her brother. It seemed their only hope.

"Charlie, why don't you call Maureen?" she murmured, unable to find the energy to talk in the calm, soothing voice she used with the child.

"Reeeen." He was rocking back and forth, arms around his knees, keening, "Reen, Reen, come for Charlie."

Not loud enough, Mae thought. "Let's try singing," she said. She couldn't find the breath to sing. Nor to call out. And Joanne had even less breath. Mae felt her pulse for the eleventh time that day. Still there. Faint and slow. She had no idea what was normal, just that the pulse was harder and harder to find, Joanne's short bursts of semi-lucidity shorter and fewer.

In the morning, Mae vowed, *I'll beat the shit out of that bitch. I don't care if she throws the acid; anything is better than this.* She felt better. She had her courage back. She dozed. She plotted and planned exactly how she would grab Moira, how she would hit her, kick her, shove the bucket, any bucket, in her face.

Then she remembered how once, in Paris, she had seen this woman's arms — the skin wrinkled and puckered, red and blue ridges standing out like roads on a map, the hands twisted, fingers missing; the damage was hideous, and the pain evident in every movement. *An accident when she worked in a factory making batteries,* a neighbor had explained.

How much worse will it be on the face, in your eyes? Her breathing was rapid again, her legs and arms twitching.

Charlie gripped Mae's hand, singing a pitch-perfect version: *Stormy weather, stormy weather, keeps raining all the time, the ti-u-mmm.*

The lock was being opened. *I'll get her this time.* Mae tried to sit up, tried to kneel. Her whole body was shaking. Her head spinning.

"Charlie?" it was a whisper. "Charlie, are you all right?"

"Reeen."

"Charlie."

"Maureen, you have to help us," Mae whispered. "Annie's mum needs a doctor,

423

she's really sick, she might . . ."

"Reen, Charlie wants to play. Charlie disnae like dark."

"Maureen? Where are you? Maureen?" The shriek was coming from the kitchen.

"Coming, Mum." The girl stepped back and began to close the padlock. "I'll be back, Charlie. Promise."

Deadline day over with, McAllister drove home. He thanked Mrs. Ross Senior for being there in case Joanne should turn up. There was no need to ask if she had turned up, or telephoned; the look and the slight shake of the head from Joanne's mother-in-law said it all.

It was now three and a half days since Joanne's disappearance. The *Highland Gazette* ran with the front-page headline they all had hoped never to publish: MISSING.

Don arrived an hour an a half later, having watched the first newspapers roll off the presses. "Someone will see the paper tomorrow, and call us with information," he said. Don had said the same thing to the compositors and printers. They had nodded before turning away, not looking at each other, not wanting to say otherwise, but thinking, *Three and a half days.*

Rob arrived two minutes later with fish-

and-chips. McAllister was pointing out that Mrs. Ross Senior had left enough food for an army when the sound of the front door opening then slamming made him look up, his eyes light up, then shut down again.

It was Annie. She was out of breath. She had a stitch in her side from cycling across town, across the river, and up the hill, in the rain, on a bike with no lights because the batteries had run out. She had a cardigan and coat over her pajamas and her school satchel on her back. She went straight to McAllister, who put his hands on her shoulders. She shook him off.

"Granny and Granddad think I'm in bed," she started. She took off her schoolbag, opened it, took out a blue Basildon Bond envelope. McAllister stared at it, and couldn't speak. Annie took out the cardboard-covered book. "It's Mum's family allowance book," she said.

All three men stared at the envelope and the book.

"Where did you get it?" Rob asked.

"It was in my bag when I took out my homework."

They were all still standing. Rob pulled out a chair for Annie, then for himself, and he and she sat down, Rob deliberately close, arms touching. He had known her since she

425

was eight. He was her babysitter, her confidant, her adoptive uncle, although she thought of him more like a big brother.

"Let's do detectives. Where was it put in your bag?"

"At school."

"Do you have an idea who put it there?"

Annie hesitated. She had thought this through. Maureen Forbes had been following her around all day, asking about her mum, asking if she was upset, if Jean was upset, if anyone knew where her mum was.

In class in the late afternoon, much to Annie's embarrassment, she had started crying. She didn't know why. Maybe because Maureen was being so nice, asking her how she was so many times.

"I was crying . . ."

Rob knew how much it took for Annie to confess this.

"The teacher took me to the office and gave me an aspirin. My bag was in the classroom. Maybe someone put the envelope in then." It was the only time she could remember leaving it unattended.

After school, Granddad had been waiting to take her and Jean home. Maureen had come up to her saying, "I hope they find your mum really soon." Annie thought Maureen was about to say more when

Granddad came over with Jean, saying, "Would your friend like to come for an ice cream wi' us?"

"No thank you, Mr. Ross, my mum will worry if I'm late." Maureen ran off and Granddad bought the ice cream, much to Jean's astonishment; ice creams were for Sundays and treats.

Annie knew as soon as she found the envelope with the family allowance book that it was important, but she didn't want to give it to Granddad, who would give it to the police. She wanted McAllister to have it. Or Rob. *They will find Mum.*

It was only as she was waiting for Jean to go to sleep, and Granny to put on the wireless, the sound turned up because Granddad was going deaf after years working in the foundry, that she thought of Maureen being so friendly. She waited until Granny came in to say night-night and switch off the light, then she waited more — fifteen minutes — and sneaked out the back door. Granny Ross didn't know she had a torch.

After explaining everything, Annie looked at Rob and said, "Mr. Forbes who works on the *Gazette* is Maureen's dad. I think maybe Maureen Forbes put it in my bag."

She expected her statement to shock them. Instead she saw McAllister look at

Mr. McLeod, and Rob look up at both of them. Then they all sat around the kitchen, planning what to do. Annie stayed with them.

It was Don who remembered to call the Rosses. It was very late for a phone call, and Granny Ross woke Granddad, telling him to answer.

"I'm too old for bad news," she'd said.

"No, I'm sorry, I've no news about Joanne," Don said, then told Mr. Ross about Annie, reassuring him the girl was fine. Hearing Granny Ross insisting on coming to fetch her, Don said, "She's asleep, let's leave her here." He knew there would be no way Annie would go home until Joanne was found.

He came back to hear McAllister and Rob discussing the options.

"No, I'm not going to the police," McAllister said.

"So what do we do?" Rob was holding the book, examining it as though it was a passport to parts unknown.

"We . . ." McAllister looked across at Annie. Saw her face was alabaster white except for dark shadows under the eyes. *This is not right that a child. . . .*

Don interrupted the thought. "Annie, can you help me?" He too wanted her out of the discussions.

She came with him, knowing full well he did not want her to hear what McAllister and Rob were discussing.

"I need to make up a bed on the couch in the sitting room." He was pretending it was for him, but was hoping Annie would sleep whilst they sat out the seconds and minutes and hours, believing that whatever happened, the child had a right to be there.

If she's alive, the girl needs to know right away, Don decided. *And if she isn't . . .* that he couldn't bear to think about.

Rob had on dark trousers. He borrowed one of McAllister's numerous black jumpers. He had a black balaclava. He put a tire iron, a torch, and a ferocious flick-knife McAllister had acquired who knew where, probably Glasgow, into a haversack. He also took a small kindling axe — blunt — the only semi-lethal implement in the house.

McAllister too was in black, but that was his usual clothing. He packed a first aid kit, left by Mrs. Ross, *just in case,* she'd said, into the glove compartment along with a flask of whisky. He threw blankets and a pillow into the rear seat. He had a torch, a kitchen knife, and a length of washing line.

"Never know if we might need to tie

429

someone up," he told Rob. He also put in two empty whisky bottles — a broken bottle being a Glaswegian's chief weapon of choice.

They raced across the river and into the road leading to Mal Forbes's house. McAllister parked close, but not too close. They got out. The house was in a gap between streetlights. McAllister nudged Rob and pointed out the high fence at the side. They went back to the car.

"The fence is new," McAllister said. "It encloses the back garden. There's a gate on the north side, but it's padlocked."

"I can climb the gean tree then drop down the other side," Rob decided, "I'll try and open the gate, but if not . . ." *I'll do this alone* he was thinking. "But it would be better if there were two of us."

"I'll climb if I have to," McAllister said.

He waited in the shadows, watching Rob climb then disappear. The rain had lessened, turning to a thick, penetrating drizzle that made halos around the streetlights. The wind had dropped but still it was a dreich night. He watched the tree, the shadows it sent out, the splats of late blossoms lying at the base of the trunk, slippery, smelly, dead. He heard the seashore sound of the next-door neighbors' larch, hoping it would disguise any noise Rob might make.

He waited. He was desperate for a cigarette and daren't light up. He waited four
minutes and it seemed like a life sentence.
He started to creep towards the side gate of
the mercifully dark house.

The snap of metal, the clatter as the lock
hit the ground was loud and sharp and ter-
rifying. A light came on in the house. Rob
was yelling, "McAllister, McAllister get over
here." McAllister had no idea how, but he
tackled the gate, bashing at it, kicking it —
useless. *There must be a second padlock.*

He heard shouting. He stepped back, took
a run. Managed to catch the top of the gate
and swung himself up and over. As he
landed, he felt something give in his ankle.
He swore but kept running.

There were two torches shining at each
other as Rob and Mal stood in a standoff.
A wailing — like a banshee — unearthly,
high-pitched, rising and falling, came from
the outbuilding.

Then a voice, faint, but unmistakable.

"Help. Help us." Then a fit of perhaps
coughing, choking, as the voice gathered
the effort to call out again. "Maureen?
McAllister? Police?"

"Mae Bell, hold on!" Rob kicked at the
window covering, the metal sheet he had

been trying to remove when Mal had come out to see what the noise was.

"Mae," Rob was yelling when he made it into the shelter, his torch shining around the room. "Where are you?"

McAllister now had his torch on Mal Forbes. And Mal was not moving. He was standing, in his pajamas, head down. Weeping. "I'm sorry. I'm really sorry. Moira never meant to harm them."

Rob found the door. The cupboard had not been put back properly. "McAllister, get in here. Come on, man, help me."

The cupboard moved easily, but the door was padlocked. Rob found a spade leaning in a corner with other garden implements. He lifted it up and was hammering at the lock. The wood gave, not the lock.

When the door opened, the stench made them choke. McAllister was shining his torch inside. He saw the huddled bodies, saw a picture akin to the pictures of survivors of Bergen-Belsen.

"She's alive," said a creature he knew was Mae Bell — from the accent only. "Get us out. Joanne needs a doctor. Get us out. Need help . . . Joanne."

McAllister was kneeling. Feeling in the dark for Joanne. He touched the child he had caught a glimpse of in the torchlight.

Joanne was silent. Not moving.

Mae was crooning, "Hush, Charlie, hush."

The boy was moaning, "Maureeen, Reen."

The sound of a fire engine bell was coming nearer.

McAllister was on the floor, touching Joanne's hair, holding her hand. "I'm here, my love. I'm here, bonnie lass."

Rob was standing in the doorway, about to lift Mae Bell out. He never knew what came first, the shriek from the boy or the shriek as Moira Forbes came running at him from the far end of the shelter.

He shone his torch. Saw the bottle in her hand. He grabbed the spade, dropping the torch. He lashed out into the dark, catching Moira Forbes on the neck.

He felt the spurt of blood shower his hands and face. He dropped the spade.

McAllister shone his torch towards them. Rob was standing over the small creature spread-eagled on her back at his feet. They both saw her nightdress, already crimson with blood, so much blood it was pooling around her shoulders. McAllister saw the head at a sharp angle, barely connected to her neck. He flashed the torch upwards. But not before Rob had seen what he had done.

The men from the fire brigade came running into the garden — Maureen Forbes was awake, hiding in her room after letting them in when they started to batter the door with an axe.

She said, "Out the back," and two giants dressed in shiny uniforms and shiny hats and shiny boots yelled *Thanks* and ran past her.

She scuttled back to her room and shut the door and tried to disappear under the eiderdown, shaking and sobbing, terrified. *It's all my fault.*

Two uniformed policemen came a minute later and ran in through the open door and out towards the commotion in the garden. The young constable shone his torch on the scene and ran into the garden to be sick. The older man, Sergeant Patience, held his arm so tightly, tears came to the constable's eyes. "Get a grip, boy, there's work to be done."

An ambulance arrived next. The men needed the firemen to help carry two stretchers. McAllister went to hospital to be with the women.

Sergeant Patience asked Rob to hold the kicking, screaming boy whilst the medical man gave him an injection. He knew he terrified children — and adults. The sedative took effect quickly — "He's just a wee bag o' bones," the ambulance man said, "better

434

bring him to hospital an' all."

Rob and the policeman were too shocked to comment on the boy's appearance.

DI Dunne arrived with WPC McPherson. She said she would take the boy to hospital, as Rob refused to move. He was sitting on the grass in the corner farthest from the shelter, saying nothing except, "I'm fine. Just need to catch my breath. I'm fine." The policewoman knew the Scottish meaning; knew that for anything from a scratch to every bone in the body broken, a Scotsman would say, "Fine."

DI Dunne took Mal Forbes into the house. It was Ann McPherson who asked where Maureen was, and found the girl. By then Maureen was mute.

"She needs a doctor too," the police-woman said, knowing she would need more than that. Her mother was dead. Her father under arrest. She was stupefied with shock.

Rob came into the house. He was trying to speak coherently, trying to give a state-ment through the stench of imprisonment and the metallic taste of blood, and the ter-ror invading his nostrils, clinging to his hair. The damp trousers, the jumper wet through, even though it was not raining, he had not noticed. Not yet.

He had stepped in the blood of Moira

Forbes. A footprint from his right boot left three full prints across the kitchen floor. WPC McPherson saw him looking, trying to work out the source and, taking his arm, she moved them into the sitting room, not caring what happened to Moira's immaculate carpet.

Without her superior's approval, Ann McPherson called Margaret McLean, saying little except the address and "Rob needs you."

Next the policewoman rang Don McLeod. It was he who had summoned help; the fire brigade first, as he knew there would be no arguments if he said there was a blaze. The ambulance next. They didn't ask either. The third and last time Don had dialed 999, he'd asked for the police, saying he was a neighbor. "There's burglars in the house next door," he said, and hung up after giving the address but not his name.

When WPC McPherson rang McAllister's house and spoke to Don, the conversation was brief. But Annie had heard the ring.

"Your mum's alive and in the hospital, but she's weak." Don told her. "They found Mae Bell with her." He knew how serious it was. As did she. He did not lie. He did not say her mother would be fine. And she was glad Mr. McLeod did not pretend.

436

"We'll visit in the morning," Annie said. "So we'd better get some sleep. Night-night, Mr. McLeod."

He reached out and lightly touched her head. "Night-night, sleep tight."

She smiled. It was what her mum always said.

And the wise wee girl, in her stripy pajamas, her hair mussed up, dark rings under her eyes, climbed the stairs to the room she usually shared with her sister and went to bed, by herself, leaving the sofa to Mr. Mc-Leod, who was finding it hard not to weep.

Margaret McLean told DI Dunne he could speak to her son in the morning. He dared not object. She took Rob home. She ran a bath for him, made him a hot toddy, put him to bed like he was still her wee boy, which he still was, even at twenty-three. She sat in the chair of his room saying nothing very much, watching and waiting until he fell asleep. She watched and waited some more, holding his hand when he called out, smoothing his hair as he cried. She watched the night turn to day and did not leave him, her boy, her son, her only child.

Only as the rooks in the trees outside began their early-morning bickering and she saw Rob turn over and this time sleep, truly sleep, did she leave him. But she left his door open, in case he should need his mother.

TWENTY-FOUR

McAllister stayed at the hospital all night and most of the next day. It was forbidden for visitors to sleep in the corridors, the waiting rooms, anywhere in the hospital. So he paced. Like Banquo's ghost he haunted the place, scaring at least one junior nurse with his chalk-white face, dark unshaven chin, and hair askew from constantly tugging at it.

A surgeon flew up from Edinburgh, arriving late next morning. During the five hours it took to perform the operation, McAllister answered questions put to him by DI Dunne, by the Reverend Macdonald, by Don McLeod, and all the other friends and relatives who called by. He chain-smoked all the while. He remembered none of what he was asked, what he said. He took the tea given to him. He took the flask Don put in his pocket. He waited.

He was alone when the theater doors

opened and the nursing sisters came out.

"How is she?"

"Are you a relative?" one of the sisters asked.

"No, she's my . . ." He didn't have a word for his role in Joanne's life.

"Sorry, relatives only."

"For Christ's sake, woman . . ."

The sister stepped backwards as though the profanity had physically struck her. "I will not tolerate such language. Please leave."

The junior staff was standing well away from the confrontation. A surgeon still in his operating gown came out. Oblivious to the standoff, he disappeared through another swing door.

"Just tell me how she is." He stepped towards the nurse, his voice that of a man in despair. Even in daylight he couldn't see what she could see; his clothes had traces of blood and mud; the smell of unwashed body and cigarettes was rank.

She shrank back from him and would not budge. "Relatives only. Those are the rules." She was the sister in charge; she would not break the rules for anyone.

"Mr. McAllister, sir, I thought I told you to go home hours ago." The lumbering juggernaut of Sergeant Patience was coming down the corridor bearing tea. In his big hams of hands the cup and saucer looked like it came from a child's tea set.

"Do you know this person?" the sister asked.

"Aye. Mr. McAllister, editor of the *Gazette.* He's Mrs. Ross's fiancé. I think we can bend the rules a wee bit since they're as good as married."

As good as married — Sister knew what that meant. She was minded to ban him from the hospital for that sin alone, never mind his blaspheming. But the policeman saw in her eyes the way her mind was thinking.

"I'll call the Reverend Macdonald," the sergeant said. "That's the patient's brother-in-law" — this part he addressed to the nurse — "he's family, and I'm sure the minister'll get permission from Matron for you to be with Mrs. Ross, sir." Then his voice changed from gentle giant to fearsome Sergeant Patience. "In the meanwhile, Sister, I'll take full responsibility for the breach of hospital rules. So please let Mr. McAllister . . ."

McAllister spotted the surgeon, now in immaculate grey-striped trousers and dark coat, come out of a room. He moved fast. Sergeant Patience stepped to the side, impeding the nurse, who was determined to stop any information being given to a blaspheming sinner, no matter he was as good as married.

"How is she?" McAllister asked.

"The operation went well," the silver-haired gentleman surgeon said. He was a man married to a woman he adored. He knew how *he* would feel. "But her condition is serious. Mr. . . . ?"

"McAllister. Mrs. Ross is soon to be my wife."

"Mr. McAllister, your fiancée suffered a hemorrhage from the blow to her temple. Although the operation went well, it is too early to be certain of a full recovery." He looked into McAllister's eyes, saw the despair, and the intelligence. He held out his hand. "I won't lie to you, there is a strong possibility of brain damage. She was left too long before being operated upon. All we can do is wait and hope for the best."

McAllister took the hand, held it that moment longer than customary, and the man, not the surgeon, kept hold, saying, "She is young. She is healthy. You and your future wife have my best wishes."

Thank God he didn't tell me to pray, McAllister thought as he watched the man leave; the editor was a man who had left faith behind on a hillside in Spain.

When McAllister was alone, Sergeant Patience came over.

"One o' the constables will drive you home." It was an order. "Get some sleep 'cos DI Dunne is wanting to talk to you. Then you can come back to see how Mrs. Ross is doing."

As he turned to leave, the sergeant said, "Congratulations on your future marriage, sir." He smiled. Then winked.

McAllister knew that hugging the man would not be appropriate. He shook his hand instead.

The first time Joanne opened her eyes, it was dark, which terrified her, and she immediately closed them. She felt sheets under her, she felt her toes, could wiggle her fingers, but not much else. She could smell laundry detergent from the pillow. The scent of cleanliness reassured her. She opened her eyes again and the dim night-light the nurses kept on threw shadows on white walls, on a metal-framed bed. She went back to sleep for another half day.

The next time she woke she knew someone was in the room. "McAllister?" Her voice was no more than a whisper.

"It's me, dear, your mother."

That made no sense to her, so she went back to sleep.

The third time she knew it was him. He was sitting so close she could feel his breath. She lifted her eyelids as much as she was able, saw him, closed them, the corners of her mouth attempting a smile. Failing. She felt his hand, stroking the back of hers, touching so lightly it was like the brush of a feather.

Five minutes passed. She looked for him. He was there. The light hurt. Again she closed her eyes. But she could listen. She could hear as the dam of emotion and love and fear broke. In the dim light, in the privacy of the room, with Joanne barely conscious, he told her everything he could never say when her eyes were upon his.

He told her of her girls, of Mae Bell, of his love, of the moon and stars and the river, and the friends and the relatives and the cheers from the printers when told she was safe.

He told her of his terror, of his absolute awareness that he could not live without her. He stripped himself bare of his fears, his manliness, his Scottishness, his past, his present. He told her how his life was worth nothing without her.

"McAllister . . ." she murmured, and went

back to sleep.

A nurse would come in every hour, always asking her the same questions.

"What is your name?"

"What's the date?"

"Who's the prime minister?"

She could answer her name. She became frustrated. "I told you! My name is Joanne Innes. No, that's not right. Joanne . . . Mrs. Joanne Ross."

When told the date, she could not remember the next time she was asked.

As for the prime minister, she said, "That stuck-up toff whatshisname." Or, "Macdonald is it?" Or, "Go away with your bloody questions." No one took offense at swearing in Intensive Care; they knew even the most mild of ladies could swear like troopers after a long period under anesthetic.

On the days that followed Joanne learned to squeeze McAllister's hand. He had to concentrate hard to feel the pressure, but day by day she became stronger.

Sometimes, trying to move her arms, which were tied down to keep her from tearing out the drips, she called out, *I'm sorry, Father. I won't do it again.* Once she said, to no one in particular, *I'm sorry, I never get anything right.*

She asked for her girls, frequently: in between waking and unconsciousness; when she opened her eyes; in between sentences; she would say, "Annie, Jean, is that you? Or, "Annie, Jean, come inside, supper is ready." Or simply, "Annie. Jean. McAllister. Wee Jean."

One time she lay back staring at the ceiling. "See yon, McAllister? See the wee fish? Coming out of the light fitting? They're lost. Can't find the sea."

He wanted to hold her but was told he shouldn't allow her to lift her head. Six days after the operation, she asked, "Annie, Jean, where are they?"

"You'll see them soon."

"I'll not live in your house, McAllister. It's *your* house."

"I'll buy a new house for us all."

"An old house. In the country."

"Anywhere you want." But she was asleep again.

Next day when he visited he said, "Your mother would like to visit."

"No."

"The girls are desperate to see you," he said, "but they're not allowed in. So . . ." He slowly wound up the bed so she could see out the window.

The room was on the ground floor, but all

Joanne could see was the top of someone's head. "Rob." She smiled. Then the head disappeared.

The shrieks and giggles were distant but unmistakable, "Annie, Jean." She tried to sit up.

"Wait." McAllister opened the window.

Annie appeared first. Rob gave her a lift up, her foot in his clasped hands. She sat on the window ledge. "You look terrible," she told her mother.

Joanne had to smile. "I know. But I'm getting better."

Annie thought she looked so ill she might never recover, but said, "Mum, when are you coming home?"

Jean appeared next, on Rob's shoulders.

"Hi, Mum. You look really weird," she said.

McAllister laughed. "Hi indeed. You've been spending too much time wi' your uncle Rob."

Joanne could barely speak. But she could smile. Smile so much her head hurt and the stitches pulled. Tears came unbidden, streaming down her face, and it frightened her children.

"Are you having a baby, Mum?" Jean asked because she'd heard that hurt.

"Don't be silly." Annie was furious.

447

"No, I'm a wee bit sick." Joanne's voice was soft, but her girls heard.

"We've a new baby brother. His name is William. He's gorgeous."

Joanne smiled again. "Really?" She had no idea what Jean was talking about.

"We have to go now," Rob told them. "Your mum needs to sleep."

As they walked back with Rob to his father's car, Jean asked, "What happened to Mum's hair?"

"The doctor had to cut it off to put stitches in where she was hurt," Rob explained.

"Mum'll no' like that."

"Mum will get better, and come home, and her hair will grow again," Annie said, her voice with a false confidence that made Rob reach for her hand. She let him. For once, she let herself be eleven again.

Mae Bell was sedated for the first two days. Dehydrated and exhausted, she had lost so much weight, her skin crinkled like a crepe bandage. As she had no relatives, no one was allowed to visit her except the Reverend Duncan Macdonald, in his capacity as hospital chaplain.

"I can't pretend she's my fiancée," McAllister told them. "Although Joanne doesn't

448

know it, I'm engaged to her — as far as the hospital is concerned."

"About time you made it official," Don told him.

On the fourth day, Mae Bell was moved into the main ward. McAllister visited, held her hand. He was not good for her; he was too distraught at the thought of Joanne having irreversible brain damage. To be cheerful and sympathetic for Mae, he needed a strength he did not have.

Mae did not want to remember the ordeal and the events leading up to them, so the second time he came to visit, she said, "Go away, McAllister. Only come back when you can cheer me up."

Rob and Frankie came together and separately; Rob was not good company either. He came in the visiting hour, asked how she was, told her Joanne was on the mend, saying nothing of the uncertainty for a full recovery, and left after ten or so minutes. Then he would drive back to work. Or home to sit with his mother.

Margaret McLean had taken him to the doctor just as she had when he was a boy. Dr. Matheson had read about the case in the *Gazette.* He and the rest of the community did not know that, when moved, Mrs. Forbes's head had parted from her body. Sleeping pills were prescribed. Rob did not take them.

Although those close to him knew his spirits were perilously close to shutdown, to most he was a hero. The prevailing wisdom was, *Rob McLean rescued Joanne Ross and the American woman — a real hero.*

So, he killed someone? So did many men in this town, this country, this world. Only recently.

Gino Corelli was Mae Bell's constant visitor. He and Chiara had attempted to visit Joanne and were told, *not yet.* Gino was left with a dozen out-of-season red roses he'd ordered from the south. He knew Mae Bell was in the hospital. As a refugee himself, released before WWII had ended from an internment camp for Italians, he knew what it was like to be a stranger in an unknown land, lost to friends and country.

He eventually found her ward in the maze of separate buildings that made up the hospital. He walked down the ward to her bed, his polished Sunday shoes squeaking on the polished linoleum floor, his hat in one hand, flowers in the other.

He made Mae smile. "Red roses are for lovers," she murmured. "Thank you, Mr. Corelli."

He blushed.

She asked after the boy. Gino had no idea who the boy was, and Mae was too tired to explain other than, "He's my son, my husband's son."

This made no sense to Gino Corelli.

Mae told him, "The nurses say I have to eat, but have you seen the food here? It's . . ." There were no words she could conjure up for the boiled potatoes, boiled cabbage, mashed turnips, and the grey pellets of what she was assured was meat. "Mince is what it is," a fellow patient told her as she examined it as though it might move. *It's the innards of a haggis,* she decided, and couldn't eat it.

Gino visited most evenings; he brought simple dishes like soup in a thermos flask, tiramisù, and fruit already cut up. Even the grapes were deseeded and cut in half. He enjoyed her company; she was almost European and knew what he was talking about when he described a place, a time, sun on the skin and grapes on the vine; she understood what it was to live away from the land of your birth.

She asked him for a pen and paper. She wrote a few words and an address. He went to the post office, sent the telegram.

She asked again about the boy. He had no news, but said he would find out. He asked

McAllister, who told him to consult Angus McLean, the solicitor and Rob's father. He told Mr. McLean that Mae Bell said the boy was her late husband's son.

"Ah, that explains it," the solicitor had said.

Gino did not know, or ask, what was meant by that but came back the same day and told Mae Bell, "Mr. McLean the solicitor will find news of your boy."

Five days after her rescue, Mae Bell insisted on discharging herself. She was told she would have to sign a form absolving the hospital of responsibility.

"Where do I sign?" she asked.

The doctor said, "You need monitoring. You need to put on weight."

"With this hospital food?" she asked.

He had the grace to smile.

Mae Bell was to stay at McAllister's house, where Granny Ross had installed herself as daytime housekeeper.

"I'll look after Mrs. Bell," she said when McAllister told her that Mae was coming out of hospital. "Where else should the poor soul be stopping except wi' friends?"

Frankie volunteered to collect Mae Bell from hospital. He asked for time off work. His superior said no and threatened to sack him. Frankie said, "Go ahead."

When he arrived, she was in a wheelchair. Mrs. Ross Senior had packed a small bag with some of Mae Bell's own clothes.

"I'll dress later," she told Frankie, "but first, take me to see Joanne."

Joanne was still in Intensive Care. It was not visiting hours. Visiting was restricted to family only.

Frankie spotted a white jacket hanging inside the open door of a sluice room. He put it on. He wheeled Mae to the Intensive Care ward. There was no need to make Mae look like she belonged there; in the hideous hospital nightie and dressing gown, her face showing every hour of her captivity, she did not look out of place. When a nurse looked up, Frankie smiled. The young nurse smiled back. Frankie carried on as though he worked there.

He found Joanne's bed. When Mae saw the drips and trappings of serious illness, she felt she would faint.

"Hi there." She leaned out of the chair and stroked Joanne's hand.

Joanne opened her eyes. "Mae Bell."

"Honey."

Joanne looked at her. "You look terrible."

"Thanks." Mae's eyes filled up. "So do you." They smiled.

"Why are you here?" Joanne asked.

453

Mae Bell couldn't answer.

Joanne closed her eyes. They were silent for so long, Frankie looked around the curtain to make sure they were both still breathing.

"See you soon, my dear dear friend," Mae whispered.

Joanne managed an upturn of the lips. "Your nightie is really horrible."

"It sure ain't Paris fashion." Mae put on a deliberate drawl, gave a deliberate slow shake of the head, which hurt. She smiled. "Night-night. Sleep tight."

Frankie pulled the wheelchair away, waving at the nurse as he passed. He took Mae to the car. As he was lifting her into the backseat, he saw the wet face, the teardrops on the gown. He felt how little she weighed. He felt every rib, every bone. The anger over Mae's imprisonment, Joanne's nearly dying, and the pain of losing his mother combined burnt a crevasse into his soul.

He walked round to the driver's side, took a moment to breath deeply. He knew then that he was not and never would be the same Frankie Urquhart — shinty player, music promoter, generally decent sunny young man whom everyone liked.

And all through that week, a week of policemen, of interviews, of death and its aftermath, a Fatal Accident Enquiry, confrontation, reflection, and recovery, those closest involved never mentioned the events to each other.

Except Don McLeod. He had a newspaper to publish.

Frankie had told Rob he had lost his job in the gentlemen's department of Arnotts and he didn't care.

Rob told Don.

Don asked, "Can he sell?"

Rob assured him Frankie could sell kilts to a fully dressed regimental pipe band and then some.

Don said, "When can he start?"

Frankie Urquhart started the next day as an advertising clerk at the *Highland Gazette*. With much help from Fiona, he quickly got the hang of it.

The *Gazette* came out. On time. Don and Hector and Fiona and Frankie and Mr. Mortimer Beauchamp Carlyle — known as Beech to friends and colleagues — were astonished at their achievement.

"Aye, well, as long as nobody spots the plagiarism," Don said to Beech as they shared a post-publication dram. "Our rivals had some good articles on what happened. All I did was a wee rewrite."

"The procurator fiscal's inquiry into

Moira Forbes's death . . ." How do you think Rob will hold up?" Beech asked.

"He'll get through it." Don was certain of that. "But he'll never be the same, right enough."

Across the river, at home in her bungalow, Margaret McLean was thinking the same. She watched her son walking around in a dwam. Others might think he was coping well, might be fooled by his normal, I'm-the-cock-o'-the-walk smiles, his black jokes. She wasn't. She vowed, *I will do everything I can to bring back my laughing, innocent son, even if it means sending him away from here, from me.*

And across town, up the steep of St. Stephen's Brae, along a wide road, past the academy, and down a crescent-shaped terrace, McAllister was home in bed. He was about to switch off the bedside light when he sat up straight, clasped his hands as though about to ask for the Lord's intervention, and said to himself, *I will bring back Joanne, bring home that laughing beautiful woman, well, and healed, and smiling, and dancing. I will look after her for the rest of our lives.*

TWENTY-FIVE

In the prison, only a few streets from McAllister's house, DI Dunne was once more interviewing Mal Forbes. For the first few days, Mal Forbes had been incoherent, sobbing, wailing, "Moira, ma poor lass. Moira."

The inspector was afraid Forbes would be declared mentally unfit for questioning. But the prison doctor was unmoved. "He's had a shock — he's been found out, his wife is dead. But no, I see no reason whatsoever to declare him of unsound mind."

When Mal Forbes was brought in, DI Dunne and WPC Ann McPherson were waiting in a prison interview room that smelled of caves. The first thing the policewoman noticed was how small the man was. Not so much short, although he wasn't much more than five foot six, but how his skeleton seemed to belong to a twelve-year-old, making his head look too big for his body.

Mal sat down. He placed his hands, clasped in prayer, on the table. He looked at WPC McPherson and asked, "How's my boy? He's scared of strangers, you know. And he doesn't like bright lights. He really likes porridge, though. And daffodils."

"He's not your boy," WPC McPherson said, her voice tight and controlled, not looking at Mal Forbes. The monster, she called him, but only to herself. "The child is being well looked after." How Mal Forbes could think the child was his was beyond her comprehension.

"Have you seen him smile?" Mal asked. "Like a wee ray o' sunshine."

The man turns my stomach, WPC McPherson was thinking, unaware of her clenched fists, her foot tapping the stone floor.

"And how's my Maureen?"

"She's back in Elgin with your family," DI Dunne answered.

"She'll like that. My cousin Effie makes great scones and . . ."

"We're not here to discuss scones, Mr. Forbes." The policewoman was barely able to control the vibrato in her voice. "You and your wife kidnapped Mrs. Mae Bell. Mrs. Joanne Ross was attacked and almost died, and one or both of you were responsible for

458

the death of Nurse Urquhart."

"No. We never . . . No. Moira, she didn't mean it, she wasnae thinking right."

"You hid the women. You and your wife kept them locked up."

"Mr. Forbes." DI Dunne felt that the anger from his colleague was appropriate and was happy to let her be the baddie. "Do you understand the charges against you?"

"The charges? No. Not really. I never did those things you say I did."

The policewoman took the official papers and summarized the charges for the third time that week. "Abduction, criminal neglect of a child, perverting the course of justice, aiding and abetting a kidnapping, attempted murder, and of course murder."

Neither the police nor the procurator fiscal could yet connect either of the Forbeses to Nurse Urquhart's death, but they knew Moira Forbes had written the letters.

"I never tried to kill anyone. And it was Moira locked them up."

"You admitted dragging Mrs. Ross into the air raid shelter."

"Well, I couldn't leave her lying out in the garden, could I?"

"She could have died," WPC McPherson said. "Your wife sent threatening letters to Nurse Urquhart, then threw acid at her,

Nurse Urquhart died. That's murder." They both knew that the charge was probably manslaughter but weren't going to tell Mal Forbes that. "Your wife could well have killed Mrs. Ross if she wasn't found in time — a second murder."

"Moira never killed anyone. Rob McLean killed *her* — that's murder." He was sobbing again, a sound Ann McPherson was sick of.

"So it was you who threw the acid at Nurse Urquhart to shut her up?" she asked.

They had been over and over the acid attack on Nurse Urquhart, and Mal still continued to deny any knowledge of it.

DI Dunne made a *calm down* gesture to his colleague. The WPC sat back, let out a breath, and left the next round of questioning to the inspector, knowing he was right, she was losing her temper.

"Could your wife have attacked the nurse without you knowing?" he asked. Again he got the same answer as before.

"No. Never. She'd never . . ." This time he conceded, "I don't know. But there was no acid in the bottle she had wi' her, it was only an empty Milk of Magnesia bottle she used to keep thon American wifie quiet." He was looking at the inspector, as he was afraid of WPC McPherson. "That shows she

460

has a kind heart, shows she'd never really harm anyone. She only wrote thon letters to scare folks, keep them out o' our private affairs. Moira, she'd never harm no one." He was back in his own dialect, a strong Moray dialect, and the officers had trouble catching every word. But his sobbing was understandable.

"We only kept the boy hidden because of his looks." Mal spoke to DI Dunne, his voice so reasonable, stating the obvious, "You know there's many a person would never understand."

When Mal Forbes was saying this he had a vision of his mother — what she would say if she saw a wee black baby. "None o' it is Moira's fault. She was right depressed after the boy was born."

He remembered coming home from work when the boy was about six months old. Moira was in the kitchen giving the baby a bath in the sink. Or at least that was what she said she was doing. But she was holding his head in the water and the wee soul had such a strength in him, wriggling like an otter, and slippery like an otter too, so she couldn't keep him under. He took the boy from her and after he'd stopped bawling, the baby had smiled at Mal, a smile he would never forget.

"So you kept the child hidden?" DI Dunne asked.

"The American, he was a decent enough fellow. I saw him a few times when I worked on the base. He was right friendly." Mal said nothing about his own friendship with Bobby Bell, about him always hanging around the American airmen, enjoying their company, their way of life oh so different from that of a man from Elgin. "Moira took a shine to Mr. Bell, and when she was in one o' her high moods, there was no resisting her, she was that persistent."

He smiled and leaned towards the inspector, one man to another. "Our Moira was a right bonnie lass when she were young." He stopped. Remembered. He started to cry. "It's no fair, it should o' been me Rob McLean hit, no' her."

Ann McPherson couldn't stop herself from interrupting. "Rob thought your wife was going to throw acid."

"I keep telling you there was never any acid. Only water."

So we're back to that, DI Dunne thought. They had taken the bottle, tested it. It was water. No acid or trace of acid could be found in the Forbes household.

"Moira read the classified in the *Gazette.* The one that was asking for information about Robert Bell," Mal explained. *My Bobby, she'd called him,* but Mal wasn't going to tell the police that. "An' ma Moira thought the idea o' it being acid in the bottle would scare the life out o' the American woman. She was right. It did."

Mal Forbes admitted keeping the boy in the shelter but denied the conditions were dangerous. "It was only at night. He was fed well, Moira always made him his favorite porridge and ham sandwiches. He had plenty milk, he had water, he only stayed in the shelter during daylight when we were away or when there were people around who might see him. Maureen, she played wi' him. We took him out in the garden nightimes."

Like taking your dog for a walk of an evening, Ann thought.

"The letters, why did your wife send the letters?" DI Dunne asked.

"That was stupid," Mal Forbes said. "She thought it would keep Nurse Urquhart from poking her nose in. Maureen told the nurse about her brother when she was checking for nits, said her brother had them too. She called round to our house. Moira told her the boy was in an institution. Then the nurse checked the hospital in Elgin and could find no health records — you know, his jabs and checks and suchlike, and no records of the boy at the institution in Aberdeen or anyplace else. That made her come round again an' then . . ." He was once again shaking his head at the interference of outsiders. "Then the American woman turned up. And Mrs. Ross. They all were nosing around . . ." He looked up at the inspector. "Why couldn't they just leave us be?"

The whine, the self-pity, the complete lack of awareness incensed WPC McPherson. "My father keeps his pigs in better conditions than you kept that child."

"The letters, Mr. Forbes. Explain to us what happened." DI Dunne's gentle questioning made Mal want to explain. *He understands,* Mal thought, *not like thon harridan next to him.*

"I didn't know at first. Moira put them in the *Gazette* mail when she brought ma morning flask o' tea. She had a wee job wi' the council, only part-time, then she was too sick to go to work. But not too sick to look after me. A right good wife is Moira."

"Who took the acid from the *Gazette* print room, you or her?" WPC McPherson asked.

"I keep telling you" — again the answer was directed at the inspector — "there was

464

never any acid. Moira got the idea to write about it from reading the newspaper, but we never had any acid."

"Aye, but your print was on the bottle." DI Dunne seemed surprised. "How did that happen?"

"I canny remember. Maybe I used it or picked it up, or more like tidied it up. Thon young fellow Alan Fordyce is right untidy."

He's lying. He knows something. He'd be no good at card games, the policewoman thought, as she saw him look at his finger-nails, which were dirty, with earth or perhaps old blood caked underneath.

"Did your wife ever visit the print room?" she asked.

"Maybe. I can't remember." His voice was fading, his body sliding down in the chair.

"Did your wife ever talk to the men in the print room? Make friends with any of them?" Ann asked.

Mal was still staring at his hands, seeing what the policewoman saw. And, for a usually immaculate man, he'd ceased caring about dirt and blood and grease. He had given up. "Maybe. I don't know."

They left him to the guard, the inspector saying, "We'll be back."

Later, when they were discussing the interview, DI Dunne told his colleague that he was inclined to believe Mal Forbes knew nothing about the acid.

Ann McPherson disagreed. "The acid, I can see Moira Forbes doing that. What I can't see is Moira digging up a grave, opening a coffin, sawing off a leg, and putting it in a shinty boot. Not without Mal's help."

The inspector groaned. "We've enough to think about. I was hoping all that business was long finished." He had considered a link in the two cases but could find none. "I'm certain that prank is down to the shinty boys."

"Fine." She agreed with her boss. Coming from the glens herself, she knew no trick was too far-fetched for the shinty boys — *a wild lot if ever there is one.* "So what about Mal Forbes's print on the bottle of acid?"

DI Dunne was weary of the whole case. There was a resolution of sorts, but both deaths had been horrific, deaths none of his constables should have had to witness. Yes, Moira Forbes had kept Mae Bell prisoner by using the threat of an acid attack, but that didn't prove she had thrown acid at Nurse Urquhart. There were still too many imponderables in the case, and he was weary to the bone.

"We'll go over it all again in the morning." He stood. "I'm away home. You should go too." He took his hat, fingered the brim until the shape was satisfactory. Before putting it on he asked, "Constable McPherson, aren't you due to sit your sergeant's exams?"

She went slightly pink. *He's been keeping track,* she thought. "Next month, sir."

"Make sure you pass. We need a senior detective on the team." He put his hat on, "Good night, Ann."

"Queer suit for a missionary," the ticket collector said to the guard as they watched the passenger alight from the train and stroll down the platform as though on his way to the opera.

"Maybe that's what they wear in Africa," the guard replied.

The gentleman also had the strangest shoes — *looked like they were made from the skin o' some kind o' big snake,* he told his wife, who, after every shift, asked him who was on and off the trains, particularly interested if someone from the town was with someone they shouldn't be with, or if someone was departing to or arriving from destinations they had no known connection with. The comings and goings of the American woman had kept his wife entertained for weeks on end, the guard remembered.

When Mrs. Ross Senior answered the

door, she had no idea what to say — or do. As she told Granddad Ross later, "I've never seen an African in real life. An' I never knew they wore clothes. Well, not clothes like thon."

When the stranger smiled, his teeth impressed her too. "Really beautiful they are," she told Granddad, who was busy thinking what excuse he could find to go over to McAllister's for a visit and see the gentleman for himself. "An' right polite."

When she showed the gentleman into the sitting room where Mae Bell was lying on the sofa looking through magazines that Margaret McLean had left for her, Mae looked up and for the first time in too long she smiled with all of herself. "Charlie."

Mrs. Ross was taken aback at the way the two of them hugged, but she was right glad, she told Granddad Ross, the way Mrs. Bell perked up.

"I got the telegram," Charlie Bell said. "But it wasn't easy getting here. Those mountains were built to keep people out."

"You'll be wanting a cup o' tea," Mrs. Ross told him, and left them alone.

"Tea? I thought they only drink Scotch."

"Charlie, tea is the national drink, and whisky — never Scotch — is a close second, along with horrible warm flat beer." She was laughing.

He was sitting back examining her. He hated what he saw. Her hair looked as though she was molting. Her skin was hanging off her bones. Her eyes, her flashing laughing eyes, were so deep in the sockets he thought they might disappear inside her head.

She could see what he was thinking. "If you think this is bad, dear brother-in-law, you should have seen me a week ago."

"Aye, she's doing well." Mrs. Ross came in with the tray and sandwiches and a plate of scones. "I don't know what foreign gentlemen eat, but there's home-made corned beef sandwiches — not thon stuff out o' a can — an' I've left a jar o' ma homemade chutney, so help yourself." She smiled at him, hoping he would smile back. He did. It was a smile that made her heart glad. And after a week of Mae's company, she was happy to see the "lass" happy.

"Thank you, Mrs. . . ." His eyes opened in a question.

"Mrs. Elsie Ross," she said. "Pleased to meet you."

"Pleased to meet you too, Elsie. I'm Charlie."

She left them alone. Standing in the kitchen, hearing the murmur of voices, the big laugh from the big man, she was lost, didn't know what to do with herself. *Elsie, he called me Elsie.* She was trying to remember when she had last been called by her name. *Not since our Bill was born.*

"I was certain something had happened to Robert's plane," Mae was saying. "You know I never accepted that an air force plane could just disappear off the map. So when I finally tracked down Robert's possessions and the letters . . ."

"That must have been a shock." Charlie held her hand, squeezed it.

"Yes, then no. I was glad I'd been proved right. He was afraid someone was out to get him."

"Then you found his son, my nephew. Another shock."

"I've been around enough to know these things happen. I never doubted Robert. I know I was his only real true love." She accepted his light and puffed on the cigarette, blowing smoke to the ceiling. "Men? Alone? Pretty girls? What can you do?"

"So Bobby put his name on the certificate? That must have caused quite a stir." Robert Bell was only Robert to Mae. To his brother, Charlie, to everyone, he was Bobby.

"No one knew. The Forbes family kept the child hidden. The mother, she's the one

I wrote to you about, and her husband, this guy Malcolm — Mal — he forgave her. I know now he loved the boy. That's why they kept him."

"A very funny way of showing love, keeping the kid hidden all these years." Charlie was shaking his head. "When I got your letter I couldn't believe what you found out. Sabotage. And yeah, I knew Bobby might have had a fling, but you were the only one for him. But a son . . ." His fingers were caressing the back of her hand as though caressing his saxophone. "I lost Bobby, I was terrified I'd lost you when you stopped writing. When the telegram came . . . Mae, honey, I can't tell you how scared I was, I had to get Max to open the envelope."

Mae knew how that felt. "How are the boys?" She needed news of the band, of Paris, of her real life, like she needed sunshine.

"All missing you. The customers too. Keep asking for 'la Belle Mae Bell.' "

She laughed. She loved the way the French said her name. "Mae Bell ain't so belle anymore, honey."

"Give it time."

"And a hairdresser."

"Mae, if you need money — or anything . . ."

"No. I'm fine. I might need help to get the adoption worked out. And if not, I'll need even more help." She didn't need to say it. He understood. And felt the same. The boy was family. There was no way they would leave him behind.

They talked the rest of the day in between Mae's naps. In the early afternoon, when she was deeply asleep, Charlie found Mrs. Ross chopping vegetable for the cock-a-leekie soup, McAllister's favorite.

"Elsie, tell me what really happened — all of it." He sat at the table, offered to help. She refused, shocked at the idea of a man chopping carrots.

As she talked, Granny Ross scraped and scrubbed, moving back and forth between table and sink and cooker.

She told him all she knew, and being in the house for nearly two weeks, she knew most of it.

"It started wi' this foot in a boot in Nurse Urquhart's washing basket."

That made him stare.

"Then there were these anonymous letters. I think they started 'cos Mrs. Bell put thon advert in the paper asking about her husband."

"My brother."

"Really? Can a darkie marry a . . ." She

stopped.

He wasn't in the least offended.

"Can a black man marry a white woman? Well, now, many think it shouldn't be so, but in Paris, things are different. They met in New York at the club we were playing in. They married in the U.S., but it wasn't easy for them there. Bobby stayed on in the service after the war, he loved aeroplanes, and he was posted to Scotland. He and Mae were apart for much of the time. Me and the band had plenty of work in Paris. We needed a singer, so Mae joined us."

"Aye, and young men being as they are, and him lonely no doubt, your brother made friends in Elgin . . ." She had no way of saying it. "The baby, he must have come out black." She looked at Charlie, took in his gentle face. "Maybe no' as black as you, he's a brown color, but with hair just like yours."

"You've seen him?"

"Oh aye, but don't tell Mrs. Bell. I have a friend works in the orphanage who let me visit, bring the wee lad some clothes and a toy, a teddy bear that was ma eldest grand-daughter's." She remembered going into the big room where the wee one played and see-ing the wee lad sitting on his own in a corner. His big eyes were staring at her, and

473

him not knowing what to do with the bear broke her heart. So she cuddled the bear and gave it back to him, and he cuddled it and smiled at her.

"He smiles just like you. He's called Charlie. Mrs. Bell said his big sister named him Charlie, but thon madwoman only called him 'the boy.' "

"I'm really pleased he has such a fine name. And you know, our grandfather was Scottish. My grandparents worked on his plantation. Robert was born much lighter-skinned than me, but definitely black." For the second time that day, Charlie Bell was close to tears. He changed the subject to one marginally less difficult. "Mae said the mother died."

"Aye. There was an accident when Mr. McAllister and young Rob McLean rescued Mrs. Bell and my daughter-in-law Joanne."

That was not what Mae told Charlie, but he accepted Mrs. Ross's version. *Probably best for this Rob character if they stick to an accident story,* he thought.

"Elsie, why did the husband go along with it all? I mean he must have known the boy wasn't his? He must have known his wife had . . ." It was his turn to search for an acceptable phrase.

"People see what they want to see," she

said. "God rest her soul, the wife — she was completely mad," Mrs. Ross said, "And what she did — locking up an innocent wee bairn, locking up Mrs. Bell and Joanne, and Joanne nearly dying, and as for Nurse Urquhart . . ." She hit a turnip a hefty whack, cutting it clean in two. "It doesn't bear thinking about."

They turned when they heard the front door open. "I'll give you a lift home, Mrs. Ross," a voice called out.

Charlie saw a tall man, in black corduroy trousers and black polo neck jumper, coming towards the kitchen, towards the smell of vegetables and chicken and the sight of Charlie Bell.

"Good heavens, you're Charlie Bell. I heard you play in Paris."

"You must be McAllister." Charlie stood, hand out, a grin so like the wee boy's it made Mrs. Ross decide to visit him again the next morning.

"Thanks for the offer of a lift, Mr. Mc-Allister." Granny Ross was taking off her apron. "I have my bicycle, so no need for you to drive me home. The soup only needs another hour or so." She finished tidying up the knife and chopping board. "You two go off to the sitting room, get yerselves a dram. No doubt Mrs. Bell will be needing your company."

McAllister insisted Charlie lodge with them. "There's a spare room." They talked late into the night but Mae left them alone after supper. Charlie helped her up the stairs.

"Night-night, Charlie. Sleep tight." When she said this, she knew she sounded like Joanne. It made her shiver. It was how they and wee Charlie comforted each other. *Night-night, sleep tight, don't let the bugs bite. Mind you cover up your nose and don't let the midgies get at your toes.*

That and "Dream Angus."

"I can't stay here a day longer," Joanne was saying as McAllister fussed with book and pillows and cards and flowers, all spilling over the bed and bedside table and floor. He'd already been told off twice for bringing in too many books. "I'll climb out the window and walk home if you won't take me." Her voice was now trembling, the tears almost there. "Please take me home." She wanted her wee house. She clung to the image of it, the feel of it. She knew she could make her life again if she was given time. How she would look after herself, and her girls, she hadn't considered.

"Have you finished this one?" He held up

a Graham Greene she had put to one side.

"Not yet."

Joanne didn't tell him she couldn't read. And that it terrified her. The letters were jumbled. She had to search for words, unable to recall the meaning. She'd asked Jean — not Annie, because Annie would know this was not good — what a word meant. *Hungry* was the word, and Jean had told her, and she was furious with herself. And scared.

Her memory was unreliable and what she could remember was unpleasant. She was trying — again and again — to recall a cheerful moment, some incident of sun and laughter, but always a darkness would appear: her father, her husband, the boy rocking, Mae Bell's voice fading in and out like the wireless on a stormy night. And the dark, the stinking, crushing dark.

"Three weeks is not a long time after an injury like yours," he said.

"McAllister, I want my home, my own bed, I want . . ." He could hear the frustration edge towards anger and felt helpless.

"Hello." The faint voice came from behind the curtain.

McAllister parted the floral screens and a woman he thought he recognized said, "Hello, I'm Joanne's mother."

From the corner of his eyes he saw the flash of panic on Joanne's face and the way she gripped the bedsheet.

"Can I come in?"

"Yes, of course." Joanne had no choice. It was a confrontation she knew she had to have, although she would have preferred it at a time and place where she could walk, talk, and do something else, like make tea or look out of a window, or anything other than lie there, stuck.

McAllister came over, kissed her forehead, and said, "I'll come back later."

"No. Stay."

Joanne's mother sat at the bedside, wanting to hold her daughter's hand. Feeling she did not have the right.

It was afternoon visiting time, and outside the two-bed room — the other bed empty — visitors with flowers and fruit and cards and smiles walked past, often glancing into the half-open doorway, hoping to see another's tragedy.

On the bus to the hospital, for she had come to visit without telling her other daughter and her son-in-law, Joanne's mother had been thinking of her late husband, their life together, their younger daughter, and the years without her.

Pride. Now he was dead, she could now

acknowledge the word. Pride. Maybe not forbidden in the Ten Commandments but certainly one of the seven deadly sins. *Perhaps the most destructive of the seven deadly sins,* she thought.

It was pride that made him the man he was; pride that made him cast out his daughter. And pride that made her acquiesce.

She had agreed to send Joanne to school when she was six. She had agreed to Joanne's joining the WAAF as soon as leaving school. Yes, there was a war on, but Joanne in the woman's army meant no Joanne at home — an eighteen-year-old, at home, in the village, at church, there for all to see. There to remind her father and her mother of that overheard conversation, the one that had been the cause of everything.

Her pregnancy with Joanne she'd tried, unsuccessfully, to hide, knowing the gossip a pregnancy at her age would cause. Her husband was more than mortified. He was furious when at five months she realized she was expecting and had to break the news to him. Furious, embarrassed, and if he could have sent her away for the duration of the pregnancy and then given the baby out for adoption, he would have. The shame of having sex at their age, even though married, was unbearable to him.

On the day of Joanne's christening, after the service, Mrs. Innes had gone to the vestry to meet her husband, baby Joanne in her arms. Her husband was hanging up his robes and did not speak. She always thought this was his time to come down from wherever celestial place he had soared to in his sermon. From the room next to the vestry, the room where the elders kept the communion wine and wafers and parish record books, came the sound of coins being poured out. Three male voices could be heard.

One said, "You count the silver, I'll take the copper and thruppences."

There was the noise of a chair being moved. Another voice, younger, said, "The minister christening his own bairn — at his age. Who'd have thought the old goat had it in him to father a child?"

Another voice said, "Hold your tongue," and another said, "Shoosh, he's next door changing out of his robes." Then came the sound of a door shutting.

Mrs. Innes did not turn, afraid to. She could feel her husband's rage. Feel her husband's shame at the words. She knew he was aware of the shifty looks at her condition from the ignorant of the parish. But that phrase — *the old goat* — he would never forget that insult. And never forgive his innocent wee baby, the cause of the gossip.

She pulled the shawl around the sleeping child's head and left. She waited ten minutes on the church porch, then went home to join her other daughter, her aunt and uncle and two family friends who were to join them for the Sunday roast she had left in the oven, and to toast the baby's head in nonalcoholic elderflower champagne she had made in the spring.

That night, when he had come back from wherever he had gone to conduct the evening service, she knew within one second of seeing the look of utter loathing he gave the baby that he would never forgive the child for bringing shame on his name.

Mrs. Innes looked at her daughter Joanne, her pale face disappearing in the hospital pillows. She was awaiting her daughter's approval, or forgiveness, or blessing. "I hope you're feeling better."

"I'm much better, thank you," Joanne said. "I'm going home soon."

"That's good." There was a silence. "Elizabeth said you and the girls can stay with them until you're fully recovered."

"Yes, she told me. But I'm living with

McAllister now." Joanne saw her mother flinch and was glad. Then she felt guilty. "Thank you for coming to visit, Mother. We'll talk properly when I'm out of here. Now I have to sleep."

Her mother nodded. She could not expect more. "I'll see you when you're better." She nodded to McAllister, uncertain if she should touch her daughter, so she didn't, and left.

A whisper of a woman, he was thinking when he saw the tears on Joanne's cheeks. "Joanne, I'm . . ."

"If you say 'sorry,' I'll murder you," she spoke with her teeth clenched, eyes shut. She opened her eyes, "For goodness' sakes, don't look so miserable. After we're married I want *our* house, not your house, to be only a wee bit out of town, with a view, and trees. But near enough to the academy so Annie can cycle — and . . . What? What are you grinning at?"

"So you will marry me?"

"McAllister, what choice do I have? You're the most annoying, interesting, intelligent . . . and I love you."

This time he was the one near to tears. "I'll start looking for a house tomorrow."

"No, *we* will start looking when I come home."

■ ■ ■ ■

There were so many visitors to McAllister's house that the kettle never went cold. Rob and Frankie, fascinated now by Charlie Bell as well as by Mae, were the most frequent.

When Mr. Angus McLean called, one morning not long after nine o'clock, Mrs. Ross was unsure whether to let him in, as Mae Bell was still in a dressing gown.

"Are you decent?" Mrs. Ross had asked Mae as she sat in the kitchen. "Only Mr. McLean the solicitor is here."

Mae laughed and later told Charlie the expression, and they laughed over the phrase for days.

"I'm sure Mr. McLean will think of me as an invalid in hospital, Mrs. Ross."

Granny Ross doubted that; no invalid she'd ever seen had a black dressing gown embroidered with red dragons.

They remained in the kitchen. Five minutes into the conversation, Charlie Bell joined them, though not in his dressing gown. Angus McLean shook hands, then continued. "As I was saying, your marriage certificate makes a great deal of difference. And no one can dispute that Malcolm Forbes is not the child's father."

"I also brought my birth certificate to show Bobby was my brother," Charlie said.

"I don't think we'll need it. The point is, no one knows what to do with the boy now his mother is dead, and the husband will be in gaol a long time. There is an inclination to grant you temporary custody of the child, and to allow your application for adoption to proceed."

"What are my chances, Mr. McLean?" All Mae Bell wanted was to have the son of Bobby Bell live with her and his uncle Charlie.

"In light of his mental difficulties and the circumstances, I believe the chances are good." He did not say that a child like Charlie had a minimal chance of being adopted otherwise. "No one wants the scandal; the welfare authorities did not follow up on Nurse Urquhart's report of a child being neglected, so . . ."

"How soon can we have him with us?"

"I believe immediately, if somewhere can be found for you to live around here for a few weeks."

"You can all live here." Mrs. Ross spoke as though it was her house, but she knew it was right.

"I have to return to Paris in two days; can wee Charlie come join us before then?"

484

Charlie asked, using the Scottish word he had learned, and delighted in, from Elsie, his new best friend.

"Unlikely, but I'll do my best." Angus McLean would do more than his best; he would shame and blackmail the department to allow the child out.

"When we, I, adopt him, can I have his name changed to Charles?" Mae shuddered every time she thought of the name on the boy's birth certificate — Malcolm.

"Of course. I can help you there."

When he left, Mae said, "Mental difficulties! The way he was treated of course he has problems. Yes, he's strange" — she smiled at Charlie — "but he has perfect pitch. I'll make a singer of him."

"And I'll teach him the sax."

When McAllister came home that evening, having gone straight to the hospital from work, Mae told him wee Charlie would be coming to stay next day. "If that's okay with you?"

"More than okay; I'm delighted. Hopefully Joanne will be out of hospital soon. She'll be delighted too. And the girls." He paused, still absorbing his news. Then he grinned, not his usual intimidating grin, more like a shy schoolboy who has won the prize grin. "Joanne and I are to be married."

Charlie and Mae Bell called out their congratulations. He and Charlie toasted the good news with his best single malt, Mae with tea.

"And Paris for the honeymoon," Mae decided.

"Where else?" McAllister smiled. "But don't tell Joanne; I want to surprise her."

TWENTY-SIX

The *Highland Gazette* limped along short-staffed, but advertising was still steady, thanks to the charms of Frankie Urquhart and the organizational skills of Fiona. Don McLean could tell from his writing that Rob was in shock; there was none of the usual vim, none of the usual superlatives Don was renowned for putting his wee red pencil through. He missed them. McAllister was spending half his time at the hospital, so his work was also suffering. Above all, in Don's opinion, with no Joanne to cover the small articles, the minutiae that made up a local newspaper, the *Gazette* was losing its character.

"The McLean residence." Margaret was trying out the accent and tone of a ladies' maid. A brochure from the Royal Scottish Academy of Music and Drama had come in the morning's post, reminding her of her youthful dreams to go on the stage, impossible for a young woman of her birth.

"How would you like the job of temporary junior reporter on the *Gazette*?" Don asked. He knew she could write. He knew she knew everyone. And he believed in the power of middle-aged women.

"When do I start?" Margaret did not have to think; the offer tied in with her scheme. Plus she was bored.

"Let's see, it's Friday, how about we meet tomorrow and you start on Monday?"

"I'll see you in the morning."

When she told her husband, he was amused; Rob, less so. "I'm not sure how I feel about working with my mother."

"Ah, I want to talk to you about that."

She gave him the brochure. She explained her plan. She knew only a small number of students were enrolled per year, and older students were encouraged to apply. She told him he would of course be accepted. She said his audition was four weeks away. "So I've arranged some coaching from Mrs. Ward, the elocution teacher. All you have to do is learn your lines."

"I'm not sure I want to be an actor." Rob was staring at the audition guidelines.

"Studying drama is an opening into television," Margaret explained. "You are now a qualified journalist. Next you study acting.

Most of all, you will be there, in a big city with a marvelous theater and television studios, and training to be an actor — think of the contacts you'll make."

You won't be continuously thinking about what happened here, remembering every time you pass that street, which is on your way home, that you killed a woman. Margaret McLean also knew that in a small town like theirs, Rob McLean would forever be the person who killed Moira Forbes with a spade, almost severing her head. The gossip was such that some people had Rob beheading Moira Forbes, à la Mary Queen o' Scots.

Rob took the brochure up to his room and studied it as he listened to late-night Radio Luxembourg. He liked the idea, saw the sense in it. And, like his mother, he was confident he would be accepted.

Frankie Urquhart was enjoying his new job. He liked talking to people. He liked the news meeting, surprising himself by how much he had to contribute.

"We might have to make you a reporter instead of advertising," Don said when Frankie suggested two stories at the Monday morning news meeting.

"Thank you, Mr. McLeod," was all Frankie said, delighted at the compliment.

That Wednesday, wanting to learn all he could, he stayed on with Rob and Don Mc-Leod to watch the edition being printed. The smell, the noise, the concentrated busy-ness, the thrill of the first of the newspapers coming off the press and knowing he had contributed to it, made Frankie feel all the more that here, in a newspaper, was where he wanted to be.

Across the floor he saw Alan Fordyce, the compositor and former player on Frank Urquhart's shinty team. Alan looked up at Frankie, who nodded. Alan turned away.

Rob waved at Frankie and they went out to watch the vans and lorries being loaded.

"So that's it for the night," Rob said. "The bundles are off to the train and the bus sta-tion and tomorrow . . ." Rob was remember-ing his forthcoming audition and trying a hard-bitten American newspaper reporter accent. "Hey presto, another edition of the *Highland Gazette* hits the streets."

Frankie was used to Rob, so he ignored his gesture of magic wand and swirl of cloak and said, "I'm liking it on the *Gazette.*"

He refused a lift home, wanting to soak in the atmosphere of the newspaper a little longer. He lit a cigarette in the shelter of the close next to the loading dock. Alan Fordyce walked out, saw Frankie, stopped and stared at him, said nothing, then hurried off down the steps to the river.

Frankie thought nothing of it, but something made him decide to follow. He was certain Alan had been behind the foot in the shinty boot in the washing hamper. *Give him a bit o' scare,* Frankie thought.

He ran to the top of the steps. He hurried after the figure halfway down the steps. They were steep, the flight long, hugging the wall to the left of the high ramparts around the castle. Below, the river was barely visible on a moonless night, and the rain intermittent.

Alan Fordyce paused. Looked up. He started to hurry. At the bottom he glanced again at the figure coming fast down towards him. He ran around the corner. By the time Frankie reached the street, Alan Fordyce had disappeared. Frankie smiled. He'd given his ex-teammate a fright. *Serves him right.*

The following Monday's news conference was taken up with an argument over the reporting of the charges against Malcolm Forbes.

"Why can't I say Moira Forbes and/or her husband were involved in Nurse Urquhart's death . . . sorry, Frankie, are you okay with

491

this?" Rob looked at Frankie, who was sitting next to him at Joanne's typewriter.

"I'm fine. I just want the bastard charged."

"That's the point," McAllister said. "There are no charges yet, as there is no direct proof."

"You know we can't print speculation," Don pointed out.

"And no one knows for sure either of them done it," Hector said.

"What do you mean?" Frankie stared at Hector. He knew him well, from their being neighbors and at school together. Over the years, he found that Hector's often preposterous pronouncements were just as often uncannily accurate.

"Mal Forbes is denying all knowledge of the attack on your mum," Rob explained, thinking he'd strangle Hector as soon as they were alone.

"I thought it was his wife who did it." Frankie's voice was calm, but his face alert; he was now certain there was information, or speculation, about the death of his mother that no one was sharing with him.

"Frankie," McAllister said, "no charges have been issued over the attack on your mother."

"Murder," Frankie said. "Mr. McAllister, it was murder."

"Yes, it was," Margaret McLean said.

The silence in the room lingered until Frankie looked around and said, "Let's hope someone discovers something soon. In the meantime, you were saying . . ." He looked at the editor, and with a slight shrug, motioned that he was ready to move on.

Rob wrote the front-page update on the charges against Malcolm Forbes. McAllister reported on the recovery of Mrs. Joanne Ross. They both contributed to a backstory on Mae Bell and her recovery and imminent departure from the Highlands, which Margaret McLean wrote, with Don heavily subbing out superlatives. *A family trait,* he thought.

"I'm not sure I can write without adjectives," Margaret had told him.

"Sure you can," Don replied. "Besides, if I can train your son, I can train anyone."

The fate of the boy — the very existence of the boy — was not mentioned outside their small circle, and news of the boy, and his parentage, never leaked out. That Angus McLean might have threatened the staff at the council department with a lawsuit for neglect, no one except those involved knew, not even his wife.

It took ten days before Frankie decided to

confront Alan Fordyce after the shinty match, a home game at Bught Park. He had to know for certain Alan had not attacked his mother.

The other players and supporters were long gone. Frankie waved cheerio to his dad, calling out that he would see him later. He told Rob they would meet up at the billiard saloon. He watched Hector leave with Rob, and soon everyone had gone. Alan was waiting in the stadium changing rooms, having agreed to talk to Frankie, albeit extremely reluctantly.

"If we've to work together," Frankie had said, "let's get all thon business out in the open."

Alan had agreed. He was nervous but didn't look particularly so.

It was light, it was clear. Frankie didn't care.

He was more worried by what their coach had said — shouted. He'd lied about his fitness. Weeks later, his foot was not fully healed and his team had lost by three goals to nil, two of which were his fault, even though he'd played only ten minutes before being substituted.

"I know it was you put the leg in the washing basket," Frankie began.

"I'm really sorry," Alan said. "I meant for

your father to find it." He was looking at the concrete floor, afraid of Frankie's anger.

"Aye. Well. It was ma mother that came across it. No' that it worried her that much, her being a nurse."

"Look, I said I'm sorry." He was now leaning against the wall, favoring his other foot. Even though he had healed remarkably well, he was hurting after all that running. "I must be getting back; the others are waiting."

"They're drowning their sorrows in the pub. They can wait."

They walked outside and were in the shadow of the stand, the short tier of seats rising up, empty of everyone including the ground staff and cleaner. Frankie had his right hand in the deep front pocket of his duffel coat.

"What I don't get," Frankie said, as though trying to puzzle out a tactic in shinty training, "is why you threw the acid."

"I never. I never threw the acid."

"Yes, you did. I know you did." Frankie pulled out the gun. It was black, heavy, and uncomfortable in the hand; Frankie had never used a gun. He had touched it once, when his father had shown him his souvenir from the war.

"German it is," Coach Frank Urquhart

had told his son. Why he kept bullets for it Frankie never knew, but when he looked for it in the trunk under the bed in the spare bedroom, he was pleased to find a full box.

"I never hurt your mother." Alan Fordyce's voice was high and shaky.

"I know you did," Frankie said again, and held out the other hand. In it was a watch, a distinctive watch, on a pin, with a ribbon. On the reverse was Nurse Urquhart's full name, her RN registration; it was the upside-down watch she had always worn, the watch that fascinated Frankie. As a child he couldn't work out how his mother could read it until she pinned it to his jumper to show him.

"I found this in your locker at work."

"You'd no right . . ." Alan started. Then stopped. Why he had taken the watch he couldn't say, even to himself. It was there, bright and shiny; the nurse was wriggling, screaming out in pain. Someone could have come. He could have been caught. It didn't matter. He wanted it the way a jackdaw wants a shiny object. He took it. He kept it. He examined it often, remembering her screams that quickly faded to a choking as she scratched at her throat, trying to tear the acid from her clothes, her skin.

Frankie was now holding the gun out,

pointing it at Alan, saying, nicely, "Tell me what happened. Then I'll let you go."

"I never meant her to die." Now Alan was crying. "I only meant to burn her a wee bit." He was on his knees. "You've got to believe me."

"Why?"

"It was her got me kicked off the team. Everyone knows your dad is no' the real coach. Everyone knows what Nurse Urquhart says goes."

"But acid? That's a terrible thing to do to a person." Frankie had not once raised his voice, not let emotion show. In these moments, he had none.

"I never meant to hurt her, I only wanted her watch; she always wore it, but she wouldn't give it to me." That was his justification. He asked her for the watch, some strange compensation for her getting him kicked off the team.

She'd laughed at him. "Don't be silly," she'd said. "I need it for ma work."

So he had no choice but to throw the acid.

Frankie remembered his mother wore her watch even when she wasn't in uniform. "Never know when I might need to take someone's pulse," she always said. It was not that — she was proud of the watch — as proud of it as any soldier with a medal.

Frankie had not lowered the gun. It was still pointed at Alan Fordyce, square in the chest.

"I only wanted to get her for kicking me off of the team," Alan whined. "I didn't mean for her to die."

"You killed my mother because you were kicked off the team," Frankie said again. "But everyone knows you were kicked off the team because you're useless. Letting in two goals today? Even though you're injured, you're still useless."

"Can I go now?" Alan was huddled on the ground, his face smeared with mud and tears and snot. Frankie still had the gun pointed at him.

"Frankie, let him go." It was Rob. "I heard it all, I'll be a witness."

"Rob, what are you doing here?"

"A man walking his dog said he thought there was someone here with a gun." The man wasn't sure, thought it must be a game. But Rob believed him. "Put down the gun, Frankie."

"Naw. I let him go; they'll only charge him with manslaughter; he'll be out in a few years."

"Put the gun down, Frankie. He's not worth it."

"Get your notebook ready, Rob, this'll be

the headline of the year."

Frankie pulled the trigger. There was a click. Nothing happened. Frankie tried again. Nothing. He turned and looked at Rob.

Rob stepped forwards, took the gun, and linked his arm through Frankie's. "Let's go."

Frankie let himself be led towards the river. They were unsteady; Frankie walked as though falling, and Rob did his best to hold him up. To a bystander it would look as though Rob was holding up a drunk.

Alan Fordyce they left in a puddle of pee and tears. Rob didn't care. Alan would be dealt with soon enough.

Rob led them across the road to the riverbank. He let go of Frankie and, holding the gun as high as he could, swung his arm back and threw the gun far out into the current. Seeing the distant splash, Rob said, as though discussing next week's football fixtures, "You forget about the safety catch."

"The safety catch?" Frankie was holding his elbows in his crossed arms, rocking himself as though chanting Orthodox prayers to the fast water. "It has a safety catch?"

"Aye. And I doubt it would fire anyhow, it's that old." This he was not certain of, only saying it to reassure himself.

"A safety catch," Frankie uncrossed his arms. He started to laugh. "A fucking safety catch."

Rob couldn't help it. He laughed. They stopped, looking where the gun went in. They looked at each other. Relief, release, hysteria made them laugh again.

They heard the shrill of police cars. They didn't look round — they were watching the river flow.

Five minutes passed.

"C'mon, Frankie," Rob said, "It's over. Let's go home."

Epilogue

Highland Gazette
17 May 1958

Missing Flight Clue Found
Norwegian ship captain Magnus Johanssen handed over to local police a life jacket he found three years ago on a Norwegian beach. The harbourmaster, Mr. John Douglass, advised the captain it may have come from the aircraft missing from RAF Kinloss airbase since 1952.

"It is not unusual for debris from shipping or from Britain to end up on Norwegian shores," said Captain Johanssen, 53, from Bergen in Norway. "I found the life jacket three years ago whilst walking my dog on the shore outside of town and kept it aboard my vessel. It can still be used in an emergency."

When asked why he took so long to inform authorities of the find, the Captain told the

Gazette reporter, "I was in the Harbourside Cafe reading the newspaper to improve my English when I saw the story of Robert Bell, the missing airman. I told the harbourmaster I had an old RAF lifejacket. He checked it and called the police."

Detective Sergeant McPherson from the local constabulary confirmed that the life jacket came from the missing aircraft: "RAF personal have identified the jacket as belonging to the flight that disappeared with five airmen on board, including Robert John Bell."

The widow of Robert Bell, Mrs. Mae Bell, who recently spent ten weeks in the Highlands looking for information on her husband's disappearance, was unavailable for comment. Charles Bell, brother of the missing, now presumed deceased, airman spoke to the Gazette via telephone from Paris.

"I guess finding the life jacket proves the plane ditched in the North Sea, but it doesn't clear up the mystery of what happened on that flight."

According to the American Air Force authorities the case remains open. The police say their case is closed. "The whereabouts of the aircraft may never be solved," said Detective Sergeant Ann McPherson.

ACKNOWLEDGMENTS

To all the lovely people who looked after me in the United States: Will and Carol Jennings, Alex Marshall, Sam Miller, Janet McKinley, Jon Hendry, Katy and Clive Hopwood, and the many kind strangers who cheered me on as I sojourned in a strange land.

To all the bookshop people and readers, thank you for the feedback and encouragement and for having me in your stores as a guest.

To Sophie Mae Young, thank you for that first spark.

To Martin and Helen McNiven, my first and most encouraging readers.

To Catherine McKinley, thank you for reading a very rough draft and giving such perceptive feedback.

To Jennifer Smart for support and feedback and laughs.

To Jan Cornall for cracking the whip.

To everyone at Atria: thank you for your support, your dedication — it was so good to meet you in the real world.

To all the usual suspects; Sheila, Peter, Sarah, Judith.

And Hugh.

Note. My foremost inspiration for this book is Annie Ross, jazz singer and actor extraordinaire. However, none of the events in this novel are in any way connected to her. As far as I know she never lived in Paris, never married an airman, never visited the Highlands. She and her music are a source of inspiration, nothing more, nothing less.

The employees of Thorndike Press hope you have enjoyed this Large Print book. All our Thorndike, Wheeler, and Kennebec Large Print titles are designed for easy reading, and all our books are made to last. Other Thorndike Press Large Print books are available at your library, through selected bookstores, or directly from us.

For information about titles, please call:
  (800) 223-1244

or visit our Web site at:
  http://gale.cengage.com/thorndike

To share your comments, please write:
  Publisher
  Thorndike Press
  10 Water St., Suite 310
  Waterville, ME 04901